Tama Janowitz's stories have appeared in magazines ranging from *The New Yorker* to *Mississippi Review* and *New York Talk*. The author of *Slaves of New York*, she is the recipient of two grants from the National Endowment for the Arts and is now an Alfred Hodder Fellow in the Humanities at Princeton University. She lives in New York City.

Also by Tama Janowitz in Picador

Slaves of New York
A Cannibal in Manhattan

Tama Janowitz

American
Dad

PICADOR

published by **Pan Books**

First published in Great Britain 1988 in this Picador edition
by Pan Books Ltd, Cavaye Place, London SW10 9PG
9 8 7 6 5 4 3 2 1
© Tama Janowitz 1981
ISBN 0 330 30267 1

Made and printed in Great Britain by
Richard Clay Ltd, Bungay, Suffolk

For my parents

When now, on its upward voyage, the earthworm reaches a stratum of hard dry soil through which it cannot penetrate by muscular effort alone, there comes to it—perhaps out of the misty realm called instinct, perhaps out of an otherwhere never to be plumbed—the knowledge of what must be done.
—Alan Devoe, *Life and Death of a Worm*

1

IN JANUARY OF LAST YEAR after cutting wood for four hours, the chain saw leaped from my father's exhausted hands, seriously and permanently maiming him.

This is only one of the dangers involved in the use of alternative energy sources. My father's house—worth, he had assured me, a quarter of a million dollars, possibly even more—was heated by wood stoves requiring vast quantities of timber.

It is true in mentioning the terrible accident of my father I may sound too callous for a son, but in this I only take after my dad himself, who at the time of his mishap was home on a weekend furlough from jail, where he was incarcerated for the murder of my mother. "Involuntary" manslaughter—"accidental," to be sure—but murder nevertheless.

Still, the thought of the whine of the buzz saw stuttering and choking on human flesh did bring certain memories to mind—to begin with, those of the day my mother told my brother and me, "We're getting a divorce."

But perhaps that was not it exactly; those were not my mother's exact words. We were getting a divorce, that much was correct. The three of us would continue to live on Marlowe Drive, in the same house, but Daddy was going to move out and live somewhere else.

My brother was weeping in the bathtub. "Shut up! Shut up,

you rotten kid!" I wanted to say. If I were you, I thought to myself, I would not say that to your little brother. But I am you, I realized with a jolt. I am you! I felt a small knot grow and bulge at the base of my spine. It felt as if I were growing a tail. It was uncomfortable to sit still.

I was ten years old.

My name is Earl Przepasniak, the same last name as my father's; a name unwieldy as a tumor, but one I have learned to live with. My hair is black, once curling, now thinning. I wear glasses and behind them my eyes are two different colors, the right blue, the left green—a minor mistake. I have worn glasses since I was eight years old. Since that time I have been protected from the rest of the world by a plastic frame and twin plates of glass.

But it did not seem then as if the plates of glass had cracked. No, it was to be expected, perfectly expected. "We're getting a divorce," my mother had said. I had been waiting for this moment since I was born, without even knowing what a divorce was. And now it had arrived, this moment.

Though those hadn't been her words exactly. "How would you feel if the three of us, you and I and Bobo, lived here by ourselves. And you could see Daddy as often as you wanted. Wouldn't we be happy?" We were sitting in the living room, where we were rarely allowed, a room that my father had designed. A statue he had made of our naked mother when she was pregnant with me stood against one wall. I looked at the statue, trying not to hear what she was saying.

"Just the three of us?"

"Yes, just the three of us."

"Without Daddy?"

"Without Daddy."

That was when my brother began to cry. I wished he had not begun to cry. It was not necessary. It was not necessary either for my mother's face to split down the seam like that, for her face to fold in on itself and her eyes to get very large. She no longer seemed like my mother. And then she—this new person, whoever she was—went and ran the bath water for my brother, and the dismal sound of the water, like the drone of an approaching airplane, began to fill up the distance.

I went into my father's office in the basement. There were bound volumes of the *American Psychiatric Journal* along one wall.

Some of the volumes were unbound and they were green and white. The air smelled of the pipe he always smoked when he saw patients, a sickly, sweetish smell. There was a leather couch. I lay down on it. It smelled of old hair.

I went back upstairs. In the bathroom my brother was still crying. The bathroom was very hot and full of steamy air. I took my clothes off and stood next to the bathtub full of soapy water. "What are you doing in here, Earl?" Bobo said. He kept crying. He couldn't seem to get enough air and made strange sounds.

"I'm going to show you how to pee in the bathtub," I said. My brother looked surprised. Then he started to giggle. I climbed into the bathtub with him. His small face was red.

After we were told about the divorce, my father took Bobo and me on a vacation. My father loaded up the car early in the morning and came to get us. The entire back seat was filled with things, so Bobo and I sat on the front seat next to him. "When do we get there?" Bobo asked.

The trip took five hours and we stopped eight times for Bobo to go to the bathroom. Once he threw up in front of a Howard Johnson's. At the bridge the traffic was so bad the car didn't move for an hour. "Bobo, why don't you sing us a song?" my father said. When Bobo started to sing he forgot he was sick to his stomach. He had a very high, clear voice and sang, "Oh, my chick-a-biddy, biddy, biddy bee."

Perspiration appeared on my father's face. "Goddamn this traffic," he said. "Bumper to bumper. It's only another twenty miles from here. If there wasn't any traffic we would have gotten there by now. You can smell the ocean already. I taste salt on my lips." I licked my lips. I tasted nothing. My father was wrong.

We drove down a dirt road. There were piles of sand and gray shrubs. "We're looking for number twenty-seven," he said. "There's supposed to be a sign in front that says 'Gulls of Heaven.'"

"I see it," Bobo said. My father pulled the car up into the driveway of a listless-looking house. Bobo jumped out of the car and ran to the front door, followed by my father, who unlocked it. It was dark inside and the curtains were closed. The air was dry and sour. Everything in it was made of yellow pine, with darker knots like eyes.

My father opened the windows. "Look, here's the bathroom!"

Bobo said. "Here's a bedroom with bunkbeds! I want the top one, Earl." He went into the kitchen and began to open drawers. "Forks, knives! This is great. Where are you going to sleep, Dad?"

"There's supposed to be a couch in the living room that unfolds into a bed. I only got us a one-bedroom place because I figured there's just the three of us. So, this is it," he said, looking around. "Kids, just a minute. Before we see everything here, let's get the stuff out of the car. I'll help you get it out and then leave you to unpack while I get stuff for dinner. Come on, there'll be plenty of time later to look around."

We went back to the car. It was late afternoon and there was no ocean in sight. To one side, beyond the houses, was a large marsh which stretched for miles. The houses were all alike, sunken in sand.

"This is going to be great," my father said. "Let's get to work." He began to unload things from the back of the car. He put the things he took out onto the driveway. Bobo and I began to carry them inside.

There were two plastic beach chairs, a hibachi and charcoal, lighter fluid, a foam ice chest, blankets, fishing equipment, tackle and reel, Audubon field books on birds and sea life, *Stalking the Wild Asparagus* (I only hoped we would not have to use it), various games, books and a ten gallon fish tank. "One day we'll go out and gather sea life in tidal pools, the way I used to when I was a kid. Then we can keep it in the tank up at the house and get fresh water or let the stuff go. It's a good way to learn about the things around us." There was Ajax, Ivory Liquid, sponges, paper towels, a lobster pot, bath towels, a bath mat, bottles of wine, a jar of marijuana, a tape recorder, harmonica, raincoats, suitcases, an umbrella, bicycles strapped to the back of the bumper, a picnic basket, a first-aid kit and a small radio.

"How long did you say we're going to be here, Dad?" Bobo said in a worried voice.

"Two weeks," my father said. "Put everything away while I'm gone. I'll be back."

"Can we go down to the water?"

"Put all the stuff away. By that time I'll be back anyway. Let's get the chores taken care of first before we have fun."

We carried the things into the house while he shopped. It took a long time to take everything out of the boxes and put it in the right place. Bobo's face was flushed with heat. "Lie down on the couch, Bobo," I said, "you don't look too good. You better go stick your head under the faucet."

My father returned from the store. "Help me get tnese groceries in from the car." In the back seat were five bags of groceries and a watermelon.

"How much stuff are we going to eat, Dad?" Bobo said.

My father began to prepare the supper while Bobo and I put the groceries away. "Where should I put this orange juice?" I said.

"Where do you think you should put the orange juice, Earl?" my father said. "Leave one out so Bobo can make it up to drink and put the rest in the freezer!" He sat down for a minute. "Hand me a beer, Earl."

"Can I have a taste, Dad?" Bobo said. He put the cold bottle up against the side of his face.

"Make up the orange juice and then you can have a taste. Earl, you scrape these carrots."

"What are we having for dinner?"

"I passed a place along the way that sold clams, and I thought we would have clam chowder. Let's get the stuff into the pot and then we'll see what we have."

"Clam chowder!" Bobo said, "Clam chowder! Ugh I don't like clam chowder. Is that all there is to eat?"

"Hey, it's going to be delicious," my father said. "Just you wait. You're going to love it."

I peeled carrots and Bobo washed the potatoes and opened the can of corn. The air reeked of fish water. It was beginning to get dark outside and it was a little cooler. When all the stuff was in the pot my father sat on one of the plastic beach chairs, watching the sun set and drinking his beer. "Ah, this is fantastic. Will you look at that sunset? This is the life."

Bobo found a very large anthill and fed the ants pieces of salami and Swiss cheese. "Hey Earl, come here!" he said. "This is really something. They can carry things that are twice as big as they are."

"Bobo, what are you doing?" my father said.

"Nothing," he said. "Feeding the ants."

"With the Swiss cheese I just bought? At a dollar eighty-nine a pound the ants don't need to eat Swiss cheese. Bring it back inside." Bobo and I broke the anthill to pieces, using little sticks.

Thousands of ants poured out of the colony, waving black feelers and looking distraught. "Wham! Kapow!" Bobo said. He jumped up and down on the mound. Dirt flew everywhere. The anthill was destroyed. "So there," I said.

"Come on, kids, suppertime," my father called from inside the house. "How about one of you setting the table."

"You do it, Bobo," I said. "My turn tomorrow night."

"Whichever of you sets the table, the other one can clear."

I set the table.

"And, voilà!" My father carried the pot of clam chowder over from the stove. "Wait until you taste this!"

Bobo and I had hamburgers for supper.

The next day Bobo and I were up early. We ate bowls of Rice Krispies and bananas. When we were finished the entire table was covered with Rice Krispies, sugar and milk. Bobo said he thought it gave the table the appearance of a beach. Some of the ants crawled up to the top of the table. "Here you go, ants," my brother said. "Lots of food." I took a napkin out of the cabinet and began to move some of the Rice Krispies around. I made them spell out my name. Into the kitchen came our father, still sleepy and rubbing at his beard. The napkin I was using grew very soggy. I went and got another out of the cabinet.

"You take a perfectly good napkin to clear the table off with?" he said. "Use the sponge! What do you think the sponge is there for?"

"The sponge smells."

"I don't care if the sponge smells, that's what it's there for! Now go and get it and do the table over again. That's not clearing the table, that's potchkeeing." He sat staring at me while I sponged. "You don't need a clean bowl to wipe the crumbs into. Use your hand! What is wrong with you?"

"I don't like to put the crumbs in my hand."

My brother stood by uneasily, hoping there would not be a fight.

"Wipe the crumbs into your hand, Earl!"

And then I wasn't sponging the surface right, I was supposed to be using circular motions and not sponging directly across and my father gave me a smack across the rear end. Tears came into my eyes. My father grabbed my hands with his and pushed them across the table in the right way, forcing the crumbs with one of my hands into the other. The crumbs were old and greasy, and the sponge stank.

My father had a cup of coffee.

"Well," he said, "time to make a picnic basket of food for lunch." He made tuna fish sandwiches with olives on rye bread, peanut butter and jelly sandwiches, and a mayonnaise sandwich for Bobo. He packed plums and a Thermos of iced tea, Milano cookies and Swiss cheese. There were also potato chips and Slim Jims. We loaded the car: two rakes, the beach chair, umbrella, suntan lotion, fishing gear and tackle, and some books.

"Hey, let's stop on the way and buy some bait for fishing."

I went into the store with him while Bobo waited in the car. From an ice cream freezer the man took out a plastic bag filled with frilly pink sea worms. "How's the fishing?" my father said. "Any striped bass yet?"

"No, it's too early for that," the man said. "Another week or so and they should be running."

"Well, we'll see what we can get." The man looked at my father as if it was apparent he knew nothing about fishing. But my father didn't appear to notice until he walked out of the store and gave Bobo the bag of worms to hold. "We'll just see about that," he said.

We parked the car in the parking lot. The beach was empty and it was very windy. "Let's go down to the end. I don't like to be in the middle of a crowd." Making all those sandwiches and buying the bait had taken up a lot of time. It was almost time to eat. Thin clouds trickled in over our heads.

"I don't know how long we're going to feel like staying," my father said, "but this is our vacation. We'll do whatever we feel like. Let's just take each minute as it comes, all right? Bring your sweaters in case it gets cold."

"I'm hungry," Bobo said.

"It's not lunchtime yet."

I carried the chair and umbrella, my father had the fishing gear and the picnic basket, and Bobo trailed behind with the blanket and a paper bag filled with the books and suntan stuff. My father was already miles ahead. "Wait," Bobo said. "Wait for me, I have sand in my shoes." He sat down on the ground, the blanket at his side, took off his shoes and socks, shook them out, and put them on again.

After a few steps I said, "Bobo, do you want me to carry some of those things?"

"No, wait, don't go on without me. It happened again."

"Bobo, why don't you just leave your shoes and socks off this time?"

"I don't like to," he said. "Then I get sand between my toes." I made him take his shoes off and put the socks into them. Then I tied the laces together and strapped them around his neck. He looked very laden down.

My father had arrived at the far end of the beach and was setting everything up. His fishing pole was already put together and he cast his line into the surf. Bobo threw the bag and blanket down and ran toward the water. "Come on, Earl," he said. "Come on!"

I followed him down to the water. We had our bathing suits on underneath our pants. The bottom of my bathing suit was too small and scraped my legs. Bobo ran to the edge of the water and ran back screaming when a wave touched his feet. The water was icy.

I went back to take my jeans off. My father took his pants off too. His legs were very thick and hairy. His bathing suit was tiny. "I need a new bathing suit," I said. "I don't like this one. It's too small."

"Why didn't you say something before we got here?" my father said. "Why didn't your mother get you a new one before we left?"

"It's not her fault. I forgot to tell her. It's too cold to swim, anyway."

The beach and ocean were not what I had expected. The sand was coarse and at the top of the beach was a narrow bathtub ring of cuttlebones, empty Clorox bottles and clam shells with small holes in them, perfectly round. "Who drilled holes in all these shells?" Bobo said.

"Some type of animal bored a hole right through them, and it ate the inside. I'll look it up in the book," my father said. I put the shells down near the blanket. My hands smelled.

All morning my father fished and read. At lunchtime Bobo and I came back to him. My father had caught something he put into the red pail filled with water. It was a large fish, speckled with black. It had a flattish head and many strange pointed spines emerging from it. It circled the dull water of the pail looking for a way out.

"Wow," Bobo said. He peered into the pail.

"I don't think there's much use in keeping this one," my father said. "I don't think it makes very good eating. I just kept it to show you."

"Let's throw it in," Bobo said. He put his hands into the pail. Then he took them out. "I don't think I should touch it."

I took the fish in my hands and threw it into the air. It smacked into the water, twisting around as it fell. Before we could see it swim away a wave broke and there was only white spray. Nothing marked where the fish had fallen.

My father brought out the sandwiches. The jelly had made the bread soggy in some, and the iced tea had melted parts of the tuna ones. Everything tasted very good. Bobo broke the crusts off the mayonnaise sandwich and ate it. "Don't pick the crusts off. You're just wasting food, Bobo."

"What are you reading, Dad?" I said. My father looked over at me. Bobo quickly buried the crusts in the sand.

"A book about the Eskimos." He stretched out on a blanket and peeled a banana. His bathing suit was really much too little. Parts of him were nearly visible. I felt bad for him. "It's a very interesting book. Maybe you'll take a look at it when I'm done. It's supposedly a true-life account about a white man who went off to live with the Eskimos. Most of the time they live in complete darkness. About nine months out of the year nobody can take a bath."

"Doesn't it smell?" Bobo said.

"You bet. The air is so cold outside, the inside of the igloo becomes steamy just from human breath. If a stranger comes to the area, the Eskimo offers the man his wife for the evening, a gesture of politeness and warmth. What do you think of that?"

"Not much fun if they haven't taken a bath in nine months," I said. My father thought this was very funny.

"You have grape jelly in your beard, Daddy," Bobo said.

My father wiped his face with a napkin.

When we were done eating it started to rain. "Maybe it will stop," my father said. He went back and cast the line in one last time, but it started to rain harder and we had a great deal of stuff to bring back to the car. There was only one other car in the parking lot. A man and a woman were sitting in it. They were smoking cigarettes. The inside of the car was white with smoke. I wondered why they didn't open the windows, how it was possible for them to breathe.

All afternoon we sat in the living room and watched the storm. My father brought out his oil paints and made a small painting, using large lumps of paint. "What is that supposed to be?" Bobo said.

"Abstract."

"Can you scratch my back, Dad?" Bobo said.

My father put the paints away in the box and Bobo climbed onto his lap. My father pulled Bobo's shirt up. They sat in front of the window. Every few minutes there was more lightning and it was raining hard. My father scratched my brother's back. Bobo's eyes were half closed like a cat's and my father drowsed.

"My turn," I said.

"One more minute," Bobo said.

"My turn."

"Earl, you don't have to compete with Bobo for my attention," he said. He rose abruptly and took his kit of marijuana and papers from the coffee table. Then he sat back down and lit a joint. I was going to say I was sorry.

"More, Daddy."

"When I'm done smoking this joint." He pulled Bobo's shirt back down. Bobo went into the bathroom and accidentally used my toothbrush instead of his own.

"Who used my toothbrush?" I said. "You jerk, mine is the red one. You slobbered all over it." I wouldn't speak to my brother for a long time. He lay on the top bunk.

"Earl? Earl? Are you mad at me? For using your toothbrush?"

"I'm trying to sleep."

"No talking in there, you guys. It's time to go to sleep."

The next day my father took us to a small beach covered with rocks. "Let's get the raincoats on, kids," he said. "Looks like it's going to rain." From his shoulder bag he took out three huge, smelly raincoats he had bought at an Army-Navy store for a quarter apiece. When Bobo got into his it came down to the ground. Inside it he looked small and demented. The arms drooped almost to his knees. My father rolled the sleeves up for him. "Guess these are a little big for you guys." He started to laugh. "But at least they'll keep the rain off."

I wrestled with mine, trying to get into it. It was made of green, cracked rubber. My father came over and hoisted me into it. When he was pulling the sleeves on over my arms he lifted me off the ground a little. "Whoops," he said.

"Whoops, you're pulling my arms off, Daddy," I said.

We carried bags filled with Tupperware and empty cole slaw containers. We left the fish tank back at the house. Far ahead of us my father carried the Audubon book of fish and sea life in one hand. He wore rubber shoes and had on a Mexican cowboy hat. It still was not sunny. Between the rocks were small pools of water, left behind when the tide went out. Soon my father disappeared behind some rocks. Large homely seagulls sat on the boulders at one side. They looked very plain, with gawky expressions on their faces. When one stood up it had red legs. "Shoo," Bobo said. There were slicks of oil on some of the rocks. We caught up with my father, bent over a pool.

"An eel," he said. "Come quickly." Bobo and I ran to him. He tried to catch the eel, but it slipped between the corners of the rocks. I saw it for a second. Black and greasy, it moved quickly. "An eel," my father said. "Now these here are hermit crabs. They take the shells from other animals—snails that have outgrown them—and crawl inside."

"Why?" I said.

"Why do you think, Earl?"

"Um. Well, maybe because—"

"For protection, of course. When the crab gets too large it moves out and finds a bigger shell."

"What happens when it doesn't have a shell?"

"It is unprotected, Earl. It's soft. It has to find another home quickly or it might be eaten." Bobo picked up a hermit crab. It pinched him on the fingers. He dropped it and started to cry. Then he looked at my father and stopped crying.

My father led us around the rocks. He knew everything about all the different things in each of the pools. There was a starfish in one. We collected small minnows in the Tupperware containers and filled them with water. He told us everything. "I used to do this during the summer when I was a kid," he said. "I went camping with my parents. My father and I would walk for miles along the beach. My mother stayed behind. My father and my uncles and aunts would take a place at the shore for part of the summer. I was very close to my father." Bobo and I climbed over the rocks, trying to keep up with him. We walked out along the sea wall. The waves broke against it, covering us with a peppery, wet dust. "Be careful kids. Don't slip."

Where the water covered the rocks at high tide, barnacles grew. "The barnacle opens at this end," he said, showing us the black, closed hole at the pointy end.

"How does it eat?" Bobo said.

"When the water covers it at high tide the barnacle opens. Small, wavy cilia reach out. It collects things from the water."

"Why doesn't it die when there is no water?"

"It closes up when the water is gone. If there was no water, it would die, but the tide comes back in."

"What if it didn't?" I said.

"The tide always comes in, Earl. Don't ask stupid questions." He broke a barnacle open to show us what was inside. I looked in the other direction. Streamers of algae and periwinkles stuck to the rocks. Some of the periwinkles grew on mussels.

"What did your mother do?" I said.

"My mother? My mother? When?"

"When you were on vacation."

"She didn't do anything. She just sat on a beach chair, eating."

"Didn't she like to look for things on the rocks?"

"No. She wasn't interested in much of anything. My father wanted to divorce her."

"Why didn't he?" Bobo said.

"She was a very sick person." My father shook his head. "You can't live your whole life for somebody else. Life is too short." He smiled at us. Then he sat down on the rocks to smoke some marijuana.

"How did you meet Mom?" Bobo said. My father waved the grass in the air, to indicate he couldn't speak until he had exhaled. "Come on, Bobo, let's play," I said. We walked down to the water where the rocks were still wet. I used a sharp rock and broke some of the mussels off. Then I smashed them open. Inside they were filled with old slime.

We put water in the red pail and brought it back to the house.

"Wash the fish tank out," my father said. "It may have soap in it. We don't want the stuff to die. The water has to be changed every day to keep it fresh. Earl, since you're the oldest, you do it."

We emptied the containers filled with crabs and snails and fish into the water. Bobo and I sat peering over the edge of the tank at the things inside, which did not move very much. The fish looked better when they were in the ocean. When my father got up and went back into the house we followed him. "Time for lunch."

He took things out of the refrigerator. On the table he put jelly, honey, rolls, butter, cheese, mustard, salami, relish, milk and pickles. Then he started to eat. "How come you eat some of everything, Dad?" Bobo said.

"How come you ask so many questions, Boborino?" My brother ate some pieces of salami and left the rinds on his plate. I didn't feel so good and didn't want anything to eat. My father mixed some clam chowder into some sour cream and ate that. Lots of food got stuck in his beard.

My father loved to eat. After lunch he went to sleep. His shirt was unbuttoned to his waist and his head leaned to one side.

"Let's get some water and put it on him," my brother said.

"I don't think so, Bobo."

One night my father invited his former secretary to dinner. She lived nearby and now did something else—sold houses and did needlepoint, from what I could understand. "Hello there," she said. Her front tooth stuck out a tiny bit.

"How do you do?" Bobo said. He shook her hand very formally and removed his baseball cap. She had a shrill, pointed face and looked around at our rented cottage.

"Bobo, you're not supposed to do that," I whispered to him when we were in the kitchen.

"Huh?" He blew his cheeks up like a balloon, then let the air out. "What do you mean?"

"I mean, don't say 'How do you do,' like that. It's too—" But I couldn't explain how my father's former secretary was baffled by my brother's dignified behavior, how people were put off by manners they weren't used to. My brother went back into the living room and explained to her how bees find their way back to the hive. My father smoked some marijuana and told Sibyl her husband was psychotic and should probably be locked up.

For dinner Sibyl and my brother ate flounder my father had

rolled up and stuffed with mushrooms. My father and I had clams. We removed each clam from its shell and pulled off a black cover from a part that stuck out. I dipped each clam directly in butter; my father put the clams in broth first, before the butter, and later drank the clam broth, hot and salty. We ate blood-red lobsters, getting out the meat with a whole set of tools my father brought along—a nutcracker, a pliers, some tiny forks and two dentist's picks. My father helped me crack open the tail and dig the juicy meat out. "This is how you have to do it," he said.

He explained the parts as we went along—how the eyes worked, where the brain was, the intestines, the roe. "Oh, how disgusting," Sibyl said. She took a dainty bite of flounder. A mushroom fell out of the corner of her mouth and onto the table. My father picked it up, dipped it in butter and put it into her mouth. Her tongue came out and wiped off some of the extra butter on my father's finger. Then my father said something I couldn't hear and the two of them laughed.

"Come on, kids, time for the fireworks," my father said. The three of them drove into town to watch the fireworks from the end of the pier. I bicycled furiously and met them there.

"Buy me some salt water taffy," my brother said.

"You spent your allowance for this week," my father told him. He and Sibyl sat down on the dock, their feet hanging over the edge. My father had his arm around her.

After it got dark the fireworks were sent above the water from the end of the pier and went off with a thud that left a hole in the base of my stomach. The reflection of the pink and green fireworks was so bright it was hard to know which way to look. At the end a lot of fireworks went off at once. My brother got very excited and wanted my father to look but my father didn't notice. He was too busy kissing Sibyl.

The crowd applauded. I was left to pedal home in the dark. "Be careful," my father said.

When I got home Bobo was already asleep. My father told me to go to sleep too. I got up later to go to the bathroom and I heard a sound like two dogs panting. I didn't turn the light on, but outside the bathroom door I stopped. In the living room my father and Sibyl were lying on the sofa that pulled out into a bed. They made a lot of noise and didn't notice me. I went to the bathroom, then went back to bed, closing the bedroom door behind me.

In the morning Sibyl was gone. "Is everything packed, kids?" my father said. "Earl, clean out the fish tank and put it into the car." I went out to the porch. Everything in the tank was dead. Minnows floated at the top. Their eyes were white. The only thing left alive in the tank was a hermit crab, scuttling at the bottom. I had forgotten to change the water.

Sometimes I thought there was no reason for my mother to have gotten married. She was like a tiny Japanese doll. Her skin had the whiteness of an almond cookie, powdered with confectioner's sugar. She did not seem to be a part of the real world.

While my father debated divorce, my mother wondered why she had married him in the first place. "Still," she said, "what choice did I have? I hated my job. And it seemed at the time that marrying a doctor would be a good thing. He was sexually attractive, and I thought he would make a good father . . ." Here she stopped herself and finished her dissection of an onion roll on the plate before her. "Your father was very gentle. In fact, he was the only man I went out with who didn't constantly attack me. The men I would meet used to take me out—a blind date, let's say. Then they drove around the block once and stopped. The first thing they said was, 'Did anyone ever tell you how beautiful you are?' Then they would leap on me like a dog on a piece of liverwurst. For a long time I believed all men were insane. Perhaps I still do."

"Even me?" Bobo said. He looked worried. He raced his cars faster under the table but he looked up at my mother.

"Your father and I fought a lot, it's true. We argued all the time. I don't remember arguing so much with anyone before. And yet I enjoyed being with him. We used to go to this place for pizza. Your father wore a white sharkskin suit and looked ridiculous. But he was very proud of his suit. Anyway, we would sit there laughing and giggling, making fun of the people we saw in the restaurant. I felt close to him.

"My father wasn't too fond of him, though. When I brought Daddy back to the apartment at night, after our date, my father would throw his alarm clock against the wall if he thought I was staying up too late." She showed me a picture of herself, only a few years older than I was at the time.

"Look at my eyes," she said. "I was stark mad, wasn't I? Don't you think? What would you think if you saw a picture of somebody looking like that?"

"I don't know. I guess you look strange."

"I was sweeping dust from under the coffee table this morning and mysteriously there I was in this photograph, seventeen and overweight. Don't you think it's strange, that it should just suddenly appear like that? I haven't seen this photograph for years."

"I don't know."

"How can you say you don't know? Look at my eyes in this picture. They're the eyes of a rabid animal."

My mother wondered—sometimes aloud—how much I really understood of what she said to me. She had trained me to listen to her, like a little parrot that sat with one side of its head tilted quizzically. She hoped she hadn't done too much damage speaking to me as if I were an adult, but still she went on.

"You don't know how lucky you are," she said. "For instance, I didn't go away to college, because we didn't have the money, and every evening I came home from school and cried."

"Why?"

"I don't know. I was miserable. An excess of hormones, perhaps. In the evening my father would play the hi-fi. It was the first hi-fi we had ever owned."

"What's a hi-fi?" Bobo said. He sat under the table, untying my shoelaces and tying them back up again.

"You know, a stereo. The three of us, my mother and father and I, sat together in the living room every night and listened to the classical music radio station. I looked forward to the program every day. When I heard the music it was as if something tired inside me was at last allowed to sleep. But each evening, as soon as the music began, my father would jump up and fiddle with the dials. As soon as he sat down he would jump up again and start adjusting things. I was ready to kill him. But I knew he was getting great pleasure from his adjustments, so instead I would go into my room, lie down on the bed and cry and cry."

"Weren't your parents upset?" I said. "What did they do?"

"What could they do? They were used to it by then."

My mother claimed to be able to remember every single thing that had ever happened to her. She remembered the name of every child in her class at elementary school, and mentioned them often. She remembered her boyfriend from when she was five years old. "His name was Cookie. In great detail he would tell me the plot of a Popeye cartoon he had seen the previous Saturday. 'And then Popeye took out his can of spinach!'"

My brother looked up from under the table, briefly interested.

My mother said, "I would stare at Cookie's eyes—he had cross eyes, I can remember—and I would watch him swagger around. Even at that age I knew what it was like to be bored by some man's stories. How many years have I known how to pretend, to listen, admiring, attentive? Is this some animal instinct only women possess?"

"Search me."

She said, "I would tell Cookie, 'Oh my!' and try to sound fascinated. My first boyfriend. Another time my uncle—the one with the removable wooden leg—sat me down on his lap and told me the story of Goldilocks and the Three Bears. Even at the age of five I had already heard that story one million times, but at least that meant I knew when I was supposed to laugh and when to act afraid. I could have been a great actress, if I had made up my mind to it. In high school I was in a play and I was terrific. But I had to do the matinee because the teacher gave the evening performance to her pet."

This was what my mother's life had been. It hadn't improved any since. She told these stories to me as if reading from the encyclopedia, even while Bobo was too young to understand what was being said. Bobo sat under the kitchen table and then moved to a chair, putting his collection of matchbox cars on top of the table and whizzing them around. My mother stared at the cars he wheeled back and forth as if memorizing these too. The red Camaro, the BP truck, something holding white plastic bottles, and then beneath them the brown and yellow Formica table. It was a wedding present from one of my father's relatives who owned a Formica factory. It was a dull, yellow speckled pattern like scrambled eggs.

"How I hated this table even then!" my mother said. "For thirteen years we haven't been able to buy another kitchen table, because this one was so solidly made. We got the worst wedding presents." She was embroidering a blue and white tablecloth, to keep her mind off cigarettes and the impending divorce, a subject my father had not completely made up his mind about.

"What were your wedding presents?" At age ten I could have recited them by heart.

"His family chipped in and bought us the set of flatware." The flatware looked as if it came from a highway restaurant.

"Did you get to pick it out?"

"No." My mother was not a materialistic person. In fact, my father was often amazed at how little she cared for possessions, how unimportant she found choosing a new toilet-seat cover. It was just that she had never been able to forget one single thing. She was burdened with detail upon detail, fact after fact, all adding up to something as yet unknown. Together we recited the litany of the wedding presents, an oral history of the past. Later, when the years before the divorce melted like snow, only these facts, articles long ago lost, remained.

"A huge silver-plated platter," she said. "The minute we took it out of the box it looked corroded. It was covered with a pattern of tiny stars and stripes. We gave it as a present later on to Daddy's friend—the one who came along on our honeymoon with us. He loved it. He thought it was wonderful. It had little claw feet that tipped over."

"He came along on your honeymoon with you?" I said. I was dismantling a broken alarm clock before my mother's eyes. This was something Bobo would have liked to do, but it was my turn. Though I had no real interest in taking apart the clock, I didn't feel it was anything Bobo was entitled to do.

"Well, we ran into him—accidentally—at the very spot in Florida we had chosen to go on our honeymoon. But I always felt he followed us there."

"Oh. What else did you get?"

"Several coffee pots, large metal coffee percolators. We gave two away and kept one for ourselves. It broke right away."

I looked at my mother. "What did you say when you and Daddy opened all that junk? Did you laugh?" Their wedding presents were a disaster from which their marriage never recovered.

"I don't know," my mother said. "We opened the presents before the wedding, when nobody else was around."

"Did the two of you have the same taste? How did you know that if you were laughing at something, Daddy might not think it was nice?"

"By then . . . we knew each other's taste well enough. We

knew, by the time we got married, that we had pretty much the same taste. His mother insisted on a large wedding party. We didn't want a large wedding party. We only wanted a few friends. But she insisted. Two hundred people in their backyard. I didn't have a good time."

When my mother was two years old she used to play under the window of her apartment out on the street. This was in Washington Heights, before her parents moved to Queens. One morning at nine o'clock she was singing to herself on the sidewalk when a man yelled out the window for her to be quiet and dropped a bucket of water on her. I often questioned her about this experience; it was one of the few things she had no personal memory of. But I, for some reason, remembered it with great vividness, though of course in reality that was impossible.

"I don't really remember much that has ever happened to me," I told her. "Only your memories. Only the things that have happened to you."

The incident of the water being poured on her head aroused the interest of the newspapers, and several reporters had come to talk to her and her mother. It was written up in the newspapers with a picture of her, aged two, now dressed in clean clothes. It was captioned, "A Minute Mystery," which I thought meant it was supposed to take only a minute to figure out what had happened. I often looked at the yellowed picture of her, when we visited my grandmother, and wondered who would ever have suspected she would grow up to become my mother, would grow up and get a divorce?

"I would have recognized you even if I didn't know that was your picture," I said. "I would always recognize you."

"Me too," Bobo said.

My mother said with pleasure, "I knew having children would give me a gang. See, I always wanted to be a member of a gang. I knew if I had you kids then I would have a gang of my own when you grew up."

My mother still kept in touch with her nursery-school teacher. "And I am the only person I know who does," she told us with some pride.

My father said he would try harder to get along with our mother and we would not get a divorce just yet. He bicycled to work, followed by the family dog, King Kong, a massive poodle with a crooked mouth that showed his lip curled in a perpetual leer. "Go home," my father yelled angrily on the driveway, as the dog ran close to his side, nipping at his heels. But the dog was not well-trained, and usually followed him all the way to the college, an expensive and luxurious school for girls, where my father worked as a psychiatrist in the health department, in addition to working at the local hospital.

When the two of them got to the school the dog went off for the day in search of girls who fed him chocolate Florentines, wads of peanut butter and other delicacies they were likely to keep in their rooms. He was a well-known dog.

My father went to his office, a room on the third floor of Reid Hall that was furnished with an antique desk and a Chesterfield couch for his young patients to lie on, black leather worn smooth and supple with age. His own chair was also leather and studded with round brass upholstery tacks. On the walls were three Chinese brush paintings of game cocks fighting—the same two cocks, one red and the other green and gold, seen battling from three different positions. In the hallway was a large avocado plant he had grown from a seed, along with several cactus plants. Often the deans and even the president would show these plants off to important guests.

Above this miniature arboretum was a sign announcing my father's title: head of the mental health department. He said this didn't mean too much, just that he had administrative duties besides seeing patients, and also the ability to hire and fire his staff. Working under him were a psychologist and two psychiatric social workers. The rest of the health department was not large either—several gynecologists, a nurse, the receptionist (huge, deflatable-looking breasts and a rather weary face, I remember) and three doctors who alternated workdays.

Although my father was not a terribly tall man he was massively built. His eyes were deep set, dark brown, under two bushy eyebrows, one of which curved up in a fierce twist that gave him a perpetually quizzical look. In his spare time he sawed and stacked cords of wood for the winter, cleared brush from the property and welded steel rods into Freudian sculptures of excessive proportions. His muscles were very developed, the envy of Bobo and me.

"I'm in better shape now than I was when I was eighteen," he used to say to us, and on Monday mornings on his way to work after the strenuous weekend, he would rub his biceps ruefully, but at the same time looking pleased.

When my father was not on call at the hospital he took us to the place in the country he said we would someday live. "Too many insects," my mother said, and waited in the car. The light filtered through the leaves and through the windows of the car, which were rolled up.

"Look, she's speckled," Bobo said as we followed our father. We had come to the property the week before, and she had gotten seven deerfly bites on her arms and legs. The swelling still had not gone down.

"I can't even bend my arm," she said. She was poisoned. She tried to make my father examine her, but he said that he had been bitten too, and it was not all that bad.

"You know, Mavis," he said, "if you don't want to get bitten, put on mosquito repellent and wear long-sleeved clothing." He looked at my mother as if he had never seen anyone so stupid in his entire life.

"The insects bite me right through my clothing," my mother said. My father opened the trunk of the car and got out his machete. My mother stayed behind, reading a book.

We tagged down the path after my father. In the lime-colored light the air was full and shrill with the sound of insects. There were small grasses and white hard fungi attached to the trees. My father went first, holding back the growths, and then Bobo, who in turn took the branches and held them carefully so they wouldn't snap in my face as I followed. Only a few feet in from the road the trees were bigger and the trunks felt warm, as if inside the bark someone was breathing.

Wielding machete and pruning fork, wearing his old Army shirt and canvas work gloves, my father snipped at one bush after the next.

"Dad, be careful," Bobo said. "The branches are flying off into my face."

My father wiped his neck and chin. He was already sweating. He had developed a particular hatred for a very large juniper bush in the center of the path about halfway down, and Bobo and I had to wait while he cut. The broken branches reeked of a piney, alcoholic scent.

"This juniper bush," my father said, "must be twenty years old at least. Look how big around the base is." The base of the bush was about three inches around, and though he gouged at it, it wouldn't get any smaller. "That means"—another grunt as he struggled to cut the trunk—"that means nobody has used this path for at least that long, or it wouldn't have grown up." He stopped for a moment and straightened up. "This path used to be the main town road."

"And now you're restoring it." This thought gave me great pleasure, that my father was rebuilding something that had come undone.

"Bam, bam, bam," my brother said, kicking restlessly at a tree.

My father gave up on the bush and my brother and I followed him through the undergrowth to the bottom of the hill, where a little stream crossed under the pathway and down the other side to the big stream below. "I don't know how large the source is," he said, looking at the water, which was still and muddy. "I'm going to have to dig a better stream bed for it, and maybe, if I can figure out where it's coming from, I can dam it up and get the water to feed into the pond."

While ripping up poison ivy plants from the ground with his gloved hand, my father told us more history of the land. When he stopped he wiped his forehead. "Hey Dad," I said, "aren't you going to get poison ivy if you were touching it with that glove and then you touched yourself?"

"I don't get poison ivy. Never have. I'm just not allergic to it."

"Maybe we're not allergic to it either," Bobo said.

"Maybe. But there's no point in taking any chances."

We walked on through the field. My father pointed out a rare wild gentian plant. He showed us where he planned to build a pond. We walked around the edge of the field, so he could survey the whole from the far end.

He spotted some grapevines, which grew up and covered branches of the trees they had long ago strangled. They were in the middle of a tremendous patch of lush, succulent poison ivy. My father was delighted. "Look at that! My own vineyard. Kids, we have our own wild grapevines here. When grapevines grow wild like this, they're called fox grapes."

Using a stick he carved on the spot, he managed to skewer some of the clusters and bring them down. "Here, try this." He popped one of them into his mouth.

The grape had a very thick skin and inside there was only a little pulp, sour and filled with two huge seeds. My father was pleased. "Let's take as many as we can and bring them home. I'll have Mavis make grape juice out of them. Maybe I can try to make wine."

My father couldn't have known that picking grapes was only the first step he would take on a downhill road to self-sufficiency. None of us could have known then that only a short time later he would learn to live off the land, fry day-lily bulbs and blossoms, spear frogs, brew tea from sassafras leaves. Shortly his life would be devoid of people and filled instead with machines making yogurt, devices to grind peanut butter, home smokers to preserve the trout he caught himself in his own stream, vats cooking jam, bottles of alfalfa sprouts on top of the refrigerator sprouting away. Signs and portents mean nothing at the time of their inception.

He looked out across the tangled field and the trees that covered the hills. Some cool air blew up from the stream. "I'm going to have all this cut down and reseeded," he said. He kicked at the dirt with his boot. "Let's go and see where I'm going to have the pond put in and come back for the grapes later." He smiled at the two of us, as if noticing for the first time that we were there.

"I guess this is all ours, huh Dad?" I said. He did not respond but scruffed up my hair.

Though it irritated him immensely when my mother went into a daydream, especially when he was talking to her—"Hello!" he would say, snapping his fingers in front of her—he didn't realize that he often went into a trance of his own, worked into a sweat chopping trees or moving rocks. The rest of the world, my mother, Bobo and I, could have disappeared and he wouldn't have noticed. Unaware that we were waiting patiently for him to wake up, he didn't realize that we weren't sharing his visions, only wishing he would play a game of ball with us.

In a small meadowland off to the side of the large field the grass was more luxuriant. It was dark green here, and the ground was a little spongy, even rubbery beneath the feet, while the tall trees shaded the area, making it cooler than out in the big field.

"There are at least three underground springs here," he said. "I've talked to the contractors, and they say it wouldn't cost too much to have the whole area dug up and made into a lake. I'm going to have a big L-shaped pond, with the deepest part right in the middle of the L. The fill they take out I'll have spread in the field—it should be very rich soil—and then on two sides there will be a beach, and I'll have white sand brought in for that."

Bobo and I waited with the grapes while he told of his plans. The house at the top of the hill, he said, would look out through the trees to the pond below. It would be the most beautiful place when he finished with it.

We went across the field and up the steep hill, instead of taking the longer, more gentle incline my father had so recently begun to clear out.

We passed three tremendous shagbark hickory trees my father had found on an earlier visit by himself. Their huge girths were covered with a shaggy, splintery bark, like shingles. A squirrel, monkeylike, chattered in the trees above our heads. My father put his grapes down on the pine needles and picked up a couple of nuts from the ground. The nuts were encased in thick wooden shells, very green, and already split from the inner nut. He pulled the case off the rest of the way and showed us the hard round nutshell, smooth and brown, inside. "I'll bet these are very hard nuts. But maybe they would make good eating. I'll try and crack them at home."

We walked through the pine forest. There was not so much undergrowth here because the pine trees were very large ones, blocking the light from the ground and making it difficult for smaller plants to grow. Where the sun shone through it made little hot spots of brightness on the ground, like tiny fires.

"It used to be that if a person wanted to get away from the twentieth century, from the rest of mankind, it wasn't hard to do," my father said. A stalk of timothy grass he had picked in the field below was sticking out of the side of his mouth. "Nowadays it's not so easy. When my father was alive he said I should become a psychiatrist to make a lot of money and get out of the rat race. I said no, I was becoming a psychiatrist because I wanted to help people. Now I'm not so sure. Is anybody really worth helping? Is any of this lousy world worth saving? I just don't know. I could be very happy living out here, if I didn't have to contend with the rest of humanity."

"Even us, Dad?" Bobo said.

My father looked up and smiled briefly. "But, God, it's a lonely existence. If there was only one person out there, one other human being who could see things as I saw them, who had my vision. Then it might not be so bad."

"I'm here, Dad," Bobo said.

I thought of my mother, waiting in the car. "Don't you think we better go make sure Mom's all right?"

"Yeah, sure," my father said. He sighed and went on ahead.

The ground was covered with tobacco-colored pine needles and the sounds of the trees and the hot wind, the cars on the road above, the occasional airplane overhead, were quieter here, in the dense, dark cover of the trees. Because nobody had been in the area for a very long time, the lower branches of the pine trees, dead and brittle, had not been chopped off. They stuck out from the chocolate bark like men's arms. At the ends they were tipped with fingers. My father broke a few of them off. The branches snapped loudly. The edges left were sharp knives.

"All this timber is very dangerous when it's so dry at this time of year. I hope we don't have any trouble with forest fires. I want to clear out all the dead wood. I've already gone through and marked all the smaller trees I want to have cut down. The house, when it is finished, should have a wonderful view if some of these trees are taken out."

"I don't like it here," Bobo said. My father was not listening. He had crushed some pine needles between his fingers and was holding them up to his nose. "I can't believe I bought the place. This is great. I feel fantastic. God, that was a smart move, Robert Przepasniak."

I touched one of the stunted pine trees my father had marked with Day-Glo tape. When I took my hand away it was covered with thick, gummy tar pitch I couldn't wipe off, as if the tree was trying to cling to me. I put my hand up to my hair. Now my hair was filled with pitch. I was afraid I would lose the grapes, so I didn't try to stop and rub my hand in the dirt or against the trunk of one of the trees.

"Let's go and take a look at the house site, kids."

"It's getting late, Dad," I said. "Mom's waiting for us."

"Yeah. Just reading in the car. I bet she hasn't gotten out of the car the entire time we've been gone. You know, sometimes your mother is like something out of a gothic novel. That she could roll up the windows and sit in the car on such a beautiful day."

"Don't you think Mom's cute, Dad?" Bobo said. He grabbed my father's sleeve.

My father snapped a branch between his fingers. "That's true. She may not be athletic, she may not be interested in the outdoors, but she does have some endearing qualities. I remember when I taught her to drive. Impossible! I never thought she'd learn. She used to shift gears like she was riding a bucking bronco. Once she backed right into a phone booth. Another time she got stuck parallel parking on a hill. What a disaster, huh kids? But it was funny."

In the car my mother had stopped reading. She was looking quietly out the window, a peaceful expression on her face. "Well," she said, when we got up to the doors of the car, "where have you been! Did you have fun? You must have been busy, you've been gone a long time."

"Were you just sitting here all this time?" my father said in an irritated voice, then tried to cover it up. "Look what we've brought you," he said quickly, showing her the grapes he had picked.

"Mm," my mother said, in an impressed tone.

"Can you make grape juice with them? We thought you could make them into grape juice."

My mother said she didn't know, but she would try.

When we got home my mother had to make dinner, and my father, rather than wait for her to finish, decided to try to make the juice on his own. It was thick and pulpy stuff when he was done, though he claimed to be pleased with the results, and was ready to try again next year. My brother liked it, too, smacking his purple lips at the results.

Neither Bobo nor I got poison ivy that week, but my mother came down with a severe case of it, picked up how or where no one knew.

My father suggested it might have come from washing our clothes that had touched some of it. "I'll be glad when the house is built and we can all move out there," he said, some days later.

"Why don't you and the kids go on over there and camp out, while I'm away at work? You don't have to wait for me."

My mother, putting calamine lotion on herself in the bathroom, did not say a thing.

The evening we moved into the new house, my father was on call at the hospital, and because our telephones were not yet installed, he stayed behind at the old house. My mother, Bobo and I were alone in the unfurnished mansion. It seemed very empty and dismal, not like a place anyone would want to live. Outside, it was very dark; unlike the house we had just moved from, there were no other houses anywhere around.

"I don't like it here," Bobo said.

My mother found some cocoa in one of the boxes and got out some of the kitchen mugs and made us all cocoa. "When your father was born," my mother said, "he was showered with love, gifts, attention and chicken soup. And he was an only child, which makes a difference. He was born in 1929, the beginning of the Depression, not a very good time to be born. When the mills closed your grandfather became a photographer and your father went with him on Saturdays to help carry the equipment. For five cents, your father used to tell me, they could get a malted milk shake at the drugstore. He has told me this rather frequently. You see, there are certain key incidents in each person's life, and your father tells his over and over."

"That's true," I said. "He doesn't have a very good memory, does he?"

"No," she said. "For instance, he likes to tell about how, when he was in college, he connived or manipulated a local waitress into making him slices of French toast for breakfast by dipping the bread a longer time into the egg batter than she was supposed to. Because of this she lost her job. I'm not sure what it means to him, but I must have heard that story a hundred times."

"What else?"

"Your grandmother Ivy likes to talk about how when Rob was a baby they would take him to the bathroom to pee and he would be asleep the whole time. All their friends would gather around the door of the bathroom, and your father never remembered any of it. This must be a key incident of some kind for her, because no matter how often your father begs her not to repeat it, she insists on doing so.

"Your grandparents were Communists, or so they claimed, but I doubt they actually joined the Party. They marched with the Wobblies and were there when the police rushed the workers on horseback. Grandma Ivy was almost trampled. She was carrying your father at the time and your grandfather pulled her to safety. Your father was supposedly an accident."

"What's an accident?" Bobo said.

"Unwanted. Grandpa Leo wanted very much to divorce Ivy."

"You told me that you and Daddy were going to stay together."

"I didn't say that, Earl. You heard what you wanted to hear. I said I don't know, I want to do what will be best for all. Now, as I was about to say: for your grandfather, every sentence Ivy spoke carried with it a gratuitous piece of advice. Leo and your father treated her horribly, made fun of her, jeered at her, called her stupid. But she never seemed to mind being treated that way. Every time Leo brought up the subject of divorce she cried, which is why, he claimed, he stayed with her. But I doubt if that was the real reason."

"What was?"

"Who knows? The three brothers and their wives used to gather at family meetings. Your grandfather was the most intelligent of the brothers. Though he had never been to college he was very interested in learning. It was always he who kept the conversation going, who asked such questions as, 'Is there life after death?' and 'Could the crater found in Siberia have been caused by a UFO?' that led to heated intellectual discussions."

"Sounds pretty good," I said.

"The women were not allowed to enter into these discussions. They could listen or prepare food in the kitchen. Your father, because he was the only child of the most important brother and because he went to medical school, was adored by everyone. He was like Freud, worshiped and doted on.

"Your father likes to say that he's a true Renaissance man— that he can do everything. He says he's a man of the future, higher on the evolutionary scale than the rest of society."

"Why?"

"Oh, you've heard him say why."

"Tell me again."

"Well, for one thing, he never got any wisdom teeth on top or bottom. He says man doesn't need these teeth, they are just a useless throwback to a more primitive time. And he has a small head, and not much of a chin. He claims that these point out the fact that he's more highly evolved. It's going to take a while for the rest of mankind to catch up with him."

In 1936 Lou Costello knocked my father's two front teeth out in a fight. He was a few years older than my father and was to go on to fame as half the team of "Abbott and Costello." Much later on, my father became addicted to Abbott and Costello movies and other forms of slapstick humor.

My father and his parents lived over a grocery store. It was a tiny apartment that looked out on the main street, but it was convenient for picking up groceries. There were three rooms: the kitchen; a bedroom, decorated with a watercolor of a foreshortened nude that my grandmother had painted; and a living room, where my father slept on a sofa next to a collection of abalone and whelk shells that his grandfather—a poet who wrote bad poems in Yiddish, then had them privately printed in books he tried to sell door-to-door—had bought on a trip to Atlantic City.

The kitchen was not very clean. All of the rooms had a thick sediment about them, due to my grandfather's habit of covering every available surface with small items. There were postcards pinned to the walls—of trips to Coney Island, Yosemite Park and Canada—all mailed to them by friends.

My grandmother had acted frequently, or perhaps not so frequently, in bit parts in the Yiddish theater. She had once met Stella Adler. "It would have been an easy thing for me to become a great actress," she reminded Bobo and me now, and my father then.

Often the bathroom mirror was smeared with greasepaint and mascara. Her photographer husband, Grandpa Leo, took occasional nude photos of her and she sometimes showed them to us to let us realize what she had once been: heavy thighs, tiny feet— she was not just somebody's grandmother.

"I spent a lot of time alone," my father told us, as he carved a huge piece of walnut down in the basement. He had gotten the walnut from a road crew cutting down unnecessary trees. Then he stored the wood out in the shed until it was aged enough to be carved. He brought it with us from the old house. It weighed at least two hundred pounds. "I hope this doesn't check."

"What's check?" my brother said.

"When the wood splits." My father used the chisel and mallet on the wood with great assurance, as if he were performing some complicated operation. Flecks of wood flew into the air.

"I hope I get hands like yours when I grow up," I said.

"Well, you have to work a lot," my father said. "I'll put you to work, develop some calluses on you. Let's see your hands." He put down the tools and picked up one of my hands. Between his, mine felt very small. "These are still little boy's hands," my father said, "but you have very wide palms, and that's a good sign. I bet you're going to have big hands when you get older."

"What about me?" Bobo said.

"You're going to have tremendous hands," my father said. He patted my brother on the head. Then he went back to his sculpting. "Hands as big as a gorilla's."

"Naw," my brother said.

"What are you making, Dad?"

"A big, naked woman," my father said.

"Oh," I said, "tell us more about when you grew up."

My father looked puzzled. "You really want to know? Well, when I was a kid I used to spend all my free time wandering alone along the Passaic River."

"Weren't you lonesome?" my brother said.

"Yeah, I guess you could say I was a pretty lonesome guy. I was an only child. I used to pretend to have friends, but even my pretend friends did not behave the way I wanted them to. Anyway, I was telling you about the Passaic. It was filled with goldfish."

"Really?" Bobo said. "How did they get there?"

"They had escaped and naturalized. Every fall, the goldfish swimming near the banks were trapped under the ice. It was like walking over a bed of writhing gold. And I used to think, if my life could just go on like this, then it would be worth living."

"And was it?" Bobo said.

"Ah, now that's a good question. I think to myself, Robert, this is it, better grab what you can, because when this is over there ain't nothing else."

"Didn't you have any pets or something to keep you company?" I said.

"Yeah. When I was a kid I had a dog called Inky. It sort of looked like the RCA Victor dog. One day, new tar was put down on the street in front of the apartment. It was a hot day, and the dog went out. So my mother decided that the way to get the tar off the dog was to soak him in kerosene in the bathtub. He died a few hours later."

Bobo got up. "I have to go now," he called from the top step.

"What was wrong with your mother?" I said. "What was she thinking of?"

My father shook his head. "Who knows?" The carving tool he was using skidded on the wood and cut him on the hand. He didn't seem to notice. "She was sick. It was a terrible thing to do." Little curls of shavings littered where he worked.

"I'm going upstairs."

"Hmm?" my father said. "What did you say?"

One night, only a short time after we moved into the new house, my parents gave a costume party. My father dressed as Fidel Castro. He wore his old Army jacket and glued on a black beard. At the last minute my mother tied a rug over her stomach, white and furry, and called herself the "Abdominal Snowman." It was terrible to see. She tied a huge white hat made of false fur over her head. Over the hat went ear muffs, and on her hands she put a pair of my father's ski mittens that were as big as boxing gloves.

On her body she wore some kind of gorilla skin, I don't remember what it was, I think a fake fur coat of some kind, or a balding bunny jacket. She looked charming and was bright and excited about having a party. Bobo and I were speechless.

"How do I look?" she said.

"Strange," I was finally able to say. Bobo only looked at her and left the room.

Meanwhile my father was writing things on pieces of my brother's construction paper before the guests arrived, such as FREE LOVE, MAKE LOVE NOT WAR, and FUCK YOU.

My mother was humiliated but could not do anything about it because it was the middle of the 1960s. "I'll avert my eyes," she said.

"Knock it off, Mavis. Jesus Christ. What a prude."

My father taped the pieces of paper onto the glass wall in the living room that looked out over the tops of the trees and spent several minutes admiring his handiwork.

Only a few guests came. A friend of my father's arrived, dressed as a penguin. He was always stopping by for a visit at times when my father was bound to be out, and when my mother, years later, grew less naive, she realized what it was he was after.

A woman named Susie Pimmer, who had once caught me in the act of drawing genitalia on models in the *New York Times Magazine* section ("What are you doing?" she had asked me gleefully. "Nothing." "Nothing?" Her voice was woozy with exaggeration and concern), was dressed as a cat. She had black whiskers penciled on her face that looked like they should be there permanently, and a long cigarette holder she kept chewing away at. Her limp husband was supposed to be an Indian rajah.

I was allowed to serve the hors d'oeuvres. Bobo did not care a bit and was watching TV in my parents' bedroom. The hors d'oeuvres were cubes of cantaloupe and fresh pineapple held together with a toothpick; an eggplant and olive mess that came from a little can and went on crackers; and cheese straws. I helped myself to a large number of them as I passed them around.

My mother said that this was the night she finally admitted to herself that her marriage was over. Where was the fun everyone was supposed to be having when they got dressed up in costumes? She imagined herself and all these adults at last allowed to play at being children, wearing brightly colored funny clothing, holding glasses with ice that tinkled gaily. She had always wanted a party where the things people said would be amusing and bright, where everyone was having a good time. That was the most important thing, that everyone enjoy themselves. My mother had looked forward to this night.

But many guests would not come because they were afraid to wear costumes. One couple had called her to say, "What if we were arrested or stopped by the police on the way to your house?" My mother couldn't get over their quivering cowardice. Another couple couldn't find a baby-sitter at the last minute. Someone else's husband had a cold. I felt very bad for my mother.

Finally she called all the guests, at least the ones who hadn't already canceled, and told them they didn't have to wear costumes if they didn't want to. She didn't bother to plan her own costume much before; she didn't want it to look too fancy, or the guests without costumes would feel out of place.

Halfway through the evening, when my mother finished getting the cheese straws out of the oven and arranging them on a tray so I could serve them, she went upstairs to make sure Bobo was all right. She pushed open the door to the guest bathroom (Were there clean towels? Had the toilet paper run out? I know how my mother's mind worked.), and there, in the middle of the room, in front of the mirrors that filled three of the four walls, my father and Susie Pimmer—her cat whiskers didn't seem to be painted on, my mother remembered thinking later, she told me, but must have been made from broom straws painted black and attached with adhesive—were wrapped around each other, two octopi in an embrace.

My father, opening one eye, saw the door swing open, and reaching out with one hand, pushed it partly shut. To my mother's surprise he caught her eye and smiled a smile that was both thin and fierce. Behind them, reflected in the mirror, she could see her own face, pinched and white. She shut the door herself.

Even at her own party my mother was not destined to have a good time.

But, as she so often reminded herself, she was not meant to. Hostesses were not the ones who were supposed to be enjoying themselves. She should never have been a psychiatrist's wife, she thought, and held her breath for as long as she could. Then she continued down the hall to check on Bobo.

Because the walls of the new house were made of glass, birds could not see them and flew straight into the house instead of around it. Many of them died. A grouse, the size of a small chicken, crashed during the end of the autumn and my father plucked it and roasted it for dinner. My mother wouldn't eat it. By then she was cooking the meals but was not there when they were ready, and I could not eat without her. Only my father and Bobo ate, as if nothing were different at all.

Bobo kept the wings of the grouse, pretty as a lady's hat, and perched them, one on each side of his head, with two of my mother's bobby pins. "Look, Earl! I'm a bird!" he said to me, and flew around the house wearing a red and blue Superman cape he had gotten for Halloween.

Sometimes the birds that crashed lived to fly away, but where a bird hit the window a greasy spot and a few feathers were left. One day I found a hummingbird on the deck. It wasn't paying enough attention to where it was going, I thought. It lay limp in my hands. It had a narrow, tubular beak, and from the end of the beak drooped a clear tongue. I stroked its feathers. They were red and green. The feathers seemed to vibrate, though the bird lay still. There was a filmy skin covering its eyes. "What have you got there?" my father said when he came out onto the deck with a newspaper in his hands.

"A hummingbird," I said. My father examined it with me. It was like a wilted jewel. It hurt my eyes to look at it too closely, and I handed it to my father.

"Put it down," my mother said to my father. "Maybe it will recover." My father paid her no attention and went on examining the bird, turning it over in his hands. "I said put it down!" my mother said. "You're going to kill it, touching it!" My father almost threw it on the ground and left it near the hammock.

"Wash your hands," my mother told me. "You don't know what kind of disease you could get."

Though I waited and waited, squatting stiffly beside it, the bird did not wake up and fly away.

My mother was upset, but what could she do? "It would break your father's heart to have to move out of this house," she said, "and so I'm letting him keep it. What do I want with it anyway, hideous place, costing too much to heat. He loves this house, let him live here. He told me"—she was crying again, but sound-lessly—"he told me, 'You and the children are millstones around my neck.'"

"What's a millstone?" my brother wanted to know.

"A rock, a type of rock."

"So what did he have to go and have kids for?" I said.

My mother sat at the top of the stairs, her pale, almost Oriental face squinched like a rubber doll's. Bobo looked uncomfortable. "You're in the way," I told him. I put my hand on my mother's shoulder. "Please don't cry," I kept saying. Bobo handed her some toilet paper to use as Kleenex.

My mother built a house at the bottom of the hill and we moved there. It was a Swiss chalet of modern design built by a company that specialized in cheaply made, rapidly put-together prefabricated homes. My father provided the land, a strip of meadow on the far side of the stream at the bottom of his property, the money for a down payment, and an antique lamp he found in a secondhand shop that gave out shocks when you turned it on.

It was a beautiful piece of acreage and except for a few difficulties—the inaccessibility of the main road in winter, the lack of water access except through my father's property, the blind driveway—it was a wonderful place to build a house.

Pieces of the new house arrived on the sides of trucks every day. My father was staying at his best friend's house until the divorce papers were finalized and the new house finished. If he came into the house, Bobo and I were told, the divorce papers wouldn't be effective. We were warned not to breathe a word about the nights he stayed over.

His best friend was living alone too. His wife, a tall coot of a blonde, had just left him, taking the four children with her but abandoning the cats and a balding beagle. One day my father took me over to show me where he was staying. The house was in the residential section of town. It was an old New England house, the kind he was contemptuous of. He preferred modern; however, the floors of his friend's house were made of ten-inch-wide planks, and that impressed him. "They just don't make floors like that anymore," he said to me, as he inspected it on his knees.

"Why?"

"There are no trees that big anymore. They've cut them all down. It would be too expensive to find them."

In the back of the house a little stairway on the second floor led up to a small apartment, separate from the rest of the house, with its own bathroom and octagonal-shaped bedroom. This was where my father was staying, though the two men did their cooking together. My father suffered frequently from indigestion, he told me, because his friend ate only healthy food. No meat was allowed in the house.

I was offered a cracker made from brown rice and cheese that reminded me of burnt cardboard. After I had nibbled at part of it I thoughtfully slipped it behind one of the couches in the living room. Though my father kept his apartment clean and soldier-neat, he could not keep up with the rest of the house and it was a disaster. Six or seven long-haired cats left their fur and droppings everywhere. My father, a hay-fever sufferer whose nose swelled up like a balloon at contact with the slightest irritant, couldn't step into the rest of the house without sneezing. Like a cocaine fiend, he was never without his bottle of Dristan Nasal Deconges-ant, which he snorted constantly. Books on mysticism, psychic phenomena and self-help were scattered with crumbs and dirty plates on every surface. When I went to get some ice from the freezer I found many small Band-Aid boxes which my father told me contained LSD and psilocybin. He believed in informing me of all the facts. The house was drafty and the windows were stuffed with tubular bolsters that were supposed to help but didn't.

It wasn't that the house was messier since Ian's wife had left, because Amanda had never been much of a housekeeper even when she was there. The four kids had no bedrooms but slept wherever they wanted.

Only a few days before she left, two of the smallest children, one eighteen months and the other four years old, had gotten into an open bottle of pills lying on the living room table and each had taken several tablets of LSD.

"What happened?" I said.

"Well," my father said, "they stood looking at the wall and giggling for several hours. Amanda called me, and I told her to give them orange juice with a lot of sugar in it."

I didn't want to mention this was the way those children acted most of the time anyway. My father didn't approve of people being so careless, or of the way they handed out marijuana brownies like tranquilizers to calm the kids, but he wouldn't have thought my telling him they were always like that was funny either. But, if I was lucky, he would have snorted gently to show he understood it was a joke.

Anyway, it was shortly after the youngest children took the LSD that Amanda ran off to California with a twenty-three-year-old boy named Kitely. Once Kitely told my father, in my presence, that I was far too tense for a kid and would no doubt grow up to have serious problems. He said I would probably become a lawyer. After this, whenever I saw Kitely I felt like flinging myself on his leg and biting him like a dog, to prove that he was indeed correct.

Amanda took the best car when she left and sold the Persian rug in the living room to raise some extra cash. Ian couldn't get over the fact that she had done this to him and lay on the floor of the living room chanting for hours, or frantically asking my bored father for advice.

The house was darker now, and chalky smelling with old sour marijuana smoke. The windows were never opened and black curtains were drawn across. On one wall, a picture of a shepherd leading a flock of starved-looking sheep was framed in an elaborate rococo frame, and stuck behind it was a mass of peacock and ostrich plumes.

Ian had a slight lisp and moaned very quietly, since he was depressed, though his voice when not depressed was hardly any different, but rather seductively graceful. He was suing for divorce now, too. He was ombudsman at the same college where my father worked, and of course hardly earned a quarter of my father's salary. This made my father the boss of their relationship, though my father, since he was a psychiatrist, was always treated with deference and even awe by his closest friends.

The four children Amanda had taken with her were all very strange in their own ways. The youngest, one of the LSD-takers, was subdued and seemed nearly retarded. He had a high, broad forehead and eyes with something called "split" pupils. They were a light blue and the pupil was very black. Instead of being round it was split and extended in a straight line like a cat's eyes. It was strangely beautiful and at first you couldn't tell what was wrong with the child. It took a lot of studying to see what gave him that blind look.

The next oldest was a sex-crazed girl. She was a blond six-year-old with a husky, Lauren Bacall voice. When she saw me she would fling herself on my lap and ask, "Do you think my mommy has nice titties?" I didn't know what to say. Sometimes she would ask if she could play "doctor" with me or she would talk about her parents' sexual relations. I dreaded going to Ian's house to visit my father before Amanda left with the kids. It was so embarrassing to be attacked by this dwarf. Had my father moved away from us only to end up in this madhouse? The two younger children were often given to acts of violence against themselves, hitting their heads against the wall, flinging themselves down flights of stairs. "What's wrong with them, Dad?" I said.

"Their mother is a very disturbed person," my father told me. "She's been in therapy for some time now. I think she should probably be committed to a mental institution, but there is no one else to look after the kids."

I played with my brother; my father came to see us on the weekends if he got a chance; my mother sat on the steps and wept. Sometimes late at night, if I looked out onto the driveway, I would see my father's car parked there, and voices coming from my parents' bedroom. But by morning the car would always be gone.

"Don't cry, Mom," Bobo said. "Please don't cry."

"I'm all right, really," my mother said. "Don't worry. I'll be fine. I have you and Earl, don't I? And there's really nothing to worry about. I don't mind, basically. It's just on the outside I feel humiliated and worthless."

"We'll take care of you, Mom." I did not care if I ever saw my father again.

In the meantime, my father's taste, along with his house, was in a terrible decline. The living room was redone, with a vast assortment of "final" touches. To replace the living room rug, the one item of furniture my mother took with us when we left, my father made his own—sheepskin pieces of various colors sewn together with the aid of a girlfriend.

Though I'm sure his original intent was to have a luxurious, colorful fur creation, the finished product was hairy and irregular—blue, red, orange, yellow, green, brown and white pieces of sheepskin. He put the rug on top of thick foam padding, and each time anyone entered his living room they were forced to remove their shoes, in what he told Bobo and me was a Japanese custom. "Take your shoes off!" he would bellow to my friends and his alike, if he caught one of them so much as bordering the rug with one soiled shoe.

Each week my brother or I was recruited to vacuum the inevitable ashes and wood shavings that fell from the fireplace onto the rug, the marijuana butts scattered from his frequent parties. The shavings and chips sank so deep into the fiber of the fur that, until it was worn down to a flat and balding mat several years later, the rug took nearly an hour to clean.

Gradually the rest of the living room deteriorated as well. I don't remember what the original lamp looked like that hung over his Eames chair, but it was replaced several times, first with one he made out of Styrofoam coffee cups glued back to back in a gigantic ball. The next one he made when he took up stained glass lamp-making as a hobby, though he took it very seriously, more seriously than his private psychiatric practice.

The largest of these lamps extended up to the ceiling, some fifteen feet high. It was in the shape of something which looked to me like a dinosaur, though my father insisted it was not. The head at the tip was a bright orange glass, and the rest—a thin, gangly necklike tube and a large round bottom—was a bright green.

At night my dad would light a fire in the huge fireplace, burn some sticks of incense and turn the ten or twelve lamps on. Some blinked, some did not, but each in its different hue and brilliance helped to illuminate his crazed acrylic paintings on the wall, the variegated rug and the peculiar artifacts my father had accumulated since the divorce: a brown pottery bowl from Mexico that appeared to be covered on the outside with rows of women's breasts; an antique hospital urinal that held peanuts; a polished ivory whale's tooth that protruded from the door.

I thought the living room looked demented. "But Dad, don't you think you have a lot of stuff in here?" My father just looked at me. It was obvious we did not think the same way at all.

By the time my twelfth birthday arrived we had been divorced for almost two months. My long term ambition was about to be fulfilled. What I wanted more than anything for a birthday present was a baby goat, a kid. Who knows, this desire may have originated in part from a story I read each year at Passover in the Haggadah, Passover being the only Jewish holiday my family bothered to celebrate, and at that it was only to please my grandmother, my mother's mother in New York, whom we visited each year at that time.

The story, at least as far as it went in the Haggadah—Anglicized editions put out by Hadassah—was that some guy's father bought him a goat for two zuzim, whatever that was, which then, through careful bargaining, proceeded to net him all kinds of other animals, along the same lines of plot as "The House That Jack Built."

Despite the objections of my mother, who wanted to know

where this goat was going to sleep, my father said he would get me one for a pet.

"He'll sleep with me," I said, and my father readily agreed, knowing it would not be living in his house. (Wrong again, Dad, I tell him now, years later—he sits on my shoulder, is always with me, even at this very minute. He was wrong because the goat, in the end, refused to stay in its little box, climbed on my chest during the night to nibble my hair, and was finally sentenced to a corner of the kitchen in my father's house.)

My mother went along with the decision to get a goat, since she had once made the unfortunate mistake of saying to Bobo and me during some of the divorce proceedings, "After the divorce nobody will be there to tell us when we have to get up or when we have to go to bed. There won't be a daddy to tell us what to do all the time."

No one to tell us when to go to bed, brush our teeth, change our socks. No one to make me take those chewable multiple vitamins each morning that my father purchased from a drug supply company for Bobo and me in gigantic bottles of one thousand. Day in, day out, each morning having to take one of those pills which stuck in my throat, leaving me with a sickening taste for the rest of the day.

One day, when we were still all married to each other, I stepped outside after breakfast with one of those very vitamins tucked away neatly in a corner of my mouth and removed it deftly between two fingers, flinging it carefully off into the woods. I went back into the kitchen, only to have my father appear moments later holding the pink tablet in his open palm. "Is this yours?" he said angrily. I had to put it back in my mouth while he watched me chew.

My father and I arranged to meet at his house on the Saturday following my birthday. "Come up around two-thirty," he told me. "I'll be done seeing my patients then, and we can go to the livestock auction. We'll see what they have."

Some time before the final divorce papers came through, my father had built a bridge over the stream that separated the two properties, in order to let Bobo and me hop back and forth from one parent to the other without undue hardship.

The stream was deepest at the point where the bridge had been built. My father had constructed it himself, with much back-breaking labor, out of white pine, with sturdy saplings for the railings. It, too, was Japanese in design and feeling, the only difference being that where the Japanese arch curves upward in a convex shape, this bridge sagged, unintentionally, in the middle.

Often it was possible to get it to swing gently from side to side, if Bobo and I together jumped up and down in the middle of it. But when it was first built, and for some years after, it was sturdy enough to hold the little tractor my father owned, so that my brother or I could mow the field that surrounded my mother's house.

It was built on the foundation of a bridge that had existed a hundred years ago, when the path that led between the two houses was part of the old town road, and it became a favorite location for trout fishermen. Eventually it was destroyed by the farm kids up the road, who, after it was weakened by a winter of heavy snows, swung back and forth on it until it collapsed into the stream a few feet below.

I could never cross the bridge without feeling guilty that I didn't pay more frequent visits to my father, after he had gone to all the trouble of building it.

On that Saturday, when I left my mother's house to begin the climb to my father's, my brother called after me. "Can I come?" he said.

"Can't I just be alone with Daddy this once? Listen, I tell you what—you can have my Spiderman sweatshirt. And next week you can go to Daddy's alone and I won't be there." My brother followed a little way behind. "Go home!" I told him. "I already said you couldn't come today!" I stopped on the bridge and peered into the water. If my brother did not return home in a few minutes, I was going to go home and tell my mother.

I peeled the bark from the green sapling railings and tossed it into the water. My brother wandered off, disappointed that I would not let him come, but not much surprised, really, and the strips of bark floated downstream and snagged in the debris of sticks and leaves caught in the dam below. In order for my father to maintain the level of his swimming pond, he had to keep a dam built in the stream so the water from the stream would be high enough to feed into the pipe, which in turn fed his pond. But it was difficult to maintain the dam, because each year spring floods would carry it away. He would rebuild the dam every summer and curse when the winter flooding ripped it apart the following spring.

One year he called all of his friends together—he was always working up projects for his friends, inviting them over for a party to pick dandelions so he could make dandelion wine, a party to chop down brush and build a bonfire, a party to gather mushrooms which he would then cook—to help him build the dam once and for all.

While cleaning out his things recently I went through one of the old photo albums and came across a photograph of this particular celebration, the "Dam Building Party," a photograph taken by whatever girlfriend he happened to have at the time, I suppose. There, looking over his shoulder, back to the camera, is my father, completely naked, lifting rocks on the dam. I guess he thought of this day as some sort of tribal ceremony—he would have loved to belong to a commune, but admitted he unfortunately did not get along with anybody for more than a few hours at a time—and insisted all his friends heave rocks in the nude. I was not invited to this day of dam building, not out of any sense of propriety on his part, but because my underdeveloped muscles would have been of little aid in heaving and cementing boulders.

It was built several years later than the time I am talking about, in any event. At this point, when my goat arrived, the dam was still only a small, slippery wall of speckled rocks and broken sticks, a shallow brook making a loud noise.

The temperature, in the area around the stream, was much cooler than the rest of the air. The mosquitoes, though it was still early in the season, were very fierce. The mosquitoes in the spring were the first insects to come out. Soon it would be black fly season, then deerfly season, and then later in the summer the swarms of gnats would come and the large bloodthirsty horse-flies—but the mosquitoes were always there, sullen and whining, raising constant welts on my brother and me, which we scratched until they bled.

In the distance my brother called for the dog, Kong, who was running at my side, to rejoin him. The dog, anxious from the pressure of these dual loyalties, jumped up against me. But he did not rejoin my brother. The stream was a great attraction to the dog, the sodden mud that surrounded it, the icy water he would rush into up to his chest and lap at eagerly. He was too great a coward to approach the stream by himself; usually he waited for Bobo or me to accompany him. He had a timid nature. If anyone ever disliked King Kong it may have been because of his condition, not his personality. He had one of the sweetest dispositions I have ever seen on a dog. His only problem was that as a puppy he had developed some sort of red mange and for years after that had to be kept inside. The disease was incurable and the dog, red and bald, with bits and pieces of fur falling out all over the house, was quite unhappy. To let him out would have insured the spread of the disease. My father, when Kong's ailment was discovered, was anxious to have him put to sleep. But my brother and I, with the help of our mother, threw a series of temper tantrums. He was allowed to live.

Finally a topical ointment was developed by a local veterinarian and after this he was allowed out. His skin was somewhat hairless and he had become incredibly human, due to the lack of contact with others of his kind. During the years indoors he had acquired a yodeling bark that bore a striking resemblance to human speech.

After the divorce my father agreed to share the dog. He said that the dog would have free run of his house, just like Bobo and me, but shortly thereafter there was a robbery in the neighborhood, and my father bolted the dog door shut, as a safeguard. Kong was intelligent, but he couldn't seem to learn that his door was closed once and for all. He cracked his head on it every time he visited my father, and would turn to look at whoever was nearby with a hurt and puzzled stare. In the end the divorce affected all of us.

There was a dank, fishy smell I associated with the stream—and with the dog—that reminded me of baby diapers, of the area under my brother's bed where he stored his old socks until my mother discovered them. In the deep section under the bridge large trout hung suspended in the water, finning to stand still against the current, flickering gently in the murky light that fell through the trees. The leaves were barely out, faint bits of cloth, the yellowest shade of green, tied to each tree. The dog tore eagerly at anything green on the ground, at the grasses and skunk cabbage springing up everywhere, nibbling as if he were a cow.

Since the divorce, since I had begun to see my father less often, he no longer seemed to be the protector he had once been.

"Sometimes I don't know who I'm supposed to be," he said to me.
"Your father? Your brother? Your friend? I can't be anybody's
father because I don't feel old enough. Just who am I, could you
tell me?"

He said this, I guess, as a joke, but he meant it.

"I don't know, Dad," I said, embarrassed. I picked burrs out of
the dog's ears. "Don't ask me." He was my father. He should grow
up and act like one. The love my father had for me had turned,
since the divorce, into something useless. The feelings he had for
me had become a bear, an old bear who sat on my head, covering
my eyes with his paws. I could not shake this bear off my head and
monthly it grew heavier. I didn't want to visit him because I was
sure that each time I did I would be kicked out, asked not to come
back. My father said, "Remember, your bedroom is still yours.
You will always have a room in my house."

But I knew better. If the bedroom was always going to be mine,
as he said, the very action of saying so meant that someday there
was a possibility that it might not be. Why did he have to keep
reminding me, unless he was secretly planning to take it away?

I had nightmares about my father having more children, who
were mysteriously named Earl and Bobo "after two other little
children who used to live here."

The previous Christmas, my fears, already established, were
confirmed. My father and his girlfriend went to Florida. Bobo and
I asked him for a house key so we could use our bedrooms and play
with the toys we hadn't taken with us when we left. My father
said, "Sure, why not?" and gave us the house key. But when we
hiked, during a blizzard, through snow up to our waists in
drifts—halfway there, even the dog turned back, legs caked with
ice—the door was locked and the key would not fit.

Grimly we circled the house, trying to slide open even one of
the glass doors, but all were locked from the inside. My brother
tried to force the dog-door open and squeeze through, but finally
we returned home.

Neither of us was upset; bewildered was more like it. My
brother insisted it had been unintentional on my father's part. For
two weeks of Christmas vacation we had nothing to do but race
back and forth in our mother's house, which was small and where
every footstep echoed because she hadn't been able to afford
anything more expensive than cement floors. When my father

returned from Florida it was apparent he was perfectly aware he had locked my brother and me out, but no explanation was ever given. My mother said it was because he was afraid she would go up there and look through his things. He had brought us all the usual presents, things no one would ever dream of wanting until they were given—jars of blackened, prehistoric sharks' teeth he had found on the beach, tiny boxes covered with seashells, placemats decorated with maps.

"This stuff is terrific," Bobo said.

"Bobo, how can you say that? He locked us out."

"Aw, I didn't want to go over there anyway. Besides, he didn't lock us out, he just had the locks changed."

My father had a tan. He was in a good mood. "You want a goat, Earl?" he said. "Another pet? A new friend? I think it's funny. Maybe you'll turn out to be a veterinarian. Okay, you want a goat, I'll get you one for your birthday. Why don't you kids come over for dinner tonight?"

He served us a tempura dinner on the fur rug in the living room. We squatted on the floor dressed in velour bathrobes he had given us, devouring large encrusted shrimps. After the meal he brought out a tray of fruit-flavored liqueurs we were allowed to sample, the fur beneath us growing sleek with drippings.

"Maybe he didn't mean to lock us out," I said later, at home.

"Told ya," my brother said.

My mother didn't say anything at all.

Before I wanted a goat I had craved a monkey, and finally, the year before we got a divorce, my parents gave me one as a Hanukkah present. After supper, they sent me down to the bathroom used by the patients who came to see my father, telling me they needed some paper towels to be brought upstairs.

There in a crate on the floor was the monkey I had longed for, a small green monkey with a black face. I carried the crate upstairs, sick with excitement. The family gathered around to examine him. We pried open the crate. I felt apprehensive about picking him up, so my father reached into the box. The monkey sank his teeth into my father's hand. Although fragile in appearance, he had a strong bite. My father couldn't shake him free. "Don't hurt him!" I said. I tried to rescue the monkey from my father's frenzied shaking, and the monkey, with greater vindictiveness released his grasp on my dad and sank his teeth into my own hand.

I decided to name him Lucky Jim.

It was concluded that the monkey was nervous and overstimulated. I settled him down for the night in my bedroom, where I placed a cardboard box filled with rags and some newspapers in one corner and then tied him to a rope by means of a small collar.

But by morning it was apparent the monkey wouldn't be able to remain in my bedroom: He was shivering uncontrollably, and my father said he would need a warmer environment. I wanted to get him some small clothes, but since he wouldn't allow me or anyone else to touch him, I realized he would have to dress himself. There was a sullen look in the monkey's eyes. Even I could tell the monkey didn't want to be my pet. I brought him into the bathroom, where it was a little warmer than the rest of the house.

During the transfer from bedroom to bath Lucky Jim escaped, nearly committing suicide when he tried to jump off the railing at the top of the stairs. My father, wearing gloves, grabbed the monkey before he could leap, while I danced around his legs, shouting that he was strangling my monkey. My mother shut herself in the bedroom; she didn't approve of wild animals being kept as pets.

I left Lucky Jim tied to the ventilator in an open space under some waist-high cabinets in "the children's bathroom," which was considered to be the guest bathroom on the nights my parents entertained.

I kept him there for a few days, but on Saturday night my parents gave a dinner party, forgetting to tell the guests that there was a monkey tied up in the bathroom. One of the guests, a bosomy, older woman who made pots somewhere out in the woods, went in and within a few minutes we heard a shrill scream. She had seated herself on the toilet and then, she told us, noticed the shrunken face observing her from under the cabinets.

She claimed not to have realized it was a monkey.

I didn't believe her; I was afraid her shrieks might have damaged the monkey's ears. He was high-strung and refused to grow any tamer. While I liked to look at him from a distance, his angry expression disturbed me, and I made sure never to touch him.

After this the monkey was transferred to the shower room. This was the room that connected my parents' bathroom to Bobo's and mine. It housed the bath and shower behind a glass wall. Here Lucky Jim was chained to the ventilator, next to the heat. My father found a five-foot section of branch for him to climb on.

Instead of adjusting to his new surroundings, however, the monkey remained angry. He had arrived with a list of instructions, among them a list of foods he would enjoy eating, but he chose not to approve of anything but monkey chow. But the monkey chow he had been shipped with ran out very quickly, and because he was my responsibility, it was left up to me to order more from the company in Florida. Even now, years later, I remember his listless and sodden expression when he would see his dinner, monkey chowless once again, and my guilt about this is still unresolved. Is this simply self-indulgence? I have tried to forgive myself, but I cannot.

Instead, I supplied him with Triscuits, pieces of apple, bits of quiche, hard-boiled eggs, an old cheese sandwich, anything I could find in the kitchen that seemed edible. He despised banana, frowned upon the lovely dinner platters I would bring to him in the shower room. He would pick through the food and stuff most of it into the slits of the heating ventilator, where it quickly rotted and solidified in the heat. His dignity prevented me from getting too close to him, and though my parents told me a number of times to clean out the ventilator, because of his presence and the hardness of the decayed food I never did. I changed his paper but did not go into the shower room more often than I could help.

The only food Lucky Jim took any joy in—the only joy he seemed to get out of life at all—was insects, spiders in particular. But these were rarely found in the house during the winter months, though during summer it is true they were plentiful. Still, spring was too many months away to imagine being able to collect any more for him. It was before the years when you could buy mealworms in bags.

When an insect was discovered and brought to him, the belligerent expression left his eyes and he would shriek with excitement, devouring it as if he had been deliberately starved and now—I felt he was looking at me as if I were an SS officer—didn't want to eat for fear it might be some sort of trap.

Although I cleaned his paper daily, the smell in the bathroom grew from the rotting food stuffed into the heating duct, and simply speaking, from the life of a monkey. The odor crept out under the door; the house began to smell like the Bronx Zoo.

When the shower or bathwater was turned on, the fearful cries Lucky Jim emitted were terrible to hear. Though he might be starving, he still had the strength to protest. To him, the noise of the shower signified the end of his life. Taking a shower became, for the whole family, a traumatic experience.

Finally the weather grew warmer, and my father built a tremendous cage, big enough for a dozen monkeys, in the downstairs workroom where we kept the television, and the monkey was again transferred.

One morning I came downstairs to find him lying limply on the floor of the cage, one long green hand opening and shutting feebly, so close to death that he was unable to take an interest in a spider which had found its way into his cage.

Later the pictures of the Biafran babies brought back many memories of him. For the first time since I had owned him he allowed me to pick him up. He didn't scream, but his face held a resigned pride. In his weakness he had given up his anger.

We brought him to a local zoo where he was doctored and placed in a cage with thirty other monkeys of the same species, all screaming happily as they dined on monkey chow. They had all been taken there from basements within a hundred-mile radius.

Once the monkey was gone I forgot about him.

Though I tried, I was, since the divorce, unable to get along with Bobo for more than a few minutes at a time. I knew he was following me at a distance in the woods on my way to my father's, because I could hear him singing to himself somewhere in the trees. He had a very pretty voice, my mother said, a lovely soprano, and I knew he was lonesome. This irritated me beyond all human endurance.

He had saved up for years, collected penny after penny, at a cost of never having enough money to buy candy or comic books or any of the purchases that always left me broke, and at last had enough money to buy himself a metal detector. After weeks of searching, the only things he turned up with it were a lot of rusted beer cans, which he stacked neatly outside the house, and a frying pan with the bottom gone from it.

Finally he decided there was something wrong with the machine and sent it back to the company. The metal detector had come with an eighty-day warranty, but when he sent it back the company had mysteriously gone bankrupt and not only did he never get his fifty-five dollars back, but they didn't return the machine either. My mother was upset and helped Bobo compose long, futile letters to the company and the Better Business Bureau, but it was of no use.

My brother was depressed. I did agree, from time to time, to play with him, to make up for his bad luck. But there was little point in that. Somehow, every time I agreed to do anything with him, by accident the baseball I was tossing would hit him on the neck, knocking him senseless, or, while utilizing him as a horse, he would collapse, claiming I had broken his knees. Once, in a spirit of jest, I tossed some pepper into his face, not realizing the effect it would have. He never cried when he was hurt. It was as if since the divorce he had used up his supply of tears, and this set me into even more of a rage against him, since I had in some way been weakened, and often felt my face dissolving like sugar in water, though I claimed always to have an allergy.

He demanded affection from me and I was not able to give it. Once his pet cat killed a rabbit and brought it into the house. Because it was his cat he was sentenced to go and bury the victim, which he did, trudging out into the night, in the rain, carrying a shovel, while my mother wiped the stain of blood from his bedroom floor. But I was not able to dissociate the dead rabbit, hot and runny, from my brother, and I saw the dirtiness in Bobo long after he was clean. Although he took a bath every day and was pink, reeking of some kind of herbal shampoo he shared with my mother, although he spent a lot of time running around dressed in white underpants and a white tee shirt, my mother's hair dryer— the old kind, a shower cap attached to a machine blowing hot air—on his head, I didn't want to touch him, was reluctant to wrestle him or tickle him as I had once done.

His room had a funny smell, chloroform he used in his killing jars—he collected insects, moldering in boxes—the smell of Testor's dope and paint he used on his model airplanes, old socks under the bed. This contributed to my feeling that my brother should never have been born.

He followed me along through the trees and I could tell he was out there.

"I'll play baseball with you when I get home!" I shouted into the trees. "Listen, wait a minute, I've changed my mind. You can come with me!"

But he didn't come out, and I knew he had left when we got to the top of the hill by the way the dog turned and disappeared off through the brush.

My father was waiting there at the top of the hill, inspecting a corner of the house. Every girlfriend he'd ever had had accidentally backed her car into the side of the house, right at that corner, due to the sharp angle of the driveway. He was filled with disgust. "Come on, come on, Earl," he said when he saw me. "I thought you wanted to get to the auction on time. Where's Bobo?"

He had changed into his work clothes. He always wore a suit when he saw his patients. He claimed that wearing a suit made them calmer, since they assumed when they saw him in it that he was sane. This was a joke.

"How were your patients?" I said, getting into the car. He still drove his 1951 Chevy, a huge black car with a rust spot in the left-hand back seat. The hole, though small, was open to the road below. I knew he planned to buy a new car, a pickup truck, as soon as he found the time. But he was proud of this car, since it had only cost him one hundred bucks, bought from the cleaning woman's husband, and ran perfectly, except for eating quarts of oil.

"My patients?" he said. He had that glazed look that told me he was a little high; probably he had smoked a joint after his last appointment. Also, he drove very slowly, perhaps only ten miles an hour, and seemed to have trouble negotiating the driveway. "This last patient I just finished seeing was the one I was telling you about before. Last week he took his clothes off and ran around downtown trying to get women to have sex with him."

"What's wrong with him?"

"The guy is a manic depressive. He thinks he's the new Messiah."

"Is he?" I said.

"He thinks he's Jesus Christ, but he can only get a few people to believe him. This week he's predicting the end of the world."

"What happened when he took his clothes off?"

"Ah, they arrested him. He was in jail overnight until his disciples could come and bail him out."

"His disciples?"

"His friends."

"Oh," I said. "How come they let him out?"

"Well, they couldn't legally keep him in jail. They called me and asked me to sign him into the state mental hospital for ten days' observation, but he didn't want to go. So I saw him this afternoon. I can't do anything for him."

My father didn't speak to me as if I were a child. We had frequent, lengthy conversations about his patients. I knew exactly what was wrong with each of them and how much they admired my dad because at Christmas we would receive dozens of homemade fruitcakes that they sent to us. Many of the cakes were stale or filled with strange ingredients.

"Wasn't your girlfriend supposed to come with us?" I said. Then I wondered if I had said the right thing; sometimes he wouldn't tell me what was going on, and a woman who had been living there the day before would suddenly be gone, no explanation given. His current girlfriend was one of his former patients, a "cure." Her problem was that for her whole life men had used her, only to discard her afterward. My father had explained to me that her queer mannerisms stemmed from the fact that she still needed constant reassurance. Each sentence she spoke ended in a giggle and a stuttering plea for acknowledgment: "You know? Don't you think?" and a rattling giggle.

"Ah, I don't know," my father said angrily. "I told her to be here at one-thirty. It was quarter to two when we left, and I didn't feel like waiting around."

"But wasn't she supposed to come over?" I said. I was relieved she wasn't coming with us, and yet it made me think. Supposing I had been a few minutes late. Would my father have left without me?

"But Dad," I said, "don't you think she's going to be upset that we left her behind?"

"I told you," he said, "it'll be okay. She'll understand." And he was quiet again, concentrating on his driving.

"What are you thinking about, Dad?" I said, after a pause. It was exciting to be driving someplace, alone, with my father. I felt whatever he must be thinking was very wise.

"Hmm," he said. "What was I thinking about? Oh, I don't know. Getting the snow tires taken off the car, I guess. I don't think it's going to snow again this year."

Disappointed, I looked out the window. I started to hum the same tune over and over again. "My dog has fleas. My dog has fleas," I sang.

"How's your mother?" my father asked me, in a voice I could easily identify as signifying that he was curious, though he made an effort to iron any inflection from his voice when he spoke about my mother.

"Fine," I said, in a noncommittal tone. I never knew what I was supposed to say. My mother was going back to school. After suddenly turning into a poet—I had known her before only as a mother, who prepared bowls of cereal each morning and opened cans of mandarin oranges—her poems were being accepted in magazines, she had received a grant from a women's college and was going back to school for a graduate degree. I could never remember what I was or was not supposed to tell my father about her, and so I tried not to say anything at all.

"When does she start school?" my father said.

"I don't know," I said. My mother was always telling me certain things and then adding, "Don't mention this to your father." Since I could not keep track of what these things were, I felt it was better not to say anything at all.

"You don't know?" my father said, and for some reason this set him off into a tirade against her. He finally calmed down by explaining, "She used her incompetency as a weapon against me." Both my parents spoke to me as if I were an adult or not there at all, and I always listened but did not reply. Because I felt so mature I was surprised to hear myself, when I spoke, sounding exactly like a twelve-year-old.

My father, his burst of talking over, was quiet again. We drove off the main road and for five or ten miles down a smaller one. The auction was held in a barn and hadn't yet started. My father parked the car and said we would go into the back room where the animals were kept before they were brought out to be sold.

My father, in his flashy Eisenhower jacket and expensive work boots, and I, dressed in chinos and loafers chosen by my mother, stuck out as if we had come from a foreign country. There were crowds of men looking at the animals and unloading them. Most of them spoke Polish. The whole place smelled of manure. The animals sold here were mostly those nobody wanted: farmyard discards, sick animals, milk cows that remained dry, the rare bargain.

It was very noisy inside. The floor was covered with muddy sawdust. There was a pen of scrawny steers, lowing and milling aimlessly, a cage of featherless geese, and a small corral of heifers that didn't look too happy—one of these had vomit on its back and I pointed this out to my father. In front of a ramp leading from the parking lot were some black and white cows. Their eyes rolling, their bodies crusted with dirt and manure, they were being prodded to step inside.

There were pigs, some several hundred pounds or more, groaning like men in the straw of their wooden crates, two thin ponies no taller than me, and messed in with the stench of the animals was the smell of pork sausages and hotdogs, a sour spoiled smell of Coca-Cola, deep fried grease of fresh cooked donuts.

At last we found some goats, a crate of them not more than three or four weeks old, standing on feeble legs. My father wrote down the ear tag number of one of them, a sturdy brown and white female. We went to the auction room next door and found two seats in the crowded amphitheater. It was very uncomfortable.

The first things that were sold off were paper bags full of cartons of eggs. "Who would want to buy so many eggs?" I said. My father, stunned or perhaps still stoned, did not reply. The helpers brought out boxes of rabbits the auctioneer held up by the ears, yellow and red chickens, some tumbler pigeons, and then they led the goats out.

"Dad," I said suddenly, "Dad, are you going to have enough money to pay for it?"

"I don't know," my father said. "I don't know how much they'll go for." I hated to see my father not in command of the situation. Suppose he didn't know how to bid? He didn't fit into the surroundings, he looked stiff, and he was the only man with a beard.

But as soon as my father started bidding on the goat we had chosen the bidding from the other people stopped. The goat I wanted went for much less than the other goats. My father was pleased. My goat cost thirteen dollars; the other goats had been sold for twenty and twenty-five. "Maybe there's something wrong with it," I said.

"I guess they thought there was no point in bidding against me," my father said, with a strange look on his face. "Maybe they knew who I was." It was true that my father's reputation, never entirely unsullied, had spread for miles.

We went up to the office to pay for the goat. A receptionist with a huge blond beehive was sitting behind a desk, and my father started to flirt with her. I was disgusted. As soon as my father opened his mouth any woman he spoke to became a sick cat. If I had come in by myself to pay for the goat the receptionist would have been a different person altogether, irritated and sullen.

"Did anyone ever tell you you looked just like Abraham Lincoln?" she said to my dad. My father laughed as if that was the funniest thing he had ever heard. Since he had grown his beard and gotten wire-rimmed glasses, I think I had heard this remark fifty times. It was true he did have a very large nose, but I felt it was needless for these ladies to say anything so cruel. I was worried for my father's feelings. "Come on, let's go," I said, dragging him by the sleeve.

"We have to go pick up this young man's goat," my father said.

"A goat!" the receptionist said. "Why, whatever are you going to do with a goat!"

"Train it," I said.

"A boy goat or a girl goat?" she said, looking at my father.

"A female."

But when we went down to pick it up, it turned out we had made a mistake. My dad had chosen a male. It had tiny horns already sprouting from its head.

A man with very baggy skin and a plaid lumberjack shirt helped us carry the kid out to the car when we showed him the receipt. "Is this animal going to be a pet?" he said, looking at us.

"Yes," I said.

"This is going to be a billy goat, you know," he said to my father.

"What does that mean?" my father said. "Is there something we have to do?"

In a low voice he told my father male goats had a high sex drive and smelled terrible. He demonstrated to my father, pinching the goat's penis tightly, how to castrate it using a rubber band. I felt a terrible sickness in my stomach. "Let's just return it, Dad," I said. I was certain it wouldn't be able to go to the bathroom, would probably explode.

I sat on the back seat with it on the way home. It went to the bathroom once, leaving a pile of droppings on the seat that I picked up and threw out the window without mentioning anything to my father. It had yellow eyes, which bothered me, and very sweet breath, reminding me in some indescribable way of my brother.

The goat proved to be a more successful pet than the monkey. It was smarter than Kong, even, learning its name, "Rover," inside of three days, following me everywhere. After it woke me up in the night, its sharp hooves on my chest, nibbling my hair, it was assigned to a box in my father's kitchen, where I brought it every day at sunset. But three weeks later, while I was holding it, it died of pneumonia, a tragic and terrible demise. I called the veterinarian, but he wouldn't make house calls, and my father, busy with his patients in his office below, was not able to help. I had to watch alone as its worried face sealed over and its small body grew cold in my arms.

Now, in looking back on this small death, I can see how I was getting used to the idea of loss, temporary or permanent. Perhaps this was at the back of my father's perceptive, psychiatric mind when he let me have these animals. Perhaps he knew they would die, and I, as a result, would become more inured, would develop like a turtle, slower and more protected against the loss of, sooner or later, nearly everyone I was dependent on. Dependency was the worst fault my father could find in anyone. He certainly disliked anyone being dependent on him. And in the end, I did learn to do without. I learned to do without him and shuck off his corporeal form, if not the shadow that huddles on my shoulder and belittles and belabors my everyday existence.

But on the afternoon of the goat's purchase, when we arrived home, my father's girlfriend was standing mournfully on the front step, red-eyed, weepy from being left behind, giggling nervously. She had been waiting for three hours. "I'm really sorry I was late, you know?" she said. "I really understand why you didn't wait for me, you know? I know it can be a real drag waiting for somebody who's late, you know?" My father gazed off into the distant trees. He went into the house and we followed.

My father, after finding a small red rubberband in the kitchen, put it around the goat's genitals and then he and his girlfriend went off to the bedroom.

I went back home to my mother and brother with the goat,

small, cloven-hoofed and sexless, in my arms. The goat seemed fonder of my brother than of me.

The chopping of forests, in spring making dandelion wine, in the autumn baking fruit cakes with over four dollars worth of nuts, fruit and brandy in each cake, growing and harvesting rare varieties of marijuana, knitting sweaters of brown and gray undyed wool, making granola, canning vegetables, boiling jam from wild strawberries he had picked himself, making maple syrup from his own trees, catching snapping turtles from the lake to stew: my father became adept at all this and much more.

My mother, Bobo and I lived a very ordinary and humdrum existence by comparison. Yet I was not without understanding for my father and the unnatural life he had chosen for himself. For one thing, as I had heard so many times before, my father had his mother to contend with.

I realize now it could not have been easy having her for a mother. When Bobo and I went to my father's at Christmas, she was there, as well as his latest girlfriend, a nurse named Rexy. A typical outfit for Grandma Ivy was a shirt patterned with figures: flowers, pagodas, pinnacles, pineapples, plum and cherry blossoms, and over this another shirt my grandmother claimed was raw silk.

In the evening she appeared in a dress with a design called L'Eventail—a light silk with a pattern of a woman's head outlined in black, the chin being hidden by an open red fan. Over it she wore a voluminous "Kolinsky" wrap with generous sleeves; tilted on her head was a black velvet toque. The wrap was to protect her from the cold—the seven wood-burning stoves my father had installed did little to heat the house, since the ceilings were too high (my father was thinking of installing several fans near the ceiling in each room in order to blow the heat down)—and the hat was to cover the fact that she had not yet put on her blond bouffant wig.

I was always amazed at my grandmother's clothes. "Royant slip-pleated skirt of white crepe de chine," she would inform when asked, or when not asked, "A jacket of blue duvetyn imitating a waistcoat. It is worn with a pleated skirt checked in black, gray and white."

I had seen my grandmother wearing a large golden-yellow

chrysanthemum fixed by one petal to the bottom of a white tulle skirt, the other petals being left free, with other silk chrysanthemums getting smaller and smaller toward the waist and winding up with a spray of buttercups. Or she would appear in a pink terrycloth jumpsuit and a baseball cap. Everything was the wrong size. Her magenta harem pants had a long tear sewn up with orange thread.

"I probably would have brought some things for you, Earl, but I thought you would object to my taste. Sometimes I go to Manhattan Shirts. For example, if you go to Jordan Marsh or Saks you see a woman's shirt and it is twenty-five dollars. But I can get it for five."

My grandmother never threw anything away.

Her days, since the death of my grandfather some fourteen years earlier, were spent searching the stores for bargains or decking herself out in the things that had filled her closets for twenty or thirty years.

"I like your outfit, Grandma," I said. Feathers of tropical birds, kingfishers or cocks, and more or less iridescent, were fastened into a wide collar around her suit.

"When I saw it I thought, this is really unusual, Earl. And if someone's taste coincidences with mine, well, that's even nicer. . . . I'm glad you like that one because—" She didn't finish her sentence but turned to look out the window. "I wish it was sunnier. I can't believe I left a hot muggy climate and here it's comfortable, if not just cold."

She had just come from Florida. My father did not like her to visit more than twice a year. "Shall I make us all a drink?" my grandmother said.

"Yeah, sure," my father sighed. He got out a jigger and handed it to her, took some of the liquor bottles from the cabinet.

"What should I measure this with?"

"Ah, a jigger, here," my father said, pressing the jigger once more against her hand.

"Do you have a jigger?"

"You're a little bit late, Ma. I *said* here's a jigger."

"Well, that's a demerit for me."

My father scowled and asked me to come with him to the basement. "I have to control myself," he said. "I shouldn't let her get to me. This is my house. I'm grown up now."

Downstairs his girlfriend's new loom was set up, various strings extending in several directions. She was weaving an uneven whitish tablecloth on it, apparently. "Pretty neat, Dad," I said.

"Rexy's weaving is one of the few things she can do," my father said. "I don't want to compete with her, so I make a point of not trying to learn anything about it."

"Oh."

My grandmother's loud voice could be heard even down there. She was talking to Rexy. "Paterson is a very depressed section," my grandmother was telling her. "It used to be middle-class Jews. Now I am Whitey. All the time they run their motorcycles. Not during the day but at night. I am afraid to complain because they might turn on me."

This was Rexy and my grandmother's first meeting. My father had never before had a Jewish girlfriend; my grandmother had asked me in a whisper if "this one" was Jewish. "I don't know, Grandma," I whispered back.

"Rexy, what is your last name?"

"Borsky, Mrs. Przepasniak."

"Borsky! Is that a Jewish name?" she said slyly.

"Is it Jewish?" Rexy said. "I don't know if the name is Jewish, but I am."

"It's a small world. You never can tell. Is that a fly in back of you? Oh, I'm going to get it. It's on your head." She swatted at Rexy's head with a thick magazine. "Oh, hold still. For fear of hurting you, I do think you're a very attractive woman, Rexy. I'm afraid to speak out. But if I think and see that you're attractive, why shouldn't I tell you? Are you such a ninny that you can't take it?"

"No, Mrs. Przepasniak."

"When I grew older I thought I would get to be wiser. One never knows about these things, at least I don't. Can I tell you something?"

"Sure."

"I'm telling you something I have never told anyone," she said in a voice that could be heard all over the house. "The doctor said to me when I went to see him—this was last week—he said, 'You know, Mrs. Przepasniak, Ivy, you have breasts a twenty-year-old girl could be proud of.' I thought, gee whiz, maybe I'm being vain, but it really made me feel good that somebody recognized that about me. It would be even nicer if I had a boyfriend. Hey, where are my grandchildren?" she shrieked suddenly. "Where are my wonderful grand-boys?"

"Go up and be with her, Earl," my father said. He went to his workbench and began hammering nails. I went upstairs. I was already taller than my grandmother. She clutched me to her, reeking of perfume.

"Isn't this wonderful!" she screamed at me.

"What is?"

"Your daddy's father, Earl, when he was alive, always used to say he was going to write a book called *Ivy Always Says,* with everything in it I had ever said. He said I have such good common sense. Over and over. If there ever was anything I wanted all my life it was to hear that, because he really was a brilliant man, Earl. I only wish you could have met him. How sad that he died before you were born. You see, I was a member of the Theatre Guild when I met him, which really was the school of the century. Unfortunately, I only had tuition for one month. Helen Hayes was a teacher there and she said undoubtedly I had great talent. But I had to prove in one month I was Sarah Bernhardt. And you cannot have two great loves in your life, and I met Leo.

"I think conversation, Earl, is the most stimulating kind of enjoyment. Maybe if I was a young kid I wouldn't say that. I would say sex is. Are you guffawing at me, Earl?"

"No, no, I'm not."

"I would say sex is. But who would want to make a pass at an old lady? So I would have to say conversation. In my life, Earl, I don't have enough stimulating people around me. I regret that very much, because I thrive on being able to speak my thoughts. And when you're thinking, your soul sings out.

"One thing I wish we could do is if we could exchange thoughts, Earl. It would give me great pleasure if you would come to me every once in a while and we could just sit and talk. And I really could be myself. If someday I knew that you really did like your Grandma Ivy. Well, I always feel I have to apologize. I was in a class, a movement workshop, and the teacher said, 'One of your problems, Ivy, is that you really underestimate yourself.' I never had inner security. If you have inner security you can be aggressive. Why not? Why shouldn't a person be aggressive? You're missing an opportunity if you're not."

Rexy lit a pipe of hashish.

"Do you smoke marijuana, Earl?'

"No."

"No, me neither," my grandmother said. "I get a kick out of life to be glad enough. If I feel depressed, then I don't want to try anything. I feel I have enough nuances within me to enjoy all the beautiful things around me. I have all these deep feelings within. I have a great joy if I can speak to someone. Anyway, I can talk silly without marijuana. What if I cry or something? . . . You know what I'm remembering, Earl?"

"What?"

"You were such bright, affectionate children, you and Bobo. You would grab my feet and say, Grandma, don't go. Whatever happened?"

"I don't know, Grandma."

"I sometimes wonder if I had come to visit you more often, would it have been any different. Well, I may have my faults, but they're not bad faults. Rexy Borsky, you can really cut a pickle beautifully."

"Thank you," Rexy said.

"After all, it isn't everyone I say that to. Did I hear that you don't eat? That you're a vegetarian?"

"No, I eat."

"Well, someday you'll make some mackerel. That doesn't have too many bones. I know one girl, a vegetarian, who ate jelly and peanut butter sandwiches for four years. The most colorless person you've ever seen."

Rexy's dog, lying under the table, made a groaning sound and turned around near my feet, trying to get comfortable. It was a boxer with pink wobbly jowls. A strong doggish odor rose up to me.

"Rexy," I said, "I hate to tell you this. But your dog really smells."

"He's not old enough, is he?" my grandmother said.

"Not old enough?" my father jeered from the fireplace. "Not old enough to smell?"

"Lettuce sandwiches. I would go out to the garden with my sister Daisy and we would pick the few lettuce leaves that there were and that would be our meal. We were so hungry that it was delicious." My grandmother could make a sandwich from anything, even just plain lettuce. She also made a very good chicken soup. All of them, when my father was growing up, spent time sucking clean even the scrawniest chicken bones in the vats of "Jewish penicillin" that my grandmother kept on the stove and served with kreplach.

Once she had made this soup for company using only one carrot and a little chicken fat. Everyone complimented her on it. I believe it was a soup for two hundred. My father, Bobo and I, even Rexy, were never allowed to forget this.

The dog sat looking at my grandmother, his eyes bloodshot, a drop of drool forming at the corner of his mouth. Was he drooling because he was hungry for the meat or for my grandmother, I thought. I shivered. The windows of the house were huge and the snow from outside seemed to have melted inward. On the branches of a few trees some birds sat listlessly. My feet were like two lumps of ice, smashing in chunks against the rugless floor.

"He does have a beautiful hindquarters," my grandmother said. "Is he a show dog?"

"Yes," Rexy said.

"When you show a dog and he makes it—whatever he does—do you make money?"

"Yes, but I can't show Itzhak. He has an undescended testicle."

"Well, what about—could there be mongoloid dogs?"

Rexy said my father thought Itzhak was retarded.

My grandmother ignored her, watching my father broil meat on the expensive indoor charcoal grill, and said, "A cookout is a man's job, even though there's women's liberation."

My father gritted his teeth, Rexy giggled in her dull way, like a snail being tickled, and offered my grandmother some hashish.

"Well, all right. I will try it, I think, because it's hashish, though I've tried marijuana."

"Are you inhaling it?" my father said, leaving the meat to approach the table and my grandmother bubbling on the water pipe. "Now inhale a little more," he said. "Maybe this will shut you up for a while."

"Oh Rob," my grandmother said.

"Inhale," Rexy said.

"Now you're getting it," my father said.

Bobo came into the room and my brother and I looked at the three of them, my grandmother, my father and his girlfriend clustered together at one end of the table. Bobo shrugged. Neither of us would touch the stuff. My grandmother's wig was slightly askew. "Like it's a straw, hmm?" my grandmother said. "It has no effect on me."

"That was good," my father said. "Keep that up." It was the first praise he had offered my grandmother since her arrival. "Now you have to do that and hold it in."

"But it's difficult to because you cough."

"But your life is going to change now," Rexy said.

"Well, as long as it changes for the better," my grandmother said. "You know, I've reached a point now where nothing is going to affect me."

"That's for sure," my father said.

"Will I be able to hear better now?" my grandmother said.

"If you do this for five or six puffs, you begin to see some changes," my father said. "Everything will slow down."

"What's this stuff called?"

"Hashish. When people ask you how it was, you say, 'I got off on it.'"

"Thank God I'm satisfied with my television," she said, sneezing several times in succession. "Oh! Look at all that sneezing. I think I'm remarkable because I can have fun without this stuff. All I need is some wine, good conversation, and thou. My goodness, what a different age this is. How many years is it you are divorced, Robby?"

"I don't know, Ma."

"Rob, as a psychiatrist, would you tell me, why does everybody hate me?"

"Ma, you do not listen to the people around you and try to make your answers fit what they are asking. You ride roughshod over people and don't even listen enough to know that."

"Oh, that's not true."

"You can ignore, deny, interpret that to suit your own needs. But you did ask it!"

"Would you make a copy of what you just said for me?"

There was a pause.

"Are you looking for some words of wisdom, Earl?" my grandmother said.

"Yeah, sure."

"When I was a young girl I was a weaver in a silk mill. It was not at all glamorous. It nearly drove me out of my mind. I think this is the kind of house where everybody can do their thing and not be in anybody's way, so I don't mind talking. I remember when we all ran out to see the first airplane. Of course there used to be horse cars. Yes, I really have led a remarkable life. Once I was the poorest person in the world and I saved and now I'm not. You would think people would appreciate that. Is that a piece of bread over there? Bobo, I think you've grown." She spoke to Rexy and me. "He's sitting tall—which means that he is taller from the waist up, I think—is that an Indian saying? I remember that from somewhere as I grew up. Most of your height is supposed to be in your legs."

"Well, what about dwarves and midgets?" Rexy said.

Great, I thought. My father might as well have picked his own mother if he was looking for intelligence in a girlfriend. How the hell did they understand each other?

"They're short," my brother said.

"Well, wait a minute," my grandmother said, "did you ever see the movie *Ship of Fools*? Well, it is true that some people are larger in the torso, which is the difference between dwarves and midgets. In Paterson we have a brother and sister the same size. One of them lives in the Federation building. Midgets. Twins. I don't know if they are twins. My sister Daisy was very close to them. Incidentally, did anyone ever look at the magazine *Hustler*? Robby, you know, if you would put a little strawberry jam that you made into the barbeque sauce that I made for the meat, it would be, I guarantee, twenty times superior."

"Ma, for crying out loud, I've told you fifteen times this evening I don't want to put strawberry jam in the barbeque sauce. I'm not going to do it! The strawberry jam is made from wild strawberries that took me forever to pick. It is meant to be used on bread! The barbeque sauce doesn't need it, and if you don't want to help with the cooking, that's fine, nobody asked you to, but please stop telling me what to do." My father was shouting now. I felt very mature.

"Holy cow, you don't really object all that strenuously. When I'm not here you won't have a mother to spoil you. It took me a long time to become a Jewish mother. And you know what? I wish *I* had a Jewish mother."

"You know, that is the psychodynamic truth of the whole

thing," my father said, lighting another bowl of hashish at a frantic pace. My grandmother straightened his shirt collar, brushed flakes of dandruff from his lapel and went over to where the meat was cooking. Using her fingers, she moved everything around.

My father threw down the pipe and went to his bedroom, locking the door behind him. My grandmother, thrusting her breasts against me, whispered that she was leaving tomorrow and that I should be kind to her. Smothered against her, I was unable to breathe.

My mother was adopted, for a time, by a couple who introduced her to "swinging." She felt that with her innocent Victorian upbringing she had been deprived of a great deal of experience, and while my father had taught her many interesting and enlightening things that she had never especially wanted to know (since she didn't know they existed in the first place), nevertheless she felt that all knowledge could only be good. The swinging couple, named Art and June, introduced her to a group of free spirits who would get together on Saturday nights for the purpose of animal comfort and warmth among themselves. Although they were divorced, my mother still felt an interest in my father and pitied his lack of knowledge of sexual pastimes. Therefore she suggested to him that they get together one night with Art and June.

My father, however, was not interested in having another man present at this orgy, since he wanted to be in control of the situation and did not care for competition.

Art said that he could not allow June to come to the house unaccompanied but said that he would pay no attention to any goings-on and would read his newspaper.

So one night my mother left Bobo and me alone in the house, informing us she was paying a visit to my father. Art and June drove up to the big glass house my father inhabited, to be greeted by my parents, stark naked in the atrium, the stained glass lamps blinking on and off, a huge fire in the living room and some psychedelic music blasting from the stereo. June was a warm, earthy person who immediately disrobed and the two women attacked my father with great gusto and a bottle of Johnson's baby oil. For once my father did not seem to worry about dripping on the fur rug. How my grandmother Ivy would have loved to have been there, my mother said later.

Sometimes I would try to think of some possible explanation for why our lives changed so abruptly and in such an unattractive and undesirable way. I, who had expected I would wake up every day to the cry and smell of my animal pets demanding to be fed, who had thought I would rise to a day exactly like the one before, had somewhere along the line been sorely deluded.

Before long my dad found someone he wanted to have around him all the time, and he married her fast and only told us casually over the telephone one afternoon. "Boys," he said to Bobo and me, "I'm getting remarried. I can't ask you to the wedding—it's just for adults, and some of them are going to be taking LSD and won't want to feel repressed."

"Dad, what's her name?" Bobo said.

"Maura O'Brian. She's a psychiatric nurse."

"Is she pretty?"

But my father wasn't listening and was already asking when Bobo or I could come over to get the tractor and mow the field.

Grandma Ivy went to the wedding, and she called afterward to say how nice a wedding it had been and how she was sorry she wasn't going to have time to see us on this visit. "A minister performed the ceremony on the deck of the house," she said. "If only you boys had come. Why weren't you there?"

I heard Bobo snickering on the other end of the phone. Here we were, the only two people in the whole world surrounded by the same set of weird circumstances, and Bobo was laughing that my father had gotten remarried. I couldn't understand it. When we hung up I poked him in the ribs and forced him to the floor. "You punk," I said. "What were you laughing at? What's so funny? That we weren't invited to the wedding?"

He lay on the floor, helpless beneath my half-tickling jabs. "I wasn't laughing," he said. "Stop! I was just coughing. I have hay fever. It's not my fault."

The Monday after they were married I called up my father. "I missed the bus, Dad. Can you give me a ride on your way to work?"

"All right," he said, "I'm leaving in fifteen minutes. Get up here by then."

The front door of his house was unlocked and I went in. "Hello!" I said, "Anybody home?"

A strange voice answered hello from the kitchen. There she was, cooking scrambled eggs in a large orange skillet I had never seen before. "Whose frying pan is that?" I said. She looked up from the eggs.

"You must be Earl," she said, "I'm Maura."

I stood in the doorway, grinning at her. I had managed to forget, in a short time, that my father had gotten married, that someone else would be living here now.

"Is something wrong?" she said.

"No," I said. "Nope. I just forgot that—is my father here anyplace? He's supposed to take me to school and I'm nearly late."

"Remember to wipe your feet the next time you stop by," she said. "You've tracked in mud everywhere."

I remember most vividly her freckles. I first noticed that she was covered with them at a picnic down at the pond for our new family. Bobo carried a coconut cake our mother had baked. There they sat, the two of them, she in a bathing suit, a blue one-piece thing with ruffles at the top and bottom.

"Now I want you boys to feel welcome to come by the house at any time," Maura said. "I don't want you to feel like things have changed."

"The one thing Maura and I would like, something that we were discussing before you got here," my father said, "is that in future you give us a call before you come by. Don't drop by without calling first. Other than that, I hope you know that your bedrooms are still your bedrooms, and I want you to remember that."

Bobo nudged me under the picnic table. "Why do we have to call first?" he whispered in my ear.

"I'll tell you later."

"Could the two of you pick up the garbage and clear the table?" Maura said. "I'm going in for a swim."

"I don't think she likes us, Dad," I said.

"That's not true," my father said, "I've told her all about you." She stepped out of the water, wet and somewhat brown with algae. Then she sat back down at the picnic table, and under her the brown boards turned dark. She looked at Bobo and me. "Well," she said, "And who do you two take after, your mother or your father?"

"Huh?" Bobo said. "I don't know."

"Dad, do you think we could buy some fruit trees and plant them?" I said.

"I don't know," my father said. "Don't you think you should ask Maura? By pretending she isn't here, that won't make her go away."

"I wasn't!" I said. "I just—!"

Maura looked pleased. "I might consider growing some plum trees," she said. "Your dad tells me you look more like your mother, Earl. I'd like to meet her. Will you send her my regards and thank her for the cake?"

"Yes," I said. "I'm cold now and I have to go home."

Bobo and I raced home across the bristly field. "Where's the leftover cake?" my mother said. "Did you eat the whole thing? You couldn't have."

"They kept it," I said. "Maura said to thank you for it and wants to meet you."

"Well, she can just wait," my mother said.

It was at this point my mother realized my father had been sleeping around long before the divorce. My father mentioned one day, as he and Maura said their goodbyes—they were off again on one of their frequent weekend trips to the Caribbean—that he had known Maura for several years. It had not been a marriage between two strangers. They had met at one of the psychiatric conventions he used to attend in various parts of the country. I repeated this to my mother, and she began to put certain things together: his secretary Sibyl, whom he once invited to move in with us for a few weeks while her divorce from her manic-depressive husband went through, for one.

"How innocent a relationship could he have had with her?" my mother asked me, while I, still ever hopeful my parents might get back together again someday, looked out the window in feigned indifference.

There were things she heard about him at a party. "Why, after all," she said to me, "did people call him 'Go-Out-And-Do-It Przepasniak'? And what about his weirdo working hours? He was screwing around before you were even born, Earl!"

The reason he had to attend those psychiatric conventions alone was because Grandma Ivy refused to stay with us and baby-sit. She said, "I'm afraid to stay alone in that great big house. But since Mavis can't go, why don't you take me, Rob?"

My father considered this. "Rob," my mother said, "none of the other psychiatrists will have their mothers with them."

My father appreciated this joke so much he repeated it as his own. "'Ma,' I said to her, 'Ma, you can't come with me. None of the other psychiatrists are going to have their mothers there.'"

"I was never given one bit of credit for that joke," my mother said, years later. "No credit for the joke, no credit for designing the house with him, no credit for raising you kids. I might as well never have existed at all."

On another occasion after his marriage to Maura, my mother asked my father if she might use the pond on his property for a picnic and a party she planned. My father, after the divorce, had told her the pond, the land, his property, was hers to use whenever she chose. "Naturally, feel free to swim at any time."

But still, my mother wasn't really surprised to hear that on the very day she was asking him for the use of the pond, my father and Maura had planned a party of their own. "It stands to reason, doesn't it?" she told me. "I just feel so alone. If I only had someone to share my life with."

My mother gave her barbeque in the field next to her own house, but after a while she noticed that everyone who had come to my father's party was standing on the bridge and peering over at my mother and her guests as if they were specimens of antelope at the zoo. "What a dirty, horrible-looking dog," one of Maura's friends from Ohio was heard to remark about Kong in a loud voice. My mother packed our belongings, rented out the house and we moved to the city.

And even though, by now, I was beginning to realize that everything my father did was out of his sense of duty and responsibility to make us all independent, so the more we hated him, the better it was, even though it hurt him terribly, even though I knew all this. Something in me had already started to toughen, like a soft shell that would someday be like the outer hairy covering of a coconut.

And would anyone ever be able to help hammer it open to get to the sweet white meat of the true Earl when all this was through?

2

M Y MOTHER RENTED THE UP-
stairs half of a two-family house in a suburb of Boston. It was
worse than anything I could have imagined. The house belonged
to a rabbi who was on sabbatical in Israel. It had been decorated,
by the rabbi himself, in ghastly blue and green overstuffed
furniture. He seemed to have the same taste as the decorators of
chain hotels along the highway.

The houses were packed close together. There was no yard at
all. Kong ran out the front door and was run over. Downstairs a
family of juvenile delinquents lived with their mother. The school
Bobo and I attended was filled with tough kids who smoked
cigarettes and knocked you down in the toilet, where they were
getting high between classes. They were picked up after school by
overweight parents in Cadillacs.

For my birthday that year, instead of a pet my father helped me
buy a stereo. I had saved some money and he put in the rest. But I
could only afford to buy one record, a whiny pop star who sang in
a minor key about Southern decadence. I played this over and over
again, lying on my bed in the room furnished with pink and white
masonite—it had been the rabbi's daughter's room—while the pop
star moaned. I didn't speak to anyone at the school. I didn't want
to. My mother and Bobo sat in the kitchen, the only room that got
any light, playing endless games of gin rummy.

My brother didn't want to make any friends here either, since the day he came home from school with a chipped tooth from being pushed off the monkey bars. His white face was thinner, he didn't speak much and uneasily fingered his tooth. "The pollution around here makes my nose run," he said, and took to carrying a spray bottle of nasal decongestant.

But at least my mother was not in tears so much of the time, and my father's supposedly secret nighttime visits to my mother—which had continued up to the time of their divorce and into his second marriage—had ceased, even if only temporarily.

When the year was up my mother asked, "What would you like to do now? Where would you like to live, you two?"

"At home," my brother said.

"I can't live there again, Bobo," she said. "I know you want to, but remember how I used to sit on the stairs and cry? I'm not like that now, am I? We'll drive around and when you see a place you like we'll move there."

My mother drove us away from the city. The houses got farther and farther apart. "It's still not the real country, though," Bobo said. "Let's just keep driving. When we run out of gas that's where we'll live."

"There's only one place I want to live," I said, "and that's home."

"Just think," my mother said. "Being a kid doesn't last forever. Soon you'll be grown up, and then you can live wherever you want to. But until then I get to decide. I'm the leader of this gang, remember?"

"I remember," my brother said. "I think I might have to go to the bathroom."

My brother and I chose a suburb of Boston, an historical area, home of the American Revolution, as a place to live in. But after we sold the little house we didn't have enough money to afford a house there, so my mother bought a house closer to Boston, in an even worse area than the house we had rented.

"It's Maura's fault," I said.

"No, it's not," my mother said. "It's mine." But I didn't pay her any attention.

My dad's second marriage lasted two and a half years.

It cost him the car, the furniture, twenty thousand dollars' settlement, and a lot of pride. It meant an expensive six-month trip to Mexico in an attempt to save their marriage, two years of analysis for Maura, clothes for her to wear, and those many brief trips to the Caribbean. He was still working to pay off his first marriage, though on that deal he had come away easy. Still, it was an annoyance to him as he had so many better things to do with the money. Two marriages had scalded him for life.

He should have gone to Europe to save his marriage. He had never been to Europe and it had always been his dream. But Maura had already been there and wanted to see Mexico.

And anyway, he didn't mind giving in, since the major part of his dream—a fact mentioned briefly to Bobo and me—was to screw hundreds of blond shiksas, which Maura probably wouldn't have looked happily on, although already at that early stage of their marriage she was getting used to what constituted my father's idea of fun.

His dreams of excess were based on making up for a time that he called "a pitifully deprived adolescence," a time when only a few of the most unattractive girls would go to bed with him. "You only live once, Earl," he said to me one Sunday afternoon when he was driving Bobo and me to a point halfway between our house and his. "You only live once," he said again, "and when it's all over, boys, all you are is dead."

"Okay, Dad."

It was at this point I believe I made up my mind to someday avenge my poor father, his unhappy life, by living out all his pipe dreams.

"I don't want you to place any value judgment on what I'm going to tell you, Earl. Bobo, are you listening?"

"Yup," he said. He was eating a box of chocolate chip cookies.

"I'm not going to be married to Maura much longer. I'm afraid the two of us are not doing well together. We're getting a divorce."

"Oh." Though I didn't say much, inside I was overjoyed. This meant my parents could be reunited. This meant we would get married and be a real family again.

"Do you know why I'm getting a divorce from her? When Maura was a girl she used to have sex with an uncle who lived with her family. This made her frigid. She's been seeing a psychiatrist for two years now, and this woman hasn't helped her. In fact, I think she's turned Maura against me. I've asked her to stop seeing this woman, but Maura won't. So, we're getting a divorce. Now, who would like an ice cream?"

"I would!" Bobo said. Bobo never entered into conversations much, which seemed pretty sensible almost ninety-five percent of the time, and it was hard to tell just what it was he was thinking. He had a game he concentrated on playing in the car most of the time. It involved finding license plates from every state. "Texas!" he said abruptly, and scribbled something down in a little note pad he carried with him. Then suddenly I felt something on my shoulder. My brother, normally unaffectionate, was resting his hand there in a seemingly nonchalant way. When I turned around, his white face, like a worried monkey, was peering into mine.

"What's the matter, Bobo?" I said to him.

"Nothing. I just wondered what flavor of ice cream you were going to get."

"Pistachio." To encourage my father I said, "Sex? Sexual intercourse? With her uncle?"

"Yup," my father said. "I'll tell you about it, but you must promise never, never to repeat it. Not to anyone—not even to your mother. Do you understand?"

"Yes, Dad," I said. "How can you think I can't keep a secret?"

So here we have it—one of the first signs of my basic untrustworthiness, my illegitimacy as a man.

"I'm glad, I'm glad, I'm glad they're getting a divorce," Bobo whispered shrilly in my ear, "and I'm getting fudge ripple." Bobo did not like Maura any more than I did. Most children, I am sure, resent their stepparents for an initial period at least. I read last week in the *National Enquirer* about a busty television star who fought tooth and nail for nine years to overcome her stepchildren's hatred for her, and finally accomplished it. No wicked stepmother here. She accomplished it through years of careful attention, never speaking harshly to the little ones, years of small doggie bags filled with food, gifts, flattery, little heart-to-hearts about birth control and great outpourings of love to the infants. This was not, however, the case with Maura, who after her marriage to my father became as nervous and febrile as a laboratory Rhesus.

Now it is perhaps true that I was not then and will never be the most lovable of characters. Awkward, pimpled—though I was already in high school I seem now to myself the way my father must have been at the same age: a walking disaster, not very attractive, unformed as a newly hatched larva.

In some ways, because of the manner in which I was brought up, I was surprisingly sophisticated. In other ways, such as relating to people, opening doors for women or even carrying on a conversation about the weather, I was a complete mess. I was like a dog who had been locked up in a garage for many years and when released was unfamiliar with the social customs of others of his kind. They sensed this about me and avoided me as if I were a leper or carried the plague.

And so I led a solitary existence. At school I lunched alone in the gloomy cafeteria, devouring my wooden meatball grinder with a sullen appetite, trying to pretend I was not there. No one spoke to me and I spoke to no one. I dozed through my classes and at night, stunned and sluggish, watched television until two or three in the morning, trying to make up for what I had lost in contact with other human beings.

At home my mother said, "But Earl, you must get out more, make friends. What's wrong with you? Bobo goes out, he has friends." Though this was not entirely true; in a way, the moment my mother said the words: "We're getting a divorce," all those years ago, it was the end of Bobo. He was a fine person, a thoughtful person, but he was a sane person. That sentence had shocked him into a kind of reality he might not have otherwise experienced. It stopped him completely from suffering an artistic sensibility, it prevented him from being a weirdo of any sort. He was a thoroughly American boy. The divorce was probably the best thing that could have happened to him. As compensation he became normal. He worked on the junior high school year book, could converse nicely and in great detail about the plots of the latest science-fiction movies, about how to build a clock, about Roman emperors and ancient coins of the world. He especially liked to sit under the car for lengthy periods of time, changing its parts and intestines.

But the question, "How do you feel?" or, "What are you thinking?" brought only a bored expression, and an "I don't know," or "Lemme alone, will ya, Earl?" He honestly thought that there were no thoughts to be found in his head. I would have liked to break down the wall he had set up for protection, but by then it was too late.

And it was true I had no friends; I almost never left the house. Sometimes as a kind gesture, Bobo invited me to hang out at the Café des Artistes, where he practiced playing pinball, but I always refused.

"But I have you, Ma," I said. "We talk, don't we? I don't need anybody else."

"Yes, but don't you understand? That's not normal. You should go out, get a girlfriend. Isn't there some girl at school that you like?"

"Nobody speaks to me there. They all went to elementary school together. It's easier for Bobo because he knew people from here in grammar school."

But I did make an attempt to find someone, anyone. I chose the most popular girl in the school, an Oriental girl named Mai Cheng, who just happened to be runner-up in that year's Miss Teenage America Pageant.

On the outside I scorned and sneered at anyone who would subscribe to such false, artificial ideas, but I felt differently when I saw her surrounded by a crowd of admiring football players in the cafeteria. From a brown paper bag she brought forth strange and exotic stuffed rolls and delicate vegetables she ate with a fastidious kittenishness, while her crowd of beaux devoured their hateful American sukiyaki—the day's offering for lunch, a kind of cat-meat glue whipped up by the school's dietician. As I watched, fascinated by the picture, she caught my eye across the room and gave me a geisha wink.

I was smitten, but how incalculably cruel my experiences with women proved to be, even at that tender age. Haunted by her little Siamese face and the words of my mother, I called her up and asked her to a movie over the weekend. "I saw you in the cafeteria today. I'm in your math class. Do you want to go out this weekend?"

"Oh, I'd love to," she said, and her thin Oriental voice was like a charming yowl on the other end of the phone. A blush came over me; yes, it was good to have friends, yes, I would be popular and cease my self-imposed reclusion. "I'm busy this weekend, but why don't we make it some other time?"

I called the following week; this time the phone was answered by her mother, who did not seem to speak English but understood after my numerous mutterings that I wished to speak to the beautiful Mai Cheng. I asked her to the high school football game. She claimed to have a bio test she was studying for, and I didn't go to the game—not that I had ever been to a football game, had ever had any interest in football or sports of any kind, it's just that I felt she would be the sort of person to go to one. But she was encouraging and told me to call again soon. Bobo later reported he had seen her there, surrounded by her chipmunk friends.

So it went; next time her giggling sister picked up the phone and told me to hang on while she got Mai. I waited fifteen minutes and when she got on the phone she was abrupt and said she couldn't talk. Each time it was a different story, but the thought that she didn't want to go out with me never occurred to me. Wasn't I interesting, with lots of unusual and warped things to say, from being in such close seclusion with my mother? Couldn't I offer weekends at Dad's ranchero, chopping wood and hiking through the mosquito-laden underbrush? "Why doesn't she just tell me, 'I don't like you. Don't bother me.' Why would anyone take the time to string me along unless they were interested in me?" I said to my mother. "What a bitch. This is torture."

"But, Earl, she obviously doesn't want to go out with you," my mother said.

"How can you tell? I think she would say if she didn't want to."

"You just don't understand. It's not that easy for people to say things like that."

It was true I didn't understand. I felt my heart had been wrung out like a washcloth, oozing old soap onto the floor. "What do you mean?" I said. "She said she wanted to go out with me. Why is she being so cruel? I keep calling her up and calling her up."

"Because it's easy to tell someone you'll see them later," my mother said. "Why don't you ask somebody else? Someone less popular."

"Oh, forget it," I said. "It's not worth it."

It seemed to me as if those years before the divorce were the only years I had really been alive. Why, then, was it that I could not remember a thing about them? Only the aftershock, a green blur, the ripples of recognition that yes, there had been a period in my life when I was completely there, when I was constantly excited about the prospect of being alive, when everything I heard or said meant something more than just words. I did not ask anyone else out; I did my homework only sporadically. I planned revenge for my mother, riches, glories, things beyond her most pitiful dreams for her and me alike.

"Your problem is you care too much," my brother said wisely when he saw me brooding in my room. He took some gum out of his mouth and stuck it on the back of his hand.

I said to my mother, "I prefer my own company and yours to anyone else's. What did he have to marry Maura for? Why didn't he just stay with you?" But I already knew the answer.

"I divorced him," she said. "If I had wanted to stay with him I could have changed. But I'm much happier without him."

Still I memorized facts: the things my father had kept after the divorce, the women he had slept with while he was still married to my mother, the contempt I believed he held us all in. I thought to myself, If for one second I could just slip out of my skin, pretend to be someone else and actually know how that person felt, then I would lose this feeling of being cut in half. To be allowed to lose myself, to not have to be connected with that ghastly, ungainly and slow brain tied by a strand of a neck to an even more useless body—this appeared to be the only answer, the only solution for escape.

Each time we visited my father my mother had to drive for an hour and a half on the highway, where she would drop us off at the Howard Johnson's. Here my father, usually late, would arrive to pick us up and drive us the hour or so to his house. For, as he said, "Why should I have to do all the driving?"

I have a snapshot taken one day when, in a joking mood, my mother brought a camera along when she dropped us off. My father agreed to pose for the picture; an innocent bystander snapped the shot. A real American family in an all-American situation! My brother, pale and white, is grinning weakly; my father scowls off into space; I am dressed in a ragged sheepskin jacket from Afghanistan, my hair is long and curly, my thin face more worried than ever; while my mother has on a most unusual hat, shaped like a white tower, pointing crookedly to the sky. Behind us is the glittering blue and orange plastic of the Howard Johnson's roof. Two cars are also in the picture—my father's white one, my mother's black one, nose to nose in the parking lot next to us, waiting for the transfer of suitcases and adolescents to occur.

My mother was not surprised to hear of my father's impending divorce.

"Do you believe it?" I said excitedly. "Is that something?" My father was getting a divorce from his second wife, therefore it was not just from my mother he sought escape, but from women in general.

"Yes, I believe it," my mother said. "By the way, I wrote a new poem."

"He's getting a divorce from her because of her incestuous past."

"Just let me go to the women's room and then you can tell me again."

Bobo and I sat in our mother's tiny car watching the windows fog over from our breath. "Well, what do you think of the whole thing?" I said to him.

"I don't know, Earl."

"What do you mean, you don't know? Don't you have any opinions about anything?"

"Yes. I guess this means it's not Mom's fault they got divorced. Is that what it means?"

"Yes, that's what it means, punk. Listen, why didn't you say something when Dad started bitching at me about not sponging the table?" I said to him irritably. I was relieved that my brother was on Mom's side, but annoyed that he had ever felt there might be any other side at all. Who had gotten custody of us after the divorce? Mom. And who had called us a millstone around his neck? Well, it wasn't Mom, that was certain. And so, as I changed subjects in my head, I changed the subject out loud, over to things less personal. My inability to sponge the table in the correct fashion was a source of constant argument between my father and me. "Why don't you ever stick up for me, Bobo?"

"I did!"

"Oh sure," I said. "You just stood there, looking out the window. I constantly have to defend you, and you never say one thing for me. And get off my seat belt. You're stepping on my seat belt!"

"I'm not going anywhere until you stop fighting," my mother said, returning from the women's room. "Every time the two of you come back from a weekend there, you're all wound up. I'm so worn out from all of your fighting, I haven't even had a chance to live myself yet."

"Just tell him to get off my seat belt."

"Tell me about this weekend. Did you have a nice time?"

There was a silence.

"They're getting a divorce," I said. "They're getting a divorce because, like I said, when she was young she had an incestuous affair with her uncle and now she doesn't like sex."

My mother was not impressed. "I didn't have to marry your father," she said. "I could have married my Contemporary Civilization teacher. Only I didn't find him physically attractive. Now, there was a character study for you, if you're interested in character studies, that is."

"I am," Bobo said. "What's a character study?"

"Anyway," my mother said, "he used to wear a black bow tie, a black suit, a little vest and steel-rimmed glasses. He used to ask questions, and then he would call on the class for an answer. No one in that class ever had a correct answer. Except for me. And even if their answers were right, he'd tell them they were wrong. But my answers were always right. 'Why don't we let Miss Marx answer that, since no one else seems to be able to?' he'd say. No matter what I said, my answers were always right. I remember on my birthday he bought me a dozen American Beauty roses. I was so surprised! But I guess I was never . . . physically attracted to him."

"Then what happened?" Bobo said.

"Then I met your father. He seemed like a real man. We fought all the time, even at first. But it was exciting. I felt like we were a team. And he was good with his hands. I admired that. After we were married, he taught me the most wonderful things in bed. At first I would say I was frightened. But your father said, 'No, when two people love each other, nothing can be wrong.'"

"What about your Contemporary Civilization teacher?" I said.

"What's Contemporary Civilization?" Bobo said.

"To get back to what I was saying," my mother said, "one summer day I was going somewhere by train. And I went to get a ticket from the little round glass ticket booth. And there he was, selling tickets."

"Who?" I said.

"Am I talking to myself? My Contemporary Civilization teacher, who else? Life imitating art once more. I asked him for a ticket, gave him the money. We made no acknowledgment. We knew each other, but he was playing a different role. The story of my life has always been a budget production. The same minor actors have to play all the bit parts."

She took a red lollipop out of her purse with one hand. "Could you take the paper off this for me?" she said. I unwrapped it and handed it to her. "So? Is this something that's happened all of a sudden? They've been married for two and a half years. He never complained at the beginning."

I was disappointed that I wasn't able to get more of a reaction from her. "Well, Daddy says at the beginning it was okay, but then things went wrong. That's why they took the trip to Mexico."

"And now he's divorcing her for it? He must have known when they got married she had this problem. What did he have to go and marry her for anyway? He could have just lived with her."

And with those words, the terrible feeling I had had was gone. When I thought about who Maura was, it didn't seem as if she should have meant that much to me. It was more the principle of the thing, that my father could ever marry anyone else after my mother. It was easy for me to see Maura in the apartment she had grown up in. Doilies and china dogs; a drab rug with a hole in it, covered by the sofa; the square flickering television set and the roll-away bed in the closet. She fit in there; she should never have been in my father's house. And I wondered about incest: outside in the heat the squeals of the ambulances, the echoes in the courtyard of the brown apartment building, and Maura in her own bed, lying wrinkled with fear and excitement, a silent hippo.

Dickie, her uncle, must have been eighteen that summer, graduated from high school and working for the summer before going off to college in Wisconsin on a scholarship. This at any rate I knew for certain: Maura had mentioned the summer her uncle lived with them, speaking of him on one occasion only, an afternoon spent boiling jars to make jam in.

"Well, g'night." That was Dickie, talking to the parents in the kitchen. And then, after that, creeping in to his wedding cake of a niece, fat and fleshy in the sticky sheets. She keeping perfectly still beneath him, tossed only by waves of her own making, an uneasy ocean liner silent except for foghorn blasts breaking the night.

"What was that?" Maura's mother to her father.

"Oh, Maura is probably having a bad dream."

"Should I go and check?"

"No, she's all right. Leave her alone."

Then, later, the mother readying herself for bed, opening Maura's bedroom to check on her and let in some air. There lay her daughter, sheets like sails spread over her, sleeping peacefully. Dickie had crept out long ago. The mother, smiling in the dark at her daughter, the small cross at the foot of the bed and the curtains, white chintz, blowing softly across the airshaft window: this, I imagined, was incest.

And at breakfast the uncle, Dickie, asking, "How'd ya sleep?" and kicking his niece under the table.

"Fine." Maura's green eyes blank slits. "What do *you* want to know for?" She salted her oatmeal.

"Just asking." He, opening the newspaper the father had left folded on the table, smirking to himself. "Anything wrong with that?"

The mother: "No, that's nice of you to ask, Dickie. Don't pay any attention to her in the mornings. She's just an old grouch. You better get going now, or you'll be late." His job, I decided, was working with the City Parks and Recreation Committee for the summer, picking up pieces of paper with a long, pointed stick. And Maura, getting up to wash her hair, all that pink, freckled flesh steamed clean in the heat.

"I'll call you boys next week," my father had said as he drove off. "I really want us to be closer now. I feel like I'm losing the two of you. Life is short, you're growing up. Let's really try to communicate with each other. I feel very close to you now."

I smiled to myself and thought: now at last my father will be alone. After a second bad marriage, he won't be so quick to have someone else move in with him. We would finally become friends.

We kept quiet for several minutes. Finally Bobo blurted out, "When we go there, Earl is so nice to me, but the minute we get back in your car he starts picking on me. Why does he hate me so? Why does everybody hate me so?"

"That's not true," I snarled. It was true I found it much easier to be nice to him when my mother wasn't around. I was worried that since my father liked him better, my mother might also. "Why does everybody hate me so?" was his most common speech at the time. "Quite frankly," I said, "that speech has lost its effectiveness." Then I felt bad I had said that and turned around to scruff his hair. But all he did was belch—a false belch he was very good at—and slide farther back on the seat.

"What did you do while you were there?"

There was no answer from Bobo or me.

"What did you eat?"

"On Friday night when we got there we had roast beef," I said.

"And for dessert, chocolate fondue," Bobo said.

"How was it?"

"Sort of sickening," Bobo said more cheerfully. It was our duty to cut everything down to size that had happened at my father's: first, to make our mother feel better about it, and second, to make us feel better. "It was pieces of banana, angel food cake, fresh pineapple, strawberries and apples in hot melted chocolate. The apple was lousy."

"The chocolate," I said, "was so sweet that one mouthful hurt your head, and it was flavored with Grand Marnier."

"Whose fondue pot was it?"

"Maura's. Or maybe they got it for a wedding present. I forget. Then for breakfast on Saturday we had bagels, Nova Scotia lox and whipped cream cheese. On Sunday we had Belgian waffles with strawberries and cream and nuts. For dinner on Saturday night we had this meat loaf that was really terrible."

"Daddy made it," Bobo said. "It had hard boiled eggs, olives, chicken livers, walnuts and some other things in it."

"There was paté inside of it, too," I said. "Canned paté. He doesn't know what he's doing anymore."

"It sounds good," my mother said.

"Well, it was lousy. It's because he smokes too much dope. Up at the crack of dawn and he gets high." If there was one thing I had learned from my dad, it was to stay away from drugs of any kind. I had never even had the slightest interest in sampling the LSD and magic mushrooms he kept wrapped in an empty Band-Aid box in the freezer. In a sense it was our rebellion: my father offered us marijuana whenever he smoked and we always refused; my father said it was just a stage we were going through. "What's for dinner at home?" I said.

"I thought we would have chicken wings. I made a sweet-and-sour sauce for a change."

How could any meal not be an anticlimax after those weekends?

My father kept himself supplied with cheeses of every nationality. "Sometimes your refrigerator reminds me of a delicatessen," my brother once told him. There was a bottle of taco sauce, more than a year old, which had congealed into a solid object, exotic fruits such as pineapples, pomegranates, Jaffa oranges at thirty-five cents apiece, Texas ruby grapefruit, strawberry-colored persimmons. Patients brought him fruitcakes and stale homemade coffee rings topped with shrill white icing; there was expensive homemade ice cream in the freezer, jars of Beni Shogi, preserved ginger and kumquats in the refrigerator door, freshly baked black breads stuffed with raisins from the bakery in town.

At my mother's house we lived on hotdogs, baked beans, chicken and cheap cuts of steak—balanced meals that tasted fine but certainly weren't the same as the dishes my father lured Bobo and me with: fresh shrimps marinated overnight in wine and ginger and then quickly fried in a fragrant oil. "I treat you right when you come to visit me, don't I, kids?" my father often said. Sometimes after breakfast all I could do was go back to sleep, but there was far too much work to be done around the place. Like his parents before him, my father saved up the chores for his children. Weeding the garden, carrying in wood, vacuuming the rug: "If you eat, you work."

And so, to compensate, it was necessary we tell my mother how lousy it all tasted. "The food I cook you is good though, isn't it?"

"Oh sure. You feel sick after eating a couple of days at their house. I mean, at Daddy's house. Maura wasn't there. She's moved out already. I think she lives in a studio apartment now. A lot of the furniture is gone. The sewing machine. The things from Mexico. But I don't know why Daddy's not as fat as a pig. I guess he doesn't eat during the week."

"He sure can eat a lot," my brother agreed cheerfully.

But my mother seemed upset by hearing about the expensive meals and began to talk again. "Well, it's nice for him that he gets to live that way. I suppose I could have asked for more money when we got divorced or I could have kept the house. I wish I didn't have to take any of his money at all, but I had you children to look after."

"How much longer until we're home?" Bobo said. "I have a TV show I want to watch."

"Okay, complain, complain," my mother said. "Where does it

get anyone, in this broken bus we're all riding to doom on. Me, you, everyone's sick and tired of women's problems. Why doesn't everything settle down, we could go back to the good old days, even though none of us has ever experienced any. We've heard speak of them at least."

"It used to be fun, once," I said.

"I remember after I divorced Dad—"

"He divorced you, as I remember it."

"After I divorced Daddy, it took me many months to have the courage to drive even a few miles alone in my car."

"I don't remember this," Bobo said.

"I was always getting lost, and since I was afraid to speak to strangers, I would drive for hours out of my way until I worked up enough courage to stop at a gas station to ask directions. I woke up in the morning crying with fright and continued crying for most of the day."

"I remember you used to cry a lot," Bobo said. "You were lonesome then. Not now. Now you write poetry."

"After about a year I realized I wasn't going to die from having been left alone. And indeed, without the nervous tension of having to respond to the criticism—although probably well-deserved, I suppose—from Daddy, and without the constant anguish of not being able to live up to what he should have had in a wife, I began to believe that there was a chance for my survival, after all."

"Daddy forgot to get us ice cream!" Bobo said.

"Well," my mother said, "I feel sorry for Maura, that's all I can say. The poor thing just didn't know what she was getting herself into."

"Daddy says she's getting a lot of money from him, and other things."

"Well, it doesn't sound as if he was too smart, either. He didn't have to marry her, as I said."

My brother had fallen asleep in the back seat. My mother pulled up into the driveway of our shabby house. She was still talking. "I remember during the first years of our marriage Daddy always used to tell me about the wonderful pickled herring his mother made. One day, to surprise him, I bought two buckets of herring. I scaled them, chopped off their heads and tails. Then I put the fish, along with spices and vinegar, into gallon jars. After several weeks Daddy was so impatient he couldn't wait any longer. We unscrewed the cover of the first jar. When I stuck a fork into the first fish the whole jar immediately turned into a gray dust."

"Yuck," I said. My brother stirred in the back seat.

"There wasn't one whole fish in the entire jar. And it was the same with the other nine gallons. I had left out some part of the process. The fish were supposed to have been smoked or salted first, I forget which. But neither Daddy nor I were surprised at the fiasco, it resembled so many others. . . . On the other hand, I suppose Maura must have been just as much of a failure, in her own way, as I was, so perhaps I was not as terrible a wife as I thought I was."

I loved to listen to her talk. Her eyes were bright and worried, the eyes of some small and active animal. "I think you're a good mother," I said. "At least I have one parent who's normal." I half-carried my brother into the house. I heard him mumbling the names of different flavors of ice cream in his sleep.

What was left that would make my father happy? He had talked for years about selling his house, but none of us ever believed he would do it. Though he thought of himself as a free spirit, it became apparent, over the years since the divorce, that he was unable to leave his cage.

But the house—the house that he and my mother had designed together, with the four of us in mind—proved to be, almost as soon as the three of us left it, an unsatisfactory habitation.

"This place sure ain't a bachelor's pad," my father said. "I'm just so discouraged. It didn't turn out at all as I planned."

Before the divorce, the contractor hired to build the place declared bankruptcy and fled to South America, leaving much of the interior and some of the exterior unfinished. And even before this had happened, my father realized the contractor was an incompetent fool. Each morning my father was forced to stand outside the unfinished dream house and scream at him about what had gone wrong.

"You can't possibly think you're doing it right," my father shouted, when he saw the massive hearthstone on the wall, four feet off the ground, instead of on the floor where my father had instructed them to put it. But it had been crushing the contractor's foot—he worked along with his men—and so they lifted it very rapidly, in order that his foot not get broken under the two hundred and fifty pound slab. While they waited for the contractor to extricate his foot, the quick drying cement hardened and the hearthstone was stuck up there. It was then too late to move it, and so the rest of the fireplace had to be installed four feet off the ground as well, as if designed for a house of giants.

The contractor left without putting in the stairs to the ground floor.

The walls peeled off in the bathroom after we took a few showers.

A nest of mice ate our cereal and scampered in front of us while we watched television. Many holes had been left in the walls which made it easy for them to get inside. Also, a pet raccoon I owned briefly climbed into the crawl space and urinated there, to my father's dismay.

The kitchen sink in the house never worked right; a leak sprung in the cesspool.

The house, a Gothic nightmare to begin with, became very nearly a crumbling ruin only a few years after the divorce. The realtor—the former secretary, Sibyl—brought prospective buyers around and my father scuttled to stand in front of cracks in the walls, forgot to mention that though the septic tank had been fixed it still backed up perpetually, and that there was a hole in the roof and another in the kitchen which no one had been able to fix. "What I'm doing isn't really dishonest," my father said, "or maybe it is, just a little. But this is the way it is in the world. If you want to sell something, there are some things you just have to forget to mention. I'm doing it, but I want you kids to know I don't really approve."

When Maura left she took most of the furniture. "I'm entitled to something, Rob," she said. "I never thought things would turn out like this." The furniture went straight into storage.

"The goddamn bitch. She's perfectly capable of taking care of herself. Wiped out my entire savings," my father said. Bobo and I agreed it was not fair. It seemed as if my father would never be happy.

The damp crept into the books my mother left behind in the library.

The cleaning woman, who had been with us when we all lived together, died of a heart attack, and my mother cried. "She used to tell me the funniest stories about the people in the different houses she cleaned," my mother said. "She didn't even know she was being funny. She used to say that near where she lived there were rabbits in the woods as big as deer." My mother went to the funeral and said our cleaning woman had led a hard life.

In the winter when we visited my father, the glass windows chilled and frosted over as the snow fell. We sat in front of the fireplace and looked out onto the treetops, huddled ourselves in sweaters and did not leave the house. The ghost voices of my parents, fighting with each other before the divorce, seeped through the walls. My brother put the spotlight on outside to illuminate the falling snow, and as the flakes fell in great heaps and drifts like dandruff, Bobo and I tried to pretend that it was the house that was rising up, a great lard-white cupcake rising through the trees, and not the snow that was falling down.

And there was yet another problem: much as my father wanted to get out, no one had the kind of money he was asking for the place, though the ads he placed in the New York papers were lushly descriptive.

Finally an older couple, who wanted the house for a summer residence, arrived from New York. I think in the end they bought the place because they were impressed with my father. Harry Katz owned a firm that published psychiatric textbooks. That may have had something to do with it.

Katz, thin, spindly, dressed in blue checked pants, past seventy, hawknosed, reminded me of one of my father's uncles. He had the same New Jersey glottal stop, and with his perpetual cough, his whining and obsequiously sarcastic ways, he doted on my father as if he had been his own son. "What's so great about this place? I'll be doing you a favor to take it off your hands, I'll tell you that."

His overweight wife, a Russian caterpillar in a babushka, toured the house. My brother and I followed her in a hesitant manner, like two baby chickens trailing a tremendous hen around the house. There was even a warm, chicken smell to her—old air escaped from under a quilt. Offhandedly she inspected my father's office, which stank of the psychiatric pipe; the bedroom with its round, cherry-framed bed, the mirrored walls; the walk-in closets scented with cloves and oranges; the eight-foot-tall statue of my mother, nude and pregnant, which graced the side of the front door; the Virginia creepers that reached out fingerlike tendrils from the atrium in the center of the house around the crumbling walls into the living room.

"See, I want to get back to nature," my father told Mr. and Mrs. Katz. "I don't have a family anymore, except for the boys, and I don't see them all that often. I can put them on sleeping bags when they come to visit. And my girlfriend, yes—but what do I need a place this big for? I don't have the money or the time to keep putting into it. I've just bought this property—a beautiful chunk of woods, a hundred acres, about forty minutes from here—and I'm going to put up a small cabin with a studio where I can do my sculpture, work on my glass lamps, raise my own vegetables. I don't want the burden of material possessions."

"You call what you do sculpture?" Mr. Katz said. Mrs. Katz looked with admiration at the large cuckoo clock on the kitchen wall. "Well, what do I know. I call it junk. But if you tell me it's sculpture, I got no right to call it anything different. After all, who am I? A nobody, that's all. I just know what I like and what I don't. But does that count for anything? Not today it doesn't."

"A pretty pessimistic attitude, isn't it?" my father said.

"Ah, what do I know? Solar heat, you say? Myself, I think it's a waste of time. A silly idea. But like I say, what do I know about anything? I'm only a poor schlemiel who made himself a million bucks. I laughed when they told me about the invention of the television."

"Harry, I don't know how you made it this far."

Mr. Katz looked at my father with admiring eyes. To Mr. Katz, as to so many others, my father was an object of adulation. They all seemed to think he was God; he took that for granted.

But on the other hand, Mr. Katz did not really exist for my father. He was just a simple admiring body to whom my father could espouse his theories. However, after the realtor left with the signed papers, my father, as a gesture of spontaneity (though it is true all his spontaneous gestures were planned well in advance) offered Mr. and Mrs. Katz a marijuana cigarette to share with him. Mr. Katz, though shocked, was thrilled.

"Will you look at that?" he said. "A real joint! Well, well. If it wasn't for my wonderful wife, who's afraid I'll be arrested, I might just go ahead. But I've lived long enough without it. I don't need to have Miss Prissy-pants sulking all the way home because I turned out. Or is it turned on? Anyway, not to change the subject, the place you have here isn't too bad. A fancy dump. My wife thinks your taste isn't too bad, though what she would know about anything I couldn't say. We have four kids," he said suddenly to Bobo. My father rested his hand on Bobo's head, which gave Bobo a sudden and unusual importance. "The kids have husbands, wives, children, pet rocks—the whole shmeer. We have a schnauzer named Misty. We wanted a place where we could all get together and go ahead and take a swim. They've been nagging me about it for so long, I went out and did it, became a country squire."

My father did not tell Mr. Katz a new pipe was needed from the stream to the pond to keep the water in it fresh and swimmable. The expense would be considerable.

"I've been in the textbook business for twenty-five years. I built it up from nothing. Who would have thought I'd wind up living in the house of a nutsy psychiatrist?"

In the contract it was written that four thousand dollars additional would be paid for my father's stained-glass lamp sculptures—two of them at two thousand apiece. What the contract did not state was that four thousand dollars from the cost of the house had been deducted and put onto the lamps instead. This was so my father could call his lamps a money-making business and deduct the expenses from his income tax. "I don't feel bad about doing that," he said. "I only wish I could sell them legitimately."

A gallery in New York had promised him a show, but when they saw the lamps up close, they changed their minds. "I like the lamps, Dad," Bobo said. "I think they're beautiful," I said. Bobo and I planned in secret to send slides of them around to galleries.

A short time later, the Katzes called my father up to ask him to come and remove the lamps.

But for now, the sale of the house at least was complete.

"Wait until you guys see my new house, when I get it built," my father said to Bobo and me later. "Just wait. It's going to be fantastic." He lit another joint and started to make little sketches of houses on a piece of paper, using a blue pen. His eyes began to close and a dreamy look came over his face. "Let's go play cards," Bobo said to me. We left my father alone in the living room.

My mother was a genius, that much was true. But what a genius! I often told her she would go on record as being the dumbest genius alive. "Even Einstein learned to tie his shoes eventually," I told her.

Anyone could take advantage of my mother. She was invited to interview for a teaching position at a college in California. "The job's yours," they told her on the telephone. "Just come out for an interview as a formality. When we give you the job we'll give you the airfare." Four weeks later she flew out there at a cost of several hundred dollars. Bobo, who had just gotten his license, had to drive her to the airport at the crack of dawn. (Have I forgotten to mention that I don't know how to drive? Shortly after I received my license, I had a traumatic accident: I backed into a tree, which put the fear of driving into me for life.) She had to wait for four hours at a layover in Chicago. When she arrived at some obscure town in California, a town she had to ride in a six-seater airplane to get to, no one was there to meet her.

"I should have gotten on the next plane and come home," my mother said. But no, she waited and waited, and called the college until finally a pimpled, silent student was sent to meet her. They drove for two hours, my mother chattering, struggling to keep the student amused. There was no reply. The luncheon where she was to read her poems took place on the floor of a sagging house where she was served a sad affair with zucchini. The interview lasted several hours and included such questions as "Why do you want to teach poetry?" ("I need to make a living somehow," my mother thought but did not say), "Why do you want to live in California?" (the college was in the middle of a miniature dust bowl; my mother had no desire to live there) and "Tell us a story." ("There was a lady poet who flew west looking for a job," my mother began.) Finally at the end of the day, she was told she did not have the job after all.

A man had driven out from the East, all his possessions tied to the roof of his car. He had sold his house. Although he had published only a few poems, did not have as much teaching experience as my mother, was not as well-known, had long, lank, greasy hair and a mountainous belly, it was only fair that the job be awarded to him. Fair? It was only typical, one of a long string of events in my mother's life all following the same pattern. My mother, crushed, was sent home, where she lay in bed, weeping. The fare for the airplane was never sent to her.

Only the week before she left for the interview, my mother and I packed away all of our books in preparation for her departure, in order to facilitate renting the house out on her return. I was to go off to college and Bobo would go with her. Though we had no furniture we did have books. My mother had made an art out of finding cheap books. We had shelf after shelf (built by my father on a long-ago promising Sunday when it had seemed likely my parents would be rejoined or at least that my father would continue to receive the sexual favors of my mother) in the living room, filled with fifteen-cent specials—remaindered paperback books with the covers ripped off that were purchased in drugstores and Woolworth's.

We had a series of disease books; books about girls murdered in Chicago and in Michigan and about young boys who were autistic, retarded or had hemophilia; a book about a priest who had contracted leprosy and lost fingers and toes; a book about a mother of five with a brain tumor, who had to have part of her skull removed and a special plate inserted that continued to bulge as the tumor grew—all true stories. There was also a psychic-phenomena section of the shelves: hundreds of *Fate* magazines; *The Life of Edgar Cayce;* strange and incomprehensible events that had transpired on the face of the earth which no one could explain—frogs dropping from the air, an amazing rain of blood and slices of meat, a hole in the Russian tundra that appeared mysteriously and was believed to have been an atomic explosion from a UFO.

All these my mother studied avidly, a pastime my father in his heyday would have had nothing but contempt for. Once when I asked him how he thought acupuncture worked, he said that the Chinese peasants had very primitive minds and it worked on them as a mild sort of hypnosis. "But what about the Americans it works on? And the Europeans?" As a neo-Freudian my father believed the primitive mentality was widespread. Why, he was only one generation removed from the Russian peasant himself. "There is no alternate reality," he told me on one of my visits to his house, which by now, by mutual consent, had been reduced to once or twice a year. "And I'm tired of all this nonsense of people trying to prove that there is."

But my mother, though she did not go in for fads, read the ESP books, and all had to be packed in boxes and stored in the attic along with everything else. What books did we have worth saving? Three boxes of the Harvard classics, rotting and mildewed, that had belonged to my grandfather, an *Encyclopaedia Britannica* from 1899 that my mother had bought somewhere for five dollars, a high-school type of encyclopedia already several years old that my mother had given to Bobo. There were "antique" books my mother had found in old shops for ten cents or a quarter apiece, with mouse-nibbled pages, stinking of age, old editions of Hardy, books on social etiquette from 1853, Godey's Lady's Books, books that contained deathbed quotes and books that purported to be scientific but in reality were about made-up wonders of the world—strange animals with the head of a bird and the body of a dog, men who ate earth, the wondrous continent of Australia— facts stranger than the strangest *Ripley's Believe-It-Or-Not.*

Each book was covered with food stains. Both my mother and I ate while we read, covering pages with drips of ketchup, blotches of fingerprint-sized grease. It was possible to see what page had been read at breakfast, where the tuna fish for lunch came in (page one hundred and nine) and by dinner (if one reviewed the book at a later date), a faint reek of onions, or perhaps some ice cream, chocolate blobs and dots. Most of the boxes were too heavy for me to lift and had to be lined up in the hall next to the linen closet until Bobo came home to help.

To get to the attic involved opening the linen closet, removing the shelves and taking down a small door held up by hooks. Bobo or I could then scramble up to the storage space above. While we packed, no mention was made of what was going to happen to me. Bobo was still young enough for it to be assumed that he would go with my mother. I think she was hoping I would suggest of my own volition that I would go off to school when she left to teach. On my part, I was waiting for her to ask me to join her in California, where I imagined myself basking like a bull seal on the beach, no matter that there was no beach for several hundred miles in the place my mother expected to have a job.

My mother didn't think it would help my future to spend a year doing nothing, a lummox at her side. "After all, I expect you to support me in my old age," my mother said to me, when I apologized for devouring great quantities of her food that I was in no way helping to pay for. "And that old age is coming very shortly."

"Maybe Bobo will be better able to support the two of us," I said. My mother and I decided that Bobo, with his logical, literal mind, would be best off operating and removing parts of other people—not a psychiatrist like Dad but a doctor nevertheless. Bobo seemed amenable to the constant suggestions that he apply for a six-year college/medical school program, that he take the right high school courses and get good grades. "After all," I said to him helpfully, "Ma and I are expecting you to support us, your feeble brother and aged mother."

But now, as long as my mother thought she had a job for the spring term, she was much happier and more relaxed about money. At least she would not have to count on either of her children for support for a short while yet. "And," she said to me, "often one job leads to the next." She was eager to begin to save money to buy a new car. She had owned her present one, a huge station wagon with only six cylinders, for almost twelve years. It groaned like a monster, it would have liked to give up and be put out of its misery, but my mother would not let it die. She couldn't afford to. "But it's not even worth fixing, Ma," my brother told her.

In the attic I arranged the cartons, stacking them one on top of the next, unable to breathe from the dust, my hands numb from the cold. It was important to try to fit the boxes of books one on top of the other, saving space as economically as possible, because there were many more boxes of books to come. My mother wanted everything put into the attic so that the tenants, whoever they were to be, would have a place downstairs to put their own belongings. She was experienced with renting out houses, because the year we moved to Boston, she had rented our house before selling it. The tenants had ruined the upstairs floor, painting the wood with a bright, plastic shellac. Also, they had stolen two valuable rocks that belonged to my mother's father—two pieces of quartz crystal, sparkling prisms, one pink and one clear, weighing about ten pounds each. Bobo and I were sick to find them gone. The tenants, who had bragged frequently to my mother that they were Van Rensaleers (what that meant I did not know), didn't deny taking the rocks, nor did they return them, so now my mother knew to pack away everything we owned.

After most of the boxes were in the attic a slight crack developed along the kitchen ceiling, which had been rebuilt by the former owner of the house, after a fire. "The world is a mess around me," my mother said. "I don't mind. I like Woody Allen films. But it was for just this very reason your father divorced me."

Sometimes my mother and I would look up and see that the spidery scrawl of cracks, like antique lettering, was spreading. When Bobo came home from school one afternoon we moved the rest of the boxes up to the attic.

"I think it's okay," he said, "but I wouldn't put any more stuff up there. What do you want to keep all that stuff for? Why don't you just throw it out? It's just a lot of junk. Why don't you get books out of the library, if you want to read." Bobo was a normal American. He rearranged all my stacking and packing in the attic, telling me I knew nothing about structure, did not know how to get the maximum out of a space and was generally incompetent. He did have a point.

I kept several rabbits in a cage in the backyard. They lived in a kind of large wooden crate, with wire sides and a heavy, one-piece roof. The floor of the cage was always damp. There were bags of rabbit feed scattered all over the yard, which was not very large. When it rained, water leaked through the roof of the cage in a number of places. I tried to keep the bottom of the cage dry, but it was always wet, and as soon as I put fresh sawdust down it was filthy. I hated to go out there. Every time a female had a litter, which was often, the babies died. I didn't have the right kind of feeder, either, and the pellets I fed them were always scattered on the bottom of the cage, swollen and mushy.

"I saw a rat in the backyard," my mother said.

"A rat in the backyard?" I said. "You're crazy. It was probably just a squirrel."

"It was a rat," my mother said.

She was right. The nearby dump had closed down, and the rats, searching for a new residence, had chosen my pellet-filled yard. The former owners of the house had been great bird lovers, and they used to put all their old food—baked beans, sugar cubes, bits of meat, cat food—out in the yard for the birds to feed on. The birds had never caught on to this diet, but the rats loved it. One day I went out to feed my rabbits, and a rat scurried out from under the cage and ran across my feet. When Bobo came out—I was shouting quite a bit, apparently—we moved the rabbit cage and found a series of holes under it, where the rats had made their home. The dirt was soft and we jumped up and down, flattening the holes. "That's that," Bobo said, wiping his hands and turning around. I looked at the area we had flattened. From out of the packed dirt a rat hauled itself, freeing itself from the thick earth, and scuttled off across the yard.

The rats did not go away. In the mornings when I looked out the window I would see a whole rat family, a mother followed by four or five romping babies. Some of the baby rats were rather cute, but the bearded, old gray rats, with their hoary complexions and large, yellow teeth, were frightening.

"What if they get into the house?" my mother said.

"Don't worry about it," I said.

"I'm calling the health department," she said. "As if I don't have enough troubles. Now I have to have rats."

At this time jobs for writers were difficult to find. In particular, jobs for poets, jobs for women poets, jobs for older women poets, jobs for older women poets who were geniuses, who had not started writing until quite late in life, who were prone to stare into space for long periods of time, who were not good at sucking up to lousy, crummy heads of departments, or who were not good at playing the games of those who imagined themselves to be poets but were in reality poem-pushers, as my mother put it.

"All I needed was this one thing to push me over the edge," my mother said when she learned she had not gotten the job and that rats were not in the jurisdiction of the health department. "Being over the edge probably wouldn't be any different from being here, though. Maybe we're already over the edge, who knows?" We decided to invest in a major load of groceries so that neither of us would ever have to leave the house again.

"I don't have to stay in too, do I?" my brother said. "Just because the two of you are nuts doesn't mean I have to be."

My mother and I went to the store to stock up. I felt this was my chance to avoid college, since my mother noticed nothing in her depression. Since it was our intention never to go out of the house again the quantities of food we purchased were vast. Together we waltzed down the aisles, filling the basket with packages of lamb chops, gallons of chocolate chip ice cream, containers of cole slaw, pickles in jars, salamis, onion rolls, frozen raspberries. There were perhaps thirty or forty cans of tuna fish in the cabinets at home, but my mother found room in the shopping basket for more because they were on sale.

My mother's hair, black and wild, cascaded down her shoulders. She wore a venomous black rain hat; we wore venomous expressions of rage and boredom on our faces, the inexpressive anger of iguanas. I wielded the shopping cart like a dangerous sports car.

"This and this and this," my mother said as we picked up chocolate chips to bake cookies with, black cocoa cookies, Triscuits, Wheat Thins, heads of cheese, bottles and bottles of diet ginger ale. The childhood fantasy of snatching down everything from the shelves had come true. "I don't ever want to leave the house again," my mother said.

"Fine with me, Mom," I said. "I already told you I didn't want to go to college. I consider it a form of prostitution. I'm not interested in sitting there absorbing knowledge simply as a means to get out of working."

The cha-cha Muzak of the supermarket loud in my ears, the inner city shoppers around us looking even stranger than we did, in their shabby beaver coats, in their ancient voluminous hats and scarves draped around their necks, all ancients themselves, trembling old people, some with canes and some in wheelchairs.

"Besides, Bobo will go to college. He's a human being. Let him support us."

"You can't dump it all on Bobo, Earl," my mother said. "I don't know what will become of us, but Bobo can't do anything about it. Not yet, anyway." My mother's glasses were dark to hide her eyes. I had on mirrored sunglasses and a pair of hospital surgeon's green pants I had picked up when my Dad had a job at an alcoholic clinic.

Actually this was the first time either of us had been out in several weeks, ever since the terrible announcement that my mother had not been accepted for the job. I had graduated from high school and didn't see any use in getting a job, despite the fury this inspired in my father. I was past caring.

Over and over the supermarket Muzak played the best loved

tunes in the nation. "Eleanor Rigby" swung right into "Those were the days, my friend." My mother grabbed my arms and together we danced down the aisles, past the shopping cart, around the infirm, fumbling with their cans of sardines, before stopping to snatch more food to bring home. We were stocking up, we were laying in for a long winter, although outside it was summer. I did not know, as I went out each morning to renew the rat poison, that the winter I was experiencing then was to last me the rest of my life.

Meanwhile my father ran into a little trouble at the women's college and lost his position as head of the mental health department.

The trouble was with a patient he slept with, a graduate student who went berserk when my father told her, in an attempt to end the affair, that she was cured.

During her frenzy she broke not only the windows—extra thick thermopane—in my father's house one evening when he was out, but also smashed all the windows on the ground floor of the medical building at the college. As they loaded her into the police car she announced to the reporters present her reasons for doing so.

It was okay with my father, losing his job I mean, because over the years the women's college had gone coed, expanded, and my father was left with mostly the administrative duties of a growing mental health service, when what he wanted to do was help people.

After that Dad bummed from job to job, trying to subsist and finish building a new mansion, maintain a couple of ex-wives and a new girlfriend, all on fifteen or twenty hours of private patients a week. Often patients would cancel and wouldn't pay for the missed hours. He tried to put away money for me to go to college, but it wasn't really his fault he couldn't. His pension fund had already gone to build the new place, and any extra cash he had went into buying up all the available acreage that surrounded the house. He didn't want to have happen again what had occurred at the old house, the one my mother and he had built: the twentieth century had crept in and had built the Glenview Homes less than a block away.

More important, my father was trying to save enough money to buy some sort of Gauguintuan getaway, a tropical island, prefera-bly in the Caribbean. "I can't take much more of this cold," he said. "If I just had an escape, a place I could get to for six months of the year. You know, if I didn't have to keep paying alimony to your mother I'd have enough money to do everything I wanted. Just because I was married to her once doesn't mean I should have to be attached to her financially for the rest of my life."

"Sure, Dad," I said. I was not pulling my own weight either. I was spending my summer in the city, a lizard of the lowest order. I slumped and moped, gaining weight, committing unspeakable acts in my room filled with old gasses and belches, wishing I could be like my dad, a success with women and men alike. Bobo had a summer job at the city swimming pool.

"How are you, Earl? I'm worried about you. Maybe you need a vacation," my father said.

So it was that he invited me and Bobo to join him and his new girlfriend, a frightened-looking dietician, to go on a trip to the Bahamas, where he planned to at least look at some property, even if he wasn't yet able to buy.

I didn't know what to say. The invitation from my father came on the day my mother received the following letter:

Dear Mavis,

Enclosed find my monthly check, which I would like to make the last of its kind. I believe your circumstances have changed. You are in a position to turn down jobs and have had a book of poems published.

I have consulted with my lawyer about going to court to sue for termination of alimony. I have been encouraged by my lawyer to offer you an opportunity to settle out of court.

It has been suggested to me to offer you in exchange for a Quit Claim of alimony payments either: 1. A lump sum of four thousand dollars. 2. Three thousand dollars this coming year, one thousand the second year, one thousand the third year, nothing thereafter.

Sincerely,
Robert Abraham Przepasniak

P.S. I would appreciate a prompt reply.

"I made one hundred and ninety-four dollars in royalty payments from my book," my mother said. "That's not enough to live on!" She started to cry. "The best tactic is not to answer him at all."

Since the dissolution of my father's second marriage and since he began to build his new house, my parents had gradually stopped speaking to one another. For a time after the divorce they had met for occasional sex; this had long ago ceased. So perhaps my father's letter was, in an obscure sense, justified. At least this is what my mother said, knowing how my father always insisted on getting something for his money. "But that's the American way, after all. It's a capitalist society we're living in. He can't really be blamed."

And how was my dad to know that when my brother and I told him our mother was undecided about whether or not to take a job in California, that meant she had not, in fact, actually gotten it?

My mother grew terrified of my father.

"Ma, he's harmless," Bobo said. "He doesn't mean anything by it. You don't have to speak to him."

"I'm not even married to him," she said. "Why should I be subjected to this?"

After several battle scenes in the Howard Johnson's parking lot when she delivered Bobo and me to my father, she grew accustomed to sitting in her car with the windows rolled up and the doors locked, looking straight ahead to avoid seeing my father decked out in his too-small beret (purchased in Montreal on a hosteling trip he took one summer when he was eighteen), the man she had been married to for almost thirteen years.

"I don't believe he's harmless," she said. "You weren't married to him. You don't know what he's capable of. And from what you tell me, I don't like the way he drives."

"Aw, Ma," Bobo said. "Just because he's run over his mailbox a couple of times. The guy smokes too much marijuana, that's all. Nothing to worry about."

"Well, I don't think it's fair," I said. "What you get in return for your years of putting my father through medical school and then taking care of all of us, is a letter saying you're no longer going to receive any alimony?"

"Your father has problems of his own, Earl. I can't feel angry with him because he doesn't even know that anyone else exists. If

I felt bad enough I could get a job. But I am a poet. I don't want to get a job selling turtles in the five-and-ten-cents store. Is it called the five-and-ten-cent store anymore?"

"They don't even sell turtles in most Woolworth's now."

"The point is this: I have many poems to write. Selling turtles in Woolworth's is not where my talents lie. Each of us has a vocation. Mine came to me much later than other people's. I don't want my life to be a waste. Sure, I worry about money. But I would rather worry and write my poems than sell turtles and not write any more poems and not worry. Because that is what selling turtles would do to me."

I wanted to tell my mother: "I want to go with Dad to the Bahamas this Christmas. I don't even mind that he is planning to take me with the money, the piddling one hundred or two hundred bucks a month he should be paying you!" But I knew I would not say this, I would not go. I felt sick at the very thought of wanting to do such a crummy thing to her.

My mother didn't say anything but brought me a poem she had just completed. It was called "The Soul Has No Morality."

"Don't you mean mortality?" I said.

"No, I mean morality," my mother said. Her eyes were a soft sea-green color.

"You know, sometimes I imagine my brains to be the exact color your eyes are," I said.

"Just read the poem," my mother said.

"It's okay," I said, when I had finished. "Not bad."

I say to myself today: "Why didn't you praise her then, Earl? It's not as if there's an abundance of praise in the world, and she above all could have used it." And I hear my father on my shoulder, laughing, laughing hoarsely into my ear.

I often wanted to scream at my mother when she handed me one of her poems, brilliant, weird, that mincing typeface crawling across the page. They upset me. My brother had no qualms about expressing this emotion. He simply refused to read the stuff, and once left the room when she begged him to read something she had written. No one wants to have a genius for a mother, some Sylvia Plath or Virginia Woolf futzing around the house while we complain and whine with our own problems, trivial by comparison.

"Not a bad poem," I said again. "But let's get down to more

realistic things. What are we going to do if Daddy stops paying you alimony? I'm not old enough to support us. I worry what will become of you."

"You liked the poem, then?" my mother said. "Really? I think it might still need some work. Don't worry so much, Earl. Your problem is you worry too much." She sat down on the chair next to my bed. I lay with the sheets pulled up to my neck, a bunch of old grapes on a plate near my head. "Aren't you hot, Earl?" I shook my head. "Anyway, don't worry. I've come up with a great idea, an idea that will make us a lot of money. I'll tell you, but don't breathe a word of it to anyone."

"Ma, who am I going to tell? I don't even go out of the house."

"All right, then." She lowered her voice to a whisper. "Here's the idea. The other day I was in the library reading some poetry books—this was before we decided not to leave the house—and I went to the women's room. While I was in there I heard different people peeing at different tones and speeds, different frequencies of pitch, like little bells. And the flushing of the toilets, the whine of the hand dryers. For some reason I was reminded of a concert I had heard on the classical radio station the day before—a concert of Baroque music, Telemann, I think it was, various Renaissance music, and so on and so forth. And I happened to think, what if someone were to go ahead and combine the two different things, this piece of Telemann with people peeing, every once in a while a toilet flushing, et cetera. It would be great! It would be a best-selling record! We'll make a fortune!"

I was silent. "Is that the idea?" I said finally.

"Yes. It's a great idea. If someone else thought of it you would think it was a great idea."

"Ma," I said, "I hate to ask you this, but who is going to buy it? No one would buy it."

"That's not true. Loads of people would buy it. College students. Undergraduates, for example. Boys in dormitories would love to own that album."

"Yeah."

"Of course, I don't know anything about it, how to record it, copyright laws—"

"Ma, these things take a lot of money to produce. I hate to tell you, if we wait for this to make us rich we'll starve first."

"Don't worry about that. You're just so discouraging all the time. How can you hope to get anywhere with your attitude? This is a great idea, you're just always skeptical. We'll be rich. Don't tell anybody about it, though."

"No, Ma."

While I lay in bed listening to my mother's plans for striking it rich, my father, probably right at that very minute, was finishing up his new house. It was going to be worth, he said, a quarter of a million dollars, on a hundred and fifty acres of valuable property, half of which was swamp.

"It's just not fair. You have to sit around thinking up these ideas and he—"

"Please don't worry so much, Earl. Try not to worry."

But I sensed something was about to go seriously wrong. Besides, as I said, "Somebody has to worry."

"That's true. Well, maybe you've found your role in life, Earl." As my mother said, it was in my nature to worry, an element found only in the blood.

Though we had stocked up on frozen groceries, my mother soon ran out of sourballs and we were out of milk. In addition, there was nothing to read. So one afternoon we went out again, to the library and the grocery store, and as I carried the bags of groceries in from the car with my mother I heard the phone ring. "The phone is ringing," I said.

"Well, answer it," my mother said.

"I'm not going to answer it. I hate answering it. You get it."

"I'm not going to get it. Supposing it's your father? Besides, I have to go to the bathroom."

It was my father. "Hello, Earl," he said.

"Hi," I said nervously. I swung the receiver, with its extra long cord, over my shoulder, so that I could unload groceries while I talked.

"I'm coming to Boston to attend a psychiatric convention. Don't much want to go, but thought I'd see you while I was there. Why don't I come by on the twenty-fifth."

"Yeah?" I said. "The twenty-fifth? That's a Saturday, isn't it? Okay, sure, about what time?" I found myself unpacking two tomatoes, huge and rancid, with several funguslike molds spread across their red flesh. I put them into the vegetable bin in the refrigerator. An egg carton revealed nothing but a broken yolk hardened in place. As I talked, I began picking out more things from the bag: an old lamb chop bone, something slimy and green and stuck to a napkin, an open can filled with solidified grease. "Goddamn it! Ugh."

"What?"

"Oh nothing, Dad. I just made a mistake. I was unloading the garbage instead of the groceries. So how long is the psychiatric convention?"

There was a pause while my father thought for a second. "The groceries? You were unloading garbage instead of groceries? Why would you do such a thing?"

Sometimes I felt as if I were older than my father. My father lived in a world of his own, unable to fathom what went on outside of it. "Aw, never mind, Dad. How long are you going to be here?"

"Just the weekend. It's on treating mental illness with drugs."

"Well, that sounds interesting," I said. Actually I didn't see how it could be. My father didn't even believe in mental illness—at least not for intelligent, unneurotic people—let alone that it might be chemically based.

I was right, because he said, "No, it's not interesting, but they've passed a new law that you have to go to a certain number of these conventions. It's all a lot of crap, but this one was on a convenient weekend. Where's the answer from your mother about the alimony? I'm planning to get remarried. Just thought I'd let you know."

After I had hung up, I went to find my mother. "That was Daddy," I said. "To be perfectly honest with you, what I feel like is just staying in my room until my life improves."

"I'm not staying in my room until my life improves because I know it's never going to improve," my mother said. "I'm just staying in my room, period. I think to myself, what am I supposed to do for the rest of my life? It's just sitting there, a great white hulk. What did Daddy say?"

"Actually, he told me he's planning to get married again."

"Are you upset?"

"No, but I said, 'Congratulations,' and Daddy said, 'You sound disbelieving, hostile, confused, and bewildered.'"

"What did you say to him?"

"I said, 'No, I'm not, you read too much into my voice, Dad. I'm only surprised since you said you were never going to marry again after the last time.'"

"And what did he say to that?"

"He said, 'That was some time ago.' Anyway, I called Bobo at his after-school job. He said he had spoken to Daddy this morning. The judge who is going to marry them is coming over to Daddy's house today so they can get to know him. I think they are trying to test him to make sure he's not religious or something. Daddy was planning to take him on a two-hour hike up the mountain, although he's seventy years old."

"Was Bobo upset?"

"No, you know Bobo. Nothing upsets him."

"I don't know, Earl. You know how he gets sometimes. He can be awful. I keep warning him, 'You're going to take after your father if you're not careful.'"

Bobo at that minute came into the kitchen. He had gotten a ride home from work and was back early. "What?" he said. "Were you talking about me? Ma, why do you sit there clutching your head that way? You look deranged."

"Oops, there you go again," my mother said to him. Bobo gave an angry imitation of a belch, winked at me and left the room. My mother sighed and poured another cup of coffee for herself. "Is there no way out of this family? It's like a thought-form that's taken physical dimensions."

"What do you mean, thought-form?" I said. "Could you just say 'thought'?"

"No, because it's more than just a thought."

"Yeah? Who thought of this 'thought-form' thing?"

"The Tibetan lama Lobsang Rampa. By the way, I changed my poem 'Euphoria.'"

I cut off a hunk of coffee cake. "To what?" I said.

"It's now called 'Depression.' Whatever possessed me to marry your father?" she said. "Why did I ever marry that maniac?"

"Well," I said, "it's a little late now to worry about it." I continued to leaf through the Sunday paper, the "News of the World." A boy had been given shock treatment as he persisted in exposing himself every time he saw a woman while jogging. He jogged ten miles a day, in populated areas. A boy kept locked up in a chicken coop and fed nothing but chicken feed was discovered at age ten, looking remarkably like a Rhode Island Red. "Talk to me," my mother said. I put the paper down.

"Dad says he's coming into Boston for the weekend to go to a psychiatric convention and he's going to stop by to talk to me," I said. "Oh, Ma, I hope he's not planning to tell me what's wrong with me again. I know I have a lot of problems, but I'm getting a little tired of hearing about them."

Although my mother had some friends, we had few visitors because we lived in a bad area of the city and my mother's friends seemed to find it difficult to reach us. So we didn't bother to clean up much; hundreds of poems with typing errors lay on all the floors. We had no furniture, either: for one thing, we were too poor; for another, the neighborhood was so dangerous, any sign of opulence would have guaranteed a robbery. As it was, we had nothing to lose but a small black-and-white television set with poor reception, and two chairs we had bought when we purchased the house—rattan with soiled leopard-print seat cushions. The rug my mother's parents had given my parents when they were still married had been put into storage when my mother thought she had a job in California. We didn't bother to get it out of storage from the Armenian rug cleaner's, Kookoo Boodakian. "There's no sense in that," my mother said. "If we got it out I would get a job instantly, and then we'd have to take it back."

Actually, this house had turned out to be something of a monstrosity in a minor key. The interior had been redone by the former owner, Mr. O'Keefe. O'Keefe and his wife had lived in the house for twenty years with their aged chihuahua and meaty son, a Viet vet, before his wife had fallen asleep with a lit cigarette in her hand. After the fire, Mr. O'Keefe wanted to do the reconstruction by himself before retiring to the country. He had not been anxious to spend money and redid everything in the cheapest way possible. The basement flooded frequently and had to be dried with old telephone books; the walls were papered with end rolls that O'Keefe had found at a bargain rate somewhere. Each wall was a different color and pattern. He had done the wiring of the house himself, using an antique fuse system that was difficult to buy as well as replace. The fuses burned out each time the garbage disposal was used.

My mother's long black hairs collected in corners of the house, along with the hundreds of poems that lay about like secret messages, each unfinished or only partly typed and reading, "Consolation Prize: I dream of someone breathing like a spider in my ear," as well as other cryptic messages. And everywhere were bags of library books. After we ran out of books and reading material we made one more trip to the library (we would send the books back when they were due via the Old Age Book Truck), to drain it of books. We loaded into shopping bags all the most delectable books in the library. My mother took out *Plague, Epidemic,* and *Tumor!* For some reason, I had taken an interest in the cannibals of New Guinea, in particular, a group in which the chief males of the tribe devoured unwanted children in order to get rid of extra mouths, and also as a means of raising the protein level of their diet. Then I had several books about a disease acquired only from eating the human brain, a disease to which these cannibals were particularly susceptible. The victims of this ailment died laughing. Or rather, I should say, died *of* laughing, which was perhaps not the worst way to go. On the way up the stairs in the library, one of the bags broke, sending the books clattering and smashing down the concrete steps.

Although the library, recently renovated at a cost of three quarters of a million dollars, was known for its liberal reading conditions (as well as its lack of books), there was a constant stream of noise from screaming kids who chased each other through the stacks, old men sleeping at the tables, snorting and farting, teenagers smoking cigars and singing loudly to music playing through headphones attached to phonographs in the music room. But when the bag of books broke, every head wheeled around to face me, scowling like a flock of hovering vultures hoping for an unmentionable meal.

My mother and I left and picked up a pizza; this I placed between stacks of books that I had to carry from the car to the house since the bag I had used to carry some of them had broken. Unfortunately, earlier in the day the doorknob had come unscrewed, and my mother, though she asked me to remind her, had forgotten to screw it back in place before we went out. Now, on our return, when she put the key in the hole, the doorknob unscrewed the rest of the way and the outside knob fell off. What remained were some screws and bolts in my mother's hand, which caused her to nervously say, "Here, Earl, take these," as she thrust the bag of books toward me. The bag broke on the front steps, and as I stooped to retrieve some of the screws that had fallen onto the ice-slicked steps, the books fell out of my hands, crashing onto my mother's feet and crushing the box of pizza between numerous volumes.

In the bitter cold I struggled to rescrew the doorknob, while my mother held open the glass storm door in front of me. Then, just as I finished screwing the knob back in, the keys on the keychain that was still attached to the keyhole slipped off the chain, leaving only the one doorkey still attached. My mother bent to hunt for the keys in the dark, letting the storm door slam into me and further devaluating the pizza.

At last we were able to get inside, in a great burst of books and gusts of wind, into the filthy living room with its dying plants—dying from lack of water, since none of us ever remembered to care for them. By now the pizza was quite cold.

Together my mother, Bobo and I dined separately, each in bed, Bobo with the television set at the foot of his. Each of us had a large bowl of chocolate chip ice cream doused with walnuts and syrup—our dinner. None of us wanted to wash dishes, so the cups, bowls, plates and coffee cups were of a plastic-coated cardboard material usually used for picnics.

"Do you have the taco sauce?" I called from my room to my mother.

"No. Did you take the Triscuits?"

My mother dipped Triscuits into a small can with an Italian label. It contained eggplant, tomato bits and olive oil, with small green olives, an old standby. I, on the other hand, favored taco chips dipped into a hot, smelly sauce which left permanent stains on the sheets. My mother, propped in her bed, surrounded by books, magazines and papers, her notebook at her side, absently ate her crackers and eggplant, or plunged her hand into a jar of peanut butter and licked her fingers while she called to me about what she was reading. Often she complained about all the poets who were getting published through politics while she industriously plugged along. Just that day she had received in the mail an influential writers' magazine with an article that advocated that writers pay to appear in magazines. In her poverty-stricken state, this felt like yet another last straw. "Do you believe it?" she shouted from her room.

"I believe it," I said. "I don't believe how naive you can still be for not expecting something like this to happen in the first place. Who told you to write poetry anyway? Writing poems is a rich person's hobby, not a starving poet's."

My mother whimpered in her bed. The radio at the side of my bed instructed: "It's wonderful to know the Scripture. It's true and if we all stick to it we will have the same thing we had in the forties and fifties. God don't change, friend, God don't change, I can tell you that. I wish I had more of an education than I had, friend, but I tell you I've been in church after church and I've seen some of the professors and doctors who came out of college who could no more preach than a chicken could—"

"Could you turn the radio down?" Bobo said. "I'm trying to watch TV."

"Ma," I said, "the days are over when they pay you for your poems. I hate to tell you this. I don't mean to be unkind, but why should an editor, why would a magazine pay you for one of your poems when there's a lot of people out there dying to be poets? These people would give their poems away for free and might even pay to have them published. And these are people with the resources to pay a great deal of money. It's time you took a look at the world around you."

"Could you two *please* be quiet?" my brother called. "You're interrupting my concentration. Is nothing sacred to you, Earl? If you would look at television you might learn something, too."

My mother, when not writing poems or recording her dreams in large black notebooks, was occupied with contacting spirits in the other world or speaking by telephone to her friends who turned to her as their guru, seeing her for the saint and great poet she was. I was not alone in my opinion of my mother as prophet, isolated in her world of doom to come. She had one friend who was very rich, and who had been seeing a psychiatrist for twenty-five years, since the age of eighteen. After her friend had been going to this psychiatrist daily for some ten years, she looked up to find him asleep in his chair, snoring gently. "Wake up," she said to him. Finally he was roused, ten minutes later, at a cost to my mother's friend of ten or fifteen dollars. He told her he had not had much sleep the night before. My mother's friend confessed that what she had to say was not very interesting.

Another friend of my mother's was recently divorced when after forty-five years of marriage she realized she was a lesbian. One friend was an epileptic, with a sister who lived with him in what appeared to be not exactly a platonic relationship. Another friend with two wives raised exotic species of fish and had long flowing locks of red hair he generally wore in a braid.

Of course, all of her friends wrote poetry, and they all called my mother at least once a day. They spoke to her for great lengths of time, asking my mother to critique their poems and their lives, or if not to critique exactly, then to give constant ego support and praise. I suggested she charge for her time. "You do as good a job as Daddy, I bet," I said, "better, even." After two hours on the phone she would emerge from her room white-faced and exhausted. Most of the women friends had high voices, and when I answered the phone they would say in a high, whispery voice, "Mavis? Where is Mavis? Do I have the right number?"

The lesbian friend was very meek and easily pushed around. Once she had had to pay for her teacher's cat to ride in a taxi. Like most of the people my mother knew, she continued to go to school long after what had once been the age of parturition—or perhaps it is matriculation I am thinking of—and her teacher asked her to take care of her cat while on vacation. The cat arrived sitting regally on the back seat of a taxicab with a nine dollar fare. Once in the house it climbed into an open suitcase in the closet and urinated copiously, ruining the suitcase forever. The lesbian, since her divorce, had lived alone, unable to find anyone she was attracted to. In fact my mother, myself and a great many of her friends, including the man with two wives (they waited on him hand and foot while he wrote sonnets to them, and I often felt that because he had two there were not enough to go around for me), all formed a group of young retirees or agoraphobes, all of us too timid or angry to leave the house for more than brief periods of time.

Our only guest was Bobo, who could not officially be considered a guest, since he did live there, after all. I guess he was given the status of a more-or-less friendly alien species-in-residence. He had to return home after school, before going to his job, and change fuses (I was afraid of being electrocuted) or fix the heating or the wiring. He was the one to mow the narrow strip of lawn, be the man around the house.

This was not entirely fair, for Bobo had to live in the smallest room in the house. His room was no wider than his bed, smaller, in fact, than a room in a college dormitory, but he had ingeniously constructed a bed built on top of dressers that fit against one wall, which left perhaps a foot of free space against the outer wall in which to navigate. Mr. O'Keefe had papered it himself, and in Bobo's room one wall was covered with a pattern of brown palm trees, one wall of pink cherry blossoms, another of a speckled, spattered brown design, and the last with a design of interwoven reptiles.

The hallway was patterned with dancing ladies at Versailles and chipmunks eating acorns. I lived in a room with a pattern of puce plaid, roses on latticework, bamboo shoots with tigers peering from behind, and finally a wall of narrow green stripes.

Unlike Bobo, I was happy to be allowed to stay in it, for the time being. I did not want to leave, nor did I want to face the real world and find that I didn't live up to the man my father was, or what he hoped I would be. I had even given up visiting him, unless he came into Boston on business and had a minute to see me. My father did not seem to notice.

My mother was invited to give a poetry reading and at last had to leave the house. She insisted I accompany her, for any moral support, however weak, was better than none.

The reading was to take place at a Cambridge coffee shop run by one of her friends. My mother read her poems to music, or played excerpts from songs before and after each poem; since she wasn't working, she had plenty of time to prepare for the reading.

The music she chose was always bizarre, songs that managed to be both awkward and embarrassing to me—"Zip-A-Dee-Do-Dah," from Walt Disney's *Song of the South;* a boys' choir singing in Japanese; obscure lieder by Schumann; or a crooning tune by Frank Sinatra or Jerry Vale.

At the reading my mother, pale and ethereal in a white faille dress donated to her by a rich friend, stood before an audience of perhaps twenty people, in a dimly lit, hot room. Ten of these people were her friends. Coffee cups clinked. A radiator plunked. Once again no one had bothered to advertise that my mother was going to be reading.

My mother placed her sheaf of poems on the podium before her. She cleared her throat, then took a sip of wine from a large plastic glass. She put on a pair of tortoiseshell half-glasses that pointed madly upward, harlequin fashion, at the corners.

She wore these while she read because she could not see with her contact lenses alone. That is, she could see with her contact lenses but she couldn't read with them. She couldn't do anything *but* read with the glasses, but then only when she had her contact lenses on beneath them.

My mother (whom I alone in the room could sense was nervous, could sense it through her professionalism) turned on the small cassette tape recorder on the shelf of the podium next to the glass of wine. From it, in the still room, emerged a thin, quavering child's voice which sang slowly in German, *"Muss i denn, muss I denn."* Another of her valuable finds from the world of records. Then a click as she switched off the machine and began to read. "When he saw me coming he arranged himself in a line," she said.

The current reading was entitled "Modern Americans." All the poems she read were about Americans in the 1970s, strange, queer characters my mother imagined the United States was peopled with. There were men who fed flies to Venus Fly Traps, mailmen in the shape of fish who nibbled on letters they refused to deliver. Fat men, tumescent cake-eaters, babies with dandruff. All these and other poems she read to her distraught and dismayed audience, who sat stiffly, painfully in shock on the floor beside me.

It was more than I could bear. I never went to my mother's readings unless I was forced to. My mother's long, black hair cascaded over her shoulders, her hand trembled invisibly as she raised the glass of wine to her lips. How painful it was for me to hear these lunatic genius poems. It was as if I was up there reading myself, the crowd spread before me. The fragments of music reached my ears only dimly, played on the tiny, tinny cassette player, quivering, speeded-up music, the music of a mad person.

Though I had read all my mother's poems many times ("You are my best critic," she was always telling me), now, listening to them read aloud, I suddenly heard things I didn't remember, things that didn't sound right. "The average American spends four years of his life in moving." I wanted to jump up in front of the audience and make an announcement. "Pay my mother no mind, ladies and gentlemen," I wanted to say. "Pay her no mind."

Still, it couldn't be denied that the poems were brilliant. The faces around me were white and disturbed looking. Sometimes a reedy laugh broke from one of the listeners, the nervous chirp of a sparrow. Some of them didn't seem to dare breathe. My mother read each poem in a voice that cracked through the room like shavings of glass.

No one, I sensed, knew quite what to make of her, knew quite what to do. She belonged to a school of her own. When my mother was finished there was a great pause and then the applause like an uneasy beast grew louder and louder. But, I thought, watching the shaken audience leave the room like frightened bunnies, at least they knew the truth. The upright lamps on the floor swayed, the shadows rocked back and forth. The room was empty.

"Was I all right?" my mother said, clutching my arm weakly. "Was I any good?"

"Yeah, yeah, you were fine," I said, drained. It was not easy being related to a genius. For one thing, my mother, her fragile dinosaur face, was unbearably strange even to me, the person closest on earth to her. I did not like to see her up there at the podium, splayed like an Aztec sacrifice in front of the unbending crowd. "You were wonderful, Ma."

But I thought: My own fame will be different. And it was then I realized that I wanted a fame of my own, something to make me into a real person, a human being. If I was famous I would know I existed, a fact I was not absolutely positive of right now.

But if I were to be famous, it would not be the torturous hell my mother went through. No, mine would perhaps be a Dorothy Parker fame, the welcoming green table in the Algonquin, the frantic look to me for a witty word, though it is true I was not in the least bit witty. Yet, I could see myself known for just this, my lack of wit. Thirty or forty years hence, I imagined, my weary, bloated face would be on the cover of *Newsweek*—aged, masculine, ringed with wrinkles. Then beneath it the caption "NOT FUNNY" or, better still "THE CHIEF PROPONENT OF THE 'NEW LACK OF WIT.'" Another possibility would be "NOT PLEASANT," though perhaps that was too similar to what my father thought already. Why, I could be one of a whole circle known for their stupidity and lack of wit.

Suddenly I felt I had something to live for, something my father would be proud of.

My mother, the woman who had invited her to read and I stepped out into the street, I carrying my mother's cassette player.

The woman invited us to go to a local bar for a drink, but my mother, still secretly trembling, refused, for which I was glad; since both of us were not used to going out, the reading with its contact with other human beings, was overwhelming in itself.

And so we went home, each in a slough of despair, to read some new books purchased from a used paperback bookstore that had just opened nearby (return two and get one free). "Okay," my mother said, looking up from her book as she nibbled on M & M's, chewing her imported Finnish gum at the same time. "Okay, so you want to be famous. But who doesn't want to be famous today. Everyone wants to be a star. But I'm telling you, you can be famous. Everyone *is* a star. The star of their own life. Every person, yes, is the main character of their own life. Of your own life you can be the director, you choose the characters, you are the main actor, the top billing. You produce it, you're the costume designer—"

"Aw, Ma, that's the auteur theory. You don't understand, it's passé now, the auteur theory."

"Oh."

"You don't understand. I *feel* famous. I don't care about being the star of my own life. I want to be the star of everyone else's. I just want to be internationally known and admired. I'm only asking for what John Travolta has. I'm only asking for—"

"I can assure you that once you are famous you will only be hated more. Most of the time with my poems nobody bothers to tell me they've seen them or read them. But if they do say, 'Oh, by the way, I saw your poem in the *Atlantic*,' then that's all they say. They don't say they liked it or anything. Well, let me tell you something, next time somebody says that to me, 'I saw your poem,' I'm going to say to them, 'Oh, I'm glad you liked it.'"

"That'll fix 'em," I said.

My mother looked disheartened for a minute and then she spoke again. "I'm sick of this! Just sick of it! What good does it do me! I won a contest judged by a poet considered the best in America, and I can't even get a job. I don't even get any publicity! I sent out a manuscript of poems, three-quarters of them had been published in important magazines. I worked for years and years on those poems, fixing commas, changing a word here and there. I had to pay a reader's fee of two dollars, four dollars, I don't know how much. They kept the manuscript for four months and then sent it back with a mimeographed slip that had a picture of a man in a tuxedo pointing at the word "REJECTED." Not even a personal note. I might as well have been somebody who dashed the poems off the night before. Couldn't they have had even the decency to include a little note? This is what will happen to you when you are famous."

"What can I say, Ma?" I said. "What do you want me to tell you?"

At the table where my mother and I now sat there was a horrific, vomitous groan and a sharp crack from the ceiling directly above our heads.

"What's happening?" my mother said. Only a few feet to the left of where we were sitting the ceiling began to buckle and sag alarmingly.

"An earthquake," I said. The two of us jumped up, books still in hand (I was reading Noreen, the story of a seventeen-year-old blind girl who died of leukemia; my mother had Leprosy!, the life story of an English leper described in detail. Persecuted as a child in India by a sadistic Anglo-Indian nurse, abandoned by his parents in New York City, he returned to India to work for a time as a used-car salesman and photojournalist. Then he caught leprosy. How this happened was not explained. For eight days on the ship he could never change his clothes or bandages, then he was found in some hidden recess of the boat, crying). With a great cloud of dust and a clatter, the ceiling caved in all the way, while box after box of books came pouring down, splitting open and scattering across the entire floor, along with the pink and white fiberglass stuffing that was supposed to be insulating the attic. Dirt, plaster, floorboards and several books narrowly missed my mother's head, who was closer to the accident than I. Only two feet to the left and we both would have been killed or seriously injured by the Encyclopaedia Britannica of 1899.

The roar of books grew in intensity, then stopped, and the cloud of dust began to settle. A gaping hole was left in the kitchen ceiling, and, as my mother and I gazed at the ruins around us, I stepped beneath the hole and looked up. I saw what seemed to be several more boxes ready to tip. "Yaa!" I screamed, and flung myself out of the way. This set off a further disruption which enabled an additional couple of boxes to plunge to where I had been standing only seconds before.

"Poltergeist," my mother said, and with a sigh took out the dustpan and broom and started to sweep around her.

After this incident my mother began to stay in her bed for longer periods of time, a shy, elongated lizard.

My father's new house finally built (it turned out, to my father's surprise, not to be the one-room cabin he had planned on originally, but something twice the size of the other one, only more primitive, more rugged, heated by wood-burning stoves that filled the house with ash. There were no bedrooms in the house except his own.), he called to tell me he was buying my plane ticket to the Bahamas and he expected me to go with him. "A real 'family' experience," he said in a grim voice. "Something we haven't shared in a long time."

I gritted my teeth, thinking, how I would like to go. But in the end I said, "I guess I don't think it's right that I go, Dad. After all, I'm not pulling my own weight, am I? I haven't gotten a job this summer."

"This doesn't have anything to do with the fact that I'm cutting your mother's alimony, does it?" my father said. "Because if your mother put you up to this, I'll—"

"No, Dad," I said, "Ma didn't put me up to this."

"Well, it's too bad," he said. "Because if this vacation had worked out, I was thinking of taking you and Bobo to the south of France next year, just the three of us. I thought you kids were finally old enough. But it's obvious you're continuing, as usual, to be sullen and unpleasant."

"I don't want to be one of those people who take from you, Dad. I know you said that I was just using you to go to college, that I should get a job."

"I only wanted your future to be a joint affair. But you're not the kind to help. What I think is going on is that your mother is very angry that I'm no longer planning to give her alimony and told you to tell me this to enrage me."

"No, I wasn't talking to my mother." Inside one part of me was screaming, "You fool, Earl! Go to the Bahamas and be a friend to your Dad!" But the rest of me muttered, "Nonsense, your Dad is not a well person at all, and to go with him would be to approve of his treatment of your mother." Still I could get no real pleasure from my sensibility, knowing that soon, probably very soon, the devilish and uncaring half of me would devour what remained of the old, sensitive Earl, and then he might be gone forever. For if it had been anybody other than my mother, I would have betrayed them.

My dad went on: "I have always made it clear that my relationship with your mother, Earl, is something completely different from my relationship with you. Yes, I don't like to have your mother taking from me, draining me year after year. She has always been passive-dependent. It pains me to see you resembling her in so many ways."

"I don't know what you're talking about, Dad." What a coward I was! Could this be the real me? "The only reason I don't want to go is that going to the Bahamas is a luxury I can do without. I can help you out in that way."

"That's not the point. I'm not going to argue with you. The offer remains. You make it sound as if your going would put our relationship on a financial basis."

"Well, Dad, let me put it like this: quite frankly, I don't want to deal later on with your saying to me that I *used* you to go to the Bahamas."

"I see." My father's voice was cold and quiet now, as if a fish had died on the other end of the line. As if I were deliberately and childishly trying to punish him and succeeding only in making a fool of myself. "Bobo says he doesn't want to go either, now. He changed his mind. Did you talk to him or something?" he said.

Couldn't my father see that something was wrong if even Bobo, his beloved, didn't want to go with him? It was not even so much that while cutting off my mother's alimony he wanted us to go on an expensive vacation. But his vacations, since the divorce, had become unbearable. Everything always had to be done his way, and that way was the way of the American Dad, lots of work and little relaxation.

But then, this had always been the case, even before the divorce. There were no other sides to his arguments. I remember as a kid I decided I needed to buy some ducklings. I did small chores around the house until I saved up several dollars. The ducklings, available from Sears, Roebuck through the mail, cost five dollars, and my father said he would make up the difference and I could work to pay him back.

When the ducklings arrived—there were thirteen of them, in a box filled with sawdust—they were covered with a sweet-smelling, yellow fuzz, and we put them in a basin of water. They paddled back and forth peeping. The dog was fascinated, and when the ducks got out of the water onto the grass his repressed instincts came out and he tried to keep them herded into a tight bunch. I brought them down to the pond, but I was afraid I wouldn't be able to get them back until I tamed them, so for the first days I let them swim only in the basin. At night I kept them under a heat lamp.

I came up with a wonderful idea: Bobo and I would sell the ducks—we didn't need thirteen of them, after all—and with the money made from selling the ducks I could pay back my father for what he had loaned me, and still have some money left over. We loaded the ducks into a wagon and pulled it the several miles to the housing development where we had once lived. All day we pulled the cart around until the ducks were looking quite seasick. When we returned home, we had managed to sell only two ducks, but at a dollar and a half each, that meant there was more than enough money to pay my father back.

He tried to explain to me that the three dollars was his money to begin with, since he was the one who had actually purchased the ducks; that while he might give me a commission on my work selling them, the payment was in fact his. I could not bring myself to understand this.

"Look," he said. "I loaned you the money. It was my money that bought the ducks. When you sold them, you were selling my ducks. All the profit is mine, because it was my investment."

"But Dad, you loaned me the money."

"I bought the ducks. They were my ducks you were selling, not yours, Earl."

I still did not understand, but finally I broke down and said I realized my mistake. I had worked all day to sell ducks I had not paid for in the first place, that much I understood. But why hadn't my father told me this before I went off to sell them? Still, I believed that what he said was right. When I confessed to this my father reneged and said, "I'll split the money with you and you can use your earnings to begin to pay me off. But I want you to understand the principles of business."

The ducks had to live in a cage he built for them in the swamp area, because he said they would murk up the pond. "We can't swim in a pond filled with a lot of duck crap," he said. The cage was very small and filled with mud. The ducks began to get large, but no tamer. They began honking at five in the morning for me to feed them, and kept the noise up all day.

I had imagined my flock of huge white ducks paddling on the still crust of the pond, back and forth, aimlessly browsing and nibbling, but instead they grew too large entirely and had nothing to do but huddle in the mud they had churned up. One of the ducks was smaller than the others and a sort of dirty brown color. The others pecked at it from time to time, but to me it had the pleasantest expression on its face of any of them.

At the end of the summer, when it began to get cold, my father said, "Well, I've spent all this money feeding them and building the cage for them. There's nowhere to keep them for the winter. Let's eat them."

It was only my mother who was able to prevent him from doing so. They were given away to the cleaning woman's husband. "What's the use of that?" my father said. "All he's going to do is slaughter them and eat them. Quite a bargain he's getting. We could have done the same thing ourselves."

The cleaning woman's husband came in a car and put the big white ducks in the trunk. When the trunk was closed and the car began to drive off I said, "Wait a minute! Let me keep the runt! Let me keep just that one!"

"Well, it's too late now," my father said. "Why didn't you think of that earlier?"

I had never let the ducks loose on the lake at all.

Now my father hung up the phone and I imagined him going out to angrily chop down tracts of trees, his mammoth army boots leaving holes the size of dinosaur tracks on the swampy earth, his fierce graying beard blue at the sides where he had dyed it (he could not bear the fact that it was graying and used Lady Clairol once a month), his hatchet flailing against the grain. Yes indeed, my father, Paul Bunyan, Abraham Lincoln, Hunter S. Thompson rolled into one, dark and strict, red and angry, a living legend.

Suddenly I realized that perhaps he was correct. I was insane; his vacation offer had been aboveboard and friendly. Not accepting it had been sheer hostility on my part. Perhaps I had only imagined what he said to me months ago: "You are using me for my money. You don't confide in me. You don't even visit me. Don't expect me to support you with nothing in return. At least

Bobo will have a job this summer. You're not working this summer deliberately to antagonize me."

In my father's mind, the dim memory of a rhinoceros, this discussion had never taken place. And since he was a psychiatrist, which made him a god, he must be correct. After all, why should a rhino remember its charges of rage? What good would it do to remember its last battle with a passing Jeep or accidental tree? No more good than it did me to worry about such dated concepts as loyalty and integrity.

I could hear my father's bull trumpet of anger as he sliced through the forest trees, triumphantly slashing and burning right and left.

I sat on the floor in my mother's room where I read an article in the *National Enquirer* about a woman who was discovered to be a man at age twenty, after she had been brought up in a French convent and taught as a schoolmistress for several years. After a short time as a man she killed himself. I could not follow the proper masculine rules either, or at least those that my father had designated as correct. I knew this; why then could I do nothing about it?

I called Bobo up at work to ask him what was going on, why he had changed his mind about going. "I thought you were going to the Bahamas with him. What happened?"

"Oh, I asked him if I could have the money it would have cost to buy a car with instead."

"Oh," I said. "I thought you weren't going because of him trying to cut off Mom's alimony. What do you think of him doing that?"

"I think he's nuts."

"Really?"

"Yeah. He's rich. He can afford it. What does he think Mom's supposed to do, anyway? Well, I got to go now." My brother's voice was always as calm and dry as a cauliflower. Never did it carry the artistic twinge of hysteria ever-present in mine. He did not feel insulted. He didn't think he was crazy or imagining things. No, he knew the truth; he liked his dad but his dad was mad.

But in my case I couldn't accept this. I thought it was me. I would probably believe anybody who told me I was sick. But particularly if those words came from my father. What did I care if he thought everybody was sick except himself? I took it personally. My mother claimed these differences in character were purely genetic. "You're exactly like me and Bobo is almost exactly like his father," my mother said. "So you see, upbringing, all my work, had nothing at all to do with the way either of you turned out. Though, of course, Bobo is much more reasonable than Daddy."

She was eating a dry piece of onion roll and a cup of coffee in the kitchen. The white, plastic kitchen table we had brought with us from the old house was brown and faded from leaving it in the house when we rented it out. There were only three chairs left from the set of four—after years of tilting backwards in it while eating dinner, Bobo had one evening, for some unknown reason, switched them around and given me his chair instead. When I sat down to dinner the chair collapsed beneath me. Bobo and my mother burst into laughter while I lay, a helpless flounder, on the floor. "Well, at least I'm good for a laugh," I said. "I could have cracked my head open, you know."

"What did your father say?" my mother said.

I told my mother my father hadn't said a thing when I told him I wasn't going with him to the Bahamas. I did not tell her, however, that I really did want to go.

"The thing is, Earl, you have to do what you want to," my brother told me. "Soon you're going to be dead and none of it is going to make any difference anyway. You know what I mean?"

The world, or at least my brother, was changing around me, while I stayed the same—weak and indiscriminate. Soon, things were to change even more.

Though I didn't want to visit my father and do his chores, nor did I particularly enjoy being analyzed by him, I did look forward to seeing him and I was pleased that he was taking the time off to come and visit me on his trip to a psychiatric convention in Boston.

Lately Bobo had been going to visit him by himself, and since he had seen my father quite recently he wasn't there on that Sunday when my father, now driving a new, white Spitfire convertible, pulled up to a screeching stop in front of our house.

"You are not to let him in the house, Earl," my mother whispered frantically as she rushed to lock herself in the bedroom.

"Aw, Ma," I said, "he's all right. He's a nice guy. He can't help it if he's a little goofy."

"I have no makeup on. I don't want to see him. Besides, *this is my house*. I don't want him coming in. Tell him to take you out somewhere for coffee."

"Aw, Ma."

From the window I saw my dashing father, resembling an animal escaped from its cage at the zoo. He had never looked right to me out of the context of the country; in the city all of his animal sleekness became awkward and somehow clumsy, as if Abraham Lincoln's statue rose and tried to free itself from the tomb of the Lincoln Memorial. He got out of his youthful car that was far too small for him, shaking his head in disgust. Why anybody would choose to live in a feces-filled city instead of a house in the country under his ready screwing jurisdiction was beyond him. I rushed down to the front door, grabbing my coat on the way, and opened it before he could ring the bell. "Dad, let's go out to the coffee shop down the street, what say, hey? We don't seem to have any—"

"I want to speak to your mother."

My father pushed past me before I could get out and shut the door behind me. Then he was in the house, my mother's private and only property. How could I explain this to my mother? How would I endure her endless recriminations for not being able to keep my father out of the house? My father did not look around him, though my mother, in fearful anticipation that someday something like this would occur (that my father might someday actually make it through the door, a door that of one kind or another he had been trying to break down for more than ten years), had specially straightened up the living room and brushed the dirt from behind the leopard-print chairs. The rest of the house remained as before; the hole in the kitchen ceiling gaped untouched. "Mavis!" My father stood at the bottom of the stairs, calling, "I want to speak to you!"

It was apparent my father had lost his mind. He was irate, he was having the temper tantrum I had feared since early childhood. All those signs he had posted around the edge of the property: "NO TRESPASSING! NO HUNTING!" And here he was now, trespassing away.

He stormed up the stairs, a storm trooper of a dad, with a red face, in a house he should have known was out of bounds. My mother had purchased this house hoping only for a little freedom, a little escape from a crime she had not committed—but one my father was determined to prove she had. He bashed on my mother's door. His knock was the same knock he had used long ago on my door or Bobo's when we would fight with him and lock ourselves in our rooms. It was a knock that could not be ignored.

"Mavis, I want to speak with you! Let me in! I know you're in there!"

"She's not home, Dad."

Why did he hate her so? He hated his mother and he hated me, too—but why? From my mother's room no sound emerged. "I want to know why you have not answered my letter. I don't want an answer from a lawyer! I want an answer from *you*. I wrote to you several months ago and I asked you for an immediate response so I could make preparations to give you your final payments. During that time I continued to pay you alimony. Well, I waited to hear from you—I am not an unfair man—but I am not going to pay anything more to you, do you hear me! Do you hear me!" He began to pound on the door. My father reeked of marijuana and booze. Had he had a fight with his girlfriend, I wondered. Usually his hysteria was controlled, the anguish of a man who knew he was the only sane man on a planet of lunatics. But now he seemed to have gone over the deep end.

From my mother's room there was no answer except the squeak of the typewriter table being wheeled across the room to help barricade herself in.

Uh-oh, I thought. And I was right, that did it. Suddenly I saw my brother Bobo, aged seven, screaming, "Let me in! Let me in!" when my mother told him he was no longer her friend and shut the door on him.

But this was my father! With a brute kick of his army boots (still the same black boots that laced up the calf like the appendages of a clubfoot; he had worn them for fifteen years or more), he pushed open the door to my mother's room—it was not much of a door, only a thin double sheet of plywood and the lock on it, I noted later, was a feeble invention that could not retain a damaged insect—and knocking over my mother's IBM Executive typewriter on its wooden stand, he stepped inside.

The shelves in my mother's room were covered with objects:

boxes of chewing gum she ordered from a health food store at an exorbitant price that came in packages of a hundred, wrapped in a blue and white metallic plastic with something strange printed on it in Finnish—a chewing gum that was supposed to be sugarless with an added ingredient that promoted health and white teeth. There were books of poetry, loose poems, notebooks, library books, an eggbeater (why an eggbeater should be there I don't know), bottles of Indian nuts, packets of old unanswered letters and M & M's, boxes of IBM typewriter ribbons, and at one end of the middle shelf a tremendous old cast-iron postage meter, army green in color, which my mother used to weigh the doughty manuscripts she sent out for publication. It was this last that my father knocked into, flinging his arms about the room in a rage, perhaps only to frighten her a bit.

He was not at all prepared to encounter anything but empty space, and this sudden jarring of a great weight tipped the shelf free from its metal brackets, and the whole thing collapsed, clobbering my mother who stood holding her ground only a few feet from my father at one side of the bed. The shelf, the books and the postage meter hit her squarely on the side of the head.

At least this is what my father told me had happened while we waited for the ambulance to arrive, and this is what he told the police when they arrived, as they sniffed suspiciously at his alcohol reek.

But in court, after I explained how my father had come to tell my mother he was no longer going to pay her any alimony despite the letter to him from her lawyer; how my father himself had built the shelves as a favor years before, proclaiming at the time that they were unshakable, would hold anything, "solid craftsmanship" that would take "a lot" to tip—after I mentioned these things, though my father was a psychiatrist and a figure of respectable justice and authority (though this may in actuality have been what tipped the scales against him, so to speak), he was given 10–15 for involuntary manslaughter.

And what was I doing at the time of this terrible event? At the time the shelf fell I was standing in my brother's room, head pressed timidly against the window as I looked out at the street, wondering why, nearly ten years after the divorce I was still being made to suffer for it.

Through the closed door I could hear the raised voices of my parents, sounding much the same as they had when I was a child. When I heard the crash, I went out to the hall and into my mother's room (I was not at all alarmed, since the shelves in reality did tip over quite easily, often waking us up unexpectedly in the middle of the night) and found my mother lying beneath the rubble of her poems, black print on the white pages, and her poetry books scattered and open before her. I picked the things off her and saw a triangular-shaped split at the side of her head, dripping onto the floor in a small spot. My father did not say a thing, nor did he help me move the pine shelf-board from my mother's chest, but instead he paced back and forth in the narrow space between the bed and the wall with its dappled pattern of bluebirds on a summer field, and nervously picked at some of the hairs on the lowest part of his beard.

While we waited for the ambulance, I gathered the poems up from where they had blown across my mother's bedroom floor. For some reason I felt I should be doing this with tweezers, as if it were wrong for me to be touching the poems with my hands, and then this reminded me in turn of the way a dentist uses tweezers to pick wet pieces of cotton out of a patient's mouth after an X ray. I could almost hear the soft plunk of the wet pieces of cotton hitting the garbage pail bottom.

Once before, my father had struck my mother on her face (I later told the court), at the beginning of her writing career. It was a year or so before the divorce, and my mother had just begun to write poems. The first poem she wrote was accepted by *The New Yorker*. As a child, she had written poems and her relatives had called her Mavis-the-Poet, a name that was enough to make her quit writing for some time. She had been embarrassed to be called a poet, because to her it meant there was nothing else she was good for. But then, before the divorce, looking around for something to do to take her mind off my father, she took a poetry writing course. She felt her fate was decided. She had been avoiding what was probably her true vocation for many years. "Still," she told me, "I don't look forward to being a poet, the poet's life and all. I'd pay somebody else to lead it for me if I could."

One evening before her class she could not find a poem she had written. My father, while accusing her of sleeping with the professor, had hauled off and belted her in the face. I stood in the room, helpless, trying to find my mother's poem so she would not cry.

And yet, curiously enough, a short time after the "accident" with the postage meter and my mother, I took a close look at myself in the mirror, and who was it that I saw? My father. Yes, I had turned my father in to revenge my mother, and yet there were those same piggy eyes, deep-set, lizard-lidded, the too sensuous mouth, a mermaid curve and ripple, the flourish of a nose.

So it was my fate to be my mother and father both, with the two halves wanting to kill each other, or at least live at opposite ends of the house. I was lonesome and it ripped through me like a great dry wind, howling and screaming about my head: I was a man; I was not a man. One thing was certain—I would never equal my father. My brother and I were drawn together by the death of my mother, yet constantly we sought to escape each other, and my brother finally went to live at my father's house and took care of it during the week while my father was in his minimal security jail. My brother drove himself to the high school every day and had a number of friends, while, who had always been so lonely in high school, envied him more and more for his confidence, for his American-Dad–like assurance, something he seemed to have acquired on reaching puberty.

Always I had with me the picture of my mother, lying on the floor with that triangular crease of blood on her forehead and I realized at last that if there was something I had ever been a part of, I was now infinitely alone.

3

AFTER MY MOTHER'S DEMISE I understood that for all my father's excesses and womanizing, he was still more of a person than I would ever be. His life at least was what he made of it.

I turned out to be a drab, beaverish person with large nostrils, full of desires but lacking ambition.

After my mother was gone I was more depressed than ever. I had slunk through high school like a hound dog with a rock tied to its tail, but now that I was to go off to college I realized just how lonely I was, and I was determined to find happiness of one kind or another.

I went off to college with strict instructions not to overspend. My dad was in jail and not able to command the salary he once had, though it is true that the publicity surrounding my mother's death and his part in it attracted many male clients seeking advice about what to do with their own wives. (He answered their letters and put together his replies in a book which sold over a million copies—but this was not until much later.)

He was legally required to put me through school, however much he resented it, according to the divorce decree. I can understand his resentment; after all, what kind of a return was he guaranteed in investing in me?

I packed my bags, rented the house, trudged off to college, all in a state of shock. I lived out of suitcases in my Columbia dorm, stuffing my dirty underwear under the bed, and dieted on nothing but Ring Dings and Pepsi Cola. I was pulled into college by strings operated by my dad.

It was during freshman orientation that I became madly obsessed with a girl named Maggie Adare. By this time, too, my father had moved in with me. He lived on my shoulder, telling me she had wrists like a man.

I tried to pay him no mind. "Dad, why don't you go home?" I said to him. "It's a little crowded in here as it is. Why don't you go chop some trees or something. Listen, I forgive you. So you killed my mother—I understand. In a sense I admire you more than ever: you do not allow convention to stop you from getting what you want. But aren't you supposed to be locked up? Can't you just leave me alone?"

And my father might have said enough foolish things to drive Maggie, my infatuation, to the opposite end of the campus, but luckily for me she was very interested in making friends with Jewish men—something to do, she said, with feeling bad about *The Diary of Anne Frank*.

To her parents' surprise, she informed them she had been Jewish in another life, probably a concentration-camp victim. I too was informed of this a short time after our first meeting, while my father snickered under his breath, "Another lunatic. Another believer in the psychic world."

In falling in love with her I seemed to take after my father, for though I heard his whispering voice saying, "Could do better. What do you see in her?" she was as much a WASP as any of the girls he had chosen after his first divorce. Her skin was so thin it was possible to see the webbed blue veins beneath it, the faintest flush of blood to her face. Often I expected to be able to see clear through to her brain, like the workings of those plexiglass clocks.

Every day she jogged on Riverside Drive, but when too many men began to harass her she took to swimming forty laps a day in the old swimming pool at Columbia. This is where we met. And this is where I fell in love—or fell in something, if not love then at least as much as I was capable of—watching her as she rose out of the small, overheated pool with its slick water, the echoing mossy room, in her tank suit with straps tied together in back with a piece of string. She was a giant fish rising out of the pool, her yellow goggles pushed from her face, leaving two white raccoon rings from the pressure around her eyes.

"Well," I said, and it came to me suddenly: the smell of the stream on the land before my father sold it, like ripe cheese dense and cool in some spring house, the thick turf underfoot, spongy and yielding, and the flowers like hot bees in the field. "So Earl," I said to myself, "I guess you are in love." And I remembered my mother, how she had been all for relationships between human beings, even though she did not really believe them possible.

"Your bathing suit is coming off in back," I said. I was desperate. This was the only thing I could think to say as she passed in front of the bleachers where I sat. The string she had used to tie the two back straps together had come undone and was hanging down her long white back. I felt her give out a little shock of anguish, as if I had made her aware that she had been stripped naked in public.

Then the Dad in me took over. Was that actually my voice, suddenly octaves lower? "Come here and I'll fix it for you," I said. She sat down beside me, dutifully. "Freshman, hmm?" I said, as if I was not one also. Even there, in that chlorine-infested room, she had a nice smell to her, a soggy baby. She nodded. She looked miserable. She sniffed. She was like the last of a species, a mammoth seal, alone in its tank.

"Too much chlorine," she said. She wrinkled her brow in the middle.

"My father recently killed my mother," I found myself saying, to attract her attention.

She agreed to come with me to the local student bar.

And what is this thing anyway, feeling more for one person above others? Why, as I myself was learning, it was the same as what my father had told me when I asked him why he was divorcing my mother. "She leaves food in little dishes," he said. "She never throws anything away—a spoonful of peas, a slice of meat turning to mold, a tiny bit of milk in the bottom of a glass—it's too much." And then, before I could stop him, he said, "And the way she puts on her underpants! I used to sit there, mornings, and watch while she slowly crawled into them. Sometimes she would drift off into a dream right in the middle, sit there for twenty minutes neither in them nor out. Someday you'll understand."

And it was true, I did understand now. Maggie was no different from anyone else I had ever seen, but when I saw her it was as if two chemical compounds necessary to each other came into contact, causing a certain reaction—a fizzing, a puffing of air.

"I was the star of all the plays in high school," she said to me when we were seated in the local college dive. The wooden table top was sticky with old food, or melted varnish. "A director from New York—"

"Won't you have a cake with that?" I said, interrupting her. I was not sure I could stand to hear about her acting career, particularly when my life story was so much more interesting. She drank tea with a wedge of lemon. The wet tea bag made a damp hump in the dirty ashtray.

"No," she said, "I have to meet my boyfriend for dinner in a little while."

"But it's only four o'clock," I said.

"He likes to eat early," Maggie said.

I gritted my teeth, thinking, Of course she already has a boyfriend.

"I went to high school with him. He was the editor of the high school newspaper. He's pre-med, a sophomore. What year are you?"

"I hope you're not one of those people who used to be popular," I said. My father groaned at the stupidity of my remark, though luckily not out loud. "What was that?" I could just imagine her saying. "Oh, nothing," I would have to say, "I—it's just that sometimes I can't shut my father up." I could already tell she would not have taken kindly to something of that nature.

"Oh no," she said abruptly. "I wasn't really popular. Though I could have been. You were not, I gather?"

"You were saying about this director from New York?"

"Oh yes," Maggie said. "She's a very well-known chanteuse. Her name is Martha Hapsbury, perhaps you've heard of her?"

"I guess. Where did you say you went to high school?"

"Massachusetts. She said I should certainly go to acting school in New York. She thought I definitely had potential. However, the theater no longer interests me. Everything seemed to come too simply to me."

I went back to the cafeteria line and bought a piece of crumb cake. I gave it to her. She paid no attention to me but began plucking at the cake excitedly. A few times she caught my eyes with hers, so sad, so blue.

"My senior year in high school I did a study in anthropology and

I was invited to go to Radcliffe. But I wanted to be here near Tad."

From beginning to end, I said to myself, this girl is a pack of lies, but so charming, so infinitely charming! That last a line from D.H. Lawrence I was fond of, *Women in Love,* I think, one of the books required in the first-year humanities class I had read in an abridged, Monarch Notes version. Now I pictured Maggie studying anthropology, out there with the meat-eating tribes in New Guinea. "Cannibals?" I said to her, startling her again. And I began to tell her about myself: how once I had been stung by fourteen wasps.

"Really."

"See, it was like this: It used to be my job to keep the field mown at my father's house. I mowed it using a little tractor. I used to drive it around and around the field, each time chopping the grass in the center so each successive time it got rechopped and it was sort of like an edible field salad, tough and blistery."

"I write poetry, and several of my poems have appeared in small anthologies," she said.

"Really? Anyhow, I went around once more and suddenly the air was filled with something happy, like a million flying grasshoppers, winging and whizzing past my ears, little flying roses or saucers. Only they started to sting, and the air was filled with the stinging, flying things, and it became apparent I was in the middle of a nest of wasps. An underground wasps' nest. I shut the tractor off and started to run, only the wasps were chasing me. My father was standing at the top of the hill and came toward me when I started running. He thought I had cut off my foot in the mower and he had always warned me to keep my feet away from the blades."

"And?"

"And so he carried me all the way up the hill and my mother was there saying, 'What happened?' They took me to the bathroom and washed me off. In the end it appeared I had received fourteen stings. You see, I would like you to know everything that has ever happened to me."

"Maybe I better go now," she said. "While you seem quite sweet to me, in a way that is a little bit different than ordinary, I prefer not to get involved."

"There's something else I wanted to tell you about. I had to go to the hospital once when my parents had been divorced for years. My father came to see me. I knew he was staying in a hotel because my parents weren't seeing each other at this point—they continued to see each other, and even sleep together, off and on, for many years. When I woke up after the operation (it was a minor operation, I'd rather not mention the details), he was next to my bed, holding a stinking trillium."

"A what?"

"A flower. He picked it in the woods near his house. It's not a kind of flower that smells good and it was already wilting because it was a wildflower, and wildflowers don't stay fresh for very long. My father must have cared for me very deeply to have driven all that distance, and yet I testified against him in court. How terrible this continues to make me feel. I remember my parents, together in that hospital room; I thought I was bringing them back together. Then I realized how much they disliked each other; they were only there for my sake and their hatred for each other was thick in the room. This made me feel sicker, and so I drifted out of consciousness again. What's it like to have parents who like each other?" I said to her. I couldn't imagine what it must be like. I asked everyone this question and no answer was satisfactory.

"Well, they are happy together. They like each other."

This seemed impossible. What did that mean, "They like each other."? It wasn't possible for anyone to like anyone else for very long. And the dredging up of all this, the syrupy dull stuff that made up the past, the memories painful and tinny like too much cotton candy that has gone all gritty and flat and lumpy between the teeth, never satisfying questions either past or present, made me feel uncomfortable and frightened, and I blamed this abruptly on Maggie.

I was like my father in that respect: anything I felt, I blamed on the person I was with. Which was fine if I was being made to feel something pleasant, but the anger and sadness that was most prevalent also got dumped on them as well.

And though I longed for the idea of love with sex, it was only an idea I was looking for. Even Maggie herself, with her chestnut hair cropped straight across at shoulder length and her clothes straight out of a Talbot's or the L. L. Bean catalog, complete with Peter Pan collars and three letter monograms on the cuffs, thought she was doing me a real favor by allowing me to be friends with her, as an act of pity on her part, for someone who was a wimpy, Woody Allen type, who did not have the social charm and wit to make up for his ineptitude.

She even told me she imagined herself a kind of Diane Keaton, with her longings to be an actress, but when I suggested I play Woody Allen to her Diane, she simply laughed.

"I already told you, I'm in love with Tad," she said. "Who needs a Woody Allen around? You can't exactly make me a star, either, at least the way it stands today, so let's just remain friends."

I heard all about her, how her mother picked out her underwear, well-constructed wire brassieres, sensible cotton underpants that came up past her naval; how she chose her clothes to emphasize shapelessness because she felt as if high heels, feminine things, would only make her too desirable. It had to be played down, or she would no doubt have to fight men off in the street.

I was grateful that she was even willing to speak to me. I tried to explain to her about myself, what my mother was like, what she had meant to me. But when I did it became only more difficult, and the person my mother had been, her wit and charm and amusing ways appeared floundering and clumsy, and I was left with not even an accurate or three dimensional portrait of a person, but only a mess and a rather strange mess at that.

I sensed by Maggie's look of resignation that she thought she of me as a millstone, though her neck was too weak to shake me off. But before I had a chance to tell her anything else, her boyfriend came in. "Maggie!" he said. "Where have you been? You were supposed to meet me for dinner in the cafeteria. Someone told me they saw you going in here. What are you doing in this crummy place? Nobody comes here except freshmen, haven't I told you?" He was six feet tall, blond in a sort of prematurely bald way, and perfectly perpendicular, as if someone had placed an invisible drop line in front of him to live up to. I observed him as my enemy, though he, obviously confident, paid no attention to my existence. I was no more than a cockroach upon the wall.

"Oh, is it late, oh, I'm so sorry," Maggie said, "I didn't realize." Flustered, she stood up to leave, knocking over her cup of tea.

"You klutz," Tad said, using the word as if it were an amusing foreign expression. "Come on, old girl," he said. Climbing into her jacket, she left her mittens behind her on the chair.

This I immediately translated as meaning she wanted to see me again. An unconscious sign, to be sure, but perfectly apparent nevertheless, and one my Dad quickly pointed out to me. Though I tried to ignore him and look at her sympathetically—as if to say: I understand your plight—she paid no attention to me but ran out after him, as if dragged by her hair, her coat flapping like the wings of a bird.

"Goodbye," I said weakly. What a disappointment I was to myself. And not only to me, Earl Przepasniak, was I a disappointment, but to the entire nation indivisible for which I stood—the trinity of mother, father and self.

This epiphany was perturbing and contributed vastly to my growing cynicism, which, although now, at times, I would like to escape from, I am welded to as to the toughest armor and the shadow of my father on my shoulder with his great beak.

I went back to the pool the next day, not to swim (she would surely have beaten me in swimming, and I needed no further humiliations) but ostensibly to return the mittens left behind in the bar. "What about coffee?" I said. "I can't swim because I've got a cold. But there's something desperate I have to tell you."

"What's that?"

"I already told you. My father killed my mother recently. It was because of me he had to go to jail. Maybe you just weren't listening." But she ignored this again and dove back into the pool. When she came out I felt that somehow I must get her attention. "In that case, I have something else I have to tell you, something vital to our mutual welfare."

She told me she couldn't join me for coffee. Her boyfriend didn't allow her to. "Oh sure," I said. "I know that excuse. Why, you must think I'm really dumb, really insensitive." And I turned to stalk off. No doubt I would have ended up in the pool, as I had taken my glasses off to look at her, but she grabbed my arm and said, "Oh no, you don't understand. Tad is really like that—"

"You fool," I wanted to say, but then to my surprise my father stepped in for me and spoke to her out loud. "I believe I'm in love with you, Maggie Adare. Naturally I can't be positive—I've never gone out with anyone before. In high school I was a very lonely person. So maybe you shouldn't let what I've just said flatter you. Really, I hardly know you. It's just something I've decided. And now my heart is broken."

We had to go for coffee after that so she could tell me why it wasn't possible, why she didn't deserve to be loved, how she wasn't a nice person, etc.

She made it perfectly clear, through signs and gestures and the way she pushed my hand away when I tried to touch her knee under the table, that there was nothing between us except friendship. So gradually, as we drank our coffee, I conquered all the evil, Dad-like desires within me. I resolved, gazing at her across the table, to fight my weaker half and not treat women the way my father had always treated them.

And it was only through my sensitive perception that I knew she preferred simply to be my friend. When I tried to speak to her about the issue, explain to her that I too was a person with needs and desires just like her, and what torture it was for me to have to look at her slim, tender body gliding up and down the length of the swimming pool, she cut me off abruptly.

"Okay, okay," I said at last. "I get the point. See, the thing is, I can't help myself. My dad is such a real man, and I have never been able to live up to his past, never been able to be the person he was at my age. I am a failure. I've never done anything in my whole life really to please him. I remember when I was a kid he said he was going to build my brother and me a tree house. It took months and months for him to build it; it was a great task, getting the material, the lumber and stuff, so high up into the tree. Only once he had finished building it, Bobo and I never used it, because there was nothing to do up there."

"Uh-huh," she said, nibbling on the cake I had bought her and sipping her watery tea. "I wonder what time I told Tad I'd meet him. I don't think he's in love with me anymore, Earl. Maybe I should try to make him jealous."

"My dad built cage after cage for my animals, and he always complained about how I had manipulated him once again into building something. But he could have refused if he wanted to."

"I realize I don't know you very well, Earl, but I wonder if you'd mind if I slept over at your dorm room this evening."

"I guess not. My father is such a swell person, but you know, he always made me feel like such a jerk and at the same time there was something wrong there, you know, so very wrong, that always after a visit with him I would suffer. He always assumed the worst about me, like I had manipulated him into building an animal cage for me when the real reason I had asked him to do it, asked him straight out, not manipulated him, was that I couldn't do it myself. Hey, did you just say you wanted to sleep over? Does this mean—"

"You talk about your dad a lot, you know that, Earl?"

"That's true. My mother and I spent hours discussing him, analyzing him, and I know everything about him. I know I can never be like him. You know, if it takes the rest of my life, I'm going to show him that I am a person and not a failure. I will lead an exciting and decorative life, the sort of life he would have liked to lead but got too bogged down in the day-to-day living, got trapped by women and children and houses and projects, to ever fully experience."

"I'm sure you'll do whatever you say," Maggie said.

And so we became friends. She stayed over in my room at school and by not allowing me to touch her, forced me to behave like a gentleman. In the middle of the night her boyfriend, drunk and enraged, staggered down the street and stood beneath my window yelling, "Maggie! Maggie! You goddamn bitch!"

The campus security guard, grunting and muttering in Spanish, shuffled over and knocked on my door to tell me I would have to get rid of my friend out on the street. Maggie, who had been sleeping on the bed, while I occupied the floor, got up wearily and went off in search of her demented boyfriend.

To make up for the disturbance, she invited me to her house in Massachusetts for the weekend. "I'm bringing a friend home for the weekend, Mother," she said when she called home on my phone. "His mother is dead, so cook something good for him. He doesn't get much home cooking. His father is in jail."

"Did you have to say that?" I said when she had finished.

"You're always saying it," she said.

But she was my friend; in a way I regarded her as I had regarded my mother: a kind figure who gave me advice and made me laugh.

And so we took the train out to her house for the weekend.

The home cooking I had been so looking forward to was in the end, spaghetti of the most watered down WASP style of cooking I had ever eaten, pale lumps of tomatoes floating glumly, large pinkish meatballs like testicles lying unstrung and heavy on the plate of thick pasta.

I met my friend's mother—five-nine, flat-chested, oversized lips painted an out-of-date fuchsia color—oh, how I felt such warmth toward her as she served this mess to the father, who looked most displeased. I remembered my own mother and her fears of my father's anger. I foresaw this dad going to the club after the meal to get something edible to eat.

Before dinner he fixed me a drink, obviously feeling something was amiss. He couldn't quite seem to remember his daughter was old enough to have a drink, or what she was doing with this weirdo for a friend when she already had a boyfriend they felt to be perfectly nice. "What do you drink, son?" he said.

"Whatever you're having, sir," I said, trying to be amiable.

He served me the most radically wrong Manhattan I have ever had, tasting as if pepper or Worcestershire sauce had been added. After one sip I came down with the worst headache and had to sit down on the mustard-colored paisley couch and look at the ghastly Christmas cards that covered every surface. Though Maggie had often reminded me in an offhand way how rich her family was: the country club membership, the University Club her dad belonged to, the kind of money a lawyer brought home; still, I couldn't believe she had been telling the truth now or ever when I saw the house she had grown up in. No wonder she had paid no attention to my own tales, probably believing them to be as fictitious as the ones she told herself.

The house was small, old but not respectably so, and shabby. The kitchen had been done in a sort of antique New Jersey style—Formica table, a broken lamp that was supposed to be adjustable over the kitchen table. How my father would have sneered! Not me though, no, not me.

In the living room the rug was full of pills and bald spots, there was a dated hi-fi system, and the couch was covered over in plastic because the dog, an evil-smelling cocker spaniel, had emotional problems and would jump onto the couch and pee on it if left alone in the house. That explained the baby fence at the foot of the stairs. It kept the dog from rushing up to urinate on the beds. He was also disturbed in other ways. A short time after I arrived, I was sitting at the dining room table and the dog jumped on top of it right in front of me and devoured the candles.

I said to Maggie, "Don't you feed your dog?" The minute he heard anyone munching, even surreptitiously in the kitchen, he went into convulsions and flung himself onto the ground, alternating ferocious growls with weeping cries for food.

"Yes, you jerk," Maggie said, and she looked at me with a condescending air.

It was disturbing, in a house of supposedly sane people, to see a dog lunge and take a pear right out of your hands. Then he would demolish the whole thing, core and all. He would not come when called, either. Sometimes Maggie and I, as a kind gesture, would take him for a walk, but if released from the leash he would not return and it took hours to retrieve him.

I stayed in her brother's room. He was away in his last year at Princeton. His room was in the attic, which had been converted to some degree with the aid of a bed and a rug. The ceiling was unfinished and nails stuck straight into the room: I had to be careful to avoid being crucified. The one window was tiny and low to the floor, and the worst thing was that the room was not heated. I was afraid to ask for more blankets the first night I was there out of politeness.

The second night I worked up enough nerve to ask Mrs. Adare for some extra blankets, and Maggie brought them up to me before I went to sleep. "Hey baboon," she said to me, bringing them up the stairs. She looked beautiful. She was wearing a bathrobe and had just taken a shower, her skin looked moist and shiny and she smelled of herbal skin lotion she constantly anointed her dry skin with. With a little smirk, she pulled back her bathrobe, revealing her naked, white body. Then she threw the blankets at me, knocking me over backward, and went back down the stairs. "Oh!" I said, "wait a minute." I banged my head against the wall as I fell again.

"What's happening up there?" her mother called from below.

"My idiot friend is very clumsy," Maggie said.

Here she had told me we were to have nothing but a platonic friendship and I, grateful for any crumb of kindness, was willing to accept that; then she had to expose herself to me, all that vanilla ice cream. When I went downstairs she was watching television in the living room and had nothing for me but a cold stare, while her sister, a thirteen-year-old shrimp with braces, kept trying to show me card tricks and her mother insisted I taste some fetid concoction she had just finished baking.

Maggie was impressed and amazed by certain things about me. "I've never met a man who was as irrational as you," she told me. "You're so basically an emotional being."

And so it was that my father's fuming and broiling at me during the summers because I could not chop wood fast enough had finally paid off. Because he had yelled I had given up in disgust, knowing I could never achieve his standards of perfection. I was the sort of nerd Maggie felt indebted to. She knew she could not give me up because she alone understood me. Without her I would be cut off from all humanity.

"But if only you didn't go out with Tad," I told her. Though it was true that since she had begun to spend time with me, she saw less of him, just returning to him to sleep and I suppose—no, what am I saying, I don't *suppose*, for she described it, in great detail—to have sex with him. But, as I told her, "No one else cares about me but you."

Bobo had moved into my father's house, and though I would have liked to leave college and caretake his house while he was in jail, this was not something he wished. First of all, I was not very competent, and it had been I who had put him in jail.

But this was not where my father's disgust for me and my weaknesses of varying degrees had begun. I think that the point where my brother and I had begun to differ, the point where it was decided that my brother would get muscles on him like a little Greek statue, had occurred years ago, when I was nine, and the three of us, my brother, my father and I were climbing up an ice-covered hill during the winter. I had slipped and fallen, and lay on the ground laughing hysterically and pleading with my father to lend me a hand up.

"Get up," my father said, snarling like a wolf on top of the hill. "Get up, Earl, you are doing this on purpose." He stalked off, followed by Bobo, who looked anxiously behind at the brother he was leaving to die in the wilderness. Yes, it was my father's own version of *The Call of the Wild*. I was wearing the wrong shoes for the ice and snow, and every time I stood up, I slipped back down the hill, laughing as I collapsed. Finally I began to shiver, and realizing the contempt my father probably—undoubtedly—viewed me with I dragged myself painfully up the hill (as the rat in the backyard had once painfully hauled itself up out of the dirt on the day when Bobo and I crushed the ratholes), holding onto rocks and pitch-covered tree trunks.

"When are you going to learn to take care of yourself, Earl?" my father said. "I'm not going to be around to help you all the time." And it was true that afterward I knew my limitations and out of spite or malice used every opportunity to demonstrate them to my father.

While my brother helped my father weld grotesque female forms, some of them ten or twenty feet high, while the two of them hauled great quantities of lumber, chopped and hacked with machetes through the underbrush of Massachusetts, I lay on a chair in the sun, reading. Sometimes when my father's disgust grew too great, when he began to snarl and roar angrily whenever he passed me, I would get up and ineffectually stack some logs in an uneasy heap, taking five or six times longer to do so than it would have taken either him or Bobo.

"You are a jerk," said Maggie. Her family seemed to agree.

"I know it," I said. "Believe me, I'm well aware of it."

My new friend spent a lot of time at the gym and at the sauna and wanted me to do the same. "God, Earl, you're such a wimp," she said. "Why don't you get in shape?"

"What should I do?"

And so I followed her dutifully down to the sauna in the basement, at the bottom of a short flight of green, corrugated metal stairs and past a thick wooden fire door that led to the tunnels. The tunnels extended around the campus below the dormitories and classroom buildings. Sometimes she would tell me to meet her in various places and then not show up, so I got to spend quite a bit of time there. It was almost ninety-five degrees, dark, the ceiling low and crowded with burning hot pipes that often swooped down on your head if you did not watch your step. Roaches several inches in diameter scurried at the sound of an approaching foot and thrived in the semitropical heat. There were piles of rubbish and a cat who lived in this fiendish environment, where often the maintenance men could be found, having escaped from work.

"Hey Earl, what's the matter with you?" one of them would say.

"Nothing."

They all perched on chairs at the side of the tunnel or in the old washrooms or linen rooms. "What are you doing down here again, huh?"

"Waiting for Maggie."

"That's some girlfriend you've got. She sleeps with everybody; won't sleep with you."

"She doesn't sleep with everybody. Just not with me."

Hours would pass. Maggie would not show up. When I met her again I said, "Where were you last night? You told me to meet you in the tunnels."

"I did not. I told you to meet me there tonight. I don't go to the sauna on Wednesdays. Are you going to be there tonight, or what?"

"Well, I don't know. Is Tad going to be there?"

"No. Tad hates to get his feet wet. He says he doesn't mind if you come, though. He calls you Pearl and says you're harmless."

"Did you have to repeat that to me? I have feelings too, you know."

Almost always Maggie was the only girl at the sauna and she found a curious thrill in it. Before stepping in she would strip and perform limbering-up exercises in the locker room, her clothes and white underwear lying in a heap next to her locker, her breasts flying up and down as she did sit-ups, push-ups, deep knee bends. "Maggie, you know you're attracting a lot of attention."

"I'm not married to you," she said. "Besides, it's coed night." When she stepped into the sauna the eyes raised, the newspapers lowered.

"You love it, Maggie. Don't tell me you don't love it." Once we were followed down the hall in the dorm by the whole football team carrying towels. When they realized we were not going to the sauna that night after all, but to the delicatessen, they groaned in chorus and turned around to go back to their rooms. I wondered how Tad could put up with her. Maggie had apparently developed a following and a reputation. In a way I was proud to be seen with her.

A three-hundred-pound wrestler who frequented the sauna

began to make overtures to her. He asked her for her phone number. As she described him, his skin was black as a buffalo, his palms pink and prawnlike, his lips like two Band-Aids stretched across his face. "What should I do, Earl? Tad refused to comment when I told him."

"Well, do you want to go out with him?"

"Oh, cut it out."

"Well, tell him to get lost, then." It was easy for me to say that. "What is he, some kind of exchange student?" It ended by her giving him my phone number. He followed her around the campus and at night he would call me, sometimes at three or four in the morning.

"But Maggie, why did you have to give him *my* phone number? He never leaves me alone."

"I didn't know what else to do, he kept asking me for it and I wanted him to leave me alone."

One night he went berserk after watching her exercise in the sauna and chased her to the library, trumpeting like a lust-maddened bull elephant. He was stopped by one of the security guards who held up a nightstick threateningly, while Maggie, one hand to her throat and the other clutching her books, ran inside to the campus phone to call me.

"All right, come on over. I hope this ends your forays to the sauna, though." I met her out on the sidewalk. She was white with fear and excitement. "You know, this reminds me of how when I was a kid my father would take us to the local town fair," I said. "There was just this same feeling of terror and thrills. I always wanted my father to win the stuffed dog for Bobo. But he never did. It was always rigged. When Bobo and I would ride the Ferris wheel, Bobo always complained he was going to be sick, but that never stopped him from wanting to ride it."

And I would have said more, talked about the green and pink lights of the fair on Memorial Day, how at that time of year in the mountains it was still cold and the grass was always soaking wet when it got dark, how my father would go around with us having more fun than we were, but Maggie cut me off abruptly, saying, "I don't want to hear about it. I'm sick of your vivid memories. Do you see the guy anyplace out there on the street?"

At last Maggie grew tired of hearing about my childhood and demanded to be taken to the scene. "I don't even believe any of it existed," she said. "Just look at you. You've got that inner-city grime about you, a kind of perpetual wheeze and facial growth. Besides, Tad's not speaking to me. I think he's got a new girlfriend. So let's get away. It'll be fun, maybe. Why don't you take me there?"

"Where, you mean my father's house?"

"What else have I been talking about? Why not? You're always talking about it."

"Well," I said, and I saw her looking at me with that little sneer in her eyes. She made up everything, lied continually, so she assumed I did too.

"Why not?" I said. "How about this weekend?"

I called up Bobo, who was still caretaking my father's house, to tell him we would be coming up for the weekend and could he give us a place to stay.

"I don't know, Earl," he said, in the same worried tone he had used when we were kids and knew he had done something wrong. "You know Dad comes here on furlough every weekend and he's not exactly on speaking terms with you since you went up as witness against him in court. I don't think there's going to be any room for you to stay here."

"All right then, Bobo," I said, and was about to hang up, hurt and shocked.

"Earl, I have to be on his side because I like it here." He blew his nose. "Once Mom died, getting Dad put in jail wasn't going to bring her back, you know."

"Yeah?"

"Listen, Earl, Dad told me something about myself and I think he's right. He said I had a schizophrenic personality. Before the accident I sided with both him and Mom. Then after Mom died— as he put it, after the opposing team lost its captain—I had a choice. I could join his team totally or be in limbo. So I did what I had to do. As Dad also put it, 'I could easily find a hundred young men, looking for a father surrogate, anxious to live off the land.' Why should I let someone else usurp my place? I'm sorry to have to tell you that you can't come here. I'm still your brother and always will be. It's just temporary, until Dad forgives you."

"Yeah, it's okay, Bobo."

I tried to explain the situation to Maggie, but all she said was, "So? Who cares about staying in a house? If there's as much land there as you say there is, let's just camp out."

I wondered if my father still continued the practice of going out in the middle of the night. It wasn't so much that he was looking for trespassers, he just liked to wander around the grounds carrying a revolver, in case one of his patients, eager for revenge, happened to steal through the woods in the night. And once a group of snow-mobilers threatened to burn his house down unless he let them use a path that cut through his property. When he showed them the revolver they sped off, leaving a trail of gasoline fumes and broken branches. Another time he came across a bobcat. At first he saw only its eyes, staring at him from a pile of brush. He wondered how long it had been stalking him. When he turned his pocket flashlight on it, the cat froze and the light revealed it feeding on the carcass of a rabbit, the white fur around its mouth rimmed with a crimson smear of blood.

But perhaps since his incarceration they had revoked his license to own and carry firearms. "I guess we could go there," I said to Maggie.

She borrowed a car from a friend and during the night I went out and removed some essential element from the motor. The next morning the car didn't start and we were forced to cancel our plans.

The next weekend, however, Maggie had found another car and announced, "This one better work, is all I can say. They've just had it tuned up. I can't understand what went wrong last week." She looked at me suspiciously.

"Juvenile delinquents," I said. "They're all over the place."

"What would they want with a distributor cap?" she said.

"Who knows? This is Manhattan. Now listen, according to the plans I have made we're not going to visit my father. We're going to visit his old house, the one I used to live in. This is the place that holds important memories for me in any case, which you seem so desirous of wringing from me."

She instructed me not to give her any back-talk and we set off—she drove, of course, while I gave the directions. Halfway there we stopped so she could call Tad. I listened from the car while she spoke to him on the pay phone. "Darling, I left you a message saying I'm going away for the weekend. Didn't you get it? Well, I left it on the desk. Are you upset? You don't sound very upset. I made you dinner. Just warm it up on the stove." When she got off the phone she was in a foul mood. "He doesn't even care that I'm gone," she said. "There's nothing I can do, not even going away for the weekend with another man, to get a rise out of him."

When we got off the highway and drove through town I could barely recognize where we were. It had changed completely, from a small town to one with many stores, crowds of people, electric traffic lights. "Oh, it's just because the college has grown so, gone coed."

But I had trouble even finding the way up to the house. The road had been rebuilt and widened, and was nearly a major highway. Everywhere there were suburban ranches combining the most hideous aspects of modern and split-level Colonial, made of redwood with big glass windows, everything about them false and glittery and bright. The yards were landscaped in a kind of natural, kempt woodsiness, the driveways were short and stunted, laden with cars.

In the midst of all this mess, house after house exactly the same, was a kind of hilltop hotel, ponderous and spread out over a bald hillside, like the clubhouse of a new golf course. "So, where are we going?" Maggie said, and then suddenly it dawned on me.

"But," I said. "That's my father's old house!"

"That? Up there? I thought you said you lived in the woods."

"Yes, I know what I said. Pull over. That's where I used to live, I tell you, in that deforested area. Let's go back." She turned the car around and went back down the road. Yes, it was unmistakably my father's house, the place I had spent those crucial twelve months before the divorce and during it. I didn't see how I could have let her drive past it. All the trees had been cut down, and the front of it had been planted with a tapering lawn and different sorts of English rosebushes. Before it had been wild and Japanese, filled with fungus.

Across the street, what had once been a cow pasture was more of the same Technicolor monstrosities. "This is ridiculous," I said. "This used to be the country. Well, we've driven all this way, at least let's get out and look around."

She parked the car and we abandoned it to hike up the hill to the driveway of the house. A number of fancy cars were parked in the driveway. "Why don't you go in, introduce yourself," she said.

"Why don't you," I said. We wandered down the path to the stream. All the brush had been cleared out. The pine tree which Bobo had once started to climb—only to be attacked by a large snake sunning itself underneath—was now gone. There was a small green bench in its place. The pathway had been tarred over, though already cracks had sprung up in it and some grasses were growing through. "There was a tree here," I said. "I once carved my initials into it. An ironwood tree, I think. It was a little farther down from here."

It was not a very big tree, and the bark was smooth, like skin. Only a faint scar remained where I had carved my brother's and my initials into it. The letters had expanded with the bark and were stretched out of recognition. The tree had sealed itself over until in the place I had once picked at it only a thin keloid was left. "It didn't last long," I said. "I thought when you carved your name into a tree it was there permanently."

"One time I saw this tree in the woods," Maggie said. "It had grown right around a strip of barbed wire fence. The rest of the fence was long gone, but the rusty strip of barbed wire was still there and the tree had grown completely around it."

"Once I went to look at the buckets the neighbors hung on the maple trees along the roadside to collect sap in during the spring thaw. They used to use those old-fashioned metal buckets with little roofs made of tin. It was raining, and I was just walking along. Anyway, I went over and for some reason I thought I would look inside it to see how full it was, I guess. And there was a dead mouse in it. It had fallen in and drowned."

"Yuck."

"Well, they didn't mind, I'm sure. They were the sort of people who would pick the mouse out and make the sap into syrup anyway."

"What's the sap like?"

"What?" I said. "Oh, it's just like water, sort of sugar water. My father was always collecting it and then he would boil it down into syrup. It takes hours to do it, though, and he always forgot and left it on the stove to burn up. What a mess."

"Hey, come on," Maggie said. She started to run across the field, over what was now a baseball diamond—all the poplars had been cut down—and I followed her, but more slowly.

When I got over to the edge of the pond I saw that most of it had filled in. It was murky and thick with algae. The white beaches were gone, grown over with grass. But there were still little pickerel, limey-green, with little muzzles, swimming back and forth, and little toads at the water's edge, the same kind I had seen one spring, when thousands of them had hatched, so many that the ground was dense with them. They squished underfoot, small toads no larger than a fingernail but perfectly formed, with tiny, delicate footpads.

I took up a stick and started stirring the water with it. Then I heard Maggie calling. "Come on, Earl, come play." She was running across the field with a stick in her hand, pretending to play baseball, darting between bases. "What's the matter," she said. "Come play, this is fun." She came over to me.

"My father used to stock this pond with all varieties of fish," I said. "He put in bass, perch, sunfish, catfish—once he even tried to stock it with goldfish, for the color, but they were quickly eaten. The pickerel came right up and grabbed them. You could see the goldfish in the bigger, wild fishes' mouths—"

But Maggie wasn't listening and snatched the stick out of my hand. Using my stick and hers as ski poles she pretended to schuss off across the field, laughing and shaking her head at me. "You're a drag, Earl. You know that? Talk, talk, talk. Come on, you're just like an old person. Let's play."

I got up and tried to romp over to her, but I felt ungainly, like some mammoth water creature on land. I was going to suggest that we go up to the car and get our stuff and find a sneaky place to camp, when a group of Little Leaguers and their coach appeared.

I realized we couldn't stay here, there were no woods in any case, no area private enough to set our tent up in. "Oh, it's all right, Earl," Maggie said.

"It's obvious we can't stay here," I said.

"What about going up to your father's, then?"

But I didn't feel like driving over there and having to contend with my father not speaking to me. Even if we hadn't let him know of our presence he might have discovered us in the woods, an event I didn't look forward to. I said we were driving back to Manhattan. Maggie sulked the entire way. I wasn't allowed to play any of the tapes I wanted to hear, and we didn't get back until after midnight.

The trip was a fiasco, and her esteem for me was lower than

ever. But I continued to feel for her with the same intensity, and there was a kind of ache in me for the perfect person she was and the one I was not.

Then something occurred to change the balance of power between Maggie and me. At first it had been a definite advantage to be weak and allow Maggie, liberated Barnard student, to open the jars of pickles. I was as thin and frail as she was strong and large. Though that thin blue blood of hers, it is true, was near the surface and visible, particularly in one large vein that pulsed under her wrist, she was not delicate in the least. She allowed me to cuddle with her in bed, during the time she suffered so much with Tad, and we pretended to be animals. "What am I now?" "A hideous biting spider! And what kind of animal am I?" "Oh, wait a minute, I've got it. You're a severe pinching crab." Totally platonic, though admittedly perverse. After all, why should I attempt anything further, when I could never hope to live up to the gorilla my father had been?

But suddenly, after several months, she would come over to my room and throw up first thing in the morning. I had to fix her tea afterward, wipe off her face, whiter than usual, while she said, "I'm fine, just fine."

"Did I ask? I didn't say a thing."

After a few more weeks of this I made her go to the Health Service, where they gave her a pregnancy test and asked whether she planned to have the kid. When confronted later, Tad denied having anything to do with it. "How do I know I'm the father," he said. "Just because I have money and your wormy friend Earl doesn't. Ha! You're not shafting me that way. Work things out for yourself, Mags. I'm not going to be around to reassure you this time."

"There's absolutely nothing between me and Earl, Tad," she said, or so she claimed she said, as she related this exchange to me. "I swear it."

"Oh sure," he said. "Why should I believe you?"

"I've never done a thing with Earl," she insisted.

This, alas, was the truth. But it was left to me to help her out. I had been sorely abused by women even from my high school days. In a way, I had something against my mother too. I could not forgive her for dying during such a crucial stage of my development. Once again I was of two minds about an attribute of mine, for while I was nostalgic for that "other" Earl, the one who was simple and loving and accepting, I found it not at all undelightful to be shielded from the constant ache of such innocence, and I felt a certain slight pleasure in exploiting others with a relatively guilt-free insouciance. For the first time in my life, I was in power. "So, Maggie," I said, "you really blew it this time." And I smiled evilly to myself. "Sorry. I didn't mean anything by it. Of course I'll help you out, in any way I can."

So we decided to get an abortion, just the two of us. We had no money—her father kept her on a fixed income, and my father was away on a trip reaching into the innermost corners of his mind (or so I hoped) up at Ithaca State Minimum Security Prison. "What to do, what to do," I fretted in my dorm room.

"Earl, why don't you get a job," Maggie said. "Help somebody else out for once in your life. How am I supposed to pay for this damn thing? Besides, I'm half coming to believe this damn fetus might be yours. Maybe you left some of your little sperm swimming about on the edge of your sink. Who knows what might have happened during all those supposedly platonic sessions in your bed."

"Maggie, you know I'm saving myself until after we get married," I said. "Besides, I did work once and I was fired when it was discovered that I moved too slowly and couldn't type, though I had passed the standard typing test. But I was able to maintain accuracy for three-minute test periods only. This was my mother's idea, learning to type, I mean, and I took a typing course my junior year in high school, the only boy in the whole gum-chewing secretarial training course. I vowed never to be fired again and the way I intend to keep that promise, made over my mother's ashes, you know, is by never working. You see, by never working I can never be fired."

"Spare me," she said wearily.

"Maggie, you know I would do anything for you. Anything but that."

"Yes, but you're not, are you? What use are you to anyone on this earth, Earl Przepasniak?"

I set out to the college employment service to look for a job. Before this terrible fate could befall me, however, I decided to place a phone call to my brother, to whom I now spoke only rarely.

"Well, Bobo, this is your brother speaking. How are things going?"

"Okay."

"Anything new? How's Dad? How's Grandma?"

"Grandma's fine. She called here—in fact, I just finished speaking to her. She says it's very cold there. 'I guess I must be getting a little senile, Robert,' she said to me. 'I'm Bobo, Grandma,' I said. She has a growth on the side of her nose that she's going to have removed next week. Yeah, I guess she is getting old, though she's never been any different. She's teaching a group of senior citizens twice a week, a course in erotic Indian art. Since Mom's gone and Dad's been locked up, she seems much more easy-going, more mature."

"Are you all right there, Bobo?"

"Yeah, I'm okay. It's just a little isolated here. I never speak to anyone except Dad on the weekends. I did pay a visit to Uncle Oran a couple of weeks back. He can't move, he has to be carried or wheeled, and he whines and carries on all the time, demanding constant attention. Partially this is senile dementia, and partially he's just suffering psychotic anxiety attacks. Anything special you called about, Earl?"

My brother had come more and more to sound like my father. "Bobo, I'll come straight to the point. I was wondering if you would send me some more money?"

"More money? What do you mean? I just sent you five hundred dollars out of the account. I can't afford any more."

"But that was months ago. That was last term, in fact. I have to buy meals on the weekends, books, clothing. The subway alone is a buck each time you go somewhere. This is New York, things are expensive!"

"I don't care, you're spending Dad's money as if it were water! I'm scraping the bottom of the barrel out here to make ends meet."

"Actually, I need the money for another reason. Remember that girl I told you about? The one I wanted you to meet? Well, she's pregnant."

"Ah."

"No, it's not what you think. I'm not sleeping with her. I mean, I sleep with her sometimes, I'm just not screwing her."

"Sure, Earl, whatever you say," my brother said. "Anyway, welcome to the Przepasniak family of breeders. Sure, I'll mail you a check."

My brother, so sophisticated, so mature, refused to believe I was not having intercourse with Maggie. But we had the money, and that was the important thing. And so it was arranged. We would leave at six the next morning to get downtown for a seven-thirty abortion call.

"Yeah, and you probably had to pretend like you're sleeping with me to get it. I know you, Earl. I know all about you and your mother-murdering father and your competent caretaker brother who can't even find a place to put you up when you decide to pay him a visit. Just don't back out on me now, as you are probably wishing you could do."

"I'm not like that, Maggie. Believe me, I wish I were, but I'm really not. I feel a deep affection for you, a deep and abiding affection. And I can never forget the person my little brother was, and perhaps still is somewhere deep in the flesh. And my father. I remember how when we were kids he once—"

"Oh, be quiet. Listen, I want you to stay over with me, and I'm going to stay in my own bed, in the room my parents rented for me in the freshman dormitory."

Of course, this is where they thought their daughter stayed, as did seventy-five percent of the other girls' parents, who were all equally adept at deluding themselves. They didn't believe Maggie lived with Tad. Nor did he, apparently—if I called up his room to speak to her and he answered the phone, he denied having any knowledge of her existence. "I don't know who you're talking about." Though this may have been all in fun.

Maggie asked her roommate if it would be all right if I slept over in Maggie's bed with her. "Yes," the roommate said, "as long as the two of you don't try to do anything."

"That's really not very likely to happen," Maggie said, "since I have this abortion first thing in the morning, and even if I didn't I have no desire to sleep with Earl." I was certain she was merely joking, and I smiled.

"Well," said the roommate, a short girl named Annie. She resembled a beached whale, at other times a lump of meat that had been left out of the refrigerator for too long—side meat. Of course I was fond of Maggie's roommate, though it is true she wore too much makeup, and at the bottom of her face was the line where she had stopped applying it, like the ring around the bathtub. "The only reason I bring it up is because one night the girl from down the hall asked me if she and her boyfriend could sleep in the extra bed—this is when you stayed at Tad's. The girl's roommate would no longer let the two of them sleep in the same room with her, and this should have warned me right there. But I said they could. That night I was awakened by a dull moan, coming from the other bed. I realized what was going on. Well, I thought, I'll just get up and go to the bathroom, to give them a minute alone to pull themselves together, to see that I was awake. But when I came back I got into bed and they started up even louder. 'Oh, that feels so nice,' Fanny was moaning. I sat up in bed. 'Get out of my room,' I said, 'I don't care where you go, just get out.'"

"Maybe they wanted you to join them," Maggie suggested.

"Well, don't worry," I said to Maggie's roommate. "We won't try anything, I guarantee it. You little cupcake." I lunged for her large rear end. She let out a squeal of terror and rage. "Oops, I'm sorry," I said. "I couldn't control myself."

"Stop picking on Annie, Earl," Maggie complained. She gave me an Indian burn on the wrist. She was quite good at it from much practice.

"Cut it out," I said. "I said I'm sorry!" Her roommate's eyes bristled out at me from beneath her bristly brow.

What had come over me? This girl and I had a great deal in common, when it came right down to it. Annie was as obsessed with Maggie as I was. For her, Maggie was the center of her life. She often pretended that she actually *was* Maggie, or so Maggie had told me. And Maggie, sorry angel that she was, had to spend much time with this mess of a girl, had to eat dinner with her, had to visit her before sleeping at night, out of the goodness of her heart. Maggie was the Florence Nightingale of the Columbia University disasters. She picked up a ruler and prodded her friend Annie on the rear end with it. "Earl's right," she said. "You really should lose some weight."

I had to admit to myself that I did like women, despite their easy inner messes and complicating lives. I thought the things of a girl were so pretty: the small bottles of lacquer red polish for their nails, like something from ancient China; the brushes, tiny and feathery; the gold and silver tweezers to pluck and pry. The soaps of a girl, the bottles arranged in the top drawer, the stink of herbal shampoo released in the air—these were the things I found almost more attractive than the girl herself. Maggie smelled of these things, of a baby powder sprinkled on after a shower like confectioners' sugar on a cake, the silver safety razors like jewelry decorating the edge of the shower, the cocoa butter lotions, the gaudy perfumes like a sort of musky fruit behind her ears with their small, gold studs.

And I thought a girl's hands were very attractive. Maggie had hands that were too large for her body. They were thin and white; she held them nervously, uncomfortably, as if she did not know what to do with them. They could pinch and jab, but they also had a touch so light, as light as the flutter of a bird's wing—white hands, sometimes red from hot water or blue from the December chill. Also a girl's nose, Maggie's nose, the way it was sweetly red and turned up at the tip so her front lip was a little short and her mouth when relaxed was not closed but showed two white teeth like small opals or pearls.

At last the dawn cracked, in front of the Palisades and the fleahop hotels. Then the beery smell of bread in the early morning; the honk of milk trucks; the line of light rising. In my half-sleep I wondered what was this blue, this blue, dark as charcoal, thick as music. I want to go home, I said to myself, I dread the whole operation. "Knock it off," my father said, and generously I did not repeat this to Maggie.

Now I saw the snow like pools of yogurt on the street; the thumbtacks on the wall, blue, green and red; and the pink brassiere; the lanolin, the crenelated fog, the persiflage, the intricate webbing. And the dust of the street, the tar in the cracks, the whirr of the street cleaners and the hotdog man. I got up, saw my face in the mirror as I shaved, green and livery, a mess behind red eyes. And what kind of disguise was this? A miter, a toad, a goitery trap? These thoughts and others came to me as I shaved, brushed my teeth. Who is the key, who the lock, where is the nasty hand that turns the knob? The baby's ear, the earwig, the waxy buildup on the kitchen floor. What is in and where is out, and this music; the jarring of the bathroom door, a doorbell rings, the schizophrenic blue. The lake that leaves a skimmy skin behind when you step out, the tadpoles between the toes. It was morning.

"Abortion time," I said.

The two of us jammed into that single bed had not had an easy night of it.

"Oh, shut up," Maggie said, huddled, a white lump under the sheets.

We took the churning subway downtown. "Talk to me, Maggie," I said.

"I'm going to throw up." She pinched my arm.

"Say something else."

"I wish Tad were here," she said. There was no one else on our subway car. "Last week I got onto the subway and there was this man sitting at the other end of the car. He kept staring at me and started to move closer. He had on a filthy pair of pants and expensive Italian shoes. I think he was a sculptor. I tried not to pay any attention to him. Finally he slid down across from me. 'Hi,' he said, 'My name's Dennis,' and unzipped his fly. He started to masturbate! He was masturbating and I just sat there. I couldn't move. I was transfixed."

"What happened?"

"We reached his stop. He got up and left."

"I guess this happens to a lot of women in New York City."

"It happens to me more! It happens to me all the time! Yesterday an Israeli psychiatrist who works at Mount Sinai stopped me on the street and asked me for a date. I go places with my sister, she doesn't get one tenth the attention I do."

"But your sister is only thirteen. And what about what happened to your roommate, when those people stayed over?"

"That? That's nothing compared to what I go through. I went out to a party with Tad last week. A homosexual art dealer I was introduced to asked me to go upstairs with him to look at his etchings. He took me into a dark passageway and tried to rape me. I couldn't push him away. Lucky for me he couldn't perform because he was homosexual. This abortion is punishment, I know, because of my desirability. There are compensations for everything. I have to endure this abortion because my physical beauty is unjustified."

"Maggie, just how am I supposed to respond to these stories?

Naturally I'm disturbed. But I'm not your boyfriend, am I? These tales only make me feel jealous, hurt, envious. I feel left out."

Then I wished I hadn't said anything at all. She stopped speaking to me. We traveled in silence.

As we entered the lobby of the clinic building we were joined by her roommate. "I got up and decided I'd come down and wait with you," she said. Her eyes were still caked over with sleep. She was wealthy, or at least her parents were, and so she was able to take a taxi and arrive at the same time we did. I noticed Maggie's hand opening and closing like a fish's mouth at her side and I tried to trap it. She ignored me and looked painfully grateful that the roommate had joined us. She clutched at her friend in a way that made me feel I didn't need to be there at all. And yet, somewhere inside me I still had fantasies that she would fall in love with me and marry me. If only she would see how right we were for each other! It was only too apparent to me that her outside attitude, one of health, jogging and boisterousness, was only a thin disguise to protect her weak shellfish interior.

The elevator rose slowly. Maggie whispered that the doorman knew exactly what we had come for. "It's legal," I reminded her. "And besides, there are twenty floors of offices in this building and we might be going to any one." Still, I supposed she was right. There was something slightly seedy about the whole thing, and for what other purpose could we have entered that coffer of a machine, dimly lit with row after row of electronic buttons to pick and choose from. A sign over our heads flashed on when I hit the button marked Nineteen, and announced PARK MEDICAL CENTER, as if we had made a wise choice. The elevator stopped, the doors sizzled open like a piece of meat being thrown on the fire.

The room was dimly lit and crowded with women, the seven-thirty shift of abortees. The magazines, missing pages and covers, were years old. The lights, only forty- and sixty-watt bulbs, were too dim to read by.

Maggie had forgotten I was with her but paced like a virginal queen about to be sacrificed, held her head high and stalked over to the glass window where a frizzy-headed receptionist sat filing her nails. Between them some sort of transaction transpired, something which appeared to be illicit but which obviously could not have been. Maggie returned to where I was sitting and whispered that she needed the money now. I handed her the roll of bills, green and crisp, as if part of the stipulation had been the money be unmarked and in small denominations. Maggie held the money unobtrusively, trying not to be ostentatious, but for whom? Who did not know what she was there for, and who cared? The fourteen-year-old girl with her boyfriend who appeared even younger? The overweight woman who had brought all four of her small children with her, running noses included? Maggie weakly, limply, handed the money to the receptionist and disappeared behind a pair of ominous doors.

"How long is this going to take?" I asked the receptionist.

"She's with the seven-thirty group? Probably around five hours."

I took out several sticks of Juicy Fruit gum and crammed them into my mouth. "Come on," I said to the roommate. "Let's go get some breakfast. It's going to be some time before she's finished." Annie nodded silently and stood up. I was surprised she did not lunge at me, angered at my coldhearted suggestion. "What? Eat? When right now they're busy removing Maggie's interior? Eat while they take out kidney and liver, stomach and intestines? You cad." But she didn't say a thing, which just went to illustrate the power food has over the human mind, I thought.

Maggie wasn't supposed to eat anything from twelve o'clock the night before. This morning I could tell it weakened her. She was used to snacking, needed the jolt from the midnight bowl of ice cream. I had given her the key to my room (hoping she might take it upon herself to seduce me) and sometimes at night she would come over to use the refrigerator while I slept. In the morning I would rise to find the remains of Swiss cheese spread with mustard and relish, banana peels flung next to the wastepaper basket, empty packages of small frozen pizzas. How could she be so stealthy, not to wake me in the night but cook and munch quietly in the dark? In the morning I would wake to find her sitting in my big, overstuffed chair, smoking a cigarette and crying. "Tad?" I would say, washing the dirty dishes and picking up my dirty socks and underwear scattered on the floor.

The roommate and I stepped onto the street. The men, in rush hour, walked with their heads down, a funereal procession of victims—one I vowed again never to become a part of. Annie was the sort of person who looked like she was wearing a bathrobe, whether she was or not. Again I noticed that sweet smell to her, like meat gone bad or something left too long in the vegetable bin. "Watch out for that one," my dad said in my ear.

"I'm really tired," I said. "Aren't you?" I was trying to compensate for my unpleasant thoughts, but Annie didn't answer.

We passed a store that sold bathtubs and faucets. The window was full of bathroom equipment, sinks in pink false marble, trumpet-shaped telephones growing like lilies on the wall. I felt like suggesting to Annie that she hire herself out to sit nude in one of those tubs, a great pink roast in a tiny ceramic basin. But I refrained, spotting at last a Hickory House Coffee Shop with a sign that said BREAKFAST SPECIALS stuck in the window. Two eggs, toast, coffee and home fries could be procured for ninety-nine cents.

"Come on," I said. "Let's eat here." I felt somewhat strange. I had gotten up too early, I decided. I was used to sleeping until ten at least. The morning had been cracked over my head like a madman breaking eggs in the wrong places, like my grandfather who before his death had demonstrated his ability to open hard-boiled eggs on his bald pate with one blow.

The air was too bright against my eyes. Flecks of soot whipped into my face, and the vision of the roommate this early in the morning was hard to take. I foresaw a lively meal. I could ask her about her courses at school, her hobbies, her pet dog (also overweight, a mongoloid dachshund named Schnitzel who suffered from an intestinal virus and was always damp from the plethora of kisses fed it by the roommate). I should not be so cruel, I reminded myself gently.

We were escorted to a booth. Annie asked for French toast, milk, sausages. I got the ninety-nine cent special and put the saucer over my coffee when it arrived to keep it warm for a few minutes longer, a custom handed down to me by my mother. "I should have told the waitress I wanted my coffee with the meal," I said in a civil voice to Annie. In return I received a look that said, "You fool." Annie said she was going to order a strawberry yogurt milkshake.

The breakfast potatoes were stiff with grease, the eggs on bread that was limp with margarine. Small tins of grape jelly as sweet as some kind of blood decorated the edge of the plate. A real winner of a meal, I thought, seeing the roommate sitting there glumly shoveling the sausages into her mouth, myself miserable, the two of us thinking of our friend being hacked up into little bits at the Heavenly Abortion Center, located high in a skyscraper overlooking Park Avenue South. "So?" I said, as we ate, "how goes it, toots?" She had a soiled look on her face.

"Fine. Just fine."

"Something wrong? The food not to your liking?"

"I'll have some coffee." Angrily she examined a businessman with a white vinyl belt strapped around his paunch. "Wrong?" she said. "What could possibly be wrong? She's just up there now being internally vacuumed while you gorge yourself down here. Wrong? No. It's just you'll never know, you'll never even try to understand. It means nothing to you that you got her pregnant and she has to pay."

"But—"

"I feel bad for her but you're very lucky. Maggie is a loyal person. You will never have to worry about losing her. She loves you. She's unique, yes, and such a beautiful person, too. I only wish you appreciated her, though that would still not be enough."

"Wait a minute. You've misinterpreted the situation."

"Oh, shut up. I don't want to hear your excuses."

If only what she was saying were true in the smallest degree! Her face, which reminded me of a boxed pie, a Tabletalk pineapple pie—easy to see the months of the wrong kind of eating that had gone into her, with yellowish fatty skin like a cheese made from sweet milk, a thick cream-colored sauce—glowered at me. A terrible thought came to me: Could Maggie's friend be a female version of myself? The cretonne shades in the restaurant, the smell of creosote and stale breakfast, the twin embryos on the plate before me: how easy it would have been to be sick right there.

If memory is organic and a chemical function, it explains why the soul pays no attention to the past when it leaves the body behind after death. How can it, when memory is something it has left along with the body? I mean, it is now known there is no place in the brain, no one area where "decision making" is located.

This is known from information handed on to me by my mother. It is the mind, separated from the body, that is up there handing out the orders. This scientific knowledge will, I am sure, lead to the discovery of the soul as a personal, existing entity. We, as a public, are being prepared for this information right now, through the flood of articles that appear in even the most respectable of magazines that purport to treat intelligently the subjects of ESP, UFOs, the workings of the brain. "Ha!" my father shrieked on my shoulder. My father, of course, had no faith in any separate reality. I only wished my father would be around when the real facts are made public. I wished only to see him experience the shock of truth, but whether this will occur in our lifetimes remains to be seen.

Of course this knowledge is going to affect life as we know it. For one thing, money will no longer matter at all. The rich will be anxious, on realizing the immortality of their souls, to dump their money on poor people like myself, thus ridding themselves of guilt. Also a time will come of great beauty and vapid art, old wine and junk foods, or at least home video recorders, I thought to myself, sitting at my dreary breakfast.

We will be the frail, happy Elois, and I can but hope no evil Morlocks will inhabit the subway systems. In addition, it will become apparent that the majority of society is quite without any soul at all, and these unfortunate beings will have to be told the truth about themselves. As much as I tried to like the roommate, I felt fairly certain Annie did have a soul that was not too pleasant at best. Perhaps I was being unkind. But I knew that this soul was no doubt recognizable anywhere, whether or not we were equipped with memories on the other side. Supposing I bumped into her after death? Aaah! More blows to my small ego, if it was still around at all.

To be on the safe side I thought I'd better make sure I could identify her, to be able to avoid her when the time came. I fretted I would be forced, later in life, to marry her, or her equivalent. And I hated to think this might be my destiny, though my father would say that I deserved no more and no less.

"You don't understand," I said, leaning across the table. "I am not the father of Maggie's unborn child. This is the truth, however sad. In any case, we must work out some kind of sign so that my soul and your soul will be able to recognize each other, when we meet in future, so we will leave each other alone and not have to go through the same thing. I know you don't like me, and in fact I sympathize with your point of view. Let's not make the same mistake in the next world. It will be in that place where age, sex, name, do not count for anything."

"Oh sure. Let's just get something straight, Earl. I don't like you, I have never liked you, I only came along for Maggie's sake. I don't know what she sees in you, though I personally think you are nuts."

I decided to try a different tactic. "I wonder if I have done something to make you angry. I am willing to try and change when I'm around you, if this is the case. Men have probably treated you badly, on the whole."

"You are a pig, Earl! As if my dislike of you was based on nothing, instead of being because of your insensitivity, your self-centered narcissism, making everyone around you unhappy. I'm perfectly aware, you know," she said, "that I have a hole and you have a thing to stick in it. Just because I don't act obsequious doesn't mean I'm not aware. Does that make you feel like a superior person, knowing that? Does that make you feel better?"

"No. No. Not at all," I said. Well, perhaps it did a little. "I do understand your feelings," I said. "But if you would only listen to me you would hear that it wasn't me who got Maggie into this mess."

"Yes, well, I'll tell her you said that. Deny the whole thing why don't you, you prick."

I said no more but I wondered why I was putting up with all this. Because she was a victim, as I was, as my mother had been. Because she was in love with Maggie. Because I was unused to any other treatment from women. "Fine. I just want to add one more thing before we finish the subject. *I didn't do it.*"

The roommate looked as if she was going to throw her plate at me. Her face was blue with rage. And I thought: I must look at her as I looked at my mother, with the same wise understanding and kindness. That I couldn't explain to her that I hadn't slept with Maggie, that in fact I was utterly undesirable as a human being—well, in truth, I gained a small pleasure from this, being thought of as Maggie's lover. Were illusion and deception to be my only joys in life? Well then, at least let me enjoy them.

The morning greased and irreparable, my father contributed to making me feel worse by whispering in my ear. "Now tell the roommate she would be better off without so many of those fried pies. Ask the roommate would she mind screwing you until the three weeks are up after the abortion and Maggie can have sex again, to keep it in the family, so to speak. Tell her you'll pay her five bucks a shot." Shut up, shut up, I thought. That's not the sort of person I am, is it? And yet, it might easily have been.

She pushed her plate away. "Well, I'm going to go back up there to wait even if you're not. *You* can always buy a piece of liver, if it is so necessary for you to find something to screw. I'm sure *you* wouldn't know the difference." And she left me to pay the bill.

In the elevator on the way down, Maggie showed us her products wrapped in a brown paper bag: a tube of raspberry-flavored diaphragm cream, free samples of nonprescription birth control, like a child who has been to a dentist and gotten a lollipop after having its cavities filled. The roommate grimaced, clutched Maggie's arm sympathetically and scowled at me.

I had almost no cash, and since the roommate did not offer to pay for a taxi we were forced to take a bus. The bus stopped half a block away from where we were. "Come on," I said, grabbing Maggie's arm at the root, "Can you make it?" I pulled her toward the bus as she stumbled along behind me. I shoved her fifty cents and mine into the token machine and the roommate suddenly remembered she had no change, smiled at me coyly, and to avoid upsetting Maggie I was forced to pay for her too. Maggie was whispering in my ear, "They tied me down. They tied rubber things on my legs, on my arms. I had no clothes on but socks and paper slippers. I wish I had remembered to shave my legs."

Now, as usual, she relished talking about anything personal having to do with sex, though it was true she also enjoyed speaking impersonally about it, insisting I buy pornographic magazines and then discussing them at great length while I looked on: this one had been retouched, this one had fake breasts, this one dyed her pubic hair. She whispered, "First they took some blood, then I had to pee in a cup. I had to be examined in a tiny triangular room where some gynecologist kept knocking me in the crotch. Then we had to hear a lecture. We had to tell them what kind of birth control we had been using and where we went wrong."

"What did you say?"

"I told them I was on the Pill but had forgotten to take it, jerk."

"For six months?"

"Well, I didn't say that. One girl was fifteen. She was in for her third abortion. She was so cute, Earl. Her name was Alma. She told me it meant soul in Spanish. I think she was a prostitute. She said first she was using an IUD but it came out and she didn't know it. Then she used foam and it didn't work; besides, it was very runny. The Pill made her gain weight and feel sick. Also she couldn't remember to take it. There were twenty of us all together, crowded into a room with five seats and two changing rooms. They couldn't even open the doors without knocking someone over. They gave us paper bags to put our belongings in, unmarked, brown paper bags, and we were called out three at a time. After they tied me down in the operating room the anesthesiologist introduced herself. That was when she told me her son went to Princeton. The nurse liked my earrings. All of a sudden, quite without warning, the anesthesiologist said, 'Goodnight, Maggie.' And poof, next thing I knew I was in the recovery room with cramps. Everyone around me was moaning and writhing. I felt sick but in a little while I was able to get up. They served me flat Coke and stale peanuts. Oh, Earl, I just feel so lousy! I feel so humiliated! And some girl kept trying to counsel me and I had to tell her to go away."

I was not spared even the most gruesome of details. This did not surprise me, because Maggie was very blunt and open in her descriptions of her sex life with Tad. I knew the details of her sexual history, past and present. Each man she had gone out with (ten, to be exact) would, after having sex, put his fingers up to his nose and sniff luxuriously, saying "Ah, delicious." Maggie wondered what the meaning was of this male trait. She looked a bit grim now, though, and her words lacked her usual glee.

When we arrived back at school Maggie went to sleep in my room. She did not wake up until the next day, when I got into the bed with her to take a nap. There was a medicinal smell to her like a cat that had been spayed. Her eyes were shut and beneath the lids I could see her eyeballs swimming, her mouth slightly open the way it always fell when she slept. I kissed her on the neck and wanted to hug her but a tiny whimper came out of her and she pushed me away.

"Get rid of her, Earl," my father whispered in my ear. "You are

Earl of the Przepasniaks. Surely you can find someone willing to screw you, Earl. I am quite ashamed of you, to be perfectly honest."

I was not willing to abandon Maggie, however. When she woke up she went out to the delicatessen to brood and buy a package of Snowballs, a sort of chocolate cupcake covered by a pink rubbery dome and topped with flakes of papery coconut. This was her favorite snack, and usually she ate it while I munched Oreos or Nabisco wafers and we drank milk in front of the television set in the beery lounge. "Earl, have I ever told you what a jerk you are?" she said, returning with her Snowballs to the lounge, and I thought she had returned to normal. But there was something wrong with the way it tasted, she said, and she looked at me as if she had never seen me before.

While we continued to be friends after her abortion, something had snapped between us. She looked at me as if the whole thing had been my fault, while I, on the other hand, longed for her more than ever, and followed her around like a beaten dog.

She did go on confiding in me, and dropped by every day. "I don't ever take my Kotex off nowadays, Earl," she said one afternoon, as I fixed her some Red Zinger in my filthy dorm room. "I'm afraid my insides are going to drop out onto the street."

"This has been known to happen to women," I said, "but I doubt it would happen to you."

"You know, I've been jogging in Riverside Park again. Recently an old lady with a tiny mustache and an ebony cane tipped with gold stopped me as I was running by. She said she was an agent for the Michael Bloom agency. She told me I have all the potential for being a really great actress. She wants me to lose forty pounds and then call her. She gave me her card."

Though I asked her if I could see this card she wouldn't show it to me, but she immediately subscribed to all the show biz magazines and took up painting her eyelids a violet-blue.

I suppose the whole thing could have been true. Stranger things have happened in New York. She stopped eating. When I invited her over for breakfast, all she had was a spoonful of Special K in a paper cup with skim milk and sugar substitute. One morning when I was preparing her tea as usual, she accidentally put her cereal in an old paper cup I had deposited some chewed pieces of Juicy Fruit in, and let out a scream of dismay when she arrived at the bottom of the cup and found the wadded lumps.

After that I could not induce her to return for breakfast, but when I met her for lunch in the cafeteria all she ate was a slice of melon. For dinner she nibbled at a few pieces of wilted lettuce. At first I paid no attention to this. But then I noticed she was getting thinner. She demonstrated to me that when she pulled some skin from her wrist it turned white and the color did not return for several seconds, the mark of her thumb and index finger remaining for much longer than normal. "I wonder how Tad is, you twerp," she would sigh, when I asked her why she insisted on demonstrating this to me. She complained it was uncomfortable to sit down, the bones in her rear end dug into the seat.

Soon it was like being friends with a skeleton. She said to me, "Sometimes I panic when I think of having to go through life with that dent over my eyebrow from when I slipped on the stairs, with the scar on my knee I got in gym in the fifth grade, with the terrible feeling I get in my stomach whenever I think about Tad. I'm damaged, Earl! Damaged!"

"Why are you punishing yourself?" I said. "You didn't do anything wrong." But I wanted to add, "Except to me."

Her ribs were like the bones of a ship. Of course it had taken several months of not eating for her to get this way. "You're not in a concentration camp," I said to her. But she was in one, of her own making, and I had somehow managed to join her there.

I was sick over her and her indifference to me, and each time I saw her pale face grown thinner I saw the face of my mother lying on the floor, the triangular mark of the United States postage meter on her forehead, the crimson streak of blood. And I imagined myself as my father, pillaging and raping, looting everyone around him, and I knew it could not be the same for me. Still, the good bits left inside me continued to shrivel and I was like a little fruit that had not been planted but shrank and grew moldy in the sun.

I even called her parents. "I don't think she's well," I said.

"I'm sorry to hear that," her mother said, and hung up. But a short time later her father returned my call. "She's going to be fine," he said. "We're coming to get her on the last day of school. I'm sure she can hold out until then. What is wrong, exactly?"

I couldn't seem to say she was not eating. I couldn't seem to tell them how the two of us were like monkeys in a laboratory on whom some terrible experiment had been performed: my mother snatched from me and replaced by a hideous wire doll, Maggie's nerves deadened until she was unable to understand that I too existed.

"I want to be an actress," she said. "I'll make millions of dollars, command adoration and love from important people. You can still be my friend, maybe. You can look after the suitcases, purchase the airline tickets. I'll find something for you to do. I know you've been a friend to me, as much as you've been able." She examined her hands in the mirror as if she had never seen them attached to her body.

"Well, why don't you at least call the agent?" I asked. "You don't need to lose any more weight." She didn't respond. "Don't worry about it," I said. "Don't worry so much." I may have forgotten to mention that I continued to harbor dreams of instant fame, though on what basis it was to be awarded to me I didn't know. "I'd prefer it if I were the one to become famous," I said. "I'm certain you would then be in love with me."

She imagined herself bedecked in furs, all eyes turning as she spoke in her imitation Katharine Hepburn voice. She worked frequently on lowering it, shrieking loudly in the shower. The Roman toga her mother had had custom-made for her as a flowing graduation dress no longer fit her. Now it appeared to be a curtain or a bedspread draped over a five-foot eight, one hundred pound girl. Out of nervousness I began to eat more. Though I was not yet fat I grew stockier and took to lifting Maggie's dumbbells, while she was now too weak to do so.

She didn't get her period again after the abortion. A doctor gave her pills and for some reason she ate a lot of yogurt, claiming that would help. Her younger sister said that if she ate a lot of meat that was barely cooked it would bring on her period. But Maggie was not enough of a carnivore. The same sister, visiting us for a weekend, perched herself on my lap while the three of us played gin rummy in Maggie's room and told me it was entirely psychological, and if she herself didn't want to get her period during any given month all she did was eat less meat and tell herself she wasn't going to get it.

Though Maggie did appear to enjoy teasing and making fun of

me, after a time her skin dried out more than ever, her jeering remarks grew weaker and it was not the same as before. On the last day of our freshman year her parents arrived in their Electra to get her. Her dad and I carried her books and clothing down from her room without speaking. He looked at me as if I had gotten her into a car accident and permanently injured her. Though they had no idea she had had an abortion, they blamed me for her current listless condition—forgetting all about Tad, of course—and blamed me for the fact that she had flunked or taken incompletes in most of her courses. If only it *had* been because of me!

Her father, in his loud, checked jacket, took me to one side and suggested I leave her alone for a few weeks, "to give her a chance to rest up." They thought of taking her and her younger sister on a trip to the Bahamas. Maggie's mother's red hands flailed about as she stood next to the long yellow car and supervised the loading of it. "Be careful, be careful," she told me as I jammed Maggie's stereo on top of boxes of clothing, and I wondered why she didn't add, "wimp." Around us, hundreds of other parents in large cars were doing the same. I noticed some girls had managed to recruit two, three, even more boys to help them pack their things, and was sure Maggie's parents were disappointed their daughter had done so poorly for herself.

I admit I was not looking well, my clothes were worn and seedy from having been through the college washing machine so many times, machines which wrung out and burned even the finest of garments. My shirt was ripped at the elbow, and I had on a pair of stinking, beat-up tennis shoes.

Maggie's father suggested we all go to an Italian restaurant for dinner, but Maggie's mother frowned and said they were in a hurry and they didn't want to get caught in rush-hour traffic, did they? "You know you hate that, Chip," she said to Maggie's father, who leaned on the side of the car wiping his forehead with a monogrammed handkerchief.

"Well, see you," I said, and after kissing Maggie on the mouth, to the dismay of her parents, I ambled off through the honking cars on Broadway. I watched as Maggie was helped into the car between them as if she was an invalid, guarded from whatever lunatic fancies she might chance to pick up next.

She called me a week later, her voice exaggerated and syrupy, to say she had been put into the hospital, she was on an IV drip after being diagnosed as having anorexia nervosa, that they kept trying to get her to eat large meals and told her she would die if she did not. Her father called and forbade me to see her, saying I was a bad influence. She had always been a sheltered girl. He did not want her to see someone like me, from an unknown background.

I admit I did not try very hard to reclaim her. But there was my father, perched on my shoulder, telling me I did not need her. And if my father's resonant voice had ordered me around for nearly two decades, and could order me still without even being near me, then what was the use of trying to escape him? I lay on my bed and went to sleep for the summer, the windows shut, the curtains drawn, the room stale. Mostly I thought about Maggie, thought of her as an indifferent, ordinary sort of person, with her timid, ordinary paintings. She was always taking classes in studio art to learn how to improve her technique. A poor portrait of me, an apple and some fruit, a pale abstract—this was her subject matter. I thought of her, a slice taken from a piece of white fruit, the fine, blond, bumblebee fur that covered her legs and the way she stuffed her clothing on the shelf at the top of her closet, sweaters stuck between brassieres, underwear on top of Levi's, the clean and dirty together. I thought of her mouth, a hybrid plum, bitten purple.

I was awash in lethargy, thinking of Maggie and her strange lies; the colors she painted her fingernails—blood red, watery blue, yellow; her handwriting that crept in a twisted arc across the page, now up, now down. Her hair fanning out behind her as she swam; her cruel, sweet look when she made fun of me; her habit of picking out the soft interior of a roll and putting tuna fish into the shell.

I knew her intimately. I would know her whoever we were, if we were to meet today, under any disguise or dismantling. The pork chops she cooked in maple syrup and mustard that left a permanent, peculiar odor to the dorm room, the way she quickly learned to make comments more sarcastic and brutal than my own. Who was she if not my own creation? I only wanted to be shut of her, I was disgusted with her mocking, queer skeleton, and yet I could not stop thinking about her. It was myself I was really thinking about when I thought of her.

I emerged now from my room only to use the bathroom or to eat my random meals. My second-rate analytic mind continued to work, evaluating her and our relationship. I made up my own neo-Freudian system of diagnosis. To her I attributed every problem known to man and some that were not. I spent many hours in the bathroom, taking baths with Maggie's brand of bath oil, the blobs floating in the hot water like paramecia, casting ringed shadows. She might as well have still been there, for the amount of time I thought about her.

And so I lived like a dog, not knowing the difference in days, only surprised to find one day it was fall and getting cold and I had not registered to return to Columbia. I had no intention of returning.

I had kept my dormitory room for the summer months, and scraping together some money, I purchased a used television, installed an extra lock on the dorm room door and locked myself in. The reception on the television was not very good but it kept up a kind of background noise and hum that made it difficult to worry or think. It seemed to keep my father quiet, now bearded and graying on my shoulder.

A short time later I received an eviction notice.

4

IT WAS TRUE IT HAD BEEN necessary to avenge my mother's death by squealing on my dad. But thoughts of him in jail preyed on me. Had I turned in my own father for any real reason?—the man who had once picked me up on his back and run down the beach into the ocean while I screamed with delight. My mother was still dead and having him locked up had not brought her back.

Having him locked up had not made me any more of a man, either, for after all my attempted intimacy with Maggie, it was no more of a relationship with a woman than any homosexual would have had, and I did not believe I was homosexual. I thought to myself: "I might be a homosexual, but the only problem is, I am not physically attracted to other men in any way. So even at that I am a failure."

And now they would not even let me see her. I called and called, longing to speak to my only friend, but her dad asked me to go away. He simply said, "You little jerk, don't call here again or I'll call the police. You've ruined my daughter's life. Go and bother somebody else."

"Someday, boys, when you get older, we'll head for France, eat bouillabaisse on the Seine and pick up some Parisian chicks," my father had told us, years before. And it came to me in a flash: broken man though I was, I would begin afresh.

With the small income from the rental of my mother's house, I purchased a plane ticket to London and set off, saying goodbye only to Bobo and writing to my father in jail to tell him what I was about to do, how I would fulfill his fantasies and win his approval. Not that this was my only aim—no, I also had it in mind to get some education, a real education such as my mother would be proud of, with trips to the Lake District to visit the watering places of Yeats and Longfellow, and jaunts over to Paris and the rest of France to see where old Oscar Wilde had been buried, and perhaps gain some poetry in myself, for I realized that by nature I was an unpoetic soul.

That too was a part of it, though winning my father's approval was perhaps my primary concern, for after my lengthy and terminal fiasco with Maggie, and with the almost daily arrival of my father's letters from jail, I was seriously considering locking myself up in a Jewish monastery, if such a thing existed, where I wouldn't have to contend with my terrible feelings of un-masculinity.

On the airplane I began to wonder why my dad felt it necessary to bring home to me my ineffectuality. But then I realized that Dad, with his constant carping and criticizing, was only attempting not to do to me what had been done to him.

He had told me often enough that he had been virtually ruined by his own parents always approving, approving, of their one and only jewel. "That sort of thing sets up unreal expectations," he wrote to me. "I had then to try to live up to them, which resulted in a chronic overachievement. Even now, can I rest upon my furloughs from listening to the complaints of people unwilling to stand on their own two feet? No, I have to come home and be with the stained-glass lamps, the massive hand-carved furniture, tend the grounds, draw water, haul wood, acquire more and more fowl for the poultry yard and in between try to satisfy as many oversexed and undersupplied women as possible, which for me is no big deal, it's just time, just finding enough time! I may be your renaissance man, but even I have to deal with a twenty-four-hour day. Naturally I'm joking, of course, I hope you understand this. After all, when would I get a chance to do any of this, since I am by some quirky accident of fate locked up in a jail five days a week and couldn't possibly fit all of this in on my weekends, heh-heh. Though Bobo is trying mightily to keep up the grounds and doesn't seem to hold it against me about your mother's accidental and tragic death, which occurred out of her own clumsiness, in any case."

I studied his letter again. No doubt what was going through my father's mind was how terrible it would be if I were unable to live up to his expectations for me. So it was again a case of my old man's wisdom and kindness when he found so much fault with me. Another display of his nearly perfect character. And I, of course, always thinking the worst, but such was the way I was bound to turn out after modeling myself on my "passive-aggressive/passive-dependent mother," as he was always pointing out. This was definitely "ego destructive" for me. And as he also said, "Your appreciation and 'reading' of other people often seems paranoid . . . very limiting for you."

These thoughts were in my head as we touched down in London's Heathrow Airport. Why was I going to London, if not in the hopes of living out his fantasies? And what did that make me? I wasn't sure. Unoriginal, at the least. How he had gone on about the trip he would someday take around the world, what he would see, the international spread of beautiful women and that ilk. You couldn't say I didn't know why I was going. It sprang from the noblest of intentions, really, so why was I always vilifying myself? From his jail cell he would get postcards from around the world and live out his dreams, at least vicariously, through me.

Oh London, city of damp! Home of the English accent! England, nation of rock stars and duchesses! How far off base could any person get? On my arrival I wrote dozens of letters to famous women:

> I am a young American student, abroad for the first time. I have always admired you, one of the most brilliant writers [or playwrights, actresses, designers, artists, etc.] of our time.
>
> I feel that it is your duty, as one of the most influential figures of modern society, to help educate the young, particularly an uncultured and uncouth American. I wonder if I might perhaps be allowed to pay a visit to honor you? No matter the time or place, even if only for a brief period of time, I'm sure my

life and yours would be changed by a meeting with you. What power you hold! I await your reply with bated breath.

I remain, Your Humble and Obedient Servant,

Earl Przepasniak

P.S. I am twenty years old and told by my friends I am very handsome.

A short time after I arrived I received an answer from one of the women I had written to, a famous English playwright in her fifties, who now lived in the south of France in an unknown town. The letter invited me to stop in when I was in the area. In the area! What the hell would I ever be doing in the area? I began to pack my bags at once. I could come for a weekend, she suggested, some time after she got back at the end of the month from filming a movie in the Aegean. That was all—a few lines scribbled on a square of cardboard with her name engraved on one side—but I was beside myself with joy. Over and over I fondled the raised letters of her name. At last the big break I had been waiting for had come. Actually, I had gotten the idea when my mother read me the Paul Bowles autobiography, *Without Stopping,* in which he had written to famous people and then spent month upon month visiting them. And he was only the son of a dentist!

What would my father say when he heard of this? At last, he would think, we men are getting back a little of what women have taken from us for so long. He would have to smile to himself, at least a little, at the thought of his son as gigolo, at his son's suaveness and sophistication, the jet-set life I planned to lead once Gillian K. met me and fell in love with me.

It was true I was more of the Woody Allen variety than the Valentino or John Travolta type of man, but then women found my kind appealing too, of that I was certain.

My letter itself was proof that I was no ordinary person. Had my father ever thought up such an unusual tactic, at my age? I remembered how he had once taken Bobo and me on a hike up a New Hampshire mountain, Mt. Monodnack, during a weekend visit after the divorce. Near the top was a plateau, and I sat there exhausted, telling him and Bobo that I could not go on, that they should continue and come back for me on the way down. "Earl," he had said, "I don't like to see that kind of attitude. Keep pushing yourself. There is always another point beyond which you can go, even when it seems as if you have reached the end of your strengths and limitations."

And so, though I was fearful, I telegraphed Gillian K. with an unsigned message that said simply, "Name the date."

But there was no reply.

Had I said the wrong thing? Was my action too hasty, too nervy? Perhaps I had gotten the address wrong. Oh Mom, Mom, I frothed and fumed in my bed-sitting room as the beginning and then the middle of November passed and there was still no response to my telegram. If only you had stayed alive, I would have known what to do, you would have given me the right advice. And though I had turned to Gillian K. in the hopes of receiving some praise and sustenance, none was forthcoming.

I hadn't read anything she had written, either. I went to the local library to read some of her plays, but I could make little sense out of any of them. Mostly they seemed quite tedious, even lifeless, though perhaps, I thought, they acted better on the stage.

Some things I read in the plays made me think Gillian K. must be very strange and possibly, like my mother, into mysticism, but then, who wasn't, nowadays? But what could ever have given me the idea, I wondered later, that she must have ears and a back covered with silky, furry down? Was it something I read in a brief biography of her and her family? Perhaps it had been something I read in one of her plays. "A fine mane of hair grew down her neck to her back." But did I even want to get involved with someone with a mane, I worried. I thought of myself gently stroking Gillian's downy, aged little ears. Well, I had always been fond of animals.

Finally, as the month drew to a close, I sent another telegram: "Arriving December 17. If this is all right, don't answer." That would teach her, I hoped, to hand out invitations and then pretend not to be at home.

I booked a seat for a shuttle flight to Paris, and then on a small airline that would take me to the region in the south of France where Gillian K. lived. Since only one plane a day went to the town where the closest airport was located, and since that plane left at ten-thirty in the morning, I had to take a seven-forty-five shuttle to Charles de Gaulle.

Trembling with fear, I tossed and turned all night in my grim room with its gas ring and grille-fronted heater. Next to my bed I had packed a tiny suitcase full of almost all my belongings. I woke in the night and remembered I had packed my toothbrush and I would need it in the morning and so I was forced to get up and pull everything out of the bag, white shirts, sweaters, underwear, and dig down to the bottom where my toothbrush had made a sodden white spot due to the fact that I didn't own a toothbrush case. Then everything once more had to be shoved back into the bag, and I went back to bed, tossing and shivering in the freezing dampness that the heater, which cost ten pence to operate for a time period of some two minutes, was never able to warm up.

In the morning I woke thinking bitterly that I should have been a rock-and-roll star. I wondered if the food I had stored under my bed, the food I was now subsisting on, was going to rot while I was away. I expected to be gone for an extended period, yet due to my upbringing I could not force myself to throw any of the stuff out. What would happen to the Tiptree raspberry jam, so much richer than any jam in the United States, with its dark, bloody fruit squeezed into the bottle, its little elegant label marked 23p? My McVitties chocolate-covered digestive biscuits, the chocolate rich and pungent, the biscuit crumbly and sweet and obviously in no way aiding the digestion; the cans marked Tunny Fish Steak, my Jacob's cream biscuits—this stuff was food these people ate all the time. For them it was just normal food, nothing strange or fancy about it! Who the hell ate Salad Cream? These people did, that's who! Vinegar-flavored crisps! Lapsang Souchong tea! Trifles, treacle, sponge pudding, boiled pudding, semolina, custard, anchovy paste, spotted dick, toad in the hole, bubble and squeak, fish and chips!

Yuck. What a country. I wanted to tell this to my father, with his plum pudding, marmite, his English breakfast tea, from the one shelf in the grocery store that was marked "Gourmet and Specialty Foods." That stuff wasn't gourmet, it was just normal! So don't give me any of that crap about your luxurious life, I said to myself, thinking of his pomegranates and Belgian waffles smothered in strawberries and confectioner's sugar he used to serve my brother and me on those weekend visits in the distant past when he was still trying to woo us. They had whole countries where the people ate nothing but Belgian waffles!

Why, right now I was in a country where a restaurant might serve baked beans on toast for breakfast. You think that's strange, Dad, a lot of people here eat *spaghetti* on toast for breakfast. Well, some, anyway. You should see the bacon they've got here, big thick strips called back bacon or streaky bacon, meaty and pink, and my mother too poor to buy anything but cereal, cold cereal day in and day out, while you spent your weekdays dieting because you pigged so much on the weekends.

And now the letters I received from Ithaca (his prison) complained that I wasn't writing to him frequently enough; he seemed to equate this with my general ineffectual weakness and insipid personality. As he said, "I've seen you manipulate me into carrying you . . . valued me only as someone you could con into giving to you . . . and when that giving and carrying stopped you were quick to shuck me off."

I was hungry but there was no time to eat my terrible biscuits and I figured I would have time to get something to eat at the airport. The roads of Finchley I walked to get to the Tube were soggy and foggy in the early morning, the rows of houses gray and blinkered, too close to one another. Each was complete with its shocking-green strip of lawn packed densely with rosebushes and dahlias that even at this time of year were still in flower.

One thing I found very disturbing was that nobody had ever told me there were palm trees in England. The road to the Tube took me past a house where three of them grew on the front lawn, the tallest some fifteen feet in height, spindly and alien. "Why didn't anybody ever tell me there were palm trees in England?" I muttered between clenched teeth each time I passed them, as if a deliberate injustice had been done to me, though what difference it would have made if I had been told I cannot now fathom.

They were not even proper palm trees to speak of, really more like overgrown yuccas. Every time I saw them I felt in some way betrayed. What was I doing here? What had I come for? Was I doing this to impress my father, or to live up to the memory of my mother? I thought of these questions and I was torn, because I understood there was no way to win.

It was apparent to me that I was in a very high-strung period in my life. I went past the mailbox, suitcase in hand. In it sat a letter, like a blunt instrument, from Maggie. She had somehow gotten hold of my address when she heard of the book my father was writing in prison, entitled *Painless Divorce*.

I could only pray that Gillian would take me out of my old life and that she would do this very shortly. Maggie's letters, when they arrived, filled me with such longing, such remorse, I really felt it would be better not to continue living. Even now, after so many months, often a craving would force itself onto me, a craving that could not be fulfilled, seemingly, by anything in the world.

It was a longing for a cigarette, chocolate, sex—something that could never be satisfied. I was aware that it was not really Maggie I was looking for, but what had passed between us—love of a primitive, flatworm kind that seemed to fill this craving more than anything else. After meals I felt it, a strong urge for something sweet. But cramming chocolate into my mouth gave an impression of satisfaction that lasted only for a second and ended with a desire for more. Sometimes too the need for a cigarette would be so strong, yet the thought of the cigarette was far more satisfying than the first puff, which only left me feeling nauseous. Masturbation, which was all I was getting, or had ever gotten, for that matter, instead of soothing me left me feeling deeply excited. Then, too, rituals and repetitions suddenly appeared and had to be followed almost compulsively. These could not exactly be called neuroses, they were more a series of thoughts and commands which interfered with my normal life only to the point of making it slightly uncomfortable—an order would come for me to take *this* bottle of juice off the shelf in the store rather than *that* one, and so on.

When the letter arrived from Maggie I ripped it open with great haste, which no doubt was a mistake, her thin, finely decorated scrawl coursing the page like a field of hounds after a rabbit: "I thought you would like to know that our dog Ginger [this was the pear- and candle-eating spaniel] died after a lengthy illness. The vet confirmed that her spine dissolved."

She herself was suffering from a broken arm which had occurred when she stepped off a bus in heels that were too high. "I am always damaging myself in unknown ways. Cuts appear on my body for no reason whatsoever. My little toes accidentally became infected down to the bone. Gentian violet stained my fingers, the walls, the dripping sink and for weeks has lingered everywhere except where I was supposed to put it, on my toes. A vicious bout with poison ivy forced me to get cortisone shots. My skin peeled off in layers. How have you been, Earl?"

Between maladies she was acting, getting many jobs, and was due to appear in a soap opera next month as a transmitter of a fatal disease. She sent some composites along with her letter. In them she was posing in lingerie, her face beautifully made up and tawny as a cat—but her body, still too skimpy, looked ridiculous, ribby and unsexy in silk underwear.

I was green with envy and lust as I read of the famous men (Lloyd Bridges, actually, was the only one) who invited her to lunch at the Plaza. An oily Arab stopped her on the street to invite her to the Gulf of Aqaba to play backgammon. And Maggie wrote she had dropped out of school. Though it was easier to believe her than not, I still could not forget the chronic liar she had been. She wrote that she was earning enough money to support herself and half a dozen others in style.

How convenient. Yes, I snarled to myself, I should have been a girl, a beautiful girl.

My father was a psychiatrist. When he told me I was a mess, told me I was unlovable, I believed him. My father, as a dad and a shrink, could only have been telling the truth. And yes, it was true nobody had told me it was going to be fair, but then nobody had told me anything! At least I should have been offered some alternatives. If I had been an amoeba I would have been divided a million times already. I would have been famous already; I would have been an entire population. I would have existed. But to be doomed to this life as a nonentity—why, even my brother, Bobo, muscle-bound and mathematical, was more of a human being than I. At least he believed in his existence and did not need fame to prove it. Well, I thought, as I embarked on this new and ambiguous adventure, perhaps *this* would prove to my Dad that I was not dependent but could carry on quite well without him or anyone, travel, have excitements separate and divorced from him.

So in my own lopsided way I trotted onto the Tube, carrying my small suitcase that had once belonged to my mother, a suitcase that had in fact been the one she had used to carry her tape cassette, manuscripts and books to sell at poetry readings. The Tube sped toward the West London Air Terminal like a plane taxiing down the runway and never getting off the ground, only churning, churning, faster and faster until it jarred to a halt at each stop like a sudden arrow. I read the subway map, pulled Maggie's letter out of my pocket, and tried to think of anything other than where this subway was taking me so early in the morning, tried not to think about the plane trip and whatever hell I would no doubt be into by the end of the day. I threw the letter bitterly to the floor. "No littering," the conductor told me.

Once again, revelation struck. I saw that without my mother I did not really exist. I was only a watered down version of her, a pitiful, stupid, male version of a not-very-bright brilliant genius. Light dawned. I felt like bawling on the subway, getting off and going back to my drab bed-sitting room. I wasn't even human! Not even human! My God! What was Earl going to do? Calm yourself, I said. In the window opposite me I practiced my facial expressions, trying to see what would be the best look to have to seduce Gillian K. All I could see was a blubbery grin, a goatish face trying to please. Perhaps it was the window, grimy and spotted, that gave me such a warped face. Or the flickering light of the subway that cast dim shadows in which even Mick Jagger would have looked inhuman.

The bus ride from the West London Air Terminal to Heathrow was an uneventful tour through miles of dreary suburbs, past an endless string of pubs named "The Frog and Nightgown," "The Pineapple and Passion," "The White Hart," "The Queen's Elm," "The Bald Peacock," "The Farrier and Fox." Each sounded like a wonderful place to have a drink (not that alcohol did anything more for me than plunge me into a treacle pit of depression), but inside, was a dreary motel-like place, a plaid rug covering the floor and a jukebox playing constant Elvis Presley, a great favorite here with the toothless clientele gathered around the dart board.

My mirrored sunglasses on, my sweater slung Americanly around my neck, I hoped I looked exotic enough to the other passengers: an Oriental gentleman; a large bumblebee of a businessman with a faceful of red fur; a few stewardi. I was weak and hungry, but by the time I had checked in at the airline terminal, my flight was almost ready to go and there was no time to grab anything to eat. After landing in Paris, I could not seem to make myself understood at a small bar in the Charles de Gaulle Airport where a Frenchman (I presumed he was a Frenchman; he didn't understand me, so I doubted he was English or American) polished glasses with a greasy rag.

Perhaps, I decided, the bar was only for drinks and did not sell anything to eat, though who would be drinking so early in the morning I couldn't say. I changed some pounds into francs at a money-changing counter, and from a booth that sold confections I bought a jar of kumquats, having decided arbitrarily that this was a suitable gift from a poor admirer.

Suddenly a panicky fear gripped me. I was wrung out from the emotions of the morning and it was only shortly after nine. I couldn't even get a cup of coffee; the microwave oven on the plane was broken and we were not offered a thing. I was blowing almost all my money on this flight to the south of France (I had to sit down, I was so weak) to visit a person who had not even acknowledged my existence, to visit some lady who was not even all that famous, a lady who obviously had no desire to see me, or wouldn't she have answered my telegram?

My God, she had not even answered my telegram!

And why had I worded my telegram—so stupidly, I now thought—to say "If this is all right, don't answer"? Even I couldn't distinguish what that meant. That meant it might now be "all right" and that she wasn't bothering to answer. Or it might mean it wasn't "all right" and she wasn't answering.

What exactly had my telegram said? I couldn't even remember. I had filled out a piece of paper at the Post Office in London, writing down my address (or so I believed) on the space provided in case there was a return message. Had I remembered to put what day I was planning to come? I knew I hadn't mentioned the time, since I hadn't yet bought a ticket. But there were so few flights to Nimes, the town next to hers, I imagined she would know to meet me at the airport. On the other hand, why would she meet me? Was she the kind of person who would meet people at the airport and if so, why? I didn't even know what she looked like!

I still had time before my connecting flight to Nimes. Perhaps I could call and find out whether she was home, whether I was in fact welcome.

Weak, pale and perspiring from lack of breakfast and deodorant, I stumbled to a series of telephone booths and a pile of telephone books that were supposed to encompass all of France.

Under her province there was no listing for Gillian K. How could she not have given me her phone number in her invitational letter? If she was not home, I thought, at least I could return to London and refund the unused portion of my ticket. Where was somebody who spoke English who would help me?

Finally I found a booth that seemed to be marked "Assistance and Information." "Do you speak English?" I said. "Speak English?" My suitcase, a great dead weight, lay at my feet. I was relieved to be able to put it down. The girl behind the counter, a delicate chimp-mustache growing on her upper lip, frowned and shook her head. "Look, you've got to help me," I said. A weak smile crossed her face. "I want to make a telephone call— *telephonez*—and I don't have the number. How am I supposed to get it?"

She shook her head again. *"Moment—moment, s'il vous plaît,"* she managed at last to squirt out. "Paul? Paul?" she called into a room that opened behind her. Then she pointed to one end of the counter. I understood I was to wait there. She picked up the phone and dialed. A conversation ensued in which I gathered she was trying to find this Paul or some other English-speaking devil.

"Why don't you speak English?" I felt like asking her. "Everybody speaks English, what is this, some kind of a joke? I don't care if French is your main language, you should be able to speak English. *Parlez-vous anglais?"* I found I was muttering out loud. Long minutes passed while we waited for Paul or somebody human to appear. "Come on, lady," I frantically tried to word in French in my head. "Come on, I'm going to miss my flight if this Paul character doesn't show up. And I don't even know whether it's a flight I'm supposed to be taking or not." The girl, bored, looked off into space. "This is a life or death matter!" I started to scream, only quietly. "If I go on this flight I'm going to be broke when I get back! At least somebody better be home!"

Finally Paul, dressed in a cheap, shiny suit, with a little wobbly French walk, swished toward us, and the girl behind the counter smiled with relief at being rescued from the maniac. "All right, you bastard," I thought to myself, "so you speak two languages, you don't have to look so smug about it, just get me out of here! Just get me Gillian K.'s phone number and I'll do all right!"

Then I had another bright idea. If I couldn't get her phone number, perhaps Paul could call the local police station in X. to ask them to drive by the house (I was sure they would know where she lived, though I myself was not positive), and then I could call them back shortly before the flight and find out if she was there.

The Paul character finished at last chattering to the girl—he was probably talking about what to eat for lunch—and turned to me. "Can I help you?" he said coldly.

"Yes!" I said, almost pouncing on him (though my New York college education never allowed both of my feet to leave the suitcase at any given time, knowing full well the minute I did the suitcase would be stolen). "Look, I'm in a little bit of trouble. I'm flying down to Nimes now" (was it Nimes I was going to? Arles? Montpelier? In glancing at the map I hadn't been able to figure out which one was the closest to where Gillian K. lived) "and I don't know whether I'm expected or not, so I want to call first, but I don't know the number and I can't figure out how to call information to get it. It may be unlisted. Is there some way I can get an unlisted telephone number?"

For a minute Paul looked at me. "I'm sorry, I don't understand."

"Look, how can I get this number? She lives in Gard, in the town of X., near Nimes. Could you help me get it?"

"You are going to visit somebody who you do not know if they are expecting you?"

So you do understand, I thought. His face turned down in a disapproving way, as if he had smelled something bad.

"Yeah, and my flight leaves in a little while and I don't know whether or not to take it."

"I am sorry." He shook his head in false sadness.

"Hey, I don't need your sympathy! Couldn't you just call and get me the phone number! That's all I'm asking. I can't seem to make myself understood when I speak French." Or English either, for that matter, I might have added.

"Okay, what do you want?"

"Look, here is her name and address. That's all the address I have, just the name of the town, actually, I guess it must be a very small place, I couldn't even find it on the map. If you could just get the number for me—"

"Okay, okay, just a minute." He took my scrap of paper and disappeared. I looked at my watch nervously. My foot began to tap involuntarily. The French girl (Some girl! She must have been thirty years old but I wouldn't have called her a woman, with that sibilant little look on her face. What did she have to look so sure of herself about except she spoke the local patois?) examined me with impassive curiosity. She had seen better specimens of chimpanzees in this zoo before.

Even if I got the phone number it was probably going to be too late for me to get a call through. There were long lines at the phone booths, and I wasn't sure, if I missed my flight, whether or not I would be able to get my money refunded. For some reason I thought you probably had to get it refunded well before actual flight time.

I opened my suitcase and began digging frantically through it. Then I stopped, forgetting what I was looking for. My passport, I realized, where was my passport! In my pocket, with my traveler's checks. Where were my glasses, my regular glasses, not my sunglasses? The floor, in my panic, became littered with my shaving kit, my white shirts; the jar of kumquats rolled into the corridor and had to be rescued from a passing Indian in a turban.

I sat down briefly on the floor and took a hard look at the lunatics waiting around in the airport: there was a man wearing shoes three sizes too large who walked like a duck; two dowagers, one in a pink raincoat, one in a blue checked polyester skirt, who approached me ominously, ignoring my outstretched limbs; a man with a head set between his shoulders like a pin; a tiny Oriental woman seemingly no more than two feet tall; a mother and daughter decked in the same wretched shade of rust; a girl wedged between two parents; an old lady with legs stuffed into stockings like sausages in casing; a girl with a nose mashed into a lip.

Every person walked past me utterly self-absorbed, seeing themselves as the center of their own existence.

Paul walked down the hall toward me at last (Where had he gone, anyway? There was a phone right here he could have used.) and I began to try to shove everything back into the suitcase so I could follow him to wherever he was going to take me: to a phone, no doubt, or an "authority," or somebody who could speak decent English. I couldn't fit everything back into the suitcase and some of it was drooping over the top of the bag, but I tried to force the zipper to close over it anyway. I gave up and left the stuff sticking out and when I stood up almost bumped into Paul. He looked at me, his cheap blue suit shiny and stinking of some strange French aftershave that had the odor of old flowers daubed with garlic, or perhaps it more closely resembled air freshener in a bathroom. He didn't smile. I smiled, however, but very nervously; it was more of a twitch than a smile. "Hi there! Did you manage to—"

"I could not get the number. It could not be gotten." He stood gazing down the hall at the oncoming rush of travelers.

"Unlisted?"

"Yes. It is—how do you say?—a number that is not available. To you. That will be five francs."

"Look, in that case, could you get me the number of the local police station down there so maybe they could tell me whether she is home or not?"

Silently he nodded and disappeared. He didn't seem to have understood me. Who knew what the hell he was going to come back with. I felt like just leaving the scene of the crime and the girl's disapproving sneer. Anyway, she was right. What kind of maniac went to an unknown place uninvited?

"I have gotten the number and I have called." Paul, back sooner than I expected, startled me into emitting a little cry like a rabbit caught by a dog.

"Oh, thanks. What did they say?"

"They do not know whether or not your friend is home. They think she may be away."

"Oh." Well, at least she did exist, at least somebody else had heard of her. And I was going to the right town. "Did they know where she lives? Is it close?"

Paul looked at me even more suspiciously. "How should I know? Here is the name of the captain of the police. He will see you when you get there." He handed me a slip of paper. "That will be eight francs. Plus five for the other call."

"Well. Thank you. What can I say." Shoving some money at him and snatching up my suitcase, I set off on a slow run to my departure gate. I had the run of a person who is considerably weakened by not eating breakfast and is wearing a too heavy sweater and is carrying a sheepskin coat in addition to the suitcase.

Charles de Gaulle was nightmarish, an airport designed by Walt Disney or a similar lunatic. The middle of the airport was a tubular glassed-in area like an aquarium with an outside circular pathway that connected to the terminals. Stretching across the center were slanted escalators, one of which I hopped onto. "Hey!" someone was yelling, and I turned around to see him pointing out to me that the seam of my suitcase had burst open, revealing to the world part of a white pair of underpants. "Thanks," I heard myself chortling in a deranged voice, though I had not meant to say anything at all.

Once more I had to ask myself, why, why, why was I doing this, what was I trying to prove by scrambling around in an unknown, unsafe country, trying to act like a native. Was all this necessary to win my Dad's approval? In that case, I could just give up, his approval, like my passport to Syria, being withheld for life. Was I trying to get one up on him? At my most grandiose, I knew better than to even begin such a fol-de-rol. Was I trying to prove that I existed? If a famous person spoke to me, would that at least be some verification? And if a famous person approved of me, would that compensate for a lifetime of disgruntled father-shrink? And on and on. One thing about having a shrink for a father was that I'd never have to pay for an expensive analysis. No, I was always analyzing myself, a do-it-yourself project, knowing all the tricks, the ropes, the right questions—and if I didn't know any answers, well, what high-priced shrink ever gave anyone any answers. And what about transference? Well, I myself was the recipient of both positive and negative transference. I was judge, I was jury, and I tried the whole case.

At last, just barely in time, I threw myself on the plane, a tiny vehicle with only four seats to a row. A short time after we were airborne I was served a cup of coffee and some salted peanuts. Some peanuts! What had ever happened to food? The stewardess, a blonde with sunken eyes encircled with purple, appeared not to understand me when I called her over and asked her if she spoke English. She called over her superior, who was servicing the front of the cabin.

"Look," I felt like saying to the first one, though I kept my mouth shut to avoid getting thrown off the plane, "I can understand your not speaking English, but surely you understand that I'm asking whether or not you do. *Sprechen-sie Deutsch? Parlez-vous anglais?* for crying out loud. I would understand a Pakistani coming over to me and asking me in his language if I spoke whatever gibberish it is they speak over there in Pakistan."

At least I would have the sense to shake my head and tell him no; I wouldn't stand there like a buffoon at the zoo trying to figure out whether that monkey in the cage was speaking or masturbating. She knew what I was saying, the stinking bitch! She knew! She just didn't want to get herself involved with my maniacal appearance and lack of true culture.

Finally her superior, a woman with an undersized pretty head with two gaping forceps dents at the temples, finished chatting with some French farmer (his hands were red, like two smashed radishes—this is how I knew he was a farmer) sitting on the opposite side of the aisle and came over to my seat. "Yes?" she said, her pretty mouth stretched in what seemed to be a permanent rictus, "Can I help you?"

"Yes," I said, and once again that tinge of desperation crept into my voice. "Look, I'm going to the town of X., and I don't know where it is and I can't seem to speak French. I wonder if you would help me and find out if anyone is going there who could give me a ride?"

Miss Forceps-face looked at me blankly. "I will see if it is all right for me to do so," she said, and disappeared up the aisle. Were my travels an escape from my father and all he stood for? Were they a living-out of all his fantasies? They were neither. They were simply a mess.

Twenty minutes later, as the plane began its descent, she returned, mincing down the aisle. "I cannot go asking everyone if he is going to X.," she said. "I am sorry, but I just cannot do so."

I looked at her. Had my thin arms been stronger, had I not been ready to faint from hunger, I might have considered strangling her. As it was, I thought of asking the passengers myself, but the idea of trying to word my request in French was beyond me, and speaking English would only have entitled me to more of the disbelieving stares the French seemed to be so good at. Which of these twenty or so people, I thought, looking around me, was going to the town of X. There would be no one at the airport to meet me, that much I was sure of. I was out here in the middle of nowhere and not only did no one know, but no one cared.

The plane descended on a parking lot next to a tiny airport terminal building. Slapping myself frequently on the pocket to make sure I still had my passport, I hiked across the parking lot to the inside of the airport, where hundreds of people eagerly searched the faces of the passengers. Much embracing, family groups, etc., but no one appeared to be looking for a young boy. Perhaps it had been a mistake to write in my letter that I was considered by many to be handsome, but I had, to tell the truth, developed from the boy my mother had grown accustomed to, and now at least my nose matched my face in a sort of Dustin Hoffmanish way. Or at least I thought so when looking at myself in the mirror and in passing windows. How else to explain Maggie's attraction to me, she who so admired Dustin Hoffman and his ilk?

Oh, all right. So maybe I'm exaggerating (for suddenly my father appeared, all the way from the U. S. of A., to sit on my shoulder and sneer) you don't need to rub it in! So I'm lying a little. Allow me this one small indulgence, this one vanity. Anyway, looks had never stopped my father from getting the girls. With his raw animal sexuality he could have been a gorilla and still attracted them like flies. I had some of that, some watered-down genetic component of dear old Dad.

I spied another information booth and after demanding *"Parlez-vous anglais?"* once again, to which I received a negative answer, I managed to stutter out in execrable French that I wanted to know how to get to X. I was informed, or at least so I believed, that in order to get there it was necessary to take a bus that was leaving immediately for Nimes—or had it already left?—and then in Nimes it would be possible to get a bus to the town of X. Throwing myself into the bus, I handed over five francs (what that sum was worth was beyond me), flung my suitcase into the rack above me and slumped with weak despair into a seat.

Though my eyes took in the surrounding countryside I could not interpret the data. The long, dirt fields that stretched endlessly on either side of the road were filled with small, stunted, leafless trees, perhaps three feet tall. Queer as bats, was all I could think about the French. What kind of people would cultivate fields of stunted trees topped with several whiplike branches?

In Nimes I stepped out at the bus terminal (though I was beginning to wonder if everything I saw wasn't a hallucination) and found a posting of the hours the buses left and where they were going to. The bus to X. was leaving in two hours.

At first I sat in the bus terminal, but as a tough-looking group of French juvenile delinquents left the pinball machines to circle me warily, swaggering in garb of studded leather, heads shaved, I got up and walked outside.

The reek of urine and bus exhaust was giving me a headache. I debated trying to find something to eat, but I could not bear the thought of fighting to make myself understood. Perhaps I was having so much difficulty because I didn't look human. Maybe on the flight from London to Paris my face had grown a covering of long reddish hair. This would explain a great deal.

Then I had an idea. I would find a phone and call the gendarmerie in X., where perhaps I could make myself understood and get directions to the house of Gillian K. If she was not at home, I could return at once to the airport without having to go all the way out there. On the other hand, possibly this had all been some sort of a test and I would arrive to find the arms of Gillian K. warm and welcoming and a hot din-din awaiting me on the stove. Possibly this was some sort of test she put all her guests through.

Lugging my suitcase, stopping every few feet to put it down, I was amazed to find no phone booths in sight, and in this way I covered what seemed to be dozens of square blocks, though I might have just been going around and around the same square.

Finally I found a row of booths in front of the *Poste Restant*. I put the correct coins in the slot (two .2 franc pieces, it said) and dialed the number that had been given to me in Paris for the X. police station. The phone rang; it was picked up. "*Allo?*"

"*Oui,*" I said, "*Je voudrais parler avec Monsieur le Capitaine.*" It was a fair rendition, I felt, of the French vocab.

"*Allo? Allo?*"

"*Oui,*" I said, more loudly. A faint irritation came over me. The man on the other end gibbered something too quickly for me to understand and hang up. All right! I thought, so my French is not so good, at least give me the chance to ask for what I want!

Perhaps the phone was broken and he had simply been unable to hear me, but when I dialed again from a different phone the same thing happened—he acted as if I didn't exist—and now it was drawing close to the time my bus was leaving. There was nothing for me but to go all the way to the town of X.

Of course, later I learned there was a small button on the telephone I was supposed to be pressing while I talked, but how was I supposed to know? The stinking French had no instructions written on the phone. At least I might have been able to figure out what to do if there had been.

I rushed back to the bus terminal where a bus was pulling out of the station, but when I flagged it down and pulled myself onto it, shouting "X.? X.?" it turned out to be the wrong one. I found the bus leaving for X., and managed to tell the driver to let me know when we arrived.

Oh Dad, how lucky you were to be missing all this!

At each step I had terrible thoughts that this was in fact the town of X., and the driver had simply not bothered to inform me. "X.? X.?" I said nervously from time to time into the driver's ear. The bus crossed over a small bridge and I saw a sign announcing the name of the town. As soon as the bus stopped I threw myself off. The wind, chilly earlier on, was fiercer now and tore through my perspiration-soaked clothes. The sky, gray for most of the day, had begun to darken into evening.

I will skip here the terrible details of how I found the police station, the discussion the captain and I had in pigeon English as he drew me a little map of how to get to the house of Gillian K. I was too fatigued to appreciate the fact that the police captain looked like Peter Sellers, and instead of examining the town, I trudged wearily down the wandering road in search of Gillian's house, crossing a wide river and several sharp turns in the road where I was nearly run over.

It had taken me an entire day to reach this godforsaken place, with not a kindly smile from anyone throughout the passage. I will avoid the details of how I reached the house, which was surrounded by a huge stone wall and iron gates through which I peered anxiously to see within the tremendous stone mansion, its windows boarded up by gigantic peeling wooden shutters.

I will not trouble you with how, as I pushed at the iron gate in the insane, vain hope that perhaps someone was home after all but only tried to hide out from me, the first big droplets of rain began to fall on my head, pittering against the leaves of the curious overgrown garden inside the walls, a garden twisted and knotted and filled with giant trees of chestnut, palm, coconut (A coconut tree? In France? Why did nobody ever tell me these things?), ivy and piles of dead leaves several feet deep, covering everything.

In a state of shock I slumped onto the ground in the driveway before the metal gate, resting my head against the suitcase. I hoped that any moment a car would turn up the driveway and it would be Gillian K.—*quelle coincidence!*

My eyes sore and gritty, my flesh pale, I rose to my feet and began to trudge back toward the police station and the center of town. In one last attempt, when I passed the gate to the front door, I tried to push it open and it swung inside with a creak of rusty iron.

I was inside the secret garden at last, probably only to be arrested for trespassing, but when I approached the huge, green, wooden front door and knocked there was not even a hollow sound—only an empty knock like someone tapping at the door to Windsor Castle.

I saw in the rapidly dimming light a gold plate on the door that bore the legend, in small letters, MADAME OLITSKY. My God, I did not even have the right house! I crept to the other side of the mansion, still lugging my suitcase, where I found a flight of stairs. I climbed up these to the side door, still hoping to find who knew what, and tacked on the door I found a small white card.

I snatched at it eagerly, hoping to find a note possibly addressed to me. Engraved on one side was the name Gillian K. At least it was the right house. On the other side of the card, scrawled in black ink, was a message: "For Information go to the Auberge au Pont Roman." Who could that have been meant for if not for me? If it had been meant for visitors or tradespeople in the area, why, it would have been written in French, *n'est-ce pas?*

The blobs of rain quickly made her beloved handwriting smear. My hands were stained and inky. But my load was now considerably lightened. I was not alone. I trudged up the road to the Auberge au Pont Roman, paying no attention to the fact that the house looked as though it had been deserted for many months. Perhaps Miss K. was at the *auberge* right now, eating dinner, or whatever it was one did at an *auberge,* and had left the note not knowing specifically when I would arrive, but wanting to make sure I could find her.

The rain fell, the lights of the little medieval town came on, it grew colder.

I threw my sheepskin coat on—a gift from my dad on my birthday several years ago, before he said no more gifts would be forthcoming, as this was part of my continuous "taking"—and changed my sunglasses for a regular pair. Though I felt more attractive in the sunglasses, at this point I felt it was more important to be able to recognize her. At the top of the road I found a sign—I dimly remembered seeing it on the way down—for the *auberge* and I turned right, more jauntily now, on my way to the Inn at the Roman Bridge.

In the gravel parking lot I spotted several elegant looking cars—a Jaguar, a Mercedes—no doubt Gillian K. and a group of her friends. I hoped I didn't look too beat up and disheveled from my day's travels. I pushed open the iron door, set in an old stone ruin of a building. Inside the restaurant the stone walls were draped with red velvet curtains and the room was lit by candles and oil lamps.

Very elegant, I thought to myself, trying to wipe some of the grit off my face. A woman, plump and thirtyish, appeared at the entranceway where I was standing, the door still open behind me. She had a small aggravated look on her face at the sight of me, the American derelict. I showed her the note I had found at Gillian's château and asked if she were here.

"Ah, yes," the woman said, and for a moment my heart jumped. Perhaps, I thought, all was not lost. But I looked again at her face, round and pielike. "I am taking care of her house," she said. "I am receiving her letters while she is gone. You are Earl? I have got your telegram but did not know with what to do. You didn't put your return on it."

She inspected me curiously, and I felt her come to the conclusion that I was nothing much. "I put my return address on it," I said.

"No, you didn't."

"Yes, I did."

"No. It is at Gillian's house or I would show you."

"Well, couldn't you have forwarded it?"

"I have no way to reach her." She had a bemused and superior look on her face. "As she is on a small boat, I have no way to send her things."

"Well, when is she supposed to be back?"

"There is a hurricane. There is a delay in filming. She should be back any day now. Weeks ago." Briefly she looked worried. "She is expecting you? Perhaps you will stay here for a few days and she will return."

"I don't know. When is she going to come back?"

"Maybe tomorrow."

"Yeah," I said, "but when she gets back she'll be tired. She's not going to want to have any guests." The woman did not answer. What a fool I had been. I was no longer sure I had put my return address on the telegram. "Is there a hotel in town?"

"This is a hotel."

The place looked expensive to me. "Another hotel," I said. "Something . . . something cheaper." Besides, I didn't feel like spending time being observed by Gillian's cleaning personnel.

"There is another hotel here, but it is not more cheaper, I do not think."

"I don't care. Just tell me how to get there." How could this be happening to me? "You will be a success," my mother had told me. "You can succeed in whatever you set your mind to." I should have listened to my father, who had said just the opposite. My whole life was now slithering between my fingers as I stood shivering and gaping here in the south of France. Yes, I said silently to the maid of Madame K., or whatever she was. Her superiority belied the fact that she claimed to be merely a caretaker. The day would come when *I* would dine at one of those tables myself! Then she would be sorry!

The other hotel turned out to be a mile and a half back down the road from which I had just come.

The interior was empty of furniture and lacked any of the cozy antiquity of the Auberge au Pont Roman, and smelled of a strong disinfectant and mothballs. The tiny lobby was decorated with peeling mock-velvet wallpaper, mildew style, and housed under a small glass counter were some wonderful *souvenirs de X.*—old cigars, old candy bars, maps of the ancient, walled medieval city, and some glass ashtrays with a picture of the Eiffel Tower. Behind the desk dozed an old man resembling pictures I had seen of Samuel Beckett, a beaked nose and birdlike eyes which popped open when I put my suitcase down, and then quickly slid shut again.

"*Je . . .*" What the hell came next? "*Je voudrais un . . .*"

The birdy eyes opened again and looked at me with distaste.

"*Je voudrais un . . . un . .* um." The guy must know what the hell I wanted. Couldn't he help me out? What did he possibly think I would come in here moaning about? "*Je voudrais un salle à coucher.* That's it! A bedroom! A *salle à coucher!*"

"*Quoi?*"

"Oh, you know what I mean! *Pour la nuit,* you old bat!"

"*Une chambre? Vous voulez une chambre pour une personne?*"

"Yeah, yeah, *oui.*"

This seemed to ease him a bit. "*Pour la nuit?*" What did he think, I was just in there for a quick nap or something? A madman recently escaped from a lunatic asylum and just out for a little rest stop before continuing on my way? "*Vous voulez une chambre avec bain?*" He added some other mumbo jumbo too quick for me to catch. "No, *une chambre sans bain. Un bain n'est pas necessaire.*" Not bad, I congratulated myself, not bad at all.

He actually understood me, for he took me to a room without a bath—I dreaded to think what the whole thing was going to cost me even for a *bain*less room—and at the door an entire conversation transpired in which I took him to mean that checkout time was at eleven, I could have breakfast (I nodded eagerly), and several other valuable bits of information which I did not quite catch but which bore that vague ring of the college French lesson entitled "The Annual Vacation," or something like that.

More and more my life was taking on the kind of slapstick quality that my father had so jeered at in my mother's own life. The things that happened to me, that had happened to my mother, were a kind of watered-down version of a Charlie Chaplin or Buster Keaton film. "At first he thought I was so cute," my mother once said, speaking about my father, "then he started to make fun of me . . ." Well, my father would certainly get a kick out of me now.

The Hôtel du Nord was sleazy and tiny, and was jammed up on the main street of the town, directly across from a café I had passed earlier and debated whether to enter, to try to coax some food. However, when I passed the door, the entire group sitting inside, consisting of some thirty or forty rugged men dressed in what appeared to be military garb and berets, ceased speaking to turn and stare at me. I realized I would be better off not going in.

I was exhausted, though it couldn't have been past eight o'clock. I was most likely going to die without food. I managed to get myself back downstairs—once again I assured Monsieur Rousseau, dozing at the desk, that I would indeed want breakfast, though he didn't seem to have the slightest idea what I was talking about. I stopped at the only store I found open, something set in the wall of an old stone passageway, where I purchased two of the few items in the store, a delicious looking, terribly expensive ball of creamy cheese, and a box of crackers. The only other food was some slabs of raw meat inside a refrigerator, and I was not yet that hungry. The store was nothing like the *boulangeries* or *pâtisseries* I had been assured of in college French. What a lie it had all been. I could not think of what I should do next.

In my room, the armoire, massively carved, reeking of moth-balls and touching the ceiling, was blocking half the window, which made it impossible to open it and get some air. The bed and the armoire were so huge as to take up the entire room, along with the hissing gold radiator. Occasionally chunks of plaster dropped from the ceiling, like bird dung. The bed tilted violently to one side, a fact I didn't notice until I was half asleep. All night I fought to stay in it, sweating profusely in the airless room. My stomach groaned and shrieked. The ball of cheese, so delicious in appearance, was not at all what I had expected. Instead it was like a great, round piece of dry chalk, with green flecks of decay. The crackers were too crumbly to force down my throat, and I hadn't bought anything to drink.

And what was that smell?

A banana I had at the last minute stuck into my suitcase, thinking only that morning of the possible hungers to come, had ripened and swelled in the heat. I took it out of my bag. It was bulging and bursting its yellow casing like a limb of some battlefield corpse. My God, I thought, I couldn't possibly eat it, starved as I was. I imagined a lengthy conversation between myself and the hotelier upon my descent the following morning.

He: *Alors, qu'est-ce que c'est que ça?* (sniff, sniff—the flexible French tusk-nose quivering at the *odeur de banane*)

Me: *Quoi?*

He: *Qu'est-ce que c'est que cette odeur formidable?*

Me: *Ah, bien sûr. Hein! Je comprends maintenant. Alors, c'est une banane plus âgé.*

He: *Mais oui! Zut alors! Pffft! Hein!*

There was nothing to do with the banana but shove it back into my suitcase. If I ever got back to London it would be the world's most widely traveled fruit. The toilet down the hall was a small piss-hole in the floor, the light a bare bulb swinging overhead. The floor slanted. How could these French ever take a crap? What did they do, stand over it and aim? A maniac population. There was a button down the hall to turn the light on, but it did not stay on long enough for me to find my way back to my room.

In the morning I trotted downstairs, wobbling and tilting from my involuntary fast. Breakfast in the dining room, an additional seven francs, was served until ten o'clock. It was glumly flung at me by a woman I assumed to be the hotelier's wife, a dour, frizzled-looking woman in some sort of ancient widow's or crone's garb. It consisted of some small, stale hunks of French bread and jelly. I wondered what my father was getting to eat in his prison, a prison which, he had written me in his letters, was very nearly the equivalent of a luxury hotel. I was dying of thirst which the lukewarm *café* and the lukewarm *au lait* did nothing to assuage.

I rapidly wolfed down the few hunks of bread. The dining room was empty except for a pinkish man in a far corner of the room who had been propped into a chair like a gigantic strawberry. He read a newspaper and hawked and coughed nearly continuously. A small girl appeared in the doorway and looked at the two of us with the greatest of curiosity.

I didn't have enough francs left to pay my bill and had to get the manager to take a traveler's check in English pounds, a difficult procedure and one that left me dripping with perspiration. I was almost positive I was being rooked, since (I may have forgotten to mention—must I recapitulate *all* my faults? Yes, Dad, very well then) I am chronically incapable of adding up even the simplest of numbers and so had to stare helplessly at the hotelier's elaborate figuring on a piece of yellow paper.

The transaction involved a lengthy wait while the hotelier's wife went to the bank to find out the daily currency exchange, but at least when it was complete I had enough francs given back to me to pay for my two bus fares back to the airport.

For this was indeed where I had decided I should go. I didn't have enough money to stay another night in a hotel, and there was no guarantee Gillian was going to be returning today or even tomorrow. I managed to inform the hotelier that I was leaving my suitcase at the desk until I left town; I headed up the street to where the bus had deposited me the day before, to find out when it would leave town to go back to Nimes. The bus—there was only one—was scheduled to leave at four that afternoon, giving me plenty of time to tour as much of the surrounding five feet of French countryside as I could possibly want to see, and also perhaps giving Gillian K. time to return from her task of film consultant and screenwriter in the Aegean.

I returned to the *auberge*, where the same plump blonde, emerging from the kitchen, looked at me with mistrust and distaste, wisps of hair falling wetly from her chignon. "Any chance she's back yet?" I said humbly. My God, it was just fabulous to be able to speak English!

"No, I don't think so," she said, wiping her hands on her huge white apron (she was a Cordon Bleu cook, I was later to find out). "What will you do?"

"I think I'll go back to London."

"You can stay here, you know. Gillian should be back any day. She was supposed to be back home time ago. You know Gillian?" she asked suspiciously.

"I'm a friend of hers, yeah," I said.

She looked nervous. "There is a chance, in that case, that she will back today or tomorrow."

I was tempted to stay, but a wave of panic overtook me. After all, I really did not feel all that welcome. "No, I think I'll take the bus to the airport this afternoon."

"Look," she said to me suddenly, as if smitten now with guilt or fearful there would be repercussions on Gillian's return (don't worry about a thing, I wanted to tell her, the dame doesn't even know me, fat lot she's going to care that I made this trip for nothing), "I will give you the number here at the *auberge*, and when you reach Nimes this afternoon, why don't you call me. It may be possible she will return this very day, and then I will tell you and you can come back . . ."

"Okay," I said. Perhaps there was some hope, after all.

I spent the rest of the day until the bus came wandering the streets, past the peculiar fields of the antlerish plants, up the ancient, Roman river to a green, still pool filled with fetid algae. In the sun it was surprisingly warm, the light of early winter making the brown earth edible looking.

Still, why would any rational English- or American-speaking person choose to live here? The locals were all out of their minds, language barrier or not. Obviously Gillian K. herself must also be a demented fool.

In Nimes I figured out how to use the telephones and called the *auberge*. But Madame had not yet returned. Good, I thought, I hope she goes down with the ship. *Quelle* hostess! I was overcome with embarrassment at the thought of what a jerk Gillian would think I was for shlepping down there.

At the little Nimes airport I boarded the plane with no fear now in my heart, only an anxious desire to turn again, Dick Whittington, and become thrice lord mayor of London.

At the airport in Paris I purchased two coiled and turdlike prepackaged cakes, something familiar at last, and devoured them frantically along with a double Scotch, which cost me the last of my francs. And so on the night of December eighteenth I found myself in the Air France terminal, pleading with the attendant to put me on the next available shuttle flight back to London. To my disgust, though I threw a minor temper tantrum, I was informed that I would be put on standby, and if there were any extra seats on the nine o'clock flight I would, perhaps, be allowed to leave on it.

If I couldn't get a flight back I really didn't know what I was going to do. Without cash, unable to speak French, I doubted I would be able to find my way to a hotel, let alone pay to stay in one. I looked around the waiting room of the airport, somehow expecting to find an answer. It was crowded with an odd assortment of people—a man in a blond mink coat, a troupe of Oriental women wearing jackets painted with dragons. All of the women were chewing huge wads of pink bubble gum. Briefly I forgot my own filthy garb, the Elvis Presley hairdo my hair had solidified into, my graying shirt, once white but now smeared with accidental banana. I had never seen such a horrific group of people. All I could do was stare and glare at them. I noted two girls, each well over six feet tall, with raspberry-colored, electrocuted hair. One was particularly striking, with milky chocolate skin and blue lips. Blue lips, I thought, how charming. More hallucinations due to my half-starved state.

Searching for a seat in the crowded waiting room, I passed a newsstand, with a series of newspapers and magazines printed with the words PRÊT-À-PORTER. That, at least, I could read, and I determined that all these grotesques and beauties were returning from the French fashion show. How my father would have enjoyed this, I thought, looking around me.

To my relief I was allowed to board a plane at nine o'clock, after the passengers with reservations had boarded. The only seat I could find was the aisle seat next to the two stunning models with the raspberry hair. I was seated next to the more beautiful of the two. "Hi there," I said, in what I prayed was a charming and sexy voice, but she did not respond, only studied the plastic card that located the emergency exits.

Well, she was not friendly. So what, I thought to myself, trying to scrape some of the dried banana off the front of my shirt. I was not the sort of person to give up so easily, after all.

The plane lifted off the ground and the lights of Paris spinkled and winkled in the dark below. I gave another friendly smile to my seat companion. She licked her blue lips and took a magazine and a bottle of blue nail polish out of her valise. "Didja have a nice weekend?" I said, only to be rudely greeted once again by silence. But why, I thought, should I give up now? I, Earl Przepasniak, living my vagabond life of unemployment, recent returnee from a brief jaunt to the south of France where I had wangled an invitation to visit a famous playwright (so what if she had turned out to be not at home), was not a "nobody" after all. No, I was a force to be reckoned with and not a person to be ignored by some beautiful and strange Watusi on an airplane from Paris to London. "You will speak to me!" I muttered, Svengali-like, under my breath. And this feeling was intensified when I was served a double Scotch on the rocks by the stewardess and I took the first sip. "Let me buy you a drink," I said loudly and insistently to Miss Blueberry Lips of the World, who sat leafing through her magazine and trying to pretend that I was not there. But above international waters I refused to be humiliated.

She was dressed, or rather covered, by a crinkly pink skin-like blouse and a pair of painfully tight jeans. As I looked over her shoulder at the magazine, it appeared to be pictures of herself she was looking at, herself dressed in a stringy black bikini and hopping about some tropical beach, rubbing greasy tanning oil on herself. "What'll it be?" I said to her, as the stewardess stood impatiently in the aisle. "What would you like to drink?"

In retrospect, the way I see my desperation to make some contact at the time is like this: I took a number of anthro courses in college: it seems primitive tribes always have rites of "coming of age" when a boy is circumcised, tattooed, stung by bees, left alone on a mountain, or whatever curious rite his tribe practices, and in that way he is guaranteed his manhood. But what have we in

America? Well, bar mitzvah, of course, but my father didn't believe in such "primitive crap." How was I to be sure of what I was? My manhood was at stake, even my existence. Therefore I had to make up my own rites by which I would prove to myself that I was at least as much a man as my father, that Priapus was alive and well even in the twentieth century, and if twentieth-century rites meant making up your own rites, well, mine would surely be as daring and original as the most primitive and advanced of societies.

And the ensuing adventures, which I relate with a slight sense of shame, were not at all pointless, as they may seem, nor even selfish, egocentric and self-aggrandizing, as some well-meaning people have observed. No, these are a young man's experiences in the world of sense and sensuousness that are, in their way, sacred and religious rituals of the highest order, a "coming of age" by an American in England, food for thought for anthropologists in every land and clime, opening the publishing doors for many volumes of photographs, footnotes, explications, bibliographies and jobs for masses of young would-be sociologists and paleontologists.

"What?" she said. She finally stopped studying herself long enough to look up. A weak smile crossed her lips. "Were you speaking to me?"

Victory was mine, my father informed me then. "Why, you're an American!" I said. There was more relief in my voice than even I was prepared for. All those days abandoned in a foreign country, unable to speak the language, and before that my many months in England, where the residents spoke an English difficult to understand, had apparently taken their toll. I brushed a few flakes of the dried banana from my shirt. "I'm glad to run into another American abroad," I said seriously, "Thank God, I won't need to play any games."

"Nice to meet you. I'm a little tired right now, though. I've been bombed out of my mind for the past—"

"That's okay," I said, "mind if I see the magazine?" And taking the magazine from her I leafed through it, proceeding to spout off some of the jargon so relentlessly indoctrinated into me by Maggie in her early days of longing to be an actress. Within a relatively short time I had succeeded in ingratiating myself completely with the model Emma Scales.

She had been brought up on an Army base in Stuttgart, Germany, and she was half black, half white, and one quarter American Indian. It was at this point I realized she was stoned out of her mind. In fact, the only thing that kept her and her friend in the other seat from falling down completely was that they were held up by their seat belts. I began to tell her my life story when she gave a sudden slump against me and I had to grab her with one hand. "What's your name?" she slushed out, looking up from where she had fallen against my chest with a somewhat surprised smile. Her eyes, the eyes of a Queen Nefertiti, very long and slanted, were glazed and filthy with old layers of mascara and kohl.

"Earl," I said, continuing with my tale.

"Earl what?" she said. But it sounded more like "Eaarrl, whut?" Her speech, though not black, very often lapsed into a parody of black or Southern speech, though that may perhaps have only been due to the drugs she was on, I couldn't really tell.

"Earl Przepasniak," I said.

"Say whut?"

"You heard me," I said. I put one finger under her chin and raised it up in a gesture not only sophisticated but sexy. Though inexperienced, I had the mannerisms down pat.

"Earl Przepasniak?" Suddenly she looked more interested. "Say, are you Jewish?"

"What do you want to know for?" I said.

"Well, it's like this," she said. "I have always been interested in the Jewish people."

"What are you, are you kidding?" I said. "You know how sick I am of that question? I mean, you don't go around asking people whether they're black, whether they're Catholic."

"Yeah, but the Jewish people are interested in books, in learning. You know, they're different."

"Well, I'm afraid to say that a question like that very definitely shows poor taste, Emma."

"Oh. I guess I didn't know," she said humbly.

"That's okay," I said. "But let me tell you something, since you asked. My grandmother was strictly from Hungary."

"Oh. Really?" Emma was paying no attention to anything that I said. Nor was I, in my excitement. It was then that I realized there was a long way to go, that a person like Emma was going to need a great deal of reeducation, a fact which I hoped I made perfectly obvious to her.

As it turned out, though, before we were fifteen minutes into the air, we were old friends. What I learned about her was this: she was twenty-eight years old and had been modeling for ten years, ever since winning a local beauty pageant in Detroit, where she moved with her mother from Stuttgart when her parents were divorced. Present at that show had been one of the owners of a New York modeling agency on the hunt for black girls to use as models, since at that time, in the late sixties, black models were just coming into demand in the fashion industry. And so Emma had left her mother and had gone off to New York.

"I see," I said. "Do you mind if I touch your hair? Why did they dye it that hideous color?"

"Oh, it is an awful color, isn't it?" she said. "It was supposed to go with my outfits, supposed to match. Everything I wore was that color." Her hair was done in soft waves of palest raspberry, like some kind of movie star out of the nineteen thirties, a dipped-below-one-eye sort of thing. She was like a strange Egyptian from the past, with her flat and flaring nose, her bridgeless profile. I barely cared that she giggled constantly and seemed not to have an IQ at all, though I did point this out to her briefly. "You should stop giggling so much," I said. "It's unbecoming. Do really top models giggle so much? I thought they were supposed to be sophisticated."

By now we were both drunk and I was exhausted. Against my will I began to tell her about my travels. "I guess you've heard of Gillian K., the famous playwright," I said. "Just got back from a little visit to her place in the south of France." I could tell that Emma was impressed, very impressed. After she ordered us both another round of drinks (which, thank God, she paid for, since I had only a minuscule amount of money left, even in traveler's checks), she proceeded to tell me how cute she thought I was and how she had always liked very young guys, that I sort of looked like Michael Caine, though I would have thought she'd say Dustin Hoffman. "You don't know what it's like most of the time in the fashion industry," she said. "It's like one long weekend after the next. Sometimes I think I'm going to go out of my mind. And then there's this horrible guy I was with in Paris—how I would love to get even with him! He's on the plane someplace, the bastard. Hey, I know what! Earl . . ." (and she licked her blueberry-colored lips while I watched with fascination), "would you do something for me?"

"That depends what it is," I said.

"Well, I'll tell you then. Why don't you just go to the toilet and I'll come a few minutes later and knock on the door."

"Why, is something the matter. Oh, you want me to get up so you can go to the bathroom?"

"That wasn't exactly what I was thinking of." And my father chimed in, "Jerk!" Emma put her hand on my crotch as I cringed, startled, and looked uneasily down the aisle. "I'll show you why when we get there. You just go and wait for me."

"My God," I said, and I gulped. "Really? Really? You've got to be kidding."

"Isn't he cute?" Emma turned and spoke to her friend in the seat beside the window. She was another beautiful giantess, though not black, and not as tall as Emma. At first I thought that this buddy was catatonic, since all she had done since I had seen her was to nod and drool in her seat, but at that point she said, "Yeah, sure," in the strongest, most garbled Cockney I had ever heard. Then she took another sip of what was her third or fourth drink since take-off, a horrible slurpy concoction she ordered from the stewardess and added to from a bottle in her bag.

I climbed out of my seat and scuttled off to the toilet.

In my rush I collided violently with the stewardess. "*Excusez-moi,*" I said, clutching her on the shoulders. For some reason I tried to physically lift her to one side, desperate to get around her and get to the bathroom before Emma changed her mind and decided not to follow me. She looked at me coldly. My voice had momentarily risen an octave, returning to preadolescent shrillness; my hands were icy with sweat. I staggered past her and flung myself into the toilet, locking the door behind me, my fantasy—my dad's fantasy—about to be fulfilled. I didn't even dare to think what kind of perversions Emma had planned in such a limited space, nor did I wonder how a six-foot-tall female and a five-foot-six male would manage to cram themselves into a space no bigger than the average-sized telephone booth.

I was trembling with excitement and shortly became plagued with doubts. What if I had misunderstood her? I was so worried that when her knock came on the door I didn't try to open it but went on inspecting myself in the mirror. How would anyone ever be able to love me, Earl P., I wondered. In the fluorescent light my little face was worried and greenish. I tried to wash myself quickly in the barely dripping, turgid water of the sink. "Let me in!" she hissed from the other side of the door.

She was there. So I mused: was I to lose my virginity in the toilet of a 747? But then, what was virginity anyway? Possibly it only mattered if one was a woman. And I would have pursued these thoughts and others, but the heavy-handed thump on the door continued.

"What?" I said. "Huh? Oh right, right."

I let her in just as the plane entered a period of turbulence.

And my father appeared to me, as if in a dream. "Earl," he said, "Earl, you may be trying to live out my fantasies. You may be trying to win my approval. But look at you. You're making a mess of the entire thing. It's embarrassing. Do you think I would behave thus? Where is your coolth?"

Before I could answer, before I could even make a stabbing attempt at defending myself, all six feet of her came smashing into the tiny room, knocking me to the toilet, where I sat down heavily. "Whoops," I said, "Heh-heh. I'll just get up now."

I tried to stand. Once again the same thing occurred—a weak and maudlin collapse onto the floor. The air was very dry and stale, there in the toilet, and the lights gave everything a greenish hue. I was reminded of how once as a kid I had gotten one of those forty-nine-cent turtles from Woolworth's, dull green with red spots on either side of the neck. It climbed out of its bowl and disappeared. Though my father was enraged that I had not put the lid back on the terrarium, though I searched for hours, the turtle was gone. It was not until months later I discovered it, mummified and desiccated, behind the toilet. "What are you doing on the floor?" Emma said. Each time I struggled to stand, holding onto the soap dispenser or clutching the toilet paper, the plane dropped through another air pocket, flinging me down again and trapping part of Emma under me.

"Get off me, you're hurting me!" she said.

"Oh, I'm sorry," I said. "Look, if you could maybe move your left leg I might be able to get up." The smell of the chemical toilet, combined with a ghastly pink soapy disinfectant smell, and the cigarette Emma insisted on smoking, as well as the great woozy dives the plane kept taking and the many drinks I suddenly remembered I had had, not only made me feel nauseated but also made me feel uninterested, at present, in having any sex, no matter how exotic. When a sign suddenly flashed on that said RETURN TO YOUR SEAT, I said in an extremely weak voice, "Maybe we better."

"What?" Emma said from her position on the floor, unable to see the message above.

"I think I might be going to be sick," I said. "Look, maybe we should go back to our seats."

"Earl," she said drunkenly, "don't you want to feel good? I can make you feel so good."

"Yeah, sure, but the sign says—"

"Oh, screw the sign." She grabbed my hand and shoved it down her expensive French jeans, which were so tight my hand jammed and would not fit.

What was I doing with this insane girl anyway, this oversexed monster—sexual fantasies or not, she most certainly wasn't mentally all there. And what kind of diseases would I be likely to get in a bathroom? Several times in her eagerness she nearly thrust me into the steaming vat of the blue chemical toilet. But my father (I am indebted to you forever once again, though I never would have admitted it to your face), disgusted at viewing his progeny trapped in such a mess, stepped in to rescue me. "Listen," I found myself saying, "we're making a lot of noise in here and the stewardess is probably going to come bursting in at any minute. Let's just go back to our seats and maybe we can finish up later on."

"Oh, all right," she said sulkily. I breathed a sigh of relief. All right, Dad, I said to myself, so I was not true adventurer material. But I could learn, I *would* learn.

"It's not that I don't want to do anything with you. It's just that I don't feel that that was the best place for it. As soon as we get back to London . . ." I promised. Though how and where anything was to be accomplished in London was going to have to be left up to Emma herself. I had no car to take us anywhere, and even if I had, I had no place to go other than the dingy bed-sitting room where I kept my belongings.

The little jaunt to the toilet seemed to wake Emma up somewhat, and she began to ask me a few questions about myself. "Why are you in London, Earl?" she said.

"Oh, I don't know. I just felt like it," I said. "My mother died recently and . . ." I managed to imply I had just come into an inheritance that enabled me to roam at will.

Then I decided it was no use going on with this game, pretending all kinds of experience I didn't have—Emma was beginning to catch on a bit and it wouldn't take her long to catch on to the rest of it. She seemed a goodhearted enough giantess in her way, big enough to take me under her condor wing. Throwing caution under the seat, I confessed to my ignorance. "Emma," I said, "that little jaunt to the toilet opened up vistas undreamed of heretofore. My ignorance cannot be allowed to continue. All must start somewhere. Can you imagine what it is for me, five-foot-six inches, to live up to a six-foot-tall Dad whose sexual prowess is mythical in the northwestern corner of a certain New England state? Such an unresolved Oedipal complex could prevent my ever coming into my manhood, the natural right of an American boy, one whose whole life may either open or shut at this crucial moment."

How humiliating it was for me, Earl P., to have to admit such frailty. But when I looked at Emma to see what her response was, her mouth was open and she was snoring in a rather pleasing, musical way in the key of C. Well, I fretted, had she heard any of this impassioned pleading?

As it turned out, I did not have to worry about a thing. I simply attached myself to her entourage, following them out to the garage where Emma's car was parked, and squeezed my way in among the various hairdressers and model friends of hers. No one spoke on the ride into London, and when she dropped the group off on some dark street, Emma was perhaps surprised to turn around and find me sitting there in the back. "Sheesh!" she said.

"Well, hi there," I said, "What about a bite to eat?"

Stunned—possibly still drunk—she drove in continued silence. Then briefly she seemed to wake up. "What the hell," she said. She pulled the little Alfa Romeo four-door over to the side of the road. "Get in the front," she said, unlocking the door on the passenger side. "I was just a little surprised to see you were still here."

Momentarily I did not know what to say and kicked slightly at the leather base of the seat. "But you told me . . ." I said. "In the bathroom, you said we'd finish later . . ."

"I don't know what the hell you're talking about," she said.

"Anyway, I'm starving. I could use a bite to eat. I tell you what. I'll take you to a delicatessen, sugar. It's the only American deli in London."

For a short time I was able to quell my sexual fantasies and desire and my anger over Emma's schizophrenic behavior and instead began to think about food. I had hardly eaten in several days, and already, simply on hearing the word deli, I was watery with the thought of devouring bagels and cream cheese, hot pastrami slathered with cole slaw and mustard and some potato salad. "And maybe a few real dill pickles on the side," I mumbled out loud. "And then maybe you for dessert." I was not unconscious of my statement. I only wanted to make certain Emma knew I had not forgotten my promise made in the toilet in the air. Often a woman like Emma, once beautiful, now older, would be very hurt if she felt her sexual advances to have been rejected—this information coming, once again, from the mouth of the oracle, my dad.

It turned out that the delicatessen was closed, and instead we went to a place called "The Great American Disaster." It was a hamburger joint, and though such a thing was a rarity in this country, the tables were inches deep in hamburger grease. Though it was chilly out, the windows buzzed, American-style, with flies. But believe me, I was not ungrateful.

"Your treat?" I asked Emma. She nodded, lighting a cigarette.

I ordered a triple hamburger plate with chili and bacon strips, as well as an order of cole slaw and French fries and three cans of a familiar brand of American beer. Never had anything looked more enticing, more adorable, than those three hamburgers as they sat there on their plate between puffy buns crowned with delicate sesame seeds and crying out for ketchup. "God, these are cute," I said.

"Thanks," Emma said, smiling for the first time since she had gotten out of the car. See, my dad said, how vain women get to be? See how quick they are to interpret everything to suit their own needs. But I couldn't bring myself to point this out to her. In my haste and general eagerness I poured half a bottle of ketchup onto the hamburger and French fries.

"Yikes, you like ketchup," Emma said, and though at first I started to scowl, I ended by grinning at her dopily (an older woman! An older woman was buying me a meal in London! Who cared if it was just a hamburger? Here I was, me, Earl Przepasniak, almost a real gigolo, and this my father would have longed to be) and giving her a little affectionate kick under the table.

"Sure!" I said, since she had put me on the defensive. "You know how it is. You start missing things about the U. S., just little things you didn't ever really think mattered before. Like ketchup, for example." And then in my embarrassment I was forced to eat the whole thing as if I had really intended to pour that much ketchup on, only it was a vinegary English ketchup, raw and bitter with hardly any tomato taste to it at all.

Nor were the limp and greasy French fries swimming in the watery blood what I had been hoping for.

Still, I didn't like to complain. I had come a long way from the previous day, alone in my hotel room with nothing to eat but an overripe banana, with an invitation to a house where nobody was home. Now, only forty-eight hours later, I was a pampered pet, at the mercy of this oversexed and beautiful creature.

As luck would have it, her generous invitation to supper extended into an invitation to come home with her. And Emma was as demanding and as insecure as I suspected. After that first night she wouldn't let me go. I had to stay in her apartment every day, taking numerous baths while she went out to be shot for an assortment of magazines.

Although Emma had all the mental capacities of a twelve-year-old, I was so in awe of her at first that I had barely even noticed this. Her vocabulary consisted totally of either one-syllable words, or those she mispronounced. Naturally, since she was paying for my board and keep, I hesitated to point these flaws out to her. And besides, there was a lot to appreciate about her. How I loved her cocoa-colored skin, how I loved to uncurl her hand like a clenched shell and see the skin of her palm so pink against the brown of her wrist.

And I was certainly learning a number of things I would not have thought possible a few months before. I was coming of age, not with a whimper, but with a bang. Not that Emma and I had what you might call an extraordinary sexual relationship. But she had a collection of books and pictures left in boxes under her bed by one Larry Flowers (more about him later) that could have been sold for an astounding price at public auction. Pornography from every land, from primitive tribes in the African veldt to unusual practices among the inhabitants of New York City, pictures that went back before the Christian era—the education I was getting would have cost at least $40,000 at a good college these days, and, as we know, with inflation, by next week it could be twice that.

So, I thought, when I get back and Dad gets out of jail, we'll at least have something to communicate about! Because he was always complaining that I never "communicated" with him, I wasn't "open" with him. Of course, I could have answered, he either screamed at me that I was spending too much money, or whatever I said was an example of my "paranoia," and the wrong "attitude." Or if he didn't respond at all, it was usually because he was wondering how many more miles he would get out of his tires, something like that.

But I knew I had hit upon it now. All my suffering and humiliation was beginning to pay off. Dad would be astounded by my amazing knowledge. And interested! Finally, a fantastic epiphany. I was beginning to realize Dad and I had a lot in common as far as interest went!

Every night, as soon as I began to make love to her, the phone would ring. Then she would be on the phone for the next three hours, by which time I had usually fallen asleep. But who cared in the end, I used to say to myself, who really cared—though she insisted I continue to pay the rent on my bed-sitting room, and leave most of my belongings there—as long as she did not kick me out and I did not have to live on my former diet of stale McVittie's Digestive Biscuits and sticky Tiptree strawberry jam.

But very quickly her habits became a drain on my nerves. She was obsessed with her looks and was constantly pushing me away from the mirror so she could look at herself in it. She had a terrible fear of losing all her hair. Complaining about a hairdresser who had spent ten hours the day before plucking and prying at her hair, she said to me one evening, "Oh Earl I think I'm losing my hair. I must be completely bald. He pulled out so much from my head. That sadistic bastard. He told me I was built like an overripe tomato. Do you think it's true?"

"Don't look at me for an answer," I said. "Whatever I told you would probably be wrong." Which was the way it was with Emma Scales, and in fact pretty much with all women: no support would ever be enough.

She snarled at me and said I had not done a very good job cleaning out the toilet. "A really lovely man I know came into the agency this morning and gave me the loveliest bunch of chrysantiniums, Earl. Are you jealous?"

"Chrysantiniums—that's pretty good!" I said, laughing. I thought she was saying chrysanthemums like that simply for my amusement, to keep me entertained, the way my mother had, before her death, always called dinner "din-din."

"No," she said, "it was a bunch of chrysantiniums."

"No, Emma, you're mispronouncing it."

"No, I'm not." This kind of argument could go on for hours, and since Emma didn't own a dictionary there was no point in my giving in. But always she was so stubborn and dense she refused to believe me and would generally end by slapping me around, an unfair tactic, I thought, since she was so much bigger than I and knew perfectly well I would never hit back on a girl.

At first, fool that I was, I used to think it was pleasant (but oh how quickly did her overly aggressive practices wear thin) to have her hand constantly thrusting itself down my pants, to have her forcing me onto the bed. It was not my fault I was not strong enough to stand up for myself once I realized how immoral her usage of me was. I doubt that to her I was even a real person. But I was not strong, as I have said. I hated to feel my weak upper arms, thin and girlish, especially now that I had gained weight in the belly region, but what was the use in my exerting myself, was my rationalization.

I will admit that it was pretty pleasant to be driven everywhere, taken out to restaurants, fed expensive food and dressed in clothes she picked up from friends in the rag trade. I had to confess to her that I was a little low on cash at the moment. "Problems with Mom's will," I lied. "One of those things that may take years to be straightened out, unfortunately."

"It's so nice to be going with someone who's not in the fashion industry," she told me one evening when she was in a comparatively good mood. "You don't know sometimes how I just hate everybody in it. I mean they're all just so eye-nane."

"I believe that's pronounced inane."

———————————⟨▤⟩———————————

"I think that's rather ig-no-mini-ous of you to tell me that, considering I'm paying for what seems to be turning into a very expensive dinner. Who asked you to order that third bottle of wine?"

"If you don't want me to eat any of this wonderful dinner then I goddamn won't," I said. Constantly Emma tried to humble me, simply because she was paying for things. For all her liberation she was not very far along spiritually. "And without meaning to put you down, I think you're supposed to pronounce it ignominious."

"Oh, shut up!" she shrieked at me like a fishwife, so loudly that the waiter turned around to look at her. And I had not even said anything at all, merely made a simple suggestion. "I tell you what, Earl," she said, regaining some control of herself, "let's change the subject."

Subject! What subject? I thought. She was not even capable of a simple conversation, let alone a subject. "Okay," I said. "What do you want to talk about?"

"Well, I got a new coat—you didn't even notice. Do you like it? It's alpalca."

"Alpalca!" At this I nearly jumped up to strangle her across the table. "It's not pronounced alpalca! It's alpaca. Alpaca, you fool!" How often she deliberately pushed me beyond all human endurance. "Alpaca!"

"Ssh, would you lower your voice? How can I ever come back here with you? What difference does it make, alpalca, alpaca, it's the same thing."

Okay, I did adore Emma. I knew the extent to which she had gone to improve me, to polish up the rough edges. My father would have longed to be taught the sophistication and panache she had taught me. The give-and-take was not mutual, however. My suggestions for her improvement made no difference at all. Whenever she referred to the coat after that it was always, "Earl, honey, could you bring me my alpalca coat?" to distinguish it from the one made of monkey fur or lynx or fox. But she knew it wasn't alpalca! She knew! She was deliberately trying to antagonize me!

And of course, little me, as usual I was vulnerable and susceptible to strong women like Emma. "Marry me," I once asked her.

"Who would want to marry you, Earl, sugar? You don't even

suspect how many requests I get from men wanting to marry me."

"But not ones like me, Emma."

"You can say that again. I'll tell you what, I'll think about it, okay? I'll write it down in my date book to spend some real serious time—maybe five minutes—thinking about your proposition next week. Anyway, I've been meaning to tell you you're going to have to scram sometime soon. Larry Flowers is going to be back soon. I'll let you know when."

Who was Larry Flowers?

He was Emma's "host" and mine too, for the time being. I guess you could say he was Emma's sugar daddy, one of the last of a dying breed, for obvious reasons, when you consider the kind of women around left to support. He was a fifty-four-year-old, five-foot-four-inch Englishman turned Texan. Complete with concha belt, Stetson hat, and what appeared to be a solid gold Neiman-Marcus credit card pinned to his lapel, he had a face that looked like the one Paul Newman would have if he had been run over by a Mack truck.

He took my presence in Emma's (or rather his) apartment quite well, I thought. "W-w-w-w-would you two care to join me for dinner?" was all he said when he let himself into the apartment with his key and found the two of us, luckily clothed, lying on the floor in the living room, watching the telly.

"Why Larry, I'm just so glad to see you!" Emma trilled, jumping up and wrapping herself around him like a slithering octopus around a stout little clam. "Darling, why didn't you tell me you were coming? This here's Earl. Now I want you two boys to keep each other entertained while I go to change." She fled the room, effectively removing herself from what I feared was going to be a sticky situation.

But all Larry Flowers said was, "What did Emma say your name is? I'm very sorry, I didn't catch it." And he offered me a huge greenish cigar.

"Earl," I said. I continued to stare at the television, rather than be forced to meet his gaze. I had no desire to be thrown out of what I had come to call my own territory by this elderly stutterer, simply because he had the cash to pay for it while I did not.

"Earl what? What is your surname, i-i-i-if you don't mind my asking."

"Przepasniak."

"You're Jewish!" he said triumphantly. I should have known at once when I saw him that he would be the sort of person to find my weak spot and grab for it. How I cringed whenever I heard that word thrust at me—"Jewish." It meant (whether or not the accuser himself was Jewish), "Let's be honest with one another, you're not really one of us. You don't fit in, Earl." As if some dark, hidden secret were being revealed to the general public for the first time—B.O. or leprosy.

It was as if I had an old, smelly fish tucked away in my pants. Larry Flowers certainly did put me in my place. For the rest of the evening I was so embarrassed I could barely think of a thing to say. I just scowled out the window in an insolent way, trying to look both intelligent and mature.

Mr. Flowers was a well-known portrait painter who painted photorealistic pictures of wealthy Texans. He took his payments for each portrait in a share of an unfinished oil well. Most of the time the wells turned out to be duds, but once in a while they came through and paid for the paintings many times over. "A k-k-k-k-calculated risk," he told me at dinner, waving magnanimously his full glass of wine in my face.

He took us to a fancy Italian restaurant on Fulham Road, where spread on a long table were a number of bright red lobsters tucked into ice like so many boiled corpses, vast platters of mussels, whole split pink melons, tropical salads festooned with shrimp and squid and piles of glazed strawberries. Yes, and platters of wrinkled salami studded with peppercorns. I began to help myself from the table before we had even sat down, until I was prevented from doing so by the ever-bourgeois Emma, who kicked me severely on the ankle and pulled me along with her to the table.

The waiters and the maître d' all knew Larry and greeted him joyfully. "Ah, Larree!" the captain shrieked in some kind of phony foreign accent, knocking off Larry's cowboy hat in the process and sending Larry into paroxysms of stuttering. After studying our weird group, however—I, in my clothes which were, as usual, somewhat grimy; Emma, a raspberry-topped Watusi—the captain thrust us at an obscure table somewhere in the back. I practically had to crawl over the table to get to my seat. Larry's shock of white hair sprouted bushily from beneath his black Stetson hat, and I couldn't even hazard a guess as to what had kept him from getting a ten-gallon hat and a holster. "Isn't this w-w-wwonderful!" he said, bending forward to get a better view of Emma's breasts, and his stuttering spewed little flecks of spittle across the table. "It sure is, pardner," I said, but my sarcasm escaped him.

For some reason all I ordered were mussels in vinaigrette and a green slab of melon. The mussels, combined with the vast quantities of wine Larry kept ordering "in celebration" (though what we were celebrating I could not have said), proceeded to make me thoroughly sick. Larry was so busy talking he didn't notice my groans, however, and Emma, as usual, was busy preening and giving the eye to every man in the room except the ones she was with. Larry was whipping out photos of his ranchero in Texas, snapshot after snapshot of himself astride his "p-p-p-palomino p-p-p-pony," his short legs dangling over the pony's fat little sides. I had the feeling the man's hand was on Emma's leg beneath the table, and I would have given him a kick to let him know I knew what was going on, but then I thought to myself, why the hell should I? I'm not the jealous type, am I? And the answer I received was, I was not.

Though I felt pretty sick, I continued to eat the mussels. They seemed to be filled with hundreds of little pearls. I had to keep surreptitiously slipping the pearls out of my mouth and putting them into my napkin. I planned to give them to Emma later on. Larry was not the only one who could give gifts, I thought angrily to myself.

Shortly after Emma excused herself to go to the ladies' room, Larry excused himself as well. When they had both been gone for what seemed like too long a time I began to suspect that Emma was using the same little trick she had employed to incur my interest in the airplane in Paris. That sneak! At first I even thought of getting up to tell the maître d' what was going on right this very minute in his so-called ladies' room. I gritted the pearly mussels all alone, crunching loudly enough for the surrounding tables of diners to turn around and look at me. They reminded me of parrots bobbing for nuts, then looking around to stare at me with birdy eyes.

I poured myself several more glasses of wine while I thought about it. Emma had ordered a calamari salad, and the calamaris, some sort of squid, I suspected, lay coiled pinkly on top of the oily pieces of lettuce. I ate this, and then I turned to Larry's dinner.

He had ordered one of those great, red chilled lobsters, and it was spread thickly with a fluffy yellow mayonnaise. The whole meal was one of the most nauseating I have ever consumed. I only devoured it out of nervous desperation. Finally, when there was nothing left to eat, I made up my mind. I would go to the ladies' room and demand to be let in. I would tell Larry Flowers that he was not the first, nor would he be the last, to be entertained in such a fashion, and I would suggest that any man who would support a woman as unfaithful as Emma was a definite fool. Keeping this thought in mind I stood up, swaying somewhat drunkenly, and marched to the back of the restaurant, where my so-called friends were keeping themselves occupied.

The restaurant was very elegant. Everywhere there was antique furniture (covered with crumbs, I noted angrily) and mirrored walls and an actual living fire in the fireplace. "Excuse me," I said to a table that accidentally got in my way.

Thank God for my name, I thought to myself. Who would I be if I hadn't been named Earl? Yes, I thought regally, I might have been a Tom or a Barry or even a Duane, unable to endure my kind of life. And obviously this was my kind of life. And there were probably more thrills to come, more postcards of my adventures to be written to my father. Who else had already had, at my age, a girlfriend named Emma who invited her boyfriend (me, that is) to come into the bathroom to sit on the edge of the bathtub and talk to her while she peed? Due to a string of urinary tract infections it took her a long time to pee, and the two of us would sit in the bathroom waiting for the tinkle and pinkle of Emma's piss like little wind chimes in the breeze, until finally, sometimes as much as twenty minutes later, that bell-like stream, notes from a Trinidad steel drum, would at last hit the water in a torrential downpour.

When I arrived, some staggering minutes later, at the door marked LADIES, I began to pound on it in a fearful beat, yelling, "Let me in, you bitch! I know what's going on in there!" All over the restaurant the eaters were turning and craning to see what was going on. "None of your business!" I yelled at them. From inside the bathroom came a muffled sound, and I continued to pound, until I turned around to find, emerging from the kitchen, Larry Flowers and the maître d', carrying a screwdriver and a pliers.

"Ah, Earl," Larry said, "what have you been doing all this time? Emma seems to have locked herself in the b-b-b-bathroom, and Giorgio and I have been trying to get her out."

"Oh," I said.

Nobody would speak to me on the way home. "I don't understand, Earl," Emma said. "You were just sitting out there, eating all of our dinners, while I was locked in the bathroom?"

"Look, so I'm a jerk. I'm a fool. My God, I'm sorry. Can't you see I'm licking your seat belt, begging you for forgiveness?"

She did not deign to answer.

We stopped at an off-license, so Larry could buy Emma a bottle of bourbon, something he had promised to bring her from the States but had forgotten. "Real American bourbon!" I said enthusiastically to Emma while we waited in the car for Larry to buy it. My enthusiasm was my way of making up. "I'll certainly look forward to drinking some of that."

"You're not going to get to drink any of it Earl," Emma said shortly.

"What?" I said. "Why not? I haven't drunk that much this evening."

"Larry is going to drop you off at your bed-sitting room. I'll have your stuff sent over tomorrow or the next day." And my stomach made a little churning sound, a pit of despair. So I had been a jerk once more. I had not been paying attention to my rotten behavior.

"I can't go back there, Emma. You can't be serious. I love you! Do you have any idea of how beautiful you are? Your face reminds me of the face of an Indian water buffalo, with your limpid eyes, your silky skin. You don't know what you mean to me. You are the first woman, aside from my mother, to be kind to me at all."

"Tell it to the Marines," she said.

"What?" I said. "You think that's a funny thing to say? You think that's clever?" I was nearly crying with bitterness and rage at the unjustness of my life. "So this is how you do things, Emma! So you think you're mature and I'm not, because you are the first woman I slept with. Opening your legs and then closing them again like a scissors. Have you no feelings, no true emotions? How can you do this to me?"

It was the first time I had been back to my stinking cell since the weekend I had met Emma on the plane, and the landlady had not even bothered to clean up the now rotting piles of fruit I had phone calls but had her new temporary roommate, a balding homosexual named Bill, tell me to leave my name and number and he would have her call me later. I tried dialing at all hours of the day and night, but always there was that same weak and toadying response.

When I finally did get to meet Gillian K., it meant nothing to me. Like my father, I was now so thoroughly detached that few things had any effect on me whatsoever. The days of trying to win my father's love were at least temporarily over, and with the end of those days had come the end of trying for anything.

To get even with Emma I called up Elmira, a friend of hers, and invited her out. Elmira was not attractive and had a nose somewhat like a foghorn (I wanted to suggest to her that the *National Enquirer* was holding a competition for the longest nose and would pay handsomely, but the *National Enquirer* did not, to my dismay, exist in England), but was terrifically built: narrow hips like a boy's, with a small, perfect ass and two, *yes, count 'em, two* (I can't help myself, this is the way I think, these are the thoughts that run in the blood) globular, huge breasts that were either built up near her shoulders or were supported by a most unusual brassiere.

Yes, yes, I know, once more flashes of that other, more vicious Earl are visible. And perhaps in truth it was not to get even with Emma that I called Elmira up but because I was lonesome and knew Elmira liked me, knew she was unattached and would not leave me for some rich Texan with a gold Neiman-Marcus credit card pinned to his lapel, would not leave me for another boy. Elmira seemed to promise an escape, as my father had promised an escape to my mother, when she decided to marry him those many years ago. But, I thought, in my case it would be different. I was looking for solace and security, and Elmira was just as anxious for those things as I. "Mutual dependency," my father would put it, which suited me just fine.

I wanted to show Elmira, herself damaged and hurt by other human beings, that men could be nice people too. If anyone could prove this to her it would be me, Earl the P.

Or so I thought.

Independently wealthy, Honourable, remnant of a fading, almost extinct class, Elmira had recently opened a dress shop off

Bond Street which she never bothered going into. Almost every day she would oversleep and then decide it wasn't worth troubling with that day. She lived alone in half of a grand old two-family Georgian house near Hampstead Heath. I had met her only after weeks of asking Emma to introduce me to some of her friends.

Also, since Emma was older than I, her friends would, no doubt, be older as well. And it was true that men reached their sexual peak at about 19 years of age, women not until 35. I had already peaked, it seemed, but I was still quite a bit more active than a woman of, let's say, 25. The ideal arrangement would be between a young man of 19 and a woman of 35. Failing to find this, the next best thing for me would be to have an educational experience with almost any woman older than me and younger than 40. I had learned all this and a great deal more from Margaret Mead, and if I had met her in her heyday I'm sure we would have found much to say to one another. She was a Barnard girl herself, once, and that was perhaps one reason for our vibes being so *simpático*.

Finally, one evening a short time before we broke up, Emma picked me up after work. I, wifelike and wrinkled after a day spent soaking in the bath at Emma's apartment, meekly climbed into her little red Alfa Romeo, took out the cocaine she kept in a squeeze bottle of nasal decongestant in the glove compartment and said, rather nastily, I suppose (but I was in a foul temper from having spent the entire day doing nothing), "So? What does Her Royal Highness have planned for this evening?"

"I don't know," Emma said grimly. "You're always asking to meet my friends, so I thought we'd go over to Elmira's tonight."

"Well, Elmira certainly is a classy name," I said. "Where is she from, New Jersey or something?"

"What's that, your idea of humor? My God, you're funny," Emma said. "Elmira is very English and just happens to be Honourable."

"I sincerely doubt that any friend of yours could be honorable. Isn't this the one you told me used to work as a go-go dancer in pubs to try and escape her background or something?"

"That's the one, but I'll thank you not to bring it up in front of her, Earl."

By the time we reached Elmira's house we were no longer speaking. Her friend greeted us at the door, snatching my coat from me in such a way as to make me feel now that I had come I was never going to be allowed to leave. She eyed me eagerly, winking at Emma. Then I was given a grand tour of the duplex.

The living room was furnished with massive, carved wooden chairs that were crawling with gargoyles—a decidedly masculine touch, I thought, since the rest of the decor was very frilly—and there was a painting that took up an entire wall. It extended from the floor to the low ceiling and went from one corner of the room almost to the other, though it was short approximately two feet, a fact which gave the whole room a crooked and lopsided appearance. I wondered if I should suggest the painting was not centered. This sort of thing irritated me beyond belief.

"What do you think of the painting, Earl?" Emma said. "Elmira just brought it. She knows the artist." She was acting nicer to me than she had in weeks, but all I could bring myself to say was, "That explains it," and quickly added on, "Very nice indeed." Though in fact I was surreptitiously trying to figure out the reason for Elmira's breasts being so unnaturally high, finally concluding that they must be the victims of one of the stunts she had performed as a go-go dancer.

The painting was a ghastly affair and portrayed two tremendous and deformed children playing on a swing set. Was it some kind of unconscious message, I wondered (only the layman, my shrink dad used to say, ever used the word *sub*conscious) that she was in the market for a husband? Or for artificial insemination? One could only imagine. Already, in my own head, I had married myself off to her and was spending what I believed to be her vast fortune, describing in letters to my father the tracts of land she and I would purchase. After all, a big affectionate girl like that, snatching my coat from me so forcefully at the door, and with those breasts too. No doubt the picture signified she was anxious to have children, though if those on the wall were representative of what she imagined her progeny would look like it would certainly take a great deal of her money to maintain them.

The painting really was dreadful. The sugary, muddy coloring of the thing! Those monsters of children at their grotesque, clumsy play! The narrow, nasty, icy eyes of them! What kind of maniac would buy that painting, I wanted to say. And the fact that it took up too much of the room and was not centered on the wall made me feel even more nervous. What kind of person was I marrying? Well, there was no understanding the English, I thought, and wondered just how much money she really did have after all. At least Emma, though not very jolly, and also comparatively flat-chested, was an American.

The rest of the house did nothing to assuage my doubts.

The kitchen was a vast, elaborate affair—Elmira informed me she had a wall torn down to accommodate it—and was lined with a vast array of electrical and kitchen equipment not normally to be found in an English household. There was a very American display of dishwasher, Cuisinart blender and a series of stainless steel items strapped to a pegboard: whips, stirrups, spatulas, egg beater, strangulators, tongs, prongs, forks, graded knives—which didn't mesh with the charming, deformed children and the cozy leather and wooden chairs clustered around the fireplace in the other room.

"The two of you will have to come over for dinner some time," Elmira said.

"She's an excellent cook," Emma said, giving me an odd look.

The two girls huddled over in one corner of the room, the expressions on their faces most strange. I felt like knocking their heads together. If there was one thing I hated, it was people whispering about me in my presence. However, all I said was, "Dinner? Dinner? That sounds great." I lacked the courage of my convictions, but as the two of them continued to whisper and giggle I became more and more furious.

Oh, I could just imagine, I thought, gazing at Elmira's elaborate coiffure, spiky wisps of hair that seemed to have been trained to grow straight up in knives of black and white and colored in dashes like salt and pepper; oh, I could just imagine, I thought, as I looked at Emma's great, soft, raspberry-colored Afro and the looks of the two women plotting against me, anxious to devour me alive. This was one time when my father would not think my "reading" of other people was paranoid. I could just imagine Elmira's wonderful meals and that wonderful dinner she wanted so badly to have me to—the visceral salads, the potted mombi, grilled and chilled tomatoes on dill bread, porcupine on a platter shivering and quivering with quills, a great, gray, greasy grackle plastered into little wooden tarts. A real gourmet cook, I thought.

"Would you like a drink, Earl?" Elmira said.

My only answer was a scowl.

Yes, here indeed was class. Elmira was in fact independently wealthy, as I had predicted. She told me this as she poured us all brandy in expensive snifters, the only kind of glass which would hold her nose. Her father, I was informed, was a sort of duke or knight. She had grown up without the aid of parents, buffered, shuttled and buffeted from boarding school in winter to a school or camp in the Swiss Alps during the rest of the year. What an introduction Emma had given me! For class, that which I had been searching for, was now before me, class was now mine. Emma, with whom I was at that time still living, was currently the most fashionable woman in London, or one of them, her face visible everywhere on the advertisements that decorated the sides of the Underground and on billboards, that infamous photo of Emma, the girlfriend who despised me, standing behind a giant sausage she was piercing with a fork and before her the caption FRY ME. What did I care if she put up with me only because I had weaseled my way into her life? I was a member now of the elite, and I was at the place where the elite meet to eat.

Yes, I thought of your meals then, Elmira, being impressed with your Honourableness and your gourmet treats—a gourmet extravaganza, a dead pigeon with two curled claws strapped down to the gynecological-looking dinner table (What normal person had a dining table so high off the ground? And what *were* those strange looking objects attached to the side of it but only at one end?), your great, friable aspics, the crumpets, strumpets and trumpets gutted and molested under gooey heaps called "Chinese," your Fingus McGingus and your piles of passion fruits. What school taught you how to cook that way, Elmira? In the summer I imagined a stinkout in the backyard, a great, fashionable stinkout around a barbecue pit in the backyard.

Suddenly I noticed the two girls looking at me most oddly. What was I saying? Why was I going on this way? "Heh-heh," I said out loud. I felt out of my mind, mad as a hatter, and in a murderous rage.

I was nearly frothing at the mouth. What good was any of it doing me? Did I appreciate any of it? Could I be happy with my present position, albeit temporary and precarious? No, I only wanted to kill the two girls, so needlessly rich and useless, and once again my wanting, something that had been quelled briefly by my trip to the south of France and my meeting Emma on the plane back to London, my wanting returned again, stronger than ever, a wanting I was unable to control.

For what I believed was that somewhere right this minute in London a party was going on, a party attended by famous and elegant people, *really* famous people, not just a model and an Honourable, but people who were not only rich but were also interesting. And when they talked they would sound . . . they would sound just like my mother, I mean, they would be *that* interesting, and this party was probably going on right that minute and I was missing it. And yet I did not dare to leave where I was, for supposing I didn't find this other party, and instead gave up where I was at present for no reason at all? Then where would I be?

Soon the two girls were clamoring to go out to a Jermyn Street disco, and then, they said, we would go to a fashionable private club Elmira belonged to. It was one that I had been dying to go to since I read about it the year before on the back page of the *National Enquirer* in a grocery store in the United States. "Oh, Earl will be glad to take us, Elmira," Emma said, a coy and cunning look on her face, knowing full well how uncomfortable I was being made. For I had no money at all, only what Emma deigned to give me, which was nothing at all outside of my room and board.

"Yeah, sure," I said. "Anyway, let's see the upstairs of this place."

Upstairs was room after room crammed full of furniture. Elmira's bedroom was occupied primarily by a huge brass bed covered with a black satin throw. It was littered with half-eaten bars of Cadbury's chocolate and empty packets of barbecue flavored crisps. What a crunchy mess. Above it and on the opposite wall were huge mirrors. I had never seen rooms filled with so much furniture. I wondered how she managed to keep the downstairs so sparsely furnished. There were huge dustballs clotted with hair that attached themselves to the bottom of my pants legs. There were oil paintings—her grim-looking ancestors, I presumed—stacks of magazines and newspapers as tall as my head, chairs from which half the stuffing was gone, stacked one on top of the next, and several beds lined up in a room, side by side. I noticed there were rugs two or three layers deep.

"Stuff from home," Elmira said with a wave of her hand. Against one wall was a black armoire that reminded me of the one I had left the banana in, in the hotel I stayed at in France, after I decided it would be better not to transport the banana across international lines. Everything appeared to be covered with a fine layer of grime, like fallout from a volcano. The air was oppressive and almost edible around me, like some tasteless Japanese soup that only later left a garbagey taste in the mouth.

"Want to see my time machine?" Elmira said.

"Sure," I said.

Elmira climbed into the armoire and began banging in it from side to side. Emma stood by, silently laughing, her raspberry-colored hair shaking as she tossed her head. "Well?" I said when she stepped out, "What am I supposed to say?" The two of them looked at me and giggled as if I was mentally retarded. Then Emma went over and began whispering something to Elmira. If I strangled both of them, I thought, I could easily stuff them both into the armoire and be on my way.

Still, in my opinion, it makes no difference how lousy and broke you are if you have that certain sympathy, that affinity with women. At least, this is what I understand according to my father. In that case, which was my case, there was no lack of them. Even if they made fun of you they were always flinging themselves on top of you, fighting over who was going to get to take care of you next. "Come on," Elmira said, grabbing my hand, "let's play Monopoly, if we're not going to get to go anywhere." Why couldn't *she* take *me* out, the silly bitch, if she was so anxious to go someplace, if she was so liberated?

We trooped back downstairs. Elmira got out the Monopoly board; Emma poured us all some more brandy. Elmira dipped her nose into her glass like a bird. Emma said, "Well gang, I can see it's going to be a hell of a party. It looks like you've even put out ashtrays, Elmira."

As we waited for Emma to hand out the money, Elmira kept telling us about why she hadn't gotten her period for several months. It turned out, she said, she had something inside her "like a bunch of grapes growing down there instead of a baby, not ugly or disgusting but like a bunch of grapes." Swell, I thought, losing what little interest I had in playing Monopoly. In any case, they were really making me nervous. Emma kept getting up to light candles. She was never there when it was her turn, too busy practicing some kind of witchcraft in the medicinal kitchen, I suspected, and Elmira insisted on buying more and more hotels, forcing me to pay nasty sums of rent. When Emma got up and went into the other room she kept talking to Elmira. Elmira had ¬aised her voice to a shriek. "Those grapes I had inside me? Well, they finally got them out with the aid of something rather like a crochet hook. It was ever so horrible. That'll be three hundred pounds, Earl, I believe." Emma let out a terrible shriek of laughter. "They just stuck this thing inside me and pulled them out. They were very deeply in."

Each time she spoke I jittered like a nervous spider. I had a feeling that the ceiling was pressing itself down my throat. I wouldn't have disbelieved it if I had been told I was drugged, or that I had been transported to another planet. A picture of Elmira's brother showed him to be a maniac of a different kind. With his white, white hair, his white circular glasses, he might have been another Andy Warhol or an albino bunny. From what I could make of Elmira's mewling English croak, her brother designed hats and had his own little company that made and sold them. The only other thing I could make out about him was that he had stayed in bed for an entire year. "Really?" Emma said, coming back into the room. She was clearly very impressed by this fact.

Other than that the game was played silently. Elmira watched me surreptitiously and lasciviously. Despite Elmira's needlessly high rents I was doing all right, and managed to buy up the English equivalents of not only Park Place but also Boardwalk, and owned most of the property by now, but there was no joy in it.

As it happened my luck began to change and Emma started to win. Of course I should have known what it would be like, playing with her. Vicious! After that the games went on every night, boring and pointless and tedious. The two girls, dim-witted as they were, loved it, and I did not dare to complain for fear that my means of subsistence, Emma, would kick me out.

Finally, one Saturday afternoon, after we had been playing for over five hours, I said I couldn't stand it any longer and knocked the board over. Emma called me a lousy sport. "The only reason you don't want to play is that you're not winning," she said.

But after the arrival of Larry Flowers, Elmira said I could move in with her if I had nowhere else to go. This I accomplished with ease, quickly realizing that there was little difference between Emma and Elmira other than the fact that while Emma went out to work modeling every day, Elmira did nothing but sleep.

While leading this crazy, nonsensical life, with Elmira demanding sex constantly like a guinea pig and I hoping against hope that I was coming closer to stardom or reality, who should I hear from but Gillian K. "I am so sorry about the mix-up and confusion," she wrote on pale pink stationery. "I was in the Aegean and a storm came up. Filming was delayed for several weeks. My caretaker had no way of forwarding your telegram. Then as soon as I returned, my entire family was down for the Christmas holidays. Would you be able to come and visit for a weekend? How about the weekend of the ninth? The weather should be lovely then and I hope it will make up for your last unfruitful expedition."

Explaining the situation to Elmira, who remained unimpressed (she didn't even know who Gillian K. was), I borrowed the money for a trip down to the south of France. Before I left she calmly dropped a tiny bomb. "I'm pregnant," she said. Pregnant! What had happened to the bunch of grapes? Why, I was as fertile as a salmon. Everywhere I went women became impregnated like rabbits! Perhaps it was something in the air I expelled from my lungs, or something I left behind me on the toilet seat.

"It's not possible," I said. "I haven't even known you very long. You must be thinking of someone else."

"Well, I'm not," she said.

"You told me you were a very sexually active person," I said. "Perhaps—"

"Well, I was lying," she said, "I'm not. I'm not what you think at all, Earl. I might have been before, but I stopped a while before I met you."

"Get an abortion, then," I said. "I don't want to hear about it! Or wait until I get back and I'll go with you to get one. There's plenty of time, if it really is me, which I doubt, considering what you told me. Anyway, even if it is true, you are no baby. I don't see why you weren't taking precautions." Then I stopped. How stupid could I get! "Unless . . ." I said hopefully, "You wouldn't like to get married, would you?" All that Honourable money!

"What?" she said, sniggering. "To you? That's a laugh, Earl."

What the hell had she gotten pregnant for, then? How could any girl who had begun her sex life screwing Swiss ski instructors when she was twelve, any girl who told me stories about a Spanish girl on the train to Italy who forced her to go into the toilet with her (those European rest rooms! Was there no end to the activity that went on in them?) where she forced Elmira to lie down on the floor and remove her panties—"Well," Elmira had said by way of explanation, "she was very aggressive. You couldn't have told her from a man, really. Very butch, with closely cropped hair."—how could anyone with a past like that (and there was more, much more) have gone and gotten herself knocked up? And by me?

"I wouldn't want to sleep with a woman again though, Earl," she told me. It had been easy, she giggled to me one night in bed, munching on a toffee bar. She hadn't had to feel any emotion, or that feeling of wanting to throw up she always felt with a new man. What business did she have having the word Honourable in front of her name? And I wanted to say that I didn't feel anything with *her* either.

But with those vicious little spike-heeled shoes with their tufted pompons that she insisted on wearing everywhere, even in bed, I didn't dare. And truth to tell, it wasn't just her I didn't feel anything for or with. It was everything. Like my dad, I could no longer feel a thing, only a pang of sympathy for myself. Everything rushed past me like a flicking picture on a flashcard. This same girl, who with her friend had already initiated me into a life of luxury, a life where nothing was important or necessary except for Monopoly games, was, despite her sophistication, nothing but a great yeasty mound of a baby herself (though to be honest I must say that I too was somewhat fatter now, gorged on all the edibles Elmira spent hours each day preparing, which perhaps was why her business on Bond Street still was not going at all well), who, though complete with breasts and ass, was simply a coward who clung to my arms. And although she did fork over the money for the plane fare she did not want to see me go.

"You'll never come back," she whimpered.

"Oh, quit nagging," I said. Her face was teary and resembled a bruised fruit. Yes, I said to myself, I had broken her spirit, but unfortunately that's the way it is in life. Break or be broken, my girl, I thought. My dad nodded wisely and appreciatively.

"I'm sorry I got pregnant, Earl," she said "It's just that I've wanted a baby for ever so long now, and I didn't care who came along to help make one. I couldn't do it on my own, you know."

"Just type this up for me while I'm gone," I said. "That is if you ever want to see me again." Not that there was much doubt of that, considering the tiny amount of money she had given me to get around on. "I'm warning you, I want it typed neatly. I wrote the address on the top where I want you to send it. And see what you can do about getting an appointment for a you-know-what. I'm in no position to support a third party at this time. Maybe later."

The letter, a stroke of genius on my part, I had concocted late one night when I was awakened by a bar of half-eaten bittersweet chocolate jabbing me in the face. It was addressed to a famous movie producer (for after receiving the invitation from Gillian K., I had thought if a letter to one famous person had worked, then why not to another) and it said:

Dear Mr. Zanuck,

Although I do not want to get your hopes up too much, I have the feeling your world-wide search for the male star of *Gone with the Wind Part II* is over.

You are a brilliant producer and I am a still yet unknown star. I feel that your singular sensitivity and intuition have directed you to my very doorstep, as it were. Although I am currently sojourning abroad, I expect to be returning to the *Etats-Unis* (as we say over here) before too long. My acting abilities are extensive; I have performed in several different films abroad.

While I am not from the South, I have spent so many summers in my ancestral home of Chattanooga, Tennessee, that I am almost indistinguishable from your true Southern gentleman. Many's the night I have spent atop Lookout Mountain reenacting the Civil War with various Southern belles. So you can see I am not one who approaches you as a neophyte.

I can be reached at the above address and number, and hope to hear from you in the near future.

> With the greatest respect and admiration,
> I am Yours Truly,
> Earl Przepasniak.

P.S. If it is not possible for me to be the star, I would be more than happy to consider a typing position or something of that sort. I can type fifty words per minute, I have been told, quite well!

A stroke of genius! I expected to return from the south of France with the role in my hands. Actually, I had never been south of Lower Manhattan, nor could I, as I may have previously mentioned, type worth shit, but there was no harm in a few small lies. I firmly expected that if the role did not come through, since there was little chance of that, that Gillian K. would ask me to remain with her forever. I was too charming to miss. And one look at Elmira's bleary face at the airport was enough to convince me I had better do my best to find an alternative solution for the rest of my life. Anybody I could upset to that degree by leaving was of no use to me whatsoever.

It was not quite as simple as I make it sound. Although truly I was getting more cynical, wiser and more sophisticated, every once in a while I would feel a slight pang of nostalgia for that other Earl, the one before the days of the divorce, simple and trusting.

In spite of the thrill of power that came over me when I exploited, used and manipulated others, weapons I had absorbed wordlessly from watching and imitating my father, there was some trace of my mother still within, some yielding, soft, submissiveness I was determined to root out of me, forcefully and grimly, if necessary, but such was the world I was inheriting, and I would need all my cunning animal nature to survive, let those who are already rich and powerful talk about goodness all they may. For I truly believed that when I became rich, famous and powerful, I would be able to give up my rottenness, give money to charity, and stop taking advantage, as was the case, of course, with the Rockefellers, the Kennedys, the Rothschilds, and others whose names I am too lowly even to know.

Such were my musings *en voyage* to meet Gillian, the mature woman who would put the finishing touches on my rites of passage, like the final colorful plumage on a matured tropical bird; like a bower bird I would then be ready to build an exotic nest for my mate with ribbons, bangles and bits of colored stone.

The flight from London to Paris, and then the one to the south of France on the little local airline were both quite easy. When I stepped off the plane (this time, unlike the first, with the assured air of a young man who is worldly, well-traveled and also knows there will be somebody there to meet him), Gillian, or an ancient woman whom I assumed to be Gillian, rushed forward to greet me as if we were old friends.

She was of course nothing like what I had expected, showing no signs of fame or even of having been well kept. She might have been my grandmother, only both of my grandmothers were under five feet tall. Nearly six feet tall, with tremendous yamlike hands, a jaundiced color to her skin and a nose like a bloat on her face, she was dressed in some sort of jodphurs and black gum boots that came up to her knees. She said at once, in a loud booming voice, "Well! I didn't expect to see *you* looking so confident!"

What was that supposed to mean? "You didn't?" was all I could manage to squeak out. "Not at all," she said firmly.

She confirmed once again that I was indeed, as she had thought, only in my twenties ("My very early twenties," I said, hoping that would make me seem remarkably mature, everything considered), sized me up and down like a piece of meat, and with the air of a horseman of the Pampas, she took my suitcase from my hand and marched it and me out to her car, a huge buslike thing with a bed in the back. "It was given me by my publisher," she said, flinging the suitcase into the back and onto the bed. I wondered if the same was going to be done to me, but luckily I was permitted to step aboard, climbing onto the seat in the front beside her, in what I hoped was a graceful and suave manner.

Before I could fully adjust myself, however, she took off, gunning the thing like Mario Andretti. I was flung to the floor, and with a roar the van jolted down the road. Almost as soon as she had started the engine she lit a cigarette and began to talk about her recent divorce, from her third husband, as well as her most recently completed play, a masterwork called *The Old Bat*, which had closed, unappreciated, on Broadway the year before.

In a fetus, the last thing to close over is the space between the nose and the lips and in my case it was almost the same thing. If the space doesn't fill in the baby is a harelip, not that I was a harelip or anything, but there was a space in me that had never fully closed over, a soft spot in the brain, and I was still waiting for it to do so. Why had I wanted to be famous? Now I was rushed about the south of France by this famous baboon, first dragged into a Roman or Romanesque church where I was forced to light a votive candle, without regard to religion, then to some kind of medieval castle and forced to view the scenery. And yet I was still no closer to fame than before, only my exhaustive quest had left me limp as a vegetable.

Obviously (and if this was ever going to sink in, it had better be as soon as possible), I realized, I was never going to be made into a famous person. No, I was never going to be allowed to have that satisfaction. Why, I was a dwarf next to this lady; both physically and mentally she was inhuman. She even looked like someone who might appear on a television program. It was true my mother had had some of those same qualities, but in her case, rather than make her a famous person, they had made a martyr of her.

Next we drove rapidly down the coastline to view some soggy brown grass and some scrubby looking, white, so-called wild horses, dashed through several towns made of mud and brown stone, and then circled, the car swaying dangerously from side to side on the narrow road, back to her house, which on this second viewing (the first had been the time she wasn't home) looked quite familiar and comforting to me.

Still I was terrified; my skin was sweating whitely and I was desperate to piss, which I rushed in to do as soon as she had parked the car. In my haste I nearly used a small room off of the living room before Gillian (or Jill, as I had been instructed to call her) boomed in her monumental and echoing voice, "Whatever are you doing in there? If you're looking for the loo it's upstairs." Embarrassed and frantic, I dashed up the stairs, almost knocking her down in my haste to get by. "I'll meet you in the kitchen, darling," she shrieked.

After easing myself upstairs, I found my way down to the

kitchen, walking in with what I hoped she would interpet once again as confidence and the quality of making oneself "at home," which I so admired in others more certain in their roles. In the clear light of the huge French kitchen, with its giant fireplace and stone floors, for the first time I was able to view her head on, as it were, and saw her tiny sacklike eyes, imbedded in her head above her red, round nose. An alcoholic of one kind or another. And indeed, this was confirmed when she asked me what I would have to drink. "Oh, something alcoholic," seemed to be the only thing I could say in this instance.

"Are you sure?" she said. "Wouldn't you rather have a cup of tea?"

I said, "Uh, well—," thinking perhaps I had been rude in my discovery of her illness, but she went into the living room and came back with two huge glasses of Scotch, into which she slipped a minuscule ice cube.

I must say that although I was petrified of this star, at the same time I felt almost nothing at all. I was now able to determine that my father, ever my constant guardian and companion, though visible only to me, was not going to allow me to have any fun, ever, at any of my experiences. I was forced to view the entire thing as if watching a B movie or television show in which I was the leading character. The whole thing was seen only from a distance. But in that case who was there instead of me? That I could not say. It may have been my father. But I personally had turned into something else, someone who was not Earl Przepasniak but was instead a spider speed-skating on ice, a crab dancing in a ballet. It seemed I had more legs than the normal person, yet a smaller brain.

After one drink, I felt barely able to stand up. Immediately upon doing so the floors began to tilt. I found myself saying the stupidest things imaginable, but luckily Gillian K. was not even listening.

We rushed through the weekend. The two of us were drinking like camels after a trip into the desert. Gillian proved to be an extremely hospitable hostess. She had arranged for dinner, the infamous local *auberge*, cooked for us by her caretaker/house-keeper, who was the Cordon Bleu cook there several nights a week. The meal consisted of slightly rank wild pheasant with two types of sauce, a dull brown one made with chestnuts and a green one made with peppercorns; *aubergine* and *courgette* (some indescribable sorts of vegetables); a salad ("You must eat the salad, darling," she told me, "a nice salad will cool you off."); cognac sorbet and quantities of wine.

For breakfast, generally there would be fluffy croissants, *mille feuilles*, brioches, *beignets*, and *tartes à l'oignon*. In our hungover states neither of us could consume a thing, but by afternoon she would be tempting my delicate palate with veal patties and fish fingers.

The drinking began at eleven in the morning, with a glass of rum. At lunch we would switch to wine, going through several bottles in the course of the afternoon, after which we moved to bourbon, shipped at great expense from a certain area of the rural south of the U.S. where it was manufactured, or else Scotch of a particularly nasty quality that was unblended, or unsterilized, or something.

At dinner it was back to wine, and then later brandy or cognac, which she poured throughout the evening while speaking constantly of her various husbands, her impending old age, and the story of her life, all while holding my hand with a frantic and earnest look. Sometimes she would place this same hand of mine on her knee. I removed it.

One night she had planned a party for me with the local celebrities—a Pulitzer Prize winner for journalism or something, an artist, a famous pop singer who lived nearby. Unfortunately I couldn't understand a word that was being said, since they insisted on conducting the conversation in French. This I really didn't think was very considerate—though I was told nobody spoke English but Everett, the pop singer, and Gillian—but there was nothing I could do about it except sit in the corner and brood.

One afternoon we toured the local countryside. I was taken to Gillian's cemetery plot, a big area filled with sand and tombstones littered with plastic flowers. "Very nice," I said. She planned to be buried in it shortly.

Or we would sit around upstairs in her studio while she painted—which is what she did when she wasn't writing—oils of giant vegetables in shades of custard green, prune-colored beets, phallic stalks of celery. "Very nice," I said. "It's the only thing I can paint," said she.

I skip through all this so briefly because it must be obvious to you that the entire experience holds memories painful and unpleasantly embarrassing to me. The first night at about three in the morning, when I became aware of what was expected of me, I fled to the room she told me was to be mine, but which she had obviously never had any intention of my staying in. The next morning at breakfast she stopped me on my way to the shower. "You certainly disappeared in a hurry last night," she said coyly.

"Oh, I guess I must have passed out," I said, "what with the trip and the alcohol and all."

The following night I was not so lucky, and after a meal (it most certainly cost at least a hundred bucks, with the wine and all) at the Auberge au Pont Roman, I was induced or seduced into returning with her to her room, where she promptly bolted the door, although I did say timidly, "What do you need so many locks for? You have me here" (my one attempt of the weekend to be gallant). My performance was, in the end, as limp as her expensive fur piece she flung dramatically to the floor, where it lay, the silver fox face glassy-eyed and stunned-looking.

Oh, her aged, papery skin! Outside, the screech of the white owls who haunted the unused water tower went on and on; I took it personally, a kind of hooting laughter, and one long wooden shutter slapped slowly and regularly, one thump after the next, against the French stone wall of the house.

She insisted I take a bath afterward—after what? There was nothing, nothing at all, in the red and black bathroom she had installed in the house at a considerable cost, the first indoor plumbing in the area, a bathroom she fondly called "Las Vegas."

"Must have had too much to drink," I said, which she kindly, though not particularly willingly, understood. The next morning, before she could wake, I slipped several hundred francs out of her purse and went downstairs, where a corniculated, corniced clock ticked on the wall like a geiger counter, counting aloud the hours I had left of my lousy life. Behind the house the sun was coming up over the grape fields, which were only beginning to sprout slim green shoots from the wooden sticks that I had learned at last were grapevines.

"In many ways," Gillian K. had told me, "you have the mind, the feelings, the thoughts of a forty-year-old." But all I could think of was the leathery feeling of her body, those shriveling breasts, the small, sagging pot of a paunch, the slackness behind the thighs. I was no forty-year-old! At least let me have a chance at youthful flesh, that of others my own age.

It was nearly a year to the day since the accident with my mother, when my father had knocked the postage meter onto her head, almost instantly killing her and ending his alimony payments. And now, I thought with despair, with this aged woman I was as close to fame as I would probably ever come. Where were the newspaper reporters, the gossip columnists, the paparazzi? It appeared that in actuality no one cared.

Well, so much for theories of the older woman and the younger man. So much for theories, period. One thing I was learning from my picaresque journeyings hither and yon, like a young Don Quixote aging rapidly, was that there was little or no connection between theories and actuality. So, whatever cobwebbed scientists locked themselves into little cubbyholes of offices and laboratories to perform had nothing to do with anything practiced or of value in the real world. Theories were one thing; they had their place, actually. Quite interesting in textbooks, good for a good read. But when it came to people there wasn't a theory on earth could catch them or pin them down. It was as if the stupidest people knew all the latest theories and were determined to outwit them. Once I thought I would read all the books I could lay my hands on until I got to be twenty or twenty-one. Then I would at last go out into the world and know what to do about people. I would know what they were thinking and feeling and could deal with them in a successful way.

But life seemed determined to make a mockery of everything about me. Where had I gone wrong? Once again I fell into one of my dark introspective moods and came up with nothing.

It was as if I had contracted before I was born to buy an expensive ticket to what was touted to be "the Greatest Show on Earth." And what ennui I was experiencing. What misery. I had been sold out completely! "A sucker born every minute." That phrase had a truer ring to it than ever before. I wanted my money back!

Well, I would go back to England as soon as I could catch a plane. But where and what was I returning to?

It seems that what I was returning to was nothing more than that game so many call, with good reason, "Monotonous." But with a switch. That evening I unloaded my weary self onto Elmira's doorstep, only to find that Emma was visiting for the night and was once again speaking to me, since enough time had passed that she had forgotten what it was she disliked about me.

Elmira had the heavy stunned look of an animal being led out of its cage for the first time, and I wondered what kind of drug she was now on, or if this new face of hers came with her pregnancy.

"Hello, girls, Daddy's home," I said, dumping my suitcase full of dirty clothes onto the floor. And then, "Oh God, not more of this," as I saw Emma bringing out the brandy snifters and clearing the usual space on the rug where we played.

Elmira's weak chipmunk face, as she brought out the Monopoly board that first evening after my return from my miserable trip, stretched into a smile, revealing a row of crooked teeth. Even the rich in England seemed to do nothing about their teeth. "Oh, don't worry, Earl," she said, "I think you'll like this game now. We're playing for stakes then, is that right?" she said to Emma.

"Of course," Emma said. "As we discussed."

The girls, while I was away, had apparently concocted some new rule to the game.

"What?" I said, "Monopoly for stakes?" Instantly a picture came into my head. Wild sexual adventures with two women? Games of Monopoly where I, the winner, forced the two lovely ladies to perform various acts with me until they were weak with exhaustion and begging for mercy? What a postcard it would make to Dad!

"Just what are these stakes?" I said, to make sure.

"Winner gets to tell the losers what to do."

"Well," I said, "I guess that's all right, then." My voice came out weakly, the sound of a mewing kitten, almost as if I were imitating Elmira, her cunning British accent.

"Think you can stand that, Earl?" Emma said sarcastically, stroking the bottom of my foot, which being bare and very ticklish made me jump and hit my elbow quite badly against a wooden gargoyle on the chair.

"Yaah!" I said.

"What's wrong with you, anyway," Emma said to me.

"Nothing, nothing," I said. I licked my lips and ye. I felt slightly worried. Something about Elmira's creepy apartment, the murky incense she insisted on lighting and the sound of the wind slapping down the streets outside made me feel homesick, for where I didn't know. Wherever I went, my behavior was a disappointment to me. It was no exception now. The details were as follows: though at first I appeared to be winning, nearly creaming in my jeans in terror and excitement, it shortly became obvious that I had been set up. The other two joined together to beat me. Still, there was a chance that I might have my first experience with a threesome, I thought. Two women at once! What every red-blooded American should come to Europe for! Win or lose, I liked the game.

My usual strategy was buy, buy, buy. Anywhere I landed. Of course I could never get used to the names of the English properties—Mayfair, Piccadilly, Marble Arch, British Rail and Kensington—they weren't at all the same as Boardwalk and Park Place, names etched into my blood from earliest childhood, when I had been initiated into the art of cheating by my dear Grandma Ivy. Money stashed in the lap or under the board, properties eased out of the bank when no one was looking. I wasn't as proficient in the English game, but I was good. Yes, I was pretty damn good! How could I have suspected that these two women, one English and brought up so charmingly in the tradition of fair play and field hockey, the other an Army brat, would actually conspire to beat me of my natural inheritance? Oh, I was to rue the day I had set out from my own land, where at least I knew that everyone cheats equally, democratically and with all good will, and come to this region of monstrous, unnatural acts.

"Undress," Emma commanded, and I was blindfolded and led into another room. When the blindfold was roughly pulled off, I found myself kneeling on the floor in the kitchen, a bucket of hot soapy water and a sponge by my side. "I want the floor perfectly clean" (this was Elmira speaking now, the unspeakable bitch). "I mean really clean."

"Imagine getting her pregnant and then just going off like that," Emma said, and her little boot jabbed me in the side. "You bastard, Earl."

"But—" I said, hot with embarrassment and rage.

"No buts," Emma said, "If it's not to our liking you'll find far worse in store for you." And it was true that the two of them, in their leather or leatherette garb, looked particularly menacing from my position, blindfold drooping over one eye, on the floor.

Then the door to the kitchen was shut and I was left alone in the room, alone except for the bucket of water and an impossible erection.

I think my Monopoly game fiasco ended my rites of passage. Either I was or was not a man; strangely, it no longer seemed to matter. I was getting a little fed up with the animal within. My brutish behavior seemed more and more to belong to someone else and I no longer admired it to the same degree. If this was "masculine" behavior, I wasn't really sure I wanted to become a man.

I viewed my life as it had occurred as a series of truncated episodes: who was I, and what was I to become, if not a man? I began to see the human condition as a ludicrous struggle against an iron law, each person being formed as part of an inextricable chain. "There is no free will," says B. F. Skinner. "We are all totally in the merciless claws of environment and heredity."

I started then on an inward journey, a journey to find the roots from whence I had sprung, those gnarled and snarled entanglements that were always tripping me up. What is there within humankind that causes us to lie, cheat, murder, steal? If I am to be blamed for my nature which isn't mine to do with what I will, let me at least know what this nature is.

With what boredom I viewed this necessary haranguing of myself by myself. I saw my father, perhaps merely a refined loafer. Why must I be the one to know this? I see man suspended like a spider from a thread. The spider spins the thread, yes. But is it his desire to dangle so?

And if I was only my father's son, was it not then important to know who he was and what effect his life had had on mine? My thoughts flickered mothlike and lighted on the familiar scene of my father, at work or at play. Was not what he claimed was hard work merely fun and games for him? And yet, for Bobo and me, it was boring work. Was it something in the genes or was it just that we were not allowed ever to exercise that tiny bit of free will that we might possibly have possessed but couldn't know if we did or didn't, if we were never allowed to give it a whirl?

And why did he hate me so much more than my brother?

My mother had claimed, "In his eyes you're just a shadow of a person, one that he has nurtured and cared for all these years and now who just ignores him, who responds with ingratitude. Because you are competition for my love."

"Why did he divorce you, then?"

"Because he didn't believe I loved him. He felt I was always someone else's—the unknown someone whom he couldn't fight. He was always waiting to be cuckolded. To have the horns put on him, as it were. Bobo is less of a threat for some reason. You are the oldest."

I didn't see it quite that way. It was more that I could never win the love of my father because—I wasn't sure why—I thought maybe it was because I was just basically unlovable. But thinking this way had only caused me to act more so, as if in revenge, to prove to him that I was as awful as he thought.

This has been my father's story, warped and distorted it is true, but the best I can do in trying to come to some kind of understanding of him. I cannot even consider myself the main character of these sparse notes. I am so much less than the sum of my parts, and I may have mentioned before that I am only a watered-down genetic version of the past and what is left to come. I have only desire (a pitiful desire that is what everyone else has, too: an All-American need to be accepted and acknowledged, a need that can only be fulfilled at the expense of putting down others) to recommend me and to prove I exist.

And did my father's life, what he accomplished with it and what he did not do, make him a good man or a bad one?

"Are you a good witch or a bad one?" I hear the voice of Glinda, the Good Witch of the North coo in *The Wizard of Oz*, only in my head the picture is of a man doing Billie Burke in drag.

No, my father was what he was, an American Dad, blind as an underground animal, unfeeling and unemotional except when it came to one subject: himself.

Why couldn't he have simply found a receptacle to screw, if this is what propelled him through his life? Couldn't he have just ordered one from the back pages of *Playboy* magazine, if this was what the whole deal had been about, instead of ruining a long chain of lives that, while they might not have been great lives, at least had been innocent enough until he stepped in and stickied them up?

But once again I, Earl the Rapacious, Earl the Carnivorous, have spoken too soon. For in the end my dad rescued me, and if it was too late for me to be saved from my own life, at least he managed to save me from ruining the life of another.

For Elmira had her baby, the baby she had always wanted, and I found myself madly in love with the little thing. We called it Robert, and it was true it was a ratlike little thing, with a red, wrinkled head and a bluish behind, but paternal instincts and outcroppings I had never known I had within me poured out like a leaky fountain and I gathered that at last I was really in love.

After the birth of the little monkey, Elmira's family refused to help her financially. Her shop on Bond Street was not yet self-sufficient, and Elmira, I'm afraid, didn't have a business oriented mind at all, having been sheltered in boarding and finishing schools all these years.

"Now, Robert," I would say to the infant, taking it from the box where we kept it under the bed, "when you get big and strong we're going to put you to work writing poems like your Grandma. You're going to be the Poet Laureate of England and America combined. After all, with your ancestry, how can you not be?" The little thing lay in its box gnawing on a Lorna Doone biscuit, not speaking but curling and uncurling one sticky fist.

"What are you saying to him?" Elmira would say, coming into the room. "This baby isn't going to be a poet. I don't want you putting any ideas into its head. After what happened to your mother, you're suggesting my baby go through that? I want this baby to be something respectable—maybe a rich American doctor. I'm on the dole and you don't even have ten pence to put into the gas meter, and you're suggesting my baby do something as foolish as write poetry. Hhmm!" And she picked up the baby and flounced away.

"It's my baby, too," I said, but she was right. The rent on the Georgian duplex in Hampstead Heath was too expensive. We had been forced to sell all those wonderful artifacts that had formerly made our house such a joyful place to live in: the carved, gargoyle-ridden chairs, the gynecological dining table, the painting of the deformed and stunted children at play. We were left with the kitchen appliances, the whips and crocks and Elmira's collection of kinky clothing (the ballerina tutu cut directly below the nipples so that they protruded above like some Renaissance style of dress, the leather jumpsuit with a zipper fitted at the crotch, the leotard of leopard print that was tattered and torn revealingly, and last but not least, a vast collection of maternity clothing—all of which, except for the latter, had done nothing for me, though as articles of sexual gear they might perhaps amuse a man who was more erotic than myself, perhaps my father) jammed into the tiny closet of our bed-sitting room at Notting Hill Gate.

After we couldn't scrape together the money for the electric bill, the interior of our room remained dark. Like the two sisters of the treacle well in *Alice in Wonderland*, we lived mostly on treacle, bread and butter. "I never expected things to turn out this way," Elmira said.

"Yes, that's just what I was trying to explain to you," I said. "You never know what may happen next. I, for one, never dreamed I'd find myself a father. When I think of how I have suffered with women, how they mocked me and jeered me and would not let me into their hearts, I realize how far I have come. Where's baby Robert?"

"Oh, Earl, you can be such a jerk," Elmira said, and would not hand over the baby. "Why don't you go out and get a job?" she said. "I'm sick of sitting in the same room with you, and I'm sick of living off bread and marmalade. I'm sure it can't be healthy."

I wasn't a British citizen. "You know it's impossible for me to get a work permit," I said. "That is, unless we get married, and you're not willing to do that."

"Bloody right I'm not," she said. Elmira couldn't work because she didn't want to leave the baby.

"I'm perfectly willing to stay home and take care of it," I said, but she could not be induced to leave, and we fought day and night over its upbringing.

What was I supposed to do? It was at this point, when I was torn in two with thoughts of the terrible things we were doing to this child by fighting over it all the time, that the telegram from my brother came:

DAD SEVERELY HURT IN ACCIDENT STOP PLEASE RETURN AT ONCE STOP PLANE TICKET FOR YOU AT HEATH-ROW STOP BOBO.

I had little choice but to leave. I wasn't doing any good over here, occupying space in the one room, eating too much bread and butter, fighting and bickering with Elmira. Once she threatened to throw the baby into the gas fire if I didn't stop speaking to it of poetry. "Quit quoting those stupid poems your mother wrote," she said. "You're going to screw up his head as much as yours is."

Besides, I knew Elmira was taken care of on the dole, and that once I left, her parents would probably welcome her home again. My son might perhaps receive an Honourable upbringing after all.

My brother met me at Bradley International Airport and on his face had grown a great weariness, a sadness as if something had happened to make the shell crack it had taken him so long to develop. "Bobo, tell me what happened," I said.

"I don't even want to talk about it," my brother said. "It happened when he was cutting wood. A terrible accident. He'll live, but he'll never be the same mentally or physically."

"And he asked to see me?"

"Yes, it was his idea you come home. And they've paroled him from prison. He won't be going back."

In my heart I felt a wonderful feeling, for whatever had happened to him and whatever he said he was still my dad, and that was something that could never be broken or untied, however much at times either of us wished for that. *He had asked me to come home.*

"I have a kid now, Bobo," I said, and I showed him the photo I had in my wallet of little Rob, an ugly turtle of a baby it is true, with a snout on him just like his paternal grandfather's—a fact I pointed out to Bobo. But though he smiled and looked interested, he said very little, almost nothing at all. "When we were kids, Bobo, I used to think: you and me are the only two people in the world with the same parents, the same set of circumstances growing up. How come you and me aren't exactly alike?"

"I'm going to drive over to the hospital now, Earl, to pick Dad up. Remember, it's going to be difficult. The accident was very hard on him. They say he's ready to come home, but he'll be going to Rehab for a long time to come. He's not taking the whole thing very well, Earl. He was always a very physical person and the adjustment is going to be hard."

Feeling tired from jet lag, unable to believe that anything too serious had happened to my invincible father, I followed Bobo down the corridors of the hospital, a dingy, ancient building reeking of antiseptic and alcohol. My father was out of bed and dressed, waiting for our arrival in a wheelchair. It was true he looked a bit pastier than I had remembered him, a bit liver-colored around the gills, but this may have been only because he had shaved off his beard, the first time I had seen his naked face since the divorce.

"Dad!" I said. "You shaved off your beard."

He did not respond, not even to smile weakly. But unmistakably he was my father, the family resemblance harsher than ever without that facial hair, and in his nose with the large pores—the nose itself large—in the small glittering eyes, deep set and fierce behind the thick lenses of his glasses, in the hairline receding and curling back onto his head, was a clear picture of myself in the short years to come, only he was broader, more massive and could not be cowed even though stuck in that hideous chair with wheels.

His powdery, peppery-cheese breath signified to me he had had an Italian grinder for lunch that day at the hospital. His dull glance, his dry mechanical hug in response to my own, were indifferent and wooden. The animal magnetism, the vibrancy which marked all of my memories of him had disappeared and in their stead sat an old man, someone I could not imagine as being my father.

Soon I knew would come the endless recriminations, his disappointment in me, his disgust for turning him in and with the way I acted. He would tell me what a fool I was for having sired a son, how all my relationships with other people were continual failures.

But to my relief, on the car ride home he was silent and asked me no questions about England, for I still feared him and believed that any answer I gave, even the most innocuous of statements, would have brought forth belicose anger and hatred directed at me and my deceased mother. I still had not come to grips with his accident and the extent of damage it had done to him.

"You're a grandfather, Dad," I said. "How does that make you feel?"

He looked out the window and mentioned that the vegetables he had grown last summer were still edible and waiting for dinner in the root cellar. Though all he discussed was the fact that he planned to cook chicken for dinner, though he seemed dulled, weary and broken down, I knew it was only a disguise, that beneath this outward silence seethed his sullen, brutal anger, his disgust with the world but mostly with me, his oldest son and least worthy part of him.

"Oh, Dad," I wanted to say, wanting to fling myself onto him and burrow into his lap the way Kong had once done when my father had picked him up from the veterinarian. "Can't you forgive me? Just this once? Couldn't you just this once tell me you think I'm great, you admire my spirit and guts, my wild and crazy European adventures? Couldn't you just this once tell me I'm worth something to somebody, that you value me at least, find me unique and astonishing?"

But no words were forthcoming, not from me nor my father.

There was no sense in stirring things up. I knew already what the answer would be. How could I forget, when I had been trained for years, already had heard all the answers from him?

In a way I was not surprised this had happened. I remembered as a child how my father had once almost cut himself in two while sawing wood. These accidents with chain saws were not really too uncommon. It was on a New Year's Eve—one of the years when Bobo and I visited my father for the Christmas holidays—when I was fourteen or perhaps fifteen and Bobo was a few years younger. I was downstairs messing around in my father's workshop in the studio, where he kept all his tools and equipment, and in a kidding way I picked up his chain saw—kidding because the damned thing weighed too much for me to pick up, let alone cut wood with, though Bobo could already split chunks of wood with an ax—and hefting it around I said, "So, when are you going to chop some more trees down, Dad?"

This too was a joke, because there had never been a time when my father did not chop wood, cut trees down in lieu of speaking to me or doing anything more personal with me, and yet what kind of a maniac would be out cutting wood on New Year's Eve in twenty below weather unless he had to?

"I'm planning to go out tomorrow and do some work. What's so funny, Earl? I'd like you to come with me. Bobo says he'll help, and I'll need the extra hands."

The next morning I trailed him dutifully down the ice- and snow-covered driveway, skidding along behind him, followed myself by Dad's watery-eyed dog. My father and I did not speak: his ears were stuffed with cotton to protect his hearing from the violent noise of the buzz saw when it was turned on. The white fluff stuck out of his ears, behind his glasses, giving him a jovial, crazed appearance.

There had been an ice storm the night before and the trees were coated with water, frozen and glassy. The branches creaked under the extra weight, bending in places almost to the ground. It was unusually cold, but there was no wind.

My father looked neither to the left nor the right, concerned only with getting to the pile of uncut logs, though once he turned to me and said, "Absolutely astonishing," referring, I could only suppose, to the glories of nature around us. The air was very still, although the branches made small aching sounds under the added weight of the ice, and when we got out to the barn (a barn my father had built so he would have a place to keep a horse), he pointed to the side of the barn where he had stacked at least a cord under the eaves to keep it dry and showed me where he wanted the logs moved to—an open area a few yards away, covered with moist sawdust and wood chips from hundreds of logs—where he would be able to cut the pieces of wood into shorter, more usable lengths.

I began to carry over the logs; my father filled the chain saw from a canister of gasoline he kept inside the barn, and, yanking the start cord on the chain saw, began to cut the wood. The air smelled of gasoline and the noise of the saw was shrill and intense.

I could not carry logs fast enough to keep him supplied with them. Each log was so long it needed to be sawed into two or three pieces to be able to fit into the fireplaces inside. It was not a great assortment of logs, speaking now in terms of their burning capacities and qualities: a lot of birch, a small amount of maple, some pine. But most of it was pine, and because I had had to take off my mittens to get a grip on the wood, my hands were very quickly rubbed raw and covered with a sticky, tarry pine pitch, reeking of turpentine and impossible to remove. My hands grew numb. Several times I stumbled, trudging back and forth, once scraping my knee on the rocky ground and once dropping a heavy log on my foot.

The whine of the buzz saw grew more monotonous; the rise and fall of the sound of the chain, ripping through the logs and then through the empty air, was making me deaf. I had a hat on. It did not, however, seem to cover my ears, which grew colder and ached. Once I stopped briefly to gaze at my father. He had removed his jacket and was sweating profusely. His face was quite red with exertion, though as I have mentioned it was bitter cold. He stopped, too, to wipe his sweating forehead and to tie his hair out of his eyes with a red bandana he pulled from his back pocket. Then he went back to his sawing.

He did it quite beautifully. Each gray and dirty log fell into two or three pieces neatly and cleanly, revealing the virgin surface, white and sharp, within. He would later split the logs lengthwise; that was accomplished with a chisel and a hatchet or mallet, a much slower and more tedious process.

I could not carry any more logs. Bobo was indoors, due to come out shortly. As I may have mentioned, I was not in the best of shape. My ears hurt and so did my hands. Though I dreaded the look I would receive from my father when he saw I was going indoors, I did not dread it enough to remain carrying the logs any longer, walking back and forth in the air brittle with ice.

Hauling a final log I placed on the ground before him, I shouted, "I'm going in!" hoping he could hear me above the roar of the chain saw engine.

"What?" I saw my father mouth, though I could not hear him. A blank look crossed his face.

My father shut the chain saw off. The chain ceased turning, the saw made several chucks and huffs before the engine turned off completely. "What?" he said.

"I'm going in!" I said. "I'm freezing."

"I still can't hear you. The noise has made me temporarily deaf."

"I have to get some warmer clothes," I said. "I'll be back out in a couple of minutes. I want to get some cotton for my ears, too." I was lying. I had no intention of returning for several hours at least, by which time I hoped he would be done. My father nodded, preoccupied as usual.

On the way back to the house I passed Bobo on his way out, clad properly in gloves and boots, wads of cotton sticking from his ears. "What's up?" he said.

"I have to get some warmer clothes on," I said. "My hands are frozen."

My brother nodded. A look of sadness crossed his face at the sight of his brother giving up so soon, his brother's lack of masculinity.

"He just wants you to move the logs over for him to cut," I said.

"Maybe I'll get to saw," my brother said.

For some reason the dog decided to follow me back to the house. He bounded up to me with a tremendous stick in his mouth, tail wagging, drool coursing to the ground. I threw the stick for him, in the process getting my hands covered with dog slobber.

I looked out over the lake. It was frozen and perfectly smooth, since there had not yet been any real snowfall. In a number of places where the water in the summer was very shallow, clusters of cranberry bushes protruded up out of the ice, growing on hummocky bogs. Even at a distance the red berries, now frostbitten, were visible on them.

I went back into the house and had some cocoa, spent the next hour watching television and talking to the dog. Finally I decided my absence would not go unnoticed over at the saw mill. I dressed again and trudged back down the road. Even the dog did not want to go out this time. The air was, if anything, even colder and the hairs in my nostrils froze and felt like splinters of glass.

From a distance it sounded as if my father was having trouble with the chain saw; it bucked and shrieked, making sounds like curses as it roared, or did not roar, through the logs. It sounded as if a hive of bees had been let loose.

My father had been out there for a good four hours. He looked tired but the stack of cut logs next to his side had grown tremendously and the cord and a half stacked against the side of the barn had diminished. Bobo, sweaty, had taken off his gloves and hat. His hair was curly with perspiration but he looked pleased with himself, fierce. "Has Dad let you use the chain saw yet?" I said to him.

"I haven't gotten a chance yet," my brother yelled, while my father went on sawing. "We're having trouble with the engine. It keeps chucking on the wood because it's too cold. We're going to quit soon." His voice, since he too had been deafened by the noise, was far too loud in compensation, nearly equaling the dismal scream of the saw.

I picked up a log, turned and stopped a moment to watch my father at his play, watch him bend over a massive log of maple, churning saw in hand, his beard and hair wild and black. My brother, too, paused in his travails to look at my father, huge, clad in plaid flannel, in the chip-filled lot. The two of us, poised thus, brothers watching a father, saw the chain saw as it spun, slipping from my father's hands at some flaw in the wood or in itself, slip and fly up, spinning, flipping wildly into the air, before slicing through his clothing and coming to a halt.

"My God," my father shouted. "My God." Bobo rushed in to shut the sputtering motor off. The saw had cut through Dad's clothing and nicked his chest. He was unharmed except for a thin line of blood, no deeper than a scratch.

This incident had scared him. From L. L. Bean he ordered a lightweight vest, like a coat of mail, made of metal and designed for just this purpose: to protect the woodsman from his saw. My father had vowed never to cut wood for more than an hour or two, when the hands begin to grow weary, when the reflexes are not so quick, had said he would never cut wood alone, but would always have someone around him. But the coat of armor, the unfulfilled vows, these things had not been enough on the afternoon of his accident.

And so the summer passed, my brother silent and mournful about the house, my father speaking to no one. I did not hear from Elmira in England, though I wrote to her almost every day.

In the morning I wheeled my father out of the house. "It's a nice day today, Dad," I said. "It will do you good to get out of the house." The gravel driveway was filled with large rocks and potholes. "I'll have to tell Bobo to bring a load of gravel over here in the truck," my father said listlessly. "Remind me, Earl."

"I will."

We stopped a minute to look out over the lake. The bronze heron my father had once made and then had cast, stood on the shore, poised as always, on the verge of flight. Some leaves had drifted down and caught on its beak. "You'll have to clean that off, Earl."

It had been a dry summer and now it was fall and the water level on the lake was low. The murky blue water stretched for acres. White rotting stumps jutted out and in the distance the low cranberry bogs were red and dark green. Behind them the mountain rose up and near the top the cliffs were gray. The trees had not yet turned colors and they were still dark, burnished green, though here and there a maple had been hit with a twinge of frost and was vermilion. There was a quietness to the air and a fine wave of cool air blew in from the surface of the lake and over to us at the house.

I pulled the blanket further up my father's lap. He did not seem to notice. His heavy hands played with a bit of leaf that had fallen from the tree above us. "You'll be out of this chair soon, Dad," I said. "You'll see. There's really no reason for you to have to stay in it, you know."

He did not respond. I had dressed him in a red flannel shirt and he looked very handsome in it. He had grown his beard again and it had become quite gray. He no longer used the Lady Clairol once a month. I wanted to break in on him, to interrupt the endless flow of thoughts he shared with no one, to connect with him in some way, even if it was only to incur his wrath once more. "What's wrong, Dad? How about snapping out of it? After all this time, the accident is a thing of the past already. Why don't you take care of yourself, dress yourself, dye your beard once again."

"What difference could it possibly make?" he said, and some of the fog lifted out of his eyes when I got him to speak. "I'm an old man now. No, that's not it—I'm not even a man. I'm less than a man, simply another worthless hunk of human being."

"But Dad, there's so much more to life than that. You loved things so much. What about your love for nature? You still have that. And the things you carve, objects that no one else can see, objects that have never existed before you conceived of them. What difference can any of the rest make? None, really. I'm lonesome for you, Dad. I miss you."

"Earl, if I can't have life on my own terms then life is impossible for me. You know that. Bobo should have left me to die that day out in the woods after the accident. I would have been better off."

"Don't say that, Dad."

"I must have things my way—always have—and if they can't be my way then I don't want them any way at all."

"Yes," I said. "I guess that's always the way you felt about me. I could never live up to your expectations, never could win your approval, no matter how I tried, and for that I did have to pay. But Dad, you know what you are saying is ridiculous. Most of us are lucky if we get anything we want at all. We have to take what is handed to us."

But the dull look had returned to my father's eyes and he was not speaking to me now.

I wheeled him down the path, pushing the chair over the bumps and rocky gravel. "Sorry, Dad." I wheeled him to the end of the drive, past the massive iron bell he had long ago riveted to a piece of extra timber left over from building the house. He had used it to call Bobo and me in to supper when we stayed to visit for a weekend. When rung it clanged loudly, with a hollow, aching sound. My father motioned for me to go and ring it. "Sorry, Dad." I kept pushing.

At the bottom of the road I turned off and pushed his chair over the soft covering of pine needles, brown and amber, thickly cradling the ground. The picnic table had turned a silky brown from being outdoors summer and winter. He had built the fireplace himself, out of rocks now blackened from smoke, a place to grill marshmallows and meat and corn over an open fire.

The water in the lake was deeper here, and beavers had long ago built a dam. A large white beaver lodge rose up out of the water, littered with bleached sticks and twigs. In the water the stumps of old trees like telephone poles were draped with algae. "All this place needs is a moose, standing up to his knees in water with plants hanging out of his mouth," I said. "And then you would have the perfect nineteenth-century American oil painting you always wanted." My father did not laugh.

I pushed him over to the white rocks of the dam. I turned his chair so that it was facing the water. He did not look out but clutched thinly at his blanket. Behind him was the dam, the slim oily trickle of water on the rocks, and the green and black water snake dozing on the heated stones.

In the small pond two mallards paddled quietly in the shallow water. The small pond had almost no water left in it. "Maybe we should drain it and turn it into a field," I said. My father took out his pouch and lit up a joint my brother had rolled for him earlier that day. His eyes closed a little.

"You and I don't smoke marijuana because we're rebelling against Daddy," Bobo had once whispered to me years ago, when he was ten or twelve. But what was left now to rebel against? And so it was that I helped myself to his marijuana and began to smoke it as I had so often watched him do. It tasted rather pleasant, though it had no effect on me at all.

A strange feeling came over me, watching my father asleep there in the chair, as I performed the activity that had previously only been done by my father. I thought: this man is not my father. He is just a man, trying to please, trying to be my friend. His pained and suffering face, the warmth that was always there, only not visible to me before—I never saw, I never realized. I never understood how his coldness was only a defense, something that was there to protect him from the rest of the world, something intended to help me from getting too dependent but was never meant to misfire the way it did. My father had not counted on my having emotions to blind me the way they did.

And lonesome—my father was alone with himself in the world and had always to live with that.

This anger that I had felt for him was for things he hadn't done. It was directed at him for things he couldn't help. I no longer wanted to hold him responsible for his criminal act, for his hedonistic behavior. I felt sorry for him.

It got cooler and my father's head drifted to one side. The wind picked up and the surface of the water ruffled. As the wind blew, the skin of the water broke and the delicate mosses, the algae and plant life under the water became agitated and waved back and forth. I saw the fronds of the plants under the water, and the minuscule creatures that lived down there in the muck, tiny insects with feelers, small fishes and one lone, lithe salamander.

As my father slept I could hear the dull drone of the buzz saw in the distance, the sound of my brother in the woods cutting down trees for the years to come. It takes a long time for the logs to dry out. My brother, determined to get next year's wood cut before the summer was completely over, was hard at work.

I had on my father's old Eisenhower jacket and his army boots. They had only needed a little bit of newspaper stuck in the ends, other than that they were still perfectly good and not at all worn out. Though I will admit it made me a trifle uncomfortable when I came down the stairs from what was formerly my father's bedroom, dressed in his clothing, and found him looking up at me from the bottom of the stairs. "Listen," I heard myself saying defensively, "you can't possibly have any use for the boots. It was you who always said not to waste things. And as for the shirt, well, until you are strong enough to dress yourself once more, I hardly think you have any choice in the matter." My father did not respond. He wheeled his chair backward and forward across the living room as if he had not heard me.

He appeared to have aged a great deal since the accident. His massive body had dwindled to that of an old man. It hurt me even to look at him. "Dad, how did this whole thing come about? I've never actually heard the full story. Why weren't you being more careful?" But my father, drowsing in the sun, did not respond, and I hesitated to press the issue.

My brother could not seem to tell me either, though he muttered something about the chain saw, and I understood that that was all I was going to be allowed to know. The rest was to remain some sort of a secret between my father and brother, yet another invincible, silent bond between them.

Still, from picking up things here and there, I was able to deduce this: that in trying to take too much on himself, in trying to cut too much wood in too short a time, on a weekend furlough as usual, my father had slipped after some four hours of cutting, the chain saw still running, and had cut himself quite severely. He had lain in the woods for hours, alone, and Bobo did not know what had happened until it grew dark and he set out to look for him. "Just leave me here," my father said, when he was found. He was very nearly dead, but Bobo managed to pick him up and carry him back to the house. There had been a great loss of blood. Bobo drove him to the emergency room of the hospital.

What do I know? What have I left out, forgotten?

What remains is cottony, as if a swish of ether or chloroform had been held under my nose, and although I am beginning to come out from under anesthesia, I still suffer from vertigo, from a torpor similar to that of a drugged slug. A drowsy groundhog, emerging from hibernation, has more life in him. In my lassitude it becomes apparent that most people love, marry and multiply out of boredom, out of not having anything better to do. These past weeks I have been thinking seriously of asking my father for the money to bring Elmira and the baby to the United States. Maybe then she would marry me. Sometimes I think of letting her put me through medical school—oh, I'm joking now of course—but after all, I do need something to occupy myself for the rest of my life. And Elmira would be good for me, fulfilling my sexual and dependency needs at the same time. And God knows, if I couldn't do a better job with little Rob than what I see resulting from a generation of fathers ahead of me, well, it would be a sad family indeed. Anyway, this is all speculation.

Late summer, and half out of the water a leopard frog sits motionless and unblinking. Large, lime green with gold spots, it sits poised between shore and water, imagining itself invisible. And yet at any moment a hand could descend from the sky, bulldoze the whole pond away, and every living thing in there would die. Or, less severe, my brother might arrive with his BB gun, looking to pick off a few frogs for our supper. There is no way to predict what may happen, after all.

A sweet and sad mood settled over me. I began to see something my father had been trying to tell me about nature and people and the fear that is always there as part of the world, how that fear is accepted and then dismissed so that animals can get on with their short but sweet lives.

And how nature makes no demands on a person but simply exists, how things grow and germinate and eat and are eaten, without expecting anything in return.

A longing for what was passed—my baby Rob, Elmira, who I had loved as much as I was able, Maggie, my mother, my brother when he was young, our lives before the divorce—rose to my shoulders like a moth. Then it took off, my life before the *now*, and fluttered a little above my head. I saw this feeling move off across the pond on dirty wings. Whether it would return or not I couldn't be certain. But I would be here waiting. My father was going to need a lot of care if he were ever going to return to normalcy. Besides, it was only fair my brother get a chance to go off to college, shake some of his anger, see the world as I had done. Then he could make his own choice as to whether or not to return.

It was getting a little too cool outside for my father's comfort. He murmured in his sleep. Some red leaves blew down and landed on his lap. The blanket crumpled at his ankles.

"Dad, Dad," I said. "Time to go inside now." I leaned forward to wake him.

Tama Janowitz
A Cannibal in Manhattan £3.50

Mgungu Yabba Mgungu is living happily on the South Sea Island of New Burnt Norton with his three wives, one hundred pigs and assorted children, the last remaining members of the tribe of the Lesser Pimbas. Into this uncivilized land comes Maria Fishburn, strange and beautiful heiress, who decides to marry Mgungu and drag him back to New York City.

From his first encounter with airline food and with rock star Kent Gable, who declares he was recently abducted by aliens, Mgungu is plunged into a world much more predatory than anything in the South Seas.

Mgungu becomes the toast of all Manhattan, meeting Parker Junius, unctuous curator of the Museum of Primitive Arts, talking philosophy with Sophie Tuckerman, deli owner, and meeting the illustrious Joey, of pizza parlour fame.

Finally, swathed in a huge fur coat and with his new gold pen through his nose, Mgungu marries Maria. After the ceremony, however, at 'that little chapel known as Tavern on the Gree', Mgungu falls in with a motley crew who come to threaten them both.

A Cannibal In Manhattan is a rich and hilarious adventure in the most formidable jungle known to modern man: the new novel from the hugely successful author of *The Slaves Of New York*.

'Laugh out loud . . . funny and wonderfully sharp' WASHINGTON POST

Tama Janowitz
Slaves of New York £3.95

'If there were a literary equivalent to a new *Talking Heads* album, *Slaves of New York* would be that book' MADEMOISELLE

'Tama Janowitz is a clever writer. She draws trendy New York popartsies to a T. These New Yorkers are slaves to high rents, migratory relationships and, most significantly, their own contagious modishness . . . Janowitz's imagination is vivid and she can invent truly memorable situations and details . . . (She) can be laugh-out loud funny and wonderfully sharp . . . A talented writer' WASHINGTON POST

'So savagely witty, so acerbic, so piercingly accurate . . . Tama Janowitz has a merciless eye for absurdity which she trains primarily on Greenwich Village "artistes". She traps them in self-conscious postering and serves them up as metaphors for her sardonic and quirky view of *au courant* urban life' LOS ANGELES HERALD EXAMINER

'Janowitz is a fearless writer. Her details are quirky, her language is lean, and her sentences sprint along with deceptive ease. The protagonists in her stories share with her a shyness and a sense of always being out of place. Although they try in earnest to fit in, they put on the wrong clothes or say the wrong thing or fail to grasp the subtle messages other people send their way . . . With the publication of *Slaves of New York*, Tama Janowitz could become the most talked-about writer of the year' NEW YORK

'With the younger generation of writers already buried under a mound of volcanic hype, it is remarkable that Janowitz, unsmothered by the critical acclaim for her novel *American Dad*, can write with such freshness' ELLE

'The shrewd observation, the skewed invention . . . are the gifts of a singular talent'
JAY MCINERNEY, author of *Bright Lights, Big City*, in the
NEW YORK TIMES

First British Publication

Kathy Acker
Blood and Guts in High School
Plus Two £4.50

A startling introduction to the writing of the *enfant terrible* of the US
literary underground. Compared to the writings of Genet and Burroughs,
these three fictions combine detailed eroticism with politics and what Acker
calls 'pop content'. Her narrative is a montage of conversation, description,
conjecture, moments snatched from history and from literature. Her eerie
exposition of anti-social values, her attack on religion, education and
government, charts the emergence of the new culture. Acker's first person
narratives make use of famous characters from life, history and fiction –
Pasolini in *My Death, My Life* and Dickens' Pip in *Great Expectations*.

'Sexy and intriguing . . . her experiments produce an authentic voice which
is a rare commodity in modern fiction' VILLAGE VOICE

Jim Crace
Continent £2.95

There and beyond is a seventh continent – seven peoples, seven masters, seven seas. And its business is trade and superstition . . .

'Jim Crace has explored this supernumerary land-mass from its impenetrable forests through the agricultural regions, sparkling with maize and sunflowers, tomatoes and melons, grazed by "fat and perfect" cows, through the acacia scrub of the central flatlands, to the bazaars, overflowing with fish and vegetable stalls, swarming with beggars and tourists. In the course of his travels he has amassed trunkloads of data about its ethnography, folklore, sexual customs, mythology, zoology, husbandry, systems of belief and manners, ways of thinking and seeing, all deployed to beguiling effect in the seven stories of *Continent*. The stories are sparsely and elegantly constructed and the whole has the accomplished inevitability of an important debut' TIMES LITERARY SUPPLEMENT

'Overtly original. It consists of seven loosely connected stories about an imaginary continent that serves as a sort of abstract model for the Third World. Highlighting conflicts that may be found in any society, but that exist in their sharpest form in countries where "progress" has been uneven, the stories are unified not by character or plot but by a common preoccupation with the nature of exploitation' OBSERVER

'He fuses folklore and political parable, moral fable and myth into something rather original and also very modern in its fragmentation . . . a new world that is strangely familiar' THE TIMES

'A remarkably original first book full of promise and achievement' GUARDIAN

Bret Easton Ellis
The Rules of Attraction £3.95

With the publication of his stunning first novel *Less Than Zero*, Bret Easton Ellis was hailed as electrifying and exceptional, a brilliantly effective voice of a new generation. He was twenty years old.

Now two years later Ellis is back. *The Rules of Attraction* is a controversial new novel as startling and original as his sensational bestselling debut. It is a bittersweet unravelling of student sex and romantic entanglements on a New England college campus.

Lauren, who changes her course subject every time she changes her sleeping partner, is the centre of a curious love triangle which involves the shrewd and passionate bisexual Paul, and Sean whose ambivalence and cynicism conceal – even from himself – his own romantic yearnings.

Through each of the characters' voices Ellis presents a kaleidoscopic view of clashing expectations and frustrations, of the dreams and tumultuous desires of youth. *The Rules of Attraction* paints a poignant and sometimes hilarious picture of the couplings and capitulations, the dramas and the downfalls of American college life in the 1980s.

'Compelling . . . and sympathetic to his "lost generation" the way only Fitzgerald was about his.' ELLE

Raymond Carver
The Stories of Raymond Carver £4.50

'Like Edward Hopper, whose landscape his characters inhabit, Carver depicts a frozen world, blue-shadowed, where time is the betrayer of lives. The men and women in these stories do no ask for much. Some common happiness – life without surprises with a touch of dignity. Sometimes they get it, more often not . . . In terse, harsh, meat-and-potato words Carver writes about a world that is lethal in its ordinariness. We wouldn't want to live there. But we do.' VOGUE

'Mr Carver's stories . . . draw upon the American voice of loneliness and stoicism, the native soul locked in this continent's space . . . They can already be counted among the masterpieces of American fiction.'
NEW YORK TIMES BOOK REVIEW

'Raymond Carver's terse gloomily funny short stories are a delight.'
IAN MCEWAN

Carrie Fisher
Postcards from the Edge £3.50

'It was like I was a car, and a maniac had gotten behind the wheel. I was driven, and I didn't know who was driving'

Suzanne Vale, the actress, is now a patient in a drug rehabilitation clinic. A victim of Hollywood's glitzy wheeling, dealing, faking it and making it, she is clawing her way back from the edge. Fast, funny and searingly realistic, Carrie Fisher's deft portraits of the inhabitants of the clinic are reminiscent of *One Flew Over the Cuckoo's Nest*, simultaneously harrowing and hilarious. A young man celebrates his rehabilitation with a wild cocaine spree. Shopping expeditions are therapy. And conversation with a psychiatrist is the order of the day.

Through the montage of diary extracts, memory flash backs and narrative shines Suzanne's (and Carrie Fisher's) sense of the absurd. This is more than a book about stardom and drugs. It is a revealing look at the dangers and delights of the obsessions of our age – career, money, sex and insecurity. In her literary debut, Carrie Fisher, star of *Shampoo*, *Star Wars* and *Hannah and Her Sisters*, reaches rare heights of perception, intelligence and imagination.

'With surprising literary artistry, Carrie Fisher swims through relationship-infested waters, braves cocaine blizzards, glitz spills . . . and *bon-mot* attacks to show us what despair is like when it refuses to take itself seriously' TOM ROBBINS

'This is a remarkable first novel. Carrie Fisher is as astounding on paper as she is in person' CANDICE BERGEN

All Pan books are available at your local bookshop or newsagent, or can be ordered direct from the publisher. Indicate the number of copies required and fill in the form below.

Send to: **CS Department, Pan Books Ltd., P.O. Box 40, Basingstoke, Hants.   RG21 2YT.**

or phone: 0256 469551 (Ansaphone), quoting title, author and Credit Card number.

Please enclose a remittance* to the value of the cover price plus: 60p for the first book plus 30p per copy for each additional book ordered to a maximum charge of £2.40 to cover postage and packing.

*Payment may be made in sterling by UK personal cheque, postal order, sterling draft or international money order, made payable to Pan Books Ltd.

Alternatively by Barclaycard/Access:

Card No. | | | | | | | | | | | | | | | | |

Signature:

Applicable only in the UK and Republic of Ireland.

While every effort is made to keep prices low, it is sometimes necessary to increase prices at short notice. Pan Books reserve the right to show on covers and charge new retail prices which may differ from those advertised in the text or elsewhere.

NAME AND ADDRESS IN BLOCK LETTERS PLEASE:

Name—————————————————————————

Address—————————————————————————

3/87